Tom Butler worked for many years for a high street bank before setting up his own light haulage business and taking up driving for a living, which he continues to do. He has attended two college creative writing courses and has written novels, short stores and poetry. Tom has lived all his life in the West Midlands, and still lives there with his wife. He has two sons and two stepsons.

CAUGHT

Tom Butler

Book Guild Publishing
Sussex, England

First published in Great Britain in 2014 by
The Book Guild Ltd
The Werks
45 Church Road
Hove, BN3 2BE

Typesetting in Baskerville by
Keyboard Services, Luton, Bedfordshire

Printed and bound in Great Britain by
4edge Ltd, Hockley, Essex

A catalogue record for this book is available from
The British Library

ISBN 978 1 84624 980 8

To Wendy, my angel, for everything you do for me.
To Pat, the best sister ever.

1

Autumn 2011

My father had two great passions. Motor cars and coarse fishing. Bizarrely it was a combination of the two that got him into trouble and, uncharacteristically, on the wrong side of the law. Thankfully no major crime had been committed, but it was a shock to my system all the same.

I had just ridden a feisty seven-year-old mare to a credible third place in the last steeplechase of the day at a rainswept Towcester when several missed calls appeared on the screen of my mobile phone as I switched it back on. They were all from my father's mobile, which immediately told me something wasn't right. Not that we weren't close or in regular contact – it was just one of those telepathic notions that one can never quite account for in life.

His voice confirmed my worst fears as he informed me he was in a police detention centre on the outskirts of Cirencester, having been arrested that morning on suspicion of malicious damage to a motor vehicle. Never, I thought. Not Father. He would be the last person to commit such a crime; he loved cars. He was a classic car collector and called them works of art. At the last count he had eleven of them, ranging from a Triumph Herald convertible to a rare 1970 Bugatti, storing every one of them in mothballs and rarely letting them see the light of day.

His stubborn obsession with them and his other chosen pastime had driven my mother to distraction and all too predictably into the arms of another man, who perversely once boasted of being 'a good friend of the family'. The man my older sister and I took to calling Uncle Jack when we were younger, long before he took a more important role in our mother's life.

It made Sam Woodall Senior sound like a bad husband and father, when in truth he was considerate and kind. He was generous with his time when he wasn't polishing a chrome bumper or trying to trick a twenty-pound pike into taking his lure. In fact, so far as Heather (my sister) and I were concerned he was just like all the other dads in the seventies and eighties, always around for school events and social get-togethers and playful to the extreme. But maybe he took Valerie (my mother) for granted and she 'lost' him to the demands of parenthood and his obsessive hobbies, until such time she felt she didn't need him anymore, rebelling in a way that caused resounding shockwaves and might so easily have brought a lesser man than my father to his knees.

Right now my father needed me. I was anxious to know what had driven him to commit a crime, if indeed charges against him were proven. So I drove on the limit, as I always did, and two hours later was waiting outside a large, purpose-built, two-storey building close to the A417 as persistent drizzle fell. It was another hour before he came out of the building accompanied by a uniformed officer, who fed a code into a keypad which opened a wrought iron gate to let him out. He stood beside my car for a while as if savouring the autumn night air and then levered himself into the passenger seat, his hair, or what was left of it, looking sadly dishevelled.

'Get me away from here, I need a bloody drink,' he said, looking straight ahead. 'The tea in that place was revolting.'

I drove for ten minutes and we hardly spoke a word. Then he made his confession as if suddenly relieved to get it off his chest. 'I bloody well did it, son,' he admitted. 'I trashed a pick-up belonging to Curtis Fielding. Of course that's not what I told them and they don't have a shred of evidence. Only his word against mine. He won't drive me out. Next time it won't be a pick-up, either. Just hark my words.'

'Father, what are you talking about? Why are you mixed up with Fielding? What's going on?'

He took his time answering all my questions, eventually divulging that he was in the middle of a feud over land at Sloane Farm where he leased a commercial coarse fishing complex originally comprising two lakes. Since taking over the site three years ago it had been a labour of love and he had only just completed the excavation of a third lake and that, he told me, had triggered the dispute. Curtis Fielding, he said, had purchased the land from its previous owner eighteen months ago and hadn't objected to the additional lake initially. But he was now angry with my father for extending the project ever so slightly onto land he had earmarked for a new static caravan park and thus losing potential revenue.

Explanation given, I was still shocked by his childish behaviour. 'But why damage a vehicle belonging to Fielding? Why make him even more angry?'

'It was tit for tat,' he replied, sounding mildly smug. 'A week ago he deliberately let a herd of dairy cattle onto the site and they made a horrible mess. One angler even got hurt and a lot of expensive tackle was wrecked. I'm facing a huge bill for compensation. Some of these modern poles the contest anglers use run into bloody thousands. Two clubs who book the venue most weekends have pulled out and others will surely follow if I can't guarantee their members' safety. That's the mentality of the man I'm dealing with. He's a real shit and I won't let him bully me.'

I responded without thinking. 'Have you tried reasoning with him?'

I knew the answer before it came. 'You don't reason with a man like Fielding, he does as he pleases,' he shrugged back. 'He's even got one of the highest-ranking police officers in the county in his back pocket. They're golfing buddies you see, so he thinks he's untouchable.'

'How much land are we talking, an acre or two?' I queried.

'Not that much, barely a strip. Says he needs it for access onto the proposed development. In reality he wants to force me out so that he can make a shedload of money by squeezing in another two dozen caravans after filling in the new lake. It's cash that motivates him. And greed, of course.'

It was sad to see my father shrouded in such bitterness but it didn't deflect me from probing the matter further. 'Surely you have a legitimate lease? In law he can't go against that?'

He rolled his weary eyes and shrugged again, suddenly looking far less defiant. 'The lease is worthless if I don't have a viable business to run on the land. The cunning bastard knows it. Ruining the business is his game, he's made that oh so obvious.'

'I had no idea this was going on, you should have told me sooner. Maybe I could have helped.'

He shook his head as though to tell me it was his fight and nobody else's. Curtis Fielding was no stranger to me but to be told he was my father's landlord had come as a complete shock. A regular visitor to racecourses in the West Country and now accepted into the ranks as a bona fide race steward, Fielding had literally galloped into racing officialdom rather as if it was his destiny to social climb. Several of my peers had already fallen foul of his thirst for discipline, overriding strictness and razor-sharp tongue. Only the previous week at Exeter he had handed out whip bans to seven individual jockeys and controversially reversed the result of the feature race, much to the chagrin of a leading trainer who called the decision a travesty of justice and made an official complaint to the British Horseracing Authority.

From my own perspective I had no reason to believe the man to be any more fierce than the next in what was a difficult post, with racing going through a period of rule changes and transition. I thought perhaps he was trying too hard to emulate firebrand Angus Gunnell, a steward of many years' standing whose reputation preceded him, giving nervy jockeys cause to shake in their boots or at the very least breathe more heavily than usual.

At Huntington two weeks ago Gunnell had dumbfounded me with a three-day ban after last year's champion jockey Bradley Somerville, egged on by an owner desperate for extra prize money, put in an objection against me for hampering his progress in the latter stages of a pretty low-key hurdle race where I had finished second and he third. In truth my horse was tiring and rolling about instinctively as tired horses are prone to do. I had no problem with Bradley, we went back a long way, even though his version of events differed a little from mine. But a pragmatic Gunnell took his side and reversed the places, and then compounded it with an enforced lay-off, which cost me dearly as bans always do. It was always the poor jockey who suffered most and counted the cost.

Whether Fielding would become another Gunnell remained to be seen, but for now he was public enemy number one so far as my father was concerned, and that in itself was enough for both of us to worry about.

What didn't quite make sense to me when I reanalysed what Father had said was the cold fact that Fielding was making money out of him, quite a substantial annual rent which was renegotiable after every twelve months and which Father was only too well aware of. I remember him coming to me before he took the plunge into buying the lease and asking me for my thoughts. He had always had a head for business and I assumed he knew what he was doing. Besides, he had dreamt about running his own commercial fishery for as long as I could remember so I gave him nothing but encouragement. There were sponsorship deals to be had with leading tackle manufacturers, he told me, which seemed a cast-iron safeguard if he struggled to make enough money out of the venture. That he had successfully doubled the turnover of the lakes and merited an expansion plan was testimony to his admirable determination and painstaking diligence, which together made his current plight as unwelcome as it was ill-timed and wholly unnecessary.

Back at my rented cottage in Stroud I poured out a large whisky and saw the beginnings of colour returning to Father's face as he first took a sip and then an animated gulp after plonking himself down on a kitchen chair.

'I might need another,' he said with a disapproving stare as I shaped to return the bottle to the cupboard where it lived. Leaving it instead on the kitchen table within easy reach I looked down at him, wondering if I should be offering him a comb for his wayward strands of hair in addition to liquid fortification.

'The police will want to speak to me again of course,' he sighed, already half-way down his glass. 'But they'll get nothing out of me.'

'So what did you do to this pick-up exactly?' I asked, intrigued.

His face distorted, but he turned it into a smile. 'It was more like one of them fancy four-by-fours with a covered back and Fielding's name on the bonnet and sides,' he corrected me. 'His farm manager left it parked close to my office while he checked some fencing. When he got back it was minus two door mirrors and had picked up a couple of punctures. How unlucky was that?'

I chastised him with my eyes but he just kept smiling into his glass.

'And of course you were careful not to be seen as you administered your revenge,' I said with no great sarcasm.

'Things get broke,' he shrugged. 'Happens all the time.'

'Not in front of your office with no one else around.'

He shook his head. 'There were people about at the time assessing the damage done by those maniac cows. Anybody could have accidentally caused those things to happen.'

'And that's what you told the police presumably?'

'Dead right. They've nothing but Fielding's accusations against me. And remember he started this. He wants to drive me out, almost said as much to my face a couple of weeks ago.'

Taking a deep breath he downed the last of the whisky and reached for the bottle. I felt as though I should stop him but backed off. He was a man who knew his limits and wouldn't welcome my interference.

'So what happens now?' I quizzed him. 'Surely you have some insurance against damage by farm animals?'

He pulled at a couple of the strands of his hair which only made them stick out more. 'Some tackle that was destroyed will be covered by its owners of course and naturally I've put in a claim myself, but it's the loss of future revenue and my reputation that will hurt most, plus the fact the new lake's now in limbo due to Fielding getting a solicitor to block the whole project. He knows that if people stay away he can put the pressure on me to get me out. That man has no scruples. I don't believe there are any lengths he won't go to. But I have to fight him, can't allow the bullies in life to win.'

'Did you report him to the police if you felt it was harassment?' I asked, attempting to put a logical slant on things.

He scoffed at the suggestion. 'What would they have done about it? It's a farming community, cows get into places they shouldn't. They'd never have believed it to be a deliberate act of vandalism. Cows don't come tooled up with baseball bats and crow bars, they trample everything in their path and are excused because they're dumb animals and go with the flow.'

I could read emotion in his eyes as he looked up at me now, but worryingly I also saw enough rage to feel the need to warn him. 'Father, don't go gung-ho with this. Study the lease you signed and get professional help. Exhaust all the legitimate channels first and do nothing to antagonise Fielding. There simply has to be an amicable solution.'

Encouragingly there seemed a flicker of resignation in his demeanour, but I still doubted that his stubbornness over the dispute would disappear completely. So I added weight to my argument by suggesting a joint offensive where Fielding was concerned, confining it to a simple approach perhaps on neutral ground with me putting my father's side and backing it with nothing but plain speaking and common sense.

He looked thoughtful as he digested my impromptu strategy, and for once I felt my education hadn't been wasted because he raised no objection and concentrated only on what was left swishing around in the bottom of his glass. And there was no objection from him either when I took the bottle away and returned it to its regular hiding place.

'Fielding will be at Cheltenham tomorrow,' I said with certainty. 'He might even be officiating at the two-day meeting. I have three rides scheduled for tomorrow and two on Saturday and there should be ample opportunity for us to have a quiet word with him. Maybe he won't seem so disagreeable in a public place and I can get him to consider a compromise to end all this nonsense. It serves no purpose to have you two at each other's throats.'

'My son the diplomat,' Father said sarcastically. 'I suppose it's worth a try. I had no idea you knew him so well.'

'I don't, he's pretty new to the racing scene and dead keen to make an impression. Maybe diplomacy is what's needed. I have nothing to lose by trying.'

'And will I gain anything if I break my golden rule of not gambling on horses and follow your rides?' he asked, changing the subject.

Not once to my knowledge had my father placed a bet before, so I was shocked to hear him say this. He might simply have been humouring me of course.

'Cheering me on from the stands will suffice,' I shrugged. 'I have yet to win at the course. Second place on five occasions and third twice sums it up.'

'Still a winner in my eyes,' he patronised me. But he hadn't always felt that way about my choice of career. He had been dead set against it.

I well remember the look on his face when I was fifteen and my mother announced she had booked riding lessons for me. He wanted me to become an engineer like he had been when he was younger, and he told my mother riding was for girls – which just propelled them into another argument to add to all the others that prevailed at the time.

'He'll see the folly when he falls off and breaks a bone or two,' he said harshly. Unknown to them both I had already ridden a friend's pony and loved every minute of it, and as if to prove Father wrong I never did fall off when I began my lessons, excelling in something for the first time in my life. Six months later I took a job as stable lad at a racing stable in Frome, Somerset. Now, nearly twenty years on and six hundred winners in fifteen years as a professional, I think he knew Mother had been right about me, though he still preached to me about getting 'a second career' to fall back on when I hung up my riding boots. I imagined he wouldn't let the subject die. At least it showed he cared.

For now he struck the pose of a man needing sleep and consolation. So I gave him my bed for the night and took to the couch with no guarantees for tomorrow, but at least a promise ringing in his ears that I would do whatever I could to ease his woes.

2

An early morning call to Cheltenham's racecourse manager confirmed my suspicions that Curtis Fielding was listed amongst the stewards for the day's meeting, with disciplinarian Angus Gunnell also presiding as chairman. A daunting prospect for any jockey with a chequered recent history, which might have filled me with dread had I not had my father uppermost on my mind.

He had slept well but was having second thoughts about the united front as we breakfasted over lightly buttered toast and strong coffee, his doubts born of his belief that his adversary would still be a hard nut to crack. I reminded him about impending police proceedings, and he reined back on his negativity enough to agree to allowing me to try peaceful negotiation with an emphasis on an ending of hostilities.

'Never imagined it would come to this,' he remarked with irony. 'Sam Woodall Junior fighting his old man's battles. I ought to be very proud of you.'

'Let's hope it doesn't turn into a battle,' I humoured him. 'That would be to no one's advantage. I shall simply appeal to his fair-mindedness and look for a common sense solution. For me there seems no other way.'

Father retained a look of scepticism but continued to praise me when I felt there was no great need. 'I never thought you had it in you, son. I always thought you followed your mother who was woefully weak-minded.'

The additional comment about someone who was no longer around to defend herself was uncalled for and I think he knew I'd ignore it.

11

'When I think there's been an injustice I speak out, it's nothing to do with bravado. I'm in a profession where you have to stand up for yourself or fall by the wayside.'

A slow nod of his head registered his approval and he looked strangely comforted. 'Good for you, Sammy boy, good for you,' he repeated.

I cringed back at him and looked at my watch. Sometimes parents made you do that. As if it was unavoidable.

Conversation en route to the course was confined to my racing prospects for the day. It was going to be a rare event to have Father along to watch me, as he had never been a natural follower of the noblest of sports, preferring instead the obsessional pursuit of specimen fish over the role of a spectator.

Cheltenham was one of the few courses I hadn't won at, and I felt unusually nervous as we drove through the entrance gates and into the section set aside for jockeys' parking. I was unsurprised to see plenty of free spaces as I had deliberately arrived early.

Barring late changes I had rides in two races as stable jockey for Dominic Ingles, and one for another local trainer Heath Coultard as stand-in for his regular jockey who was serving a whip ban, the current scourge of over-scrutinised jump jockeys. Father had been astute enough to notice my nervousness upon our arrival and squeezed my arm with a reassuring hand, which he hadn't done for many a year and which meant much more than he could ever have imagined.

I led him purposefully towards a perfectly manicured grassed area in front of a building that housed the stewards' room where a well-dressed group of people had already collected, most of them wearing wind-defying overcoats and carrying identical-looking clipboards. Predictably in the middle of the group stood the bulky figure of Angus Gunnell who had forgone his overcoat and seemed to be making some sort of speech as the others listened. Standing immediately to his right as if in rank and file was the taller, slimmer, Curtis Fielding whose dark-brown waxed jacket looked new. He sported a bright-yellow identity rosette.

Looking fresh-faced and as keen as mustard, Fielding, who I guessed was in his mid to late forties, then handed out paperwork to some of the others and joined a cut-off group of four men in a regimented huddle as if they were some sort of secret society, leaving Gunnell to herd up the rest. My father swore under his breath and I grunted at him with disapproval, despite feeling the same.

Fielding's voice was less than discreet and I think he must have cracked a joke, as suddenly the four men laughed loudly and became much more animated in their movements. It was then that he saw us, which rendered an immediate change in his expression almost as though he had seen a ghost instead of the spectre of two generations of the Woodall family. He ran an unsteady hand across his black wavy hair and looked temporarily hesitant. As the group disbanded, still in jocular mood, he pretended he hadn't noticed us at all and went back over to speak to Gunnell, now talking to the racecourse vet, a man called Anthony Thompson who was shivering with cold.

It seemed as good a time as any to make a polite approach, so I moved in with my father tucked in behind me, to ask Fielding if he could spare us a few minutes of his precious time, trying hard not to make it sound like an ultimatum. He looked back at me with an indignant smirk and scowled over my shoulder at my father, telling us both with economy of words that he was far too busy and whatever it was would have to wait.

'Too busy or just plain rude,' Father muttered a little too audibly, clearly to wrestle the man's attention.

Fielding straightened his back and looked around uneasily. 'This is neither the time nor place to discuss whatever it is you have come for. Frankly I'm amazed you have the nerve to try, given what we are all here to do.'

'Seems as good a place as anywhere,' I countered. 'We were hoping you'd hear us out.'

My pulse was racing and my voice wavered, probably something to do with the fear of making my father's plight worse by confronting the enemy.

Glancing at his watch and saying something I couldn't hear to Gunnell, our quarry suddenly gestured to us to follow him, stopping abruptly after a dozen brisk strides and backing us both up against a security rail close to the jockeys' weighing room. We both looked up at a face that resembled an impending thunderstorm and waited with bated breath.

'Say what you came to say and make it quick, I really don't have much time,' he said, glaring at us with unfriendly eyes.

My father shaped his mouth to speak but I got the words out first.

'Well obviously it's about the dispute and recent bad feeling between you and my father,' I began, desperately trying to remain composed. 'He does appear to have a legitimate lease and has no intention of vacating the site, so I was hoping we could reach a compromise. The complex is his livelihood and he has invested a substantial amount of money into improvements there. Surely you and he can work something out so that there is no animosity between you?'

Fielding rocked on the balls of his feet as he listened, then shook his head in blatant defiance. 'But your father broke the terms of the lease by encroaching onto land he doesn't pay rent for. The very same land I had plans to develop,' he said coldly. 'So I have every right to take legal action against him. Anyone would do the same in my position.'

'And does this "legal action" include turning animals out

onto the rented land to cause damage and endanger life?'
I responded.

There was lightning in his deep-set eyes to accompany
the thunder, and his narrow shoulders became menacingly
hunched. 'That had nothing to do with me,' he insisted.
'I don't own the cattle and the police were quite happy
with my explanation of events. But wanton vandalism to
one of my vehicles is a different matter.'

'Perhaps a stray cow caused the damage,' Father piped
up, not helping at all.

Fielding blew out his cheeks and checked his watch before
making his position clear. 'I've put matters in the hands of
my solicitor so this little charade is pointless. I didn't start
any of this and as the landowner I'm perfectly entitled to
tackle any tenant who flouts the terms of their lease. I think
I've been as patient as any man could be – and it wasn't
me who took matters into their own hands and chose to
break the law.' He paused. 'Now if you'll excuse me I have
much to do. You of all people should know that. I won't
wish you luck for later on because I must remain impartial.'

His voice became sarcastic and his body language
unbending. Alongside me, Dad was as close as he could be
to striking out so I made one last impassioned plea to the
man as he began backing away.

'Mr Fielding, can't we resolve this with sensible negotiation?
My father's too old to be engulfed in legal jargon. Can we
please talk again soon to find an amicable solution?'

Fielding listened but simply threw his arms up in the air,
said a curt 'Not possible', and turned tail back towards the
stewards' room.

We stood watching him open-mouthed before I said the
first thing that came into my head. 'That man has no heart.
Of all the people to pick on to annoy, you chose him. I
must be careful not to attract his attention today, I need
another ban like a hole in the head.'

15

'He wouldn't dare extend the feud to you, that would be wholly unprofessional,' Father said naively.

'Same name, similar treatment; enemies come in all guises,' I surmised.

Before he had the chance to summon a response a familiar voice prised his attention away from me and I had to wait for the inevitable loud greeting to subside. Lavender Thompson was a woman with a few too many masculine mannerisms to ever be described as dainty. Father was overwhelmed by the celebrity status she bestowed upon him and the haphazard kiss she aimed in the general vicinity of his mouth. Mother of Anthony, the official course vet whom we had spotted talking to Angus Gunnell earlier, she was also the proud custodian of a 1952 Bentley which was once owned by royalty and was responsible for her meeting Father whilst exhibiting at the same classic car show. Her 'priceless asset' had been inherited and was currently on loan to a motor museum in Warwickshire.

Cheltenham was a regular haunt for her too where she tended to preside over various charity events especially those that raised money in support of the Injured Jockeys Fund which was fine by me and my many appreciative peers. I think in truth she had a soft spot for my father despite being married to Anthony's late father for more than thirty years. In spite of what we had come here to do and his current predicament I found it mildly amusing to watch him try to extricate himself from her overbearing clutches.

She was wearing an expensive-looking red, full-length coat and a Russian-style fur hat that sat to one side of her head. Her hair, a mix of bluish grey and light auburn, looked like it had been professionally sculpted around her heavily rouged face, and her eyes were a dark shade of green. It appeared she had lost weight since I had seen her last but feminine grace still eluded her, making her seem like the embarrassingly awkward aunt you tried deliberately to avoid when your paths were about to cross in a public place.

Father looked at me, fully expecting me to rescue him, but I was already edging away and leaving him to cope as best he could. I was rather surprised that he was suddenly allowing her to pull him to one side as if she was eager to speak to him out of the earshot of other jockeys and race officials who were gathering around them. Even her loud and piercing voice was replaced by a covert whisper and it soon became obvious that whatever she wanted to tell him was serious enough to command his undivided attention.

Predictably I added to the growing number of jockeys now collecting outside the weighing room for the usual pre-race banter, the topic on most lips being another amendment to rules governing the use of the whip following yet another series of complaints from those at the sharp end of the industry. I doubted there was a jockey in the group who hadn't fallen foul of the whip guidelines which were immensely hard to comply with in the cut and thrust of a race, especially in larger fields where errant horses needed to be corrected if running too freely or wavering off line.

One with more to say than most on the subject was Nathan Scully who had finished a close runner-up in the jump jockey championship last season and narrowly led the way six weeks into the new season. His thick Yorkshire accent bristled with condemnation for the newest guidelines, and it was as though the group had elected him to speak on their behalf or at the very least to echo their thoughts and major concerns which they considered a threat to their livelihoods.

Only last week Nathan had threatened to boycott steeplechase racing in this country unless something was done about what he described as 'ludicrous short sightedness' on behalf of the BHA which introduced an unworkable totting up system of whip use during a race.

'It's impossible to expect jockeys to count the number of times they employ the whip during a three mile chase,' he had said forcibly at a hastily convened meeting a few days earlier, making sure there was someone from the racing press present to record it. Not one of the sixty-odd jockeys who attended, including me, disagreed though not one backed a collective boycott which meant lost revenue. I even suspected Nathan wouldn't have carried out his threat due to his loyalty to the handful of top owners and trainers who queued up to have him ride for them, especially at the most prestigious of meetings like today's.

Notably Nathan was nicknamed 'Safe Bet Scully' and his Cheltenham winning ratio was second to none, which probably influenced his decision not to turn his back on eight chances to improve his record over the next two days. Thankfully he wasn't in too much of a preaching mood today. Most of the discussion had moved on to focus upon concerns over the close proximity of the first fence to the start, a change made by the Cheltenham hierarchy to prevent headstrong horses from approaching the fence too quickly.

It had met with a mixed reaction but 'Safe Bet' seemed to accept it, as I did. Anything aimed at safety and putting the welfare of horse and rider first was OK in my book but several wanted to take a precautionary look. They quickly arranged with a steward to get a lift down to the revised start which broke up the impromptu gathering and left me dithering over whether to join them or not. With Lavender Thompson still deep in conversation with Father, who didn't look at all stressed, I chose to hitch a ride on a four-by-four to familiarise myself with the amended start at the bottom of the famous Cheltenham hill.

On my return I noticed Lavender and Father had been joined by her son Anthony, a lean-looking man in his late thirties with a receding hairline and narrow, clean-shaven face. The three of them were soldered together in discussion, almost looking as though they were about to plot some dastardly deed. When I reached them Father was shaking Anthony's hand and the man acknowledged me with a wave before hurrying away to carry out his pre-race examinations. Father met my inquisitive stare with raised eyebrows and spoke only a few guarded words. 'Not enough time now, son, go ride some winners and I'll fill you in later.'

'I never thought you had any time for the Thompsons,' I quizzed him, careful not to let Lavender hear me.

'They have their uses,' he replied, tapping the bridge of his nose which only heightened my intrigue. 'I'm off to get a drink,' he added, looking in the direction of the nearest bar. 'Good luck for later on, I might risk a pound or two on the tote.'

With that he was gone, gesturing a hand in the direction of Lavender Thompson who was now waving furiously at someone else she recognised amongst the next influx of racing connections to enter the VIP arena.

With no interest in the first race, I ambled into the jockeys' changing room and found the designated space where my colours for the second race hung from a hook. The scarlet with two bold yellow stripes together with a conspicuous yellow cap were the registered colours of a newly formed syndicate headed by an ex-school chum of trainer Dominic Ingles. He had recently obtained a five-year-old chaser named Capital Gain from its previous disillusioned owner, who had lost patience with the horse following two unsuccessful years as a temperamental novice. Ingles believed it would come good eventually and was perfect for the six syndicate members to cut their collective teeth on.

I had schooled Capital Gain the previous week. He seemed both willing and the progressive type despite having an annoying habit of holding his head to the left which meant he naturally pulled to that side, plus a tendency to leave little to spare when negotiating his fences. If any trainer could turn him into a winner Dominic could, his mantra being to focus on the positives and not dwell too much on any historic negatives, albeit he took every flaw in a horse at face value. It had made Dominic into arguably the king of the Cotswolds in training terms, with only one other trainer successful enough to rival him. That distinction went to Heath Coultard for whom I had a ride in the third race of the day on a useful hurdler aptly named Leap of Faith. The horse was owned by Heath's racing-obsessed wife Felicity who rode regularly herself at point-to-point meetings but left it to the likes of me on the mainstream courses.

Around me the changing room was soon a hive of activity as jockeys due out for the opening hurdle race made last minute preparations, many of them still carping about the new whip regulations but trying to smile about it as jockeys tended to do. Behind me Nathan Scully was part of one of these discussion groups with a few jockeys at various stages of undress, and to my right there was a smaller group who looked ready to race. Just to my left on his own sat the rather forlorn figure of Paul Eddison, a veteran jump jockey who by his own confession was never much of a conversationalist and thus kept himself on the periphery of things.

'This lot are never happy unless they've got something to moan about,' I said to him, only half expecting a reply.

Although looking as if he was in a self-induced trance he had clearly heard what I had said and delivered a profound if unhurried response. 'Everything's changing, Sam,' he sighed with cold inevitability. 'We are always the ones who suffer.'

Paul was a man in his mid-forties who had retired from racing two years ago with over eight hundred career winners to his name, only to be persuaded back into the saddle at the start of this current season. Though he had a face full of wrinkles and his hair was turning grey he was as fit as any jockey half his age, and only last week I had ridden against him at Exeter and noted a determination to prove those doubting his decision wrong. He had cantered home twenty lengths clear of the field in one race and beaten me by half a length in another, which made his glum expression today even more of a mystery – considering he had good rides in four races over Cheltenham's challenging fences and the green and white colours he wore for the first race belonged to wealthy industrialist Tristan Jolly and wife Trudy.

For them to show such faith in Paul when every other jockey yearned to ride their classy string of Oxfordshire trained horses was indeed an honour, but as I glanced into his glazed-over eyes I wondered if he really saw the significance of it himself. There had been many raised eyebrows when Tristan announced he was turning to Paul as stable jockey to replace Australian-born Judd Fisher, who had tragically died in a motorway pile-up in May. It was a decision that hadn't looked great a month ago until Paul began racking up winners to revive the Jollys' reputation.

'We bounce back and get on with it like the mugs we are. Lambs and slaughter comes to mind,' I replied after a lengthy pause, attempting to inject some humour.

Paul shrugged his bony shoulders and at least mustered a grimace which was the nearest thing to a smile I was likely to get. With that he rose to his feet, secured his green cap to his riding hat, tucked his shirt into his breeches and, anticipating the call, edged slowly towards the open door before filing out with his rival jockeys to form the familiar procession en route to the parade ring.

The room was now empty except for one other jockey and two of the regular valets who were busy tidying anything remotely out of place. When he saw me sitting alone the other jockey, Liam Dowdy, sidled over to join me, passing an immediate remark in a thick Southern Irish accent with reference to Paul Eddison's restrained demeanour. 'Poor sod, surprised you even got a word out of him. When I tried earlier he practically told me to piss off. Anybody would think he was the first bloke to find out his missus was playing away,' he shrugged.

My eyes mirrored my surprise but Liam wasn't really looking at me to monitor my reaction. 'Not as if it hadn't happened before,' he continued. 'He's a damn sight better off without her if you ask me, the cheating bitch.'

His bitterness gave his voice an edge I hadn't encountered before, but then he threw me a wry smile.

'Odd thing though,' he mused, 'since he found out he's ridden twice as many winners as usual and owners are suddenly turning to him for rides. I've been trying to get to ride for the Jollys for ages and never had a sniff.'

Strangely I had put Paul's standoffishness at Exeter down to his dislike of the West Country course and never imagined that domestic disharmony had befallen him, perversely triggering a sudden run of success. Seven wins from his last dozen outings was impressive indeed, a ratio all jockeys aspired to but rarely achieved.

'He's certainly riding as though his life depended on it,' I acknowledged, thinking back a week and remembering the way he had edged me out over the last few yards of a gruelling slog in bottomless ground. 'Motivation comes in all sorts of ways. Good luck to him, hope some of it rubs off on me.'

As I said that, Liam looked at me with eyes that expressed the same sentiments. We were both going through a barren spell and winners were becoming increasingly scarce. Cheltenham was undoubtedly the place to stop the rot. There was nowhere better.

3

Paul Eddison's fancied ride won the opening race of the day with six lengths to spare but he still appeared far too solemn a figure when weighing in and no one seemed keen to congratulate him. I think the much younger jockeys were suddenly in awe of him because of his winning streak, whilst others like me were just plain curious as to why he had hit such a rich vein of form, doubting it to be the bizarre result of his wife's infidelity.

Because it felt like the right thing to do, I did offer him a subdued 'Well done' but the man's modesty prevailed, barely allowing him a response though he did bow his head in my direction before making a bold prediction. 'That horse will be a champion hurdler one day,' he said with a resounding sigh. 'I didn't really have to do much, just sit tight.'

'Those Jollys have it made, they can afford the best,' I said with envy.

'They paid peanuts for Gala Prince,' he corrected me. 'They owe it to the trainer; he'd turn a donkey into a three-mile stayer.'

Paul had ridden for trainer David Miles's dad Cyril when he first turned professional over twenty years ago and though there had been reports of friction it appeared that Miles Junior had won him over with his modern training methods.

'One down, three to go,' I said, building him up when it wasn't necessary and noticeably failing to induce any reaction from him. He started undressing and I wondered if Liam Dowdy was indeed right about him and whether it had been the onset of marital adversity that inadvertently played a role in unlocking the hidden secret of winning more races than he lost. Something akin to him being able to channel the anger that he must have felt inside and harnessing it so that it gave him a previously untapped energy force. However, to watch him almost dithering over the change of kit for the second race you would have thought he was a man very much down on his luck out on the racecourse, instead of someone scaring the bookmakers to death with his upturned form.

I remember once hitting a purple patch myself when I won three high-profile races on three consecutive days at different meetings which got me a mention in the *Racing Post* as well as some daily newspapers. It felt good at the time but also put me under huge pressure to maintain a consistency of form from then on; sadly something I couldn't manage, which said everything about how fickle a jockey's life can be. The following week I suffered several ignominious falls including one at Sandown where I cracked two ribs and spent a painful few hours in hospital before being laid off for the whole of the next week. Accolades and disappointments went together like toast and jam, and I suppose Paul knew that only too well having plied his trade for longer than most and experienced the highs and lows of what was still a lucrative career.

Right now he was wearing the blue and white of another owner who wanted the magic to continue in the first three-mile chase of the day, his slightly curly, greying hair that was in need of a sympathetic trim being lazily combed back into place as though through habit and not vanity.

'Have you ridden Master Middleman before?' I asked him, trying to legitimately find out something about the opposition.

He shook his head and finished grooming his hair. 'Not in a race, only at the yard,' he replied. 'He's a big bugger and pulls a bit.'

24

That was all I was likely to get, but at least he was conversing and beginning to look interested.

'Mine's a bit temperamental and he won't have seen fences like the ones here before,' I said, with profound honesty. 'I may have to fiddle about a bit and see how he approaches them.'

He nodded back and muttered something along the lines that sometimes that was the only way at Cheltenham. He needn't have reminded me where we were, I was already suffering from stomach cramps, knowing only too well they would depart as soon as I was mounted and out on the racecourse, awaiting the start of the race.

When it was time to leave for the parade ring Paul surprised me with a friendly nudge and wished me luck. Whether it was sincerely meant or not, I returned the sentiment though I didn't for a minute believe he needed any help from lady luck. He met the bespectacled owner of Master Middleman with a curt smile before I peeled away to join Dominic who had been courting the syndicated owners of an impatient-looking Capital Gain and hopefully singing my praises.

The race itself in the early stages went very much to plan, both Paul and I tucking in close behind a leading bunch on the first circuit and then tracking a strong front running grey called Powder Keg ridden by Liam Dowdy. That was until his horse took off too early and rattled the third last fence to lose vital ground. Still Liam kept the strong grey in front of us though he wavered off line and I switched mine to the outside, whilst a diligent Paul stuck to the rails and overtook Liam on the approach to the final fence. Liam and I got mightily close to each other on landing and actually bumped which lost us both impetus, but thankfully Capital Gain responded to my urgings to pull away and draw alongside Paul whose horse was tiring as the infamous Cheltenham hill took its toll. Though I tried to get Capital Gain to run straight he was naturally drawn to the rails and there was little if any room between us at the finish, though I was a clear half a length ahead as we struggled past the post.

Feeling exhausted but elated at the same time I shook hands with both Paul and third-placed Liam – the former did so grudgingly as though denying him another victory hadn't been part of the script. He muttered something about me muscling him out and taking his ground, and then seemed to hold a post mortem on the finish with Liam on the way back to being met by our respective grooms. A smiling Dominic Ingles ran a considerable way to meet me and I readied myself for the greeting I would receive from the ecstatic syndicate members.

Nothing is certain in racing, however, and those dreaded words 'stewards' inquiry' cast an immediate shadow over post-race celebrations. Dominic's expression changed from joy to apprehension after I dismounted and several of the joint owners offered me only subdued plaudits whilst others were more forthcoming, appearing to be more than happy with their investment.

'Did you impede anyone on the run in?' the anxious trainer asked before I had a chance to get away to weigh in. 'It looked like you got there fairly from here but obviously somebody thinks different.'

'I think I left them enough room,' I answered hastily, my voiced edged with uncertainty. 'There were three very tired horses, they were a good match and gave their all.'

It mattered to a lot of people who had won and who hadn't, and no one more than me. Capital Gain had given me everything. He had jumped better than I thought he might and picked up speed when I had asked him to, giving me a near faultless ride. But his tendency to hang to the left on a left-handed course like Cheltenham hadn't helped me at the finish, especially with a rival determined to stick to my inside and race me all the way to the winning post.

I was hurried to the stewards' room still with Tannoy announcements being made regarding the suspension of bets awaiting the official outcome of the inquiry. As I reached the door where Messrs Fielding and Gunnell were waiting inside, Paul Eddison came striding up breathlessly behind me and we virtually tumbled in together to find the chairman of the stewards and his accomplice watching the final throes of the race on one of several TV screens. We stood to attention and Angus Gunnell spun around to address Paul, asking him if he felt his horse had been stopped from winning the race.

Paul took a deep breath and nodded. 'I was in front and the other horse got too close so I had no chance to use my whip on the run in. I don't think it was a deliberate move by Sam because both horses were tired but I do feel it affected the result,' he said.

My heart sank as Gunnell turned to Fielding, who I sensed had already made up his mind about my involvement, then he turned back and asked me for my account.

'Well, as Paul said, both horses were pretty tired and as far as I'm concerned it was just a typical race for the line between two game horses. I feel I did nothing wrong and my horse was marginally quicker at the finish.'

'Why didn't you keep your horse straight, Mr Woodall? It's clear to us you came across towards the rail where Mr Eddison was,' Gunnell said.

I grimaced. 'It wasn't intentional, Sir, just tiredness shown by a very honest horse.'

My eyes met Fielding's across the room and I feared the worst.

'Thank you both,' Gunnell said, dismissing us.

Paul escaped first and was legging it back to the weighing room at breakneck speed as if he couldn't bear to walk with me. I hadn't even reached the changing room when the result of the stewards' inquiry was broadcast, demoting Capital Gain to second and gifting Paul another winner. There were heavy drones of disappointment mixed with cheers and genuine words of consolation. Nathan Scully said I had been robbed and Liam Dowdy, who had obviously witnessed the finish, said I was just plain unlucky.

My head was spinning and there was no sign of Paul who I felt had exaggerated his account of the finish to get sympathy from the deliberating stewards. But I think if I'm honest Curtis Fielding had swayed the chairman and the words 'sour grapes' stuck solidly in my throat without the likelihood of ever being set free.

There was no time to dwell on what ifs, incriminations and hard-luck stories. Heath Coultard would expect only my best in the third race where I was to be united with his wife's pride and joy Leap of Faith for the first time. I was blatantly aware if I made an impression on both of them they might use me on an ad hoc basis to fit in with Dominic Ingles' demands on me. But a call to attend the stewards' room again before I had chance to even change into Felicity's colours had me expecting further retribution from the law makers. It came in the form of a three-day ban for careless riding and was meted out by a smug-faced, revenge-fuelled Curtis Fielding who said he was acting on Angus Gunnell's behalf and written confirmation would follow.

He said that it gave him no pleasure to be handing out the punishment, which I knew wasn't true. I think he would have enjoyed it even more had I questioned both his authority and the decision that had been made by appealing against the ban. To have done that might have made me feel better in the short term but it would only prolong the agony and would serve no real purpose other than making me even more unpopular. So I chose to say nothing except to call him 'Sir' and accept my fate, though I felt inwardly sick at having to be so subservient. But then the trials and tribulations you put up with as a jockey tended to make you feel that way.

I was soon meeting the Coultards in the parade ring with a genuine air of optimism helped by encouraging words from several of my peers who, like Nathan Scully, felt I had been wrongly deprived of my first victory at the course. Likewise Dominic had not held me in any way responsible nor had the owners, who in truth hadn't expected a visit to the winner's enclosure so soon after acquiring the horse. A horse which, when all was said and done, had met his fences like an old pro, shown undeniable staying power and demonstrated impressive finishing speed.

Predictably, Felicity Coultard looked a picture in a dusky pink floral dress, and her horse took the rosette for the best turned out, behaving impeccably in the ring and showing up well in the early stages of the race before fading to finish fourth, a good twenty lengths behind the winner guided skilfully home by Nathan. Paul Eddison didn't have a ride in the race but he was up in the next on the clear favourite Chez La Fur in the green and white of the Jollys. I was back on a Dominic-trained two-mile chaser called Hillsong owned by a reclusive Gloucestershire millionaire.

Any awkwardness between Paul and me had dispersed and he even threw me a makeshift smile as we got ready to do battle in the fourth race of the day, which I graciously returned. It was supposedly a competitive novice handicap but Liam Dowdy's Irish-trained mount Drumladen soon had the rest of the field trailing in its wake. When I tried to regain some ground to at least secure a minor place, Millsong unceremoniously unshipped me at the next open ditch and gave me a stiff shoulder to remember him by. As I sat in an ambulance waiting for clearance to head back, the news filtered through that Liam's horse had unseated him at the last and man of the moment Paul Eddison had profited to complete an unlikely hat-trick. Someone was watching over him all right. There were such things as guardian angels.

The day was over for me with no more scheduled rides, which was a blessing in disguise given another racing injury had me wincing as I undressed and showered. The pain had left me by the time I had found Father, who stood watching the runners for the fifth race leaving the parade ring, a look of abject indecision on his face.

'I should have listened to you all those years ago and become an engineer,' I said to him with no little sarcasm. 'But at least I know what it's like to be first past the post here now.'

Father blew out his cheeks and swore, making heads turn as he said the offending words. Like quite a few others I imagined he had lost money on the result of the inquiry. 'It's scandalous, son, from where I was you did nothing wrong. I've even watched it back on the monitors and the TV pundits all thought you were hard done by. Am I right in thinking you-know-who had something to do with it. Did Fielding reverse the places?'

I nodded. 'If I'm brutally honest the horse did run off course but many do when they're tired. That's what I said in my defence but I could tell from the look in the man's eye what he was thinking. And he gave me a three-day ban to boot.'

Another expletive passed Father's lips but thankfully it was inaudible. 'He ought to be reported for abusing his authority or at the very least for exceeding it. The man is an out and out shit. I just wish I was twenty years younger, he'd not be so keen to meddle with me then.'

'Angus Gunnell was the chairman so the decision was, in theory, a joint one,' I conceded.

Father thought I shouldn't be apportioning the blame;

there was only one protagonist in his eyes. 'Fielding is a manipulator. He saw a quick way to get back at you for standing up for me – if that's not abuse of authority I don't know what is. You must appeal against the ban and get the authorities to see the man responsible was overzealous to the extreme. That at least would wipe some of the ugly smirk off his face and might even get his wrists slapped.'

I felt he was right, but if you challenged a decision in racing you went up against the might of the BHA, risking making matters much worse and labelling you a troublemaker.

'I won't be the first jockey to cry injustice, it goes with the territory,' I shrugged, trying to sound philosophical. 'Didn't I say you had to be mad to do what I do for a living?'

He said nothing and began hurriedly scanning his race card with the start of the next race imminent.

'Nathan Scully's on an improving horse and Paul's luck must run out soon,' I told him, though I considered myself a lousy tipster.

'Let's not bother,' he said after another quick glance at the dozen or so hopefuls on the card. 'Let's get a drink and I'll tell you some news. You might know it concerns Curtis Fielding. He appears to be public enemy number one.'

4

We watched the race from the warmth of a bar. For once Paul Eddison had no joy at all on another Jolly-owned horse which he sparingly pulled up as it laboured with quarter of a mile to go. An outsider craftily ridden by Bradley Somerville, who was having his only ride of the day, triumphed. I was especially pleased for Bradley because we once lodged together in digs as impoverished stable hands and he had struggled of late after his championship-winning exploits of the previous season.

With the excitement of the race over and the bar now less populated I looked to Father to expand on his news, unsurprised to learn it had emanated from Lavender Thompson with whom he now had much more in common. He explained that she had spotted us having words with Curtis Fielding, rightly guessing from our body language it was no friendly chat and deciding immediately to divulge to Father her and son Anthony's recent dealings with the man. It did not make for easy listening.

'Seems he's been making the Thompsons' life hell too,' Father said with irony. 'They've only just got themselves straight after a horrendous year and it's all because of Fielding's insatiable greed. Lavender claims their involvement with him almost lost Anthony his veterinary business when the ratbag unexpectedly demanded repayment in full of a loan he had given them to fund the building of an extension and hydro pool. They both wish they'd never let the man talk them into letting him help them with the scheme in the first place, they reckon he was a complete nightmare.'

'So why borrow off him in the first place, couldn't they have gone to a bank?' I asked.

'Fielding boasted to them that he had the money at his disposal, that it was part of his inheritance and he would lend to them at a very low rate of interest. A proper loan agreement was drawn up and both Lavender and Anthony said Fielding was perfectly charming at the time and seemed genuinely interested in helping them expand the business. But as it transpired the bastard had an ulterior motive for helping them out in the first place and used the loan to muscle in on an invention that Anthony was on the brink of getting patented.'

'What invention?'

'Some kind of heated wrap that used electrodes to speed up the healing of minor horse injuries like pulls or tears and mild bouts of tendonitis. Not a new idea in principle but one that seemed to work quicker so that trainers could get their horses fit to race in half the time, which would obviously be popular with owners.'

'And Fielding wanted a share of the action, I presume?'

Father distorted his face. 'Dead right, son. He persuaded Anthony to cut him in for a percentage of sales once the patent had been obtained for what he called "services rendered" and then Anthony naively made him a partner in the business which was a major mistake. Fielding simply insisted on a bigger slice of the cake after threatening to call in the loan and he knew he had Anthony over a barrel.'

'So why call in the loan when he had a foothold in the business? That makes no sense.'

'Because he'd got what he wanted out of it, I suppose,' Father shrugged. 'He said he needed the money back asap and just kept hounding Anthony. The recession was making it hard for businesses to borrow off the banks so Lavender was forced to draw out all her life savings, sell assets and even re-mortgage her house to raise enough to pay Fielding off. At one point she considered selling her prize possession, the beloved Bentley, but it's been in her family a long time and she just couldn't part with it. All the worry made Lavender quite ill and Anthony's reputation suffered because Fielding got someone to spread quite nasty rumours about him which made some owners shy away from using him.'

'The same way he got somebody to direct a herd of cows onto your complex presumably?'

Father nodded his head slowly, said nothing and sat with a pained expression on his face for a little while.

'Does Lavender know about the current state of affairs with you and Fielding?' I asked him.

'I told her about what I did to his pick-up and she almost wet herself laughing. But she also warned me not to go up against him again. I doubt there's anybody on this planet that could get her to swear but Fielding managed it. I won't even tell you what she called him, very unladylike.'

It was all well and good getting warnings from somebody who had seriously fallen foul of such an unsavoury character, but it didn't make it any easier to deal with and as Father was suddenly deep in thought again I didn't try to ascertain his next move. But what he then said did shake me.

'I suppose you already know Fielding's younger half-brother is shagging Paul Edison's wife?' he said quite matter-of-factly, as if it was common knowledge. 'Lavender even made a joke about it, suggesting that they both liked screwing people, which for her was really quite good.'

I wasn't tempted to raise a smile, not even a false one. 'I'd heard on the grapevine earlier that Connie's been seeing someone else but didn't know who. Wasn't even aware there was a half-brother.'

Father enlightened me. 'He apparently crawled out of the woodwork about three years ago and his name's Bruce. He's the product of an affair Curtis's old man had with a much younger woman, and lived in America for a time. It

came as a bombshell to the whole family when Bruce
suddenly turned up just weeks after the old man died.
According to Lavender he tried to claim half of his brother's
vast inheritance but settled on enough to live off instead
and returned to the States. But now he's back and causing
havoc. Rumours are the jockey's wife isn't the first woman
to end up in his bed since his return and she won't be the
last. Doesn't it make you want to puke.'

It did but then I was just one of many who must have
felt that way. 'Could this Bruce have been the reason behind
his brother wanting to raise some quick cash?' I suggested.
'Maybe he demanded more money, after all old man Fielding
was considerably rich when he died and there were unlikely
to be any other benefactors drawing off his estate.'

'That's a possibility I suppose.'

'Or then again, Curtis Fielding might have needed the
capital to buy the static homes you told me about plus
money to redevelop the site. None of that comes cheap.'

'Maybe,' Father muttered, looking unsure.

His brain had soaked up a lot of information since he
was taken aside by Lavender Thompson and I wondered if
by speculating on Fielding's motives I was causing it to
overload. Though still a very astute man, Father didn't deal
well with pressure in general, preferring to keep a lid on
his emotions and not to play his cards out in the open. In
the past twenty-four hours I had watched him virtually age
before my eyes and also seen his anger bubble and boil to
the surface, both events leaving me in a kind of mental
disarray that was a parallel of his own bemusement.

But at least we could both glean some comfort from the
knowledge that Curtis Fielding had made other enemies of
late, and that it appeared he now had a marauding, and
considerably younger half-brother to contend with, all of
which would surely make his efforts to ingratiate himself
with the British Horseracing Authorities a damned sight

TOM BUTLER

harder. With that in mind I decided to find out more about what was making the enemy tick, planning to set aside any spare time that might happen my way the following week. I had hopes of raking up anything that could help Father resolve his current plight and maybe put me at less of a disadvantage in the future, should another racing incident like the one today occur.

Father was in no mood to argue with my proposal and quite bluntly asked me to find him a last race winner from the eight contenders, blaming me for his failure to bet on the previous contest. Another Jolly-owned horse with Paul Eddison aboard immediately drew my attention, but for no other reason than the name. I pointed to one ridden by a young amateur jockey and called No Friend of Mine, which Father got a generous twelve to one for with a bookie who looked down on his luck. Needless to say it finished last of the five who got round but at least Paul could only manage a disappointing third.

Next morning Father spent the whole day at his complex whilst I tried again to break my duck at Cheltenham. My cause was not helped by the late withdrawal by Dominic of a promising chaser in the second race due to the ground being a tad too firm, although I did pick up a bonus ride for Northumberland trainer Malcolm Clough in the first. Malcolm rarely brought his horses down south but told me Mugshot had travelled to the course this time last year and won handsomely, immediately putting me under extra pressure. Well if Mugshot was familiar with the surroundings he didn't show it, dispatching me at the fifth hurdle after completely forgetting to get his feet off the ground. That tested the shoulder I had bruised yesterday but thankfully I secured myself a relatively soft landing.

Predictably Paul Eddison fought out the finish with another

36

older jockey who just held on to win. Back in the changing room he reprised his dull body language of the previous day despite his three winners. No wins today, I thought, might make him suicidal given his glum expression. But at least when he saw me rubbing my shoulder he offered me some comfort.

'I used to ride regularly for Malcolm at the northern courses when he first started training and I never had much joy. He's a genuine bloke but that can't be said of some of the nags he trains up there. I'm surprised he hasn't called it a day.'

I couldn't disagree. 'Well today was a wasted trip, his horse never settled and couldn't cope with the pace you and some of the others set. It didn't even fall if I'm honest, just bumped me off.'

'Happens to the best of us,' he shrugged, stripping down to his body protector.

He then referred to the previous day's controversial race and gave me his version of an apology, stating categorically that I should not have been banned. 'Shit happens when you least need it,' he said, profoundly. 'It's one of the reasons I jacked it in when I did, and keep asking myself why I came back.'

'Judging by your recent success rate I'd say you made a pretty good decision.'

He looked sheepish as though he was as overwhelmed by it all as was everyone else. Then leaning over towards me and lowering his voice he confided in me. 'I came back because I couldn't stand being at home. I suppose you've heard the rumours circulating about Connie and Bruce Fielding,' he paused awkwardly. 'Well he's welcome to the bitch. She'll do exactly the same to him.'

Connie Eddison was what I would describe as a trophy wife, twelve years younger than Paul and the ultimate head turner. She was daughter of a wealthy owner Paul had regularly ridden for in his early thirties, supposedly out of his league in the looks department, and with a string of eligible suitors always a footfall from her doorstep. But Paul was the one she chose to marry and have children with, and despite infrequent stories about her straying they appeared to have survived and stayed on track in the ever tricky marriage stakes. Until now that is. Paul seemed resigned to his fate and the bitterness he was harbouring was only to be expected. It had me lost for words.

'I'll make sure the kids are OK of course,' he went on. 'Craig is a natural in the saddle and he's only ten and Lucy's just had her first pony.' He looked like any proud dad would and somehow temporarily stowed his bitter feelings towards Connie and her boyfriend away.

'Kids are resilient,' I said, having had it said to me many times not so long ago, a reference to my own estranged daughter Grace.

Recognising there was a common bond between us had undoubtedly loosened Paul's tongue and he seemed all the better mentally for talking about it. 'When I was not much older than my son I fell off a big clumsy horse at a riding stable and swore I would never climb aboard another one,' he grinned. 'Look at me now, why didn't I become a doctor like my father? He encouraged it enough and he could afford to put me through medical school.'

I returned the grin, though it was fuelled by sarcasm. 'Perhaps it wasn't exciting enough? In racing there aren't so many dull moments. We race about like blue-arsed whatsits nearly every day of the week and rarely get a break unless we fall foul of the lawmakers.'

Paul looked thoughtful, aware I was having a dig at officialdom. 'I've no truck with Curtis Fielding myself in spite of the actions of a close relative he never knew he had, but I gather he's none too popular in some quarters. I shall have to avoid being called in front of him, wouldn't want that. Despising one brother is enough.'

He remained melancholy and had now changed into his normal clothes as he wasn't due to ride again until the last two races on the card. 'Off to the bar to overindulge,' he joked. 'Maybe I'll risk two tonic waters.'

My only other ride was now in the fourth race so I asked if I could join him.

He politely declined me. 'Got to see a man about a dog,' he replied mysteriously. 'Another time, when we are both free.'

I watched him go with no more of a spring in his step than yesterday but felt that I had at least helped by listening and humouring him.

The immaculately dressed and distinguished-looking man I later saw him talking to as they sat at a corner table didn't come across as a racing man to me. It took old friend and rival Bradley who had followed me into the bar to educate me.

'That's Christopher Southgate, Chief Superintendent Southgate to be precise. Perhaps Paul's been doping the other runners and they've found out about him,' he joked. 'Why else would he be chatting to one of Gloucestershire Constabulary's most senior policemen?'

Remembering what Paul had said about seeing a man about a dog waylaid my immediate thoughts. Then I recalled what Father had said about Curtis Fielding and a top notch policeman being pals and my mind meandered. After all there weren't many who could boast to have reached the pinnacle of their profession so it seemed a natural assumption.

Bradley confirmed my suspicions when he conveniently told me the Chief Superintendent was indeed Fielding's golfing partner and was one of several high profile guests who had been invited along to present trophies at today's event.

I watched the two men from a safe distance as Bradley sloped off to meet some friends, and noted it was the policeman doing most if not all of the talking. Paul was listening intently but also looking like the naughty schoolboy who had courted trouble and was now getting the obligatory lecture from a head teacher. At one point he went to get up but the Chief Superintendent half rose to stop him, and they then sat glaring at each other until the temperature cooled and they conversed again. Whatever it was they were discussing had nothing to do with racing for sure and when the grey-haired policeman did eventually rise fully to his feet he did so with one last parting shot that left Paul open-mouthed. His mouth was still gaping when I reached him.

'You look as if you're in need of something stronger than tonic water. Let me get you another,' I suggested, at which he snapped his jaw shut and pretended everything was fine.

I noted a bead of sweat on his wrinkled forehead and a sense of fear in his small, deep-set eyes. I was expecting him to get up and leave but he nodded, accepted my offer of a refill and finished his first one. The bar was busy and it took me five minutes to get served, by which time Paul was sitting with his arms crossed looking relaxed, focusing on a TV monitor showing a re-run of the second race.

'Nathan will be insufferable now,' he commented. 'And he's got three more great rides to come.'

'Maybe between us we can spoil his day,' I shrugged. Looking down at the half-full glass the Chief Superintendent had left, I casually levered the conversation away from racing. 'Your friend left in a hurry, a sheer waste of good whisky is that,' I said as I sat down.

Paul didn't move his eyes from the monitor but at least he obliged me with a reply. 'Not a friend exactly. Well it started out as a friendly chat but finished up all wrong. I won't bore you with the detail.'

'I'm not easily bored and I'm a very good listener. Maybe I can help.'

He ran a hand over a day's growth of stubble and shook his head slowly. 'Nice of you to offer. You're a good bloke, Sam, and I know you've been through it yourself but I doubt you ever took it too far. That's my problem, I overstepped the mark and now I've got the bloody police on my case – and not just some beat bobby either.'

'Are you saying he was from the law?' I asked, deviously.

Paul focused his eyes on me as I turned on the sincerity. 'Surprised you didn't recognise him. He's always in the local newspapers banging on about reduced crime since his appointment,' he replied. 'Last week he even made the *Racing Post*. Apparently he's bought his precious daughter a racehorse for her twenty-first, doesn't that sort of thing make you sick.'

'So he's pretty senior then?' I asked naively.

Paul puffed out his cheeks. 'A Chief Super no less. And a more intimidating bastard you would not wish to meet,' he said with real disdain.

I barely took a breath before quizzing him again. 'So what kind of trouble are you in, Paul? It surely can't be that serious?'

I sensed he was putting on a brave face for my benefit and his answer stunned me. 'A couple of weeks ago I threatened to kill Bruce Fielding, even had a shotgun in my hand when I said it, though it wasn't loaded at the time but of course he wasn't to know that.'

'Shit, that's serious enough nowadays,' I reacted.

'I also made silly threats against Connie, just things that you say in the heat of the moment, though I'd never harm a hair on her head, honestly I wouldn't.'

'I believe you, Paul. But idle threats can be misconstrued.'

'She knows me well enough to know I couldn't hurt her or the kids. They'd be the ones to suffer most.'

41

'So was it Bruce or Connie who reported it to the police, or both?'

'Neither as it turns out. That was courtesy of Bruce's brother, well half-brother to be exact. He got on to the Chief Super who contacted me to arrange today's informal chat, except it sounded anything but informal to me. Basically if I don't back off he said he would make sure I spent a few years at Her Majesty's pleasure and would never ride again. He said to doubt his words would be a grave mistake. That if I wanted to be around to watch my kids grow into teenagers I should creep back into my hole and in his words, "Shut the fuck up".'

'Intimidation from on high,' I said aloud, a sour taste in my mouth.

He stared helplessly at me and nodded, then swigged back his tonic water in one. 'I'd appreciate your secrecy on this, Sam, and thanks for listening.' He straightened his back in readiness to stand.

'Not a word to anyone, I promise,' I agreed.

As soon as I said it I knew I would have difficulty in maintaining an oath of silence on the matter. It wasn't just my father's skin Curtis Fielding had got under. Now he had ruffled my feathers too.

5

After digesting Paul Eddison's confession and deciding I would almost certainly have to break my promise to him, I caught up with Dominic down at the stables. He was pacing about outside Hologram's box looking mightily worried. The big chestnut with the tell-tale white blaze running the whole length of his head had been kicking up his right hind foot and behaving erratically, and Dominic had called for the vet to take a closer look. Hologram was a spirited type and I had partnered him to success as a novice on several occasions. He was now competing against seasoned chasers and looking every bit a Gold Cup prospect. He had twice finished in the frame with me aboard at the course and until this untimely scare he had trained well, with today's race targeted by both trainer and owner Dame Olivia Blackwood.

Dame Olivia was an ex-Olympic gold medal winning show jumper from Wiltshire who had long retired from the sport and bought a small string of racehorses to pursue her secondary passion, and not without modest success. She had switched her string to Dominic only last year after a fallout with a Lambourn-based trainer and I had selfish reasons for wanting their allegiance to last a long time. I had fallen head over heels in love with her youngest daughter, divorcee Tamara, who as yet regrettably hadn't divulged her true feelings for me nor arrived at the racecourse as promised when we last spoke two days before. Only forty-eight hours but it felt more like a week.

Not for the first time today my mind wandered, but seeing

Dominic's relief as the vet gave the horse the thumbs up reeled me back in. I began to think about racing again rather than the other uncertainties in life such as romantic interludes which might or might not happen.

'He's walking OK again now, the lad thinks he might have banged his foot when he exited the box this morning,' Dominic said to anyone willing to listen, reverting back to type and wearing a face that could be described as quietly confident.

'He looks a picture,' I complimented, lost for something more original to say and adding, 'No sign of the owner yet.'

Dominic Ingles took off his trademark trilby-style hat and risked a small smile, knowing it was the no-show of somebody else that bothered me. 'They'll get here in time, don't you fret. The Blackwoods have never missed a race yet since I began training for them.' The 'them' he referred to included husband Joe and eldest daughter Ann Marie.

I pretended not to know what he was talking about, and he just lengthened the smile and re-engaged his hat in almost haphazard fashion.

Sure enough before I had reached the jockeys' changing room again I spotted the Blackwood family and a group of friends mingling with other owners, lapping up the occasion as they were prone to do, and Dominic, hat now properly secured, homing in on them at a rate of knots. I imagined he wouldn't mention his earlier concerns over Hologram's welfare to them, nor would he tell Tamara how much I was pining for her, preferring instead to hobnob with the rich and famous and accept their hospitality.

The third race was due to start in a matter of minutes and as it had the biggest field of the day there weren't many jockeys about, basically me and perhaps three others plus the valets who were trying their best to look busy. Nathan Scully was one of the others which surprised me because I had understood he was declared to ride one of the favourites in the race. I think he guessed what I was thinking because he sauntered across and as he did he appeared to be limping.

'Injured?' I asked.

He straightened the leg that was causing him to hobble and shook his head. 'Turned my ankle as I dismounted after the second race and that idiot doctor grounded me for the rest of the meeting. It's nothing really, I've ridden with much worse,' he moaned. 'Not my day at all,' he went on. 'The buggers have slapped a five-day ban on me plus a fine for over-striking with the whip which is fast becoming a farce. Don't know whether to appeal or not. Might as well all give up and buy ourselves bleeding greyhounds instead, they don't have to have jockeys on their backs.'

I found his stating of the obvious amusing but not his fate at the hands of the overzealous stewards. 'Not another to fall foul of Curtis Fielding?' I asked, making an assumption.

'Does it matter who?' he complained, not revealing which steward had administered the ban. 'All right for them sitting in that room with state of the art all around them to help them out,' he began ranting. 'We're the poor bastards who have to go out and try to keep half a bloody ton of horse running in a reasonably straight line, and be sure they're not gonna have us for not riding the horse out on its merits. I'm getting a bit sick of it; it's making our jobs ten times harder.'

The self-appointed spokesman for hard-done-by jockeys was now sitting down, his face flushed and fists clenched. Though he was never the most articulate of men, I could see the role suited him because he was probably the most committed jockey on the current scene and the one that trainers, owners and punters alike trusted unreservedly.

I was still of a mind that Curtis Fielding was probably the cause of Nathan's frustration and no doubt enjoying every minute of the authority that had been bestowed on him and the sense of power that it gave him over lesser mortals. It meant I would have to be doubly sure I didn't over-exercise the whip on Hologram over the two-and-a-half mile course, knowing that he had needed a few reminders on our last outing here at the Festival meeting in March when he finished second behind one of today's contenders, a David Miles trained horse called Westside Glory.

Noting that I was looking pensive and guessing why, Nathan threw me a telling smile and stowed away his anger for long enough to champion my horse. 'If I wasn't a cripple,' he joked, 'and had the choice of any I'd plump for yours, Sam. I think he's got a much bigger race in him than today's and I'll eat a bucket of horseshit if I'm wrong. Just don't give him one too many taps though otherwise the racing Gestapo will get you.'

I suddenly felt as though I had more pressure to contend with which I'm sure hadn't been his intention. Jockeys were notorious sometimes for getting wound up by praise for themselves or the horses they were due to ride and I was no different.

'I'm not going to use it unless absolutely necessary,' I said, referring to the whip. He smiled again and just looked up at the ceiling which masked his disbelief.

Ten minutes later he was still in the room though it had now filled up after completion of the third race. His ankle was the topic of conversation for anyone prepared to listen and no doubt his latest ban too. I was kitted out in Olivia Blackwood's blue and green quarters, trying to remain calm as I waited to be called into the weighing room, thinking that this might be a prelude to my Cheltenham dream and growing ever nervous inside at seeing Tamara again at the same time.

As befitted the occasion the Blackwoods were all immaculately attired and appropriately colour-coded, making it hard for me to miss them when I and the seven other jockeys were herded into the parade ring to mount up. Mother in lilac two-piece with pea-green broad-brimmed hat, older sister in green flower-patterned dress with blue shoulder shawl, and Tamara in mid-blue with complementary lighter blue pillbox hat and pale-green accessories. Not to be outdone, Joe Blackwood wore a bold pin-striped navy-blue suit, silky green waistcoat and turquoise cravat. Trainer Dominic looked positively drab by comparison in plain grey functional suit that had perhaps seen better days and an understated, mismatched tie.

Tamara waved a restrained hand in my direction when she saw me and joined the others in giving Hologram the lion's share of attention as he was led across prior to Dominic helping me into the saddle and delivering his final instruction. There was a simultaneous chorus of good luck from the gathered group and Tamara flashed her pretty brown eyes at me as though it might help galvanise me for the job ahead.

With a drying wind having accounted for any dampness in the ground the pace set from the off was quicker than Hologram might have preferred, and Westside Glory ridden by the trainer's eighteen-year-old son Lee Miles soon had the field stretched out with some clearly floundering in his wake. Hologram was big and bold at his fences as usual, a legacy of being honed on point-to-points when he was younger and testimony to his owner's previous career. Although prone to be temperamental and therefore difficult to handle, his ability and resolve were unquestionable and we rapidly closed the gap on Lee on the back straight with no other horses now in serious contention. Westside Glory clattered the fence before the last turn but Lee held on despite being propelled forward onto the horse's neck to make a recovery his father and late grandfather would have been proud of. But I wasn't hanging around to admire him, landing alongside him and giving Hologram only a glimpse of the whip as we gained a clear advantage. I stuck doggedly to the rail and asked for one more unerring leap which I duly got at the last, but Lee had rallied to get within two lengths of me. Like a slow motion replay the race was won and lost as the post didn't meet me soon enough and Lee stood proud in his stirrups to punch the air in triumph. Half a length, second place again, it was becoming a habit I couldn't shake.

My heart sank but I was man enough to give Lee a deserved pat on the back for a monumental effort. To rub salt in, he said it was the first time he had ever ridden the horse in a competitive race and had no idea how good he was. It was also his first ever ride over the Cheltenham fences and he couldn't wait for his next. I was also riding winners at eighteen but not at such a prestigious place as this, and now I had an all too real and irritating monkey on my back.

None of the Blackwoods showed any disappointment upon my return but Dominic skirted around me with rounded shoulders as I dismounted, and waited for my thoughts on the climax of the race.

'He was trying all the way to the line, he couldn't have given any more,' I said, unbuckling the saddle.

The trainer had rarely ever questioned my commitment in riding out a finish and he just stared back at me as if to say, 'If you say so,' before closely inspecting the right hind foot that had caused the earlier scare. Olivia seemed happy with my assessment while both Ann Marie and Tamara smiled at me in unison as I swept past them, mouthing the words, 'See you later,' to the youngest and eligible sibling which was greeted with positivity in her eyes.

With my racing duties over I dressed with a rapidity that drew a comment from Paul Eddison, who was now back to ride in the last two races of the day and looking surprisingly cool about it considering his earlier experience. 'Rushing off for a peck on the cheek or will it be something more?' he said impertinently. 'Don't go upsetting mother, I hear she can be a pretty fierce woman when she wants to be. Joe Blackwood must wear ear plugs, only way he's ever going to get some peace and quiet.'

'I'll be on my best behaviour,' I shrugged, deciding I had spent enough time with him already and hastening my exit.

As previously arranged I rejoined Olivia and her party in a hospitality area, sampling the side of her that Paul hadn't highlighted in the shape of her very buoyant mood which was echoed by her daughters and husband who always turned race days into an occasion to remember no matter what the outcome. I found Olivia deep in discussion with Dominic who had disposed of his hat and seemed to be in agreement with her over forthcoming plans for Hologram. Joe Blackwood was first to speak to me and as always he mixed generosity with honesty.

'Pity you couldn't quite pull it off, Sam, at the last I thought we had it. Don't know how that other horse stayed upright at the fence before the bend. Next time he won't be so lucky. So damned bloody close, you must think the gods are against you.'

The thought had already occurred to me but I tried not to dwell on it. 'That jockey must have had superglue on his breeches,' I agreed, after briefly shaking his hand. 'Like you I thought he was a goner.'

Joe was a thick-set man in his early sixties and by and large I had never seen him in anything but a philosophical mood, perhaps in keeping with the consistent rumours that he was well under Olivia's thumb and ever so slightly outnumbered by womenfolk.

'Don't exactly know what those two are cooking up,' he nodded towards his wife and her trainer. 'If it was up to me I'd send the horse to Sandown next in preparation for bringing him back here in March. What do you think, Sam?'

I didn't give it a great deal of thought. 'They know best, I'm sure they'll make the right decision.'

My eyes were now set on Tamara. Her father, sensing he wouldn't be able to compete with her in the attention stakes, backed off and quite deliberately prised the sisters apart to talk to Ann Marie.

'You look stunning,' I told Tamara without hesitation, backing it with a peck on her cheek. 'Sorry I couldn't quite pull it off. Now I know exactly how a bridesmaid must feel.'

She smiled and flashed her eyes at me again which made coming second a lot less annoying. 'It was such a close thing, Sam, the finish was unbearable,' she sympathised.

Tamara could so easily have been adopted because she barely resembled either parent but she did share her mother's philosophy on racing. 'You'll win on Hologram next time, I'm sure of it. You have nothing to be sorry for. You always do your best and I thought you rode a brilliant race.'

I could barely take my eyes off her. There didn't seem to be a hair on her head out of place. I wondered how anyone could have sunk so low as to physically hurt her like her ex-husband had, and whether she would ever fully trust a man again. It had never been a topic for discussion between us but always in the back of my mind I imagined it must have made her wary when she eventually re-emerged from her shell to begin dating again. Coincidently I had met her at Cheltenham last year and been arguably brave in asking her out, which left her mother speechless and Dominic verbally cursing me in private afterwards, believing it to be a possible threat to his newly established allegiance with Olivia who was paying him handsomely for his services. And it still rankled with him when he saw us together, although Tamara's mother had long since given me her blessing and Joe had positively encouraged me 'to bring a little light' into his daughter's life.

That said, my relationship with Tamara was not without

the usual frustrations you got with a slowly blossoming courtship, nor was it as yet set in stone. We had holidayed together, slept together infrequently, gone quite long periods apart and at times felt inseparable. My obligations to Dominic and other trainers made it hard for me and she had a busy life dividing her time between her nine-year-old daughter Emilia and running a modelling agency she had set up with a friend in central London. It was a juggling act sometimes just to see each other, so days like today were priceless.

Encouragingly she asked me if I was free later to join the Blackwood clan for the usual post-race get together at their palatial home The Willows on the outskirts of Chippenham. I savoured the thought that I might get her on her own or better still stay over. Only fly in the ointment was Dominic who would want me bright-eyed and bushy-tailed for two scheduled rides at Kempton Park tomorrow and might even suggest we travel to Middlesex together. Whoever said Sunday was a day of rest?

Both having a daughter of a similar age gave Tamara and me something else in common apart from stormy marriages we had endured, and when she asked me about Grace I struggled to hide my guilt at not seeing her for several weeks.

'My ex and her partner have been abroad a lot,' I said by way of an excuse. 'It's becoming harder but it's half term next week and Grace will be spending the whole of Monday with me due to a blank day in the racing calendar giving me a rare day off. Perhaps we can meet up. I remember the last time and the hours they spent playing together in the garden. That was such a good day.'

She liked the idea. 'Emmy asks about Grace all the time. Yes that would be nice, we must make it happen,' she said enthusiastically.

'And maybe we could bribe them to come racing depending when and where it is of course. I'll check my diary.'

'Sounds good, you know how much Emmy loves horses. Mother is already on the hunt for a suitable pony in readiness for her tenth birthday as I had insisted she didn't have one before then.'

'A budding jockey in the making, eh?' I suggested.

Tamara pulled a face. 'I think somebody else has other plans. She never forgave me for hating riding at that age though Ann Marie was so different from me and loved it, even if she didn't quite make top show jumping grade.'

She had deliberately lowered her voice so as not to be overheard and almost on cue her older sister had parked herself next to me and offered me her cheek.

'Bad luck, Sam,' she said without overdoing the politeness she wasn't renowned for. 'Just too bad you couldn't quite do it.'

Unlike her younger sibling, Ann Marie was the spitting image of her mother. Same distinctive bone structure, hair and eye colouring and upright posture. She was seven years older than Tamara and noticeably taller, married to a Dutch art dealer with an unpronounceable name and mother to three livewire sons.

I was never quite sure where I stood with her if I'm truthful. Perhaps something to do with having to gaze upwards at her, making me feel either awkward or inferior, or both. Nothing to do with sibling rivalry for sure because in the twelve months I had known them there had been no jealousy or cross words between them, and Dame Olivia was always keen to stress to all that the closeness of her family was as essential as it was unquestionable.

With Dominic rushing off somewhere as was his way, she now gave me her full attention as well as a brief insight into Hologram's future following the inevitable owner/trainer post mortem on the race that had so cruelly eluded me.

'Providing he's well recovered we're thinking of running

him at Wincanton in a fortnight. What's your opinion, Sam?'
she asked.

'Makes a lot of sense, I don't imagine his fitness is an
issue,' I replied.

'Then the plan would be to give him a break before
sending him to Sandown in the new year and after that
well ... we'll see.'

'Great,' I exclaimed, noting she wouldn't be drawn on
any further plans. 'Hologram's an absolute dream to ride.'

She looked at me and read my mind. Such praise was
tantamount to me telling her that I would not wish for
anything or anybody to come between me and a horse that
I genuinely admired so much and rated so highly.
Reassuringly, Dame Olivia smiled and looked pretty
contented. Then suddenly she changed the subject and
looked a little less far into the future. 'We're having the
usual party at the house and of course you have an open
invitation. Dominic won't be there to watch what you drink,
he's got something else on. Don't let Tammy down, she's
been missing you. Stay over.'

She deliberately avoided eye contact with me, peering
across to see if Tamara had heard her. She too, like her
father, was wearing a happy face. I took it that she had.
Now all I had to do was think of a reason for driving to
Kempton on my own and convey it to Dominic without
having to field any awkward questions.

6

I was woken by an incoming text message on my phone at twenty minutes past three. Tamara lay naked beside me, our bodies entwined, but she didn't rouse as I read the message before gently extricating myself from her warm limbs, pulling on a shirt and phoning Father from the safety of the en suite bathroom.

'Dad, what's up?' I stuttered.

He sounded even more frantic than he did on Thursday. 'I'm at Swindon General with Big Dave, I found him collapsed a couple of hours ago, he's in a bad way.'

'Where did you find him?'

'At Sloane Farm. Some bastard tried to cave his skull in and left him for dead.'

'But what was he doing there at that time?' I asked, puzzled.

Father enlightened me. 'All I know is that I left him there to lock up at dusk and got a phone call at midnight from his missus to say he hadn't come home.' he explained. 'I found him lying a few feet from the quad bike on the far side of the match lake and thought he'd had a heart attack. There was a lot of blood – I just thought he'd hit his head when he fell. But that's not what the paramedics told me when they'd finished checking him out. They said if I hadn't found him when I did he would surely have died from his injuries.'

'What do you want me to do?' I asked him. 'I have to be at Kempton by midday but I can be with you in half an hour.'

He was hesitant so I made up his mind for him and told him to sit tight, waking Tamara to inform her and leaving soon after with her blessing and the sweet taste of her lips still lingering on mine.

Big Dave or Dave Burrows to be exact was Father's right-hand man and general dogsbody who worked long hours for the pittance my dad considered a living wage. He was forty-five, twenty stone (hence the word 'big'), lived in a static caravan with an equally large wife and chubby child, and knew everything one needed to know about freshwater fish. Father had sort of inherited him when he took over the lease and the man had become irreplaceable. Nobody would dare not stump up money for a day ticket or break the strict rules of the fishery when Big Dave was around and it was hard to believe that anyone could get the better of him let alone come so close to killing him.

When I reached Father at the hospital he looked pale and weary. His imagination had been working overtime to offer me a pretty strong theory as to what had happened to Dave, who thankfully had now regained consciousness and had his wife at his bedside.

'This has Fielding written all over it, Sam,' he speculated. 'Only the other day Dave said he'd chased some undesirables away who he suspected were up to no good and we both decided to do more sweeps of the site in view of what happened with those blasted cows.'

I was immediately sceptical. 'How can you be sure he didn't disturb some poachers? You said yourself a while back you suspected you'd had some of the fish taken at night.'

He shrugged his shoulders but still dismissed it. 'I doubt any poacher would have done what some animal did to Dave. You weren't there to see the blood, it was just awful.'

'Has Dave said what exactly happened yet?'

'Not as yet. They want him to rest, the police will interview him when they eventually bother to send someone round,' he said, sounding bitter.

'How come you left Dave on his own to clear up anyway? I thought you usually locked up together?' I asked him.

He looked sheepish and said he had somewhere to go so left early.

'Where were you?' I pressed.

'I was invited out,' he admitted reluctantly. 'I had a meal with Lavender round at hers.'

'Just the two of you?'

'Anthony left just after I got there, I think he felt put out.'

I stared at him disapprovingly. 'Not wise to come between mother and son.'

'It was only a meal, don't read anything else into it. She invited me and I didn't like to say no.'

'Didn't or couldn't?'

He scolded me with heavy eyes for my ill-timed teasing and I got the message.

'Well,' I said, 'there's not much you can do here, his wife's with him and you said he's going to be OK. He's in good hands.'

'But what if he's told her something, assuming he's remembered. Don't you think we should...'

'No!' I interrupted him. 'I think you should go home and get some sleep, forget about the fishery today. If there's a contest cancel it. No one will be surprised if you close up for the day.'

Father shook his head and looked grimly back at me. For the second time in days he looked down in the dumps but he remained defiant. 'I'll try and get a couple of hours and then go and see what's what. I won't shut the fishery down, we stay open for business. I won't be beaten.'

Arguing with him was futile so I just didn't waste energy, driving him back to collect his car which he had left, in a

panic, on the fishery car park. For no good reason he
showed me where he had found Dave and then began
swearing loudly, turning the night air blue. He had spotted
something thrown against a bush and retrieved it. The large,
empty plastic container didn't have a cap on it and he stuck
his nostril close enough to the opening to identify what
had been inside before it had been emptied and discarded.

'Smells like caustic soda or something equally as nasty,
maybe strong bleach. What did I tell you, Sam? Somebody's
out to poison the lake.'

We searched around and found three more identical
containers within a twenty-yard radius and I noted there'd
been no real attempt to hide them. Still being dark made
it impossible to search further so I practically frogmarched
Father back to his car and told him I would follow him
home. Though not for a minute did I think he'd be in any
kind of mental state to fall asleep.

After I left him at the Cricklade house he was renting
prior to buying it I headed for the M4, stopping just short
of it in a lay-by as dawn broke to hopefully sleep until my
phone alarm woke me in good time to resume my journey.
I had agreed to meet Dominic at Reading Services at ten
and accompany him and an owner I was riding for to the
racecourse from there. I was fully expecting him to grill
me about last night's party at the Blackwoods' and badger
me for an update on my love life.

When Dominic saw me he said it looked like I'd slept in
a hedge all night but I skirted around the issue of my
appearance for the sake of the owner, a practising lawyer
named Grant Ibbotson who had spent a lot of his incoming
fees on buying horses and was addicted to the sport. The
last thing I wanted was to lose face in front of an owner,
though I think Dominic was just playing games and enjoying
watching me squirm, revelling in the entertainment I was
providing.

Predictably he asked me about the party at the Blackwoods', which I idly summed up as boring and with a playful glint in his eye he waited a while before bringing up the inevitable. 'Well, Sam, how are things between you and Tamara progressing?' he asked, making it sound as if it really mattered to him.

'Well, I think,' I replied casually.

With Grant's ears twitching he went on. 'She's so different from the others, just like a delicate flower and so beautiful with it of course.'

'She's good company,' I admitted.

'A bit too quiet at times, never quite sure what she's thinking,' he sighed.

'Hadn't really noticed, perhaps she prefers it that way. And she does have a lot to compete with.' I shrugged knowingly.

'Yes, maybe that's it. At least you appear to have hit it off with her. The steeplechase jockey and the ex-model eh? Material for a film. Make sure you treat her right,' he pontificated.

I sensed he had said all he intended to on the subject and was relieved that he hadn't asked me about sleeping arrangements last night. That might have put him off his driving. Not wise at eighty in the fast lane.

Understandably Dominic prided himself on his relationships with owners and the attention to detail he gave them, as though they were the most important people on earth and never to be taken for granted. He tried hard not to favour one over the other but I always thought he made an exception where Dame Olivia was concerned and wondered where Grant Ibbotson came if there was indeed a pecking order. Grant the lawyer was never more happy than when he watched his horses run. He owned one of the stars of Dominic's stable, a light grey by the name of Informed who had won seven of its last nine races including the King George VI chase on Boxing Day last year, coincidentally at today's racing venue. For a man whose working vocabulary could be described at eloquent he was an excitable sort who possessed much racing knowledge to back his judgement when it came to investing in bloodstock, though oddly I found him in the main cold, aloof and frankly uninteresting. Much, I think, to do with his illogical habit of talking down to jockeys and stable lads alike, almost as if he wanted to stress to them that they owed him for their existence and were in his eyes deemed to be dispensable. This, Dominic let slip to me a while back, was probably due to Grant finding a previous girlfriend in bed with an Irish jockey that neither of us had ever heard of. It brought tar and a brush into mind and didn't stand up as a defence or improve my opinion of him.

Today in the first race on the card I was riding another of the eight horses Dominic trained for the legal eagle, a former flat race specialist named Code Excel who had taken to hurdling like a duck to water and at the grand old age of twelve was still going strong. When discussing its chances as we closed in on the M25 Grant did what he always did, by conversing with Dominic as though there was no one else there worthy of an opinion, which the trainer compounded by giving me little scope to add to the conversation. I just kept telling myself I was there to do a job of work and hopefully if I won help to mellow the owner's prejudices. But if I didn't win it wouldn't worry me.

Subsequently a good Sunday turnout at Kempton basked in the autumn sunlight but sadly Code Excel was neither as bright as the weather nor as fleet-footed as usual and I could only coax him to finish a well-beaten sixth. That sparked a debate between owner and trainer even before I had left the unsaddling enclosure to weigh in, which had me wondering if I was the subject rather than the horse and whether there would be repercussions.

I decided not to worry either way and found somewhere relatively quiet to chill out for a couple of hours until the penultimate race of the day when I was due aboard the promising first-time novice chaser Sir Matt, owned by Dominic himself and schooled by me last week.

A call to Tamara apologising for my hasty exit was followed by another to Father, who had done as expected and partially opened up the fishery despite only a handful of die-hard pleasure anglers to provide for. Confirming his worst fears he said there had been an attempt to contaminate an area of the match lake with, as yet, unidentified toxic substances, reporting with a mixture of anger and sadness that he'd also discovered a few small dead or dying silver fish near the spot where the water looked discoloured. He had notified the Environment Agency who were responsible for inland waterways and was waiting for a visit from the local police who, according to Big Dave's wife, still hadn't interviewed him yet. He said he'd keep me posted.

With Kempton being the only National Hunt meeting of the day all the usual suspects were there. Paul Eddison had already steered a Miles-trained, Jolly-owned horse to victory in the second and was up on the favourite in the third race. I thought about what he had told me yesterday. It chilled me to think that he had resorted to pointing a gun at Bruce Fielding's head and now had one of Gloucestershire's most senior policemen on his case, albeit in an unofficial capacity, plus the spectre of Curtis Fielding overseeing it all making it seem even more like a figment of fantasy.

The third race eluded Paul and then he suffered the indignity of falling in the fourth, when he got so badly hampered by a stray horse his only course of action was to literally try to change direction in mid-air, something his relatively inexperienced horse didn't cope well with, sending them both crashing to the floor. I saw him walking with the suspicion of a limp afterwards back into the changing room where he threw off his colours and swore loudly, and I watched others around him secretively smirk whilst offering him false sympathy with their eyes. There didn't seem any point to me in shying away from talking to him, though I did so with caution.

'That looked bad,' I suggested, not overdoing the sincerity. 'Not much you can do but hold on and pray at times like that.'

He took a big breath and rubbed the top of his thigh through his heavily grass-stained breeches, disguising any pain he was in. 'Just when you think you have things under control the worst can happen,' he groaned.

'Occupational hazard,' I philosophised.

'Bloody Eddie Gifford's fault,' he lamented. 'He practically committed hara-kiri at the fence before, and had no choice but to jump off and leave the horse that baulked me to run on in full flow. That horse had no intention of running out and without a jockey well ... it was an accident waiting to happen.'

'Not much more you could have done,' I tried convincing him.

He shrugged, peeled off the soiled breeches and stepped into a clean pair as though it was a race in itself, which at least signalled his determination to put adversity behind him and perhaps scupper my own chances.

Whilst one would never describe Paul as a racing machine, his apparent rebirth had him focused to a frightening degree and it was never more evident than when the fifth race of the day got under way. He galloped off into the distance leaving a following bunch, including me, wondering if his horse, a fairly moderate chaser called Do You Mind, was jet propelled. It rendered Dominic's pre-race instructional chat pretty useless, as he had hoped I would force the pace on Sir Matt, the young horse having shown to be something of a bold frontrunner in training.

After the first circuit Paul was still twenty lengths clear and Do You Mind was jumping faultlessly so I put plan B into action, born out of pure panic and replicated by others who could see the gap lengthening if they didn't react. I led a small group of four into the chase and with about half a mile to go and three more fences to clear Do You Mind's lead had been halved. A whip-waving Nathan Scully on board the favourite went past me but Sir Matt instinctively quickened and by the time he had jumped the second last I got that immeasurable feeling inside that nothing was going to stop him from winning on his racing debut. Nathan's horse looked strong on landing as all three of us took the last fence together with Paul now asking everything of Do You Mind, despite him beginning to tire. I gave Sir Matt two flicks of my whip, kept him straight and he did the rest like a seasoned performer, leaving Paul to battle with Nathan for the places and Dominic no doubt the happiest man alive.

When he met me on our way back the words cat and cream came to mind and exactly what he said to me was just a blur. Nathan and Paul had been gracious in defeat and understandably surprised by the speed and stamina of a horse having his first outing under National Hunt rules. It was a feeling shared by most of the Sunday crowd who had left Sir Matt well alone on the tote and in bookies' alley which meant it became the biggest priced horse of the day to win, at a cool thirty-three to one.

Naturally Dominic forgot all about Code Excel and its pretty dismal sixth place in the opening race of the day and even lawyer Grant, who I suspected had just won a handsome wager, didn't seem to be holding it against me on the way back to being reunited with my car. Tomorrow I was riding another of his horses at Plumpton and it was edifying to know that he was talking with a positive air and telling the trainer he had good vibes about the horse which of course wouldn't make a shred of difference on the day.

Back in Stroud I called Tamara and asked to see her, and she didn't let me down. She congratulated me on my victory which had been relayed to her by her mother and added that she had some information that might help my father, which naturally intrigued me. But before I could arrange a place and time to meet her I was in the presence of a sudden and unwelcome visitor and there had been no polite knock on my door. It had all happened too quickly.

The man wore a black hooded top, suggesting evil intent, and the strength of his grip from behind had me immediately at a disadvantage, numbing the speed of my reactions, my brain still coming to terms with such an act of bravado.

'Don't struggle, you bastard,' the man said, his voice educated and with no rough edges. 'If you do I'll hurt you and if you don't I won't break your arm.'

I still had my mobile in my hand and Tamara on the other end but the man shook it free from my grasp and it ricocheted off a hardwood coffee table on to the wooden floor of my lounge. But I could still hear her voice as she tried to make sense of what was going on. The man's grip on me tightened, he dug his fingernails into my flesh and after kicking over the coffee table as we struggled he somehow located my phone with his foot and stamped down hard on to it. Tamara's voice was gone.

'What the fuck do you want?' I demanded, struggling to catch any kind of breath.

The man raised his voice a little. 'I want you to tell your father to leave Sloane Farm. Tell him hospital food is shit and that's the only place he'll be heading if he doesn't move out. You too if you don't make him see sense.'

'Who wants him out so badly? The landlord?' I asked, sounding understandably hoarse.

'I'm not here to have a conversation, just tell him.'

The urge to fight him if I could was too great now and I managed to jab my heel into the shin of his right leg. It only made him grip me harder which confirmed that he was bigger and stronger than me and singularly determined to get his message across. I thought then that if I complied with his wishes he would have to release me to make his exit and that might be my best chance of finding something I could fight him with or at least get to see what the hell my uninvited guest looked like.

As I thought this he eased the grip with his right hand and delivered a short but breathtakingly effective punch to the bottom of my ribcage which bent me double. For good measure and with revenge in mind he trod hard on the backs of both my legs as I crumpled to the floor.

'That's payback, you miserable bastard. Remember to tell your old man what I said or he'll be on the receiving end next time.'

His last words faded fast as he left me to check the severity of the damage he had inflicted on me. I cursed myself for not being able to get up to look out of the window or make it to the door. All I had was the sound of a powerful car screeching away into the dark and the distinct impression the man had not been born into villainy. For that I should have felt grateful. At least, unlike Big Dave, there had been no attempt to cave my skull in with a piece of concrete. I was in pain all right but I felt sure this had not been his main intent. It was merely a warning.

7

Having troubled a neighbour and borrowed a phone that worked, I had called Tamara and she had driven from the Willows to administer her as yet undiscovered nursing skills. Racing injuries were nuisance enough but this was different, though the aches and pains felt the same. Luckily I had plenty of bandages, sticking plaster and soothing ointments in my bathroom cabinet which Tamara now had all over the same coffee table that was unscathed from my earlier struggle – unlike the phone that still lay in bits on the floor.

'Take my phone, I have a spare pay-as-you-go at home. Keep it until you sort out another,' Tamara said as I fretted over my shattered handset. She had asked me no questions at first and only did so once she knew my injuries weren't more serious and after I had been unconvincing in playing them down.

'Whoever did this was just trying to make a point,' I told her. 'This wasn't the work of a thug. He left his mark and got his message over.'

'How can you be so cool about it, Sam? Somebody breaks in and does this and you just shrug your shoulders. This is serious,' she remonstrated.

She then reacted with horror when I revealed my front door hadn't been locked and was the sort that could be opened from the outside. An oh-so-common design fault that wasn't offered in my defence.

'And what about your father, what if the same thing should happen to him?' she feared.

TOM BUTLER

'It won't. I'll warn him of course but this was for my benefit only.'

She looked totally unconvinced. 'Some date this is turning out to be,' she muttered after shaking her head at me before kneeling down to weigh up the task ahead of her.

'Sorry,' I mouthed back. 'It'll be champagne and caviar next time,' I promised.

'Make it oysters instead,' she suggested, playfully tossing her honey-blonde hair. Tamara had given up posing in front of cameras a while back, preferring to stay out of the limelight, but she had been careful to retain her size eight figure and easily outshone the nurses who had administered to me following my inevitable racing injuries.

Trusting her implicitly, I endeavoured to tell her everything whilst she carefully wrapped a bandage around my battered midriff and tried not to pull it too tight. She raised her perfectly presented eyebrows several times during my revelations and then watched me raise mine when it became her turn to tell me what she had learned via her mother earlier today.

'Somebody she knows who works for the British Horseracing Authority phoned her in strict confidence this morning to warn her that they had heard Anthony Thompson, who currently treats her horses, was in breach of certain regulations regarding veterinarian certificates and is also being investigated regarding treatments employed at his surgery,' she explained. 'Her contact on the phone also confirmed he was at risk of being suspended and was likely to be struck off if serious irregularities were found.'

I asked questions straight away. 'Has your mother spoken to Anthony about it? What does he have to say?'

'You know Mother, she didn't waste a minute and phoned him immediately. He just laughed it off and said somebody with a grudge had tampered with his files. He assured her she had nothing to worry about and not to listen to tittle

66

tattle. Then he told her he had his suspicions and was spending the rest of today checking his records.'

'Did he elaborate on his suspicions?' I asked her, having already put Curtis Fielding in the frame.

She thought back but shook her head. 'He wouldn't say. I think he just wanted to be left alone to go through his files so that he could report back to the authorities.'

I didn't tell her precisely what I was thinking, but it looked like the work of Fielding who was probably still bitter at the Thompsons and hell bent on some sort of retribution.

'Don't tell Mother you heard this from me,' she said suddenly, noticing the intensity with which I had received the news. 'And in view of what you've just been through please don't try to be a hero, Sam, you're no good to me with broken body parts. And please double lock your door in future.'

She threw me a wry smile, finished the bandaging and kissed me on the lips to support what she had just said. I tried to make the kiss last longer but she pulled away and began tidying the table.

'I feel better already, you should think of joining the St John Ambulance team, jockeys would be queuing to fall off just to have you attend them,' I smiled.

With not much of Sunday left and upon Tamara's insistence I called Father to tell him about my uninvited visitor and the message he had got across. He said very little except sorry and that it was all his fault which I totally ignored. I told him to be extra vigilant but not to lose sleep over it, and let it slip I was in good hands which had him guessing what I meant and thinking maybe I had planned it all along.

Afterwards I sat with Tamara pinned to my side on my sofa and we watched the end of an old Michael Caine movie that didn't tax our brains too much. When I asked her to stay over she politely declined and said I needed to rest without what she cheekily described as 'distractions'. My attempts to make her reconsider went unheeded and by eleven she was on her way home, promising me a phone call to confirm when she got there.

The call came through just after midnight and she ended it by reminding me to report my attack to the police and to spend tomorrow in bed resting my bruised torso. I wondered what she would think if she found out there were no plans to do either. A mix of stupidity and stubbornness.

Even without bruised ribs it seemed ludicrous to be spending the whole of Monday morning travelling to East Sussex for one scheduled ride plus the possibility of picking up a bonus spare or two if I was lucky. But there was much to say for loyalty. Though naturally stiff I could move my body sufficiently, and certainly Bradley was none the wiser when he picked me up from our arranged rendezvous at eight thirty. With him in the car was the same Eddie Gifford who had been lambasted by Paul Eddison yesterday for having the temerity to fall off a horse he then later collided with, almost if it had been done deliberately to stop him winning yet another race.

To pass the time we indulged ourselves in racing gossip and when Tamara called me at ten to see how I was feeling both my fellow jockeys seemed puzzled by my answer and could tell the person on the other end was not best pleased.

'In trouble, Sam?' Eddie asked nosily.

'Who me? No, nothing like that,' I lied.

The two of them smirked at each other and allowed me to change the subject quickly. Secretly I was cursing that Tamara might disown me and I carried that thought heavily all the way to the weighing room at a windy Plumpton, where one jockey seemed to be the main topic of conversation. Details were sketchy but it appeared Paul Eddison had been arrested and for sure he would not be riding any winners here today. Quite a few jockeys with 'spare capacity' pricked their ears at the news, as did I, and it was I who got summoned outside to meet the Jollys, who had brought two of their prized string an awfully long way and looked visibly shellshocked at Paul's no-show.

'We need a jockey, Sam, in the first and third races,' Tristan Jolly said, his face ashen. Trudy, as always just one step behind, pulled hair out of her eyes and fixed me with a stare that was almost intimidating but also strangely sincere. I had almost given up hope of ever riding for them and today of all days, when I probably should have stayed in bed, they were shoving priceless work my way and pinning their faith in me.

'Of course,' I said without a hint of uncertainty. 'Do you know why Paul was arrested?' I asked both of them.

Tristan probably knew but clearly wasn't about to elucidate. 'We know as much as everybody else, Sam,' he shrugged. 'It's unfortunate but the horses have travelled well and are raring to go. I'll give you instructions when I've spoken to the trainer; he's been held up in traffic but should get here in time.'

With that they were gone, Tristan anxiously punching numbers on his mobile phone and his wife, a yard from his shoulder, having to fit in extra strides to keep up with him. The Jollys were not in the habit of spending vast amounts on transportation for their precious cargos unless they felt there was money to be made, which made me curious given today's first race was a pretty low-key two-mile, mares-only novice chase with a small purse at stake. I knew nothing of the six-year-old Fancy Nance except that she had pulled up in her last race still with a circuit to go. A quick glance at somebody's *Racing Post* indicated she was the least able of the seven mares in contention and likely to be a firm outsider.

As I began my preparation I started to wonder how Paul

Eddison would approach it if he was here and whether he might feel as nervous as I was, which for someone with my years of experience seemed crazy. It didn't help that Bradley and Nathan kept making wisecracks at Paul's expense, with the changing room still abuzz with surprise and speculation. And it didn't do anything for my confidence when another jockey taking part in the race innocently nudged me in the ribs to register a painful reminder of why I maybe shouldn't have been decked out in racing colours at all. The dull ache had gone by the time I had mounted and received my instructions from a recently arrived David Miles and like so many two-mile races it was over too soon and a creditable third place attained. Fancy Nance had proved to be much better than her lack of form had suggested and I was commended for my efforts in extracting the best out of her. Not even in-form Paul could have done better, I convinced myself.

The pressure was now on, however, to give them a winner in the third race which was a competitive three-mile chase and would see me paired with a recent French import with Gold Cup or Grand National ambitions, the sweetly named Sucre Bleu. He was a horse the racing press had been lording ever since he demolished a useful field on his English debut at Newton Abbot in September and the one that my ten rival jockeys would surely be most wary of. That said, I began having doubts about my level of fitness with my ribs still aching and a bruise on one of my calves testing my pain threshold further with constant rubbing from the top of my riding boot.

With much intrigue I made a couple of phone calls during the running of the second race to usually well-informed contacts but Paul Eddison's arrest was news to them, so I had to rely on the grapevine which for once shed no more light on what exactly had happened to him. I didn't trade in speculation and there was still plenty of that floating around the changing room when I returned there, still wearing the green and white Jolly colours and parking myself next to Eddie Gifford who was looking dapper in crimson.

'Try to stay on today, don't want lightning striking twice do we,' I joked, seeing straight away he understood the reason for my mirth.

'Best keep well away from me, Sam,' he ordered, his tongue hidden well inside his cheek.

'I plan to,' I said back.

'Listen to that lot, anybody would think Paul's been done for murder,' Eddie said, preferring not to join in.

His last word conjured a picture in my mind of the normally mild-mannered Paul pointing a shotgun at Bruce Fielding. Perhaps it wasn't so far off the mark. Maybe he had found some live cartridges and confronted the man again. And pulled the trigger. Another crime of passion.

I cleared my head of the negatives and returned to the job ahead, trying to put one of those ear-to-ear smiles on the face of Trudy Jolly and make her and her husband a tad more money. It was a task that didn't look any easier when I caught my first glimpse of Sucre Bleu who was diminutive by comparison with some of the others and sweating up badly.

David Miles told me to hold him back and let him settle into a rhythm, which might have worked if the horse had fully understood the English language or responded to my attempts to curb his natural instinct to power on ahead and set the pace. I could almost hear the trainer shouting at me from his vantage point to apply the brakes, and by the end of the first full circuit of the course it did seem the horse had settled though we were still several lengths ahead of a crowded bunch who were no doubt patiently watching, waiting, and expecting Sucre Bleu to tire.

But one thing the French inbreeding had given the horse was a surplus of stamina and by the time I had steered him unerringly over the second last fence we still had many lengths to spare and my only fear was if he suddenly got lazy and threw away his advantage. Two relatively light strikes of the whip relayed my fears to the horse's inner senses and he gave me his best, meeting the last in stride and fairly bounding up and beyond the post with nothing else in sight.

There was a look of cold envy on the faces of both Bradley and Eddie who had taken the minor places. They shook my hand as if to say I must have somehow inherited Paul Eddison's winning streak which I suppose was a backhanded compliment. When my groom took the reins to lead us back in he gave horse and jockey equal praise and I wondered if the trainer whose orders had seemingly been ignored would be so generous. David Miles was a pretty earthy character and straight away after doing a quick inspection of the horse he expressed his concerns. 'Thought you were never going to get him back at one point,' he sighed, looking relieved that the victorious Sucre Bleu had returned unscathed.

'He'll get three and a half or four miles easily,' I enthused, ignoring his comment. 'He had plenty left in the tank.'

The beaming Jollys both applauded me and I had never seen them happier. They, I supposed, had not been party to my racing instructions from their trainer and thought everything had gone perfectly to plan. Had they really found themselves a gem who would go on to win one of National Hunt's prestige races? Judging from their euphoria they couldn't be thinking anything else.

I didn't have time to gloat too much as I was due to ride in the next two-mile hurdle for Dominic, who hadn't made the long trip himself but sent his head lad to oversee proceedings. I had ridden Bookends several times and he was a favourite at the stable, owned by a very modest man who was content so long as the horse covered its own upkeep, which perhaps explained why this was its fourth race already this current season.

For whatever reason the owner had chosen a combination of bright orange and shocking pink with a bold chevron design which made me (and others) smile every time I saw it hanging from a peg and drew even more guffaws when I wore it. To the ten-year-old horse with a chequered history it mattered not, and his honest endeavours out on the course soon had me believing that despite the pain I was in this could turn out to be a very good day. As I coaxed him over the final hurdle he had every chance with two others either side of him making their challenge and as always he gave his all, only conceding defeat to one of the others at the line by less than half a length.

Gratifyingly both head lad and owner seemed happy enough on my return and the latter was already mentally adding the second place prize money to the horse's total winnings and, in addition, no doubt planning its next race. I left him to it, and back in the weighing room my body was keen to tell me it had nothing more to give, endorsed emphatically by the length of time I stood soaking in a shower that helped to physically rejuvenate me.

I sat with Bradley in a bar later as we watched Eddie plod around on a no-hoper in the last race still no better informed about Paul's plight. The jibes had long since subsided as fellow jockeys now realised it was perhaps cruel to poke fun at his expense when he wasn't around to defend himself. Bradley had vied with Paul more than most over the years and famously the two had fought out one of the classic finishes in the Gold Cup at Cheltenham six seasons ago that still got regular airtime from appreciative racing pundits.

'I remember feeling quite relieved when Paul retired and less than pleased when he decided to come back,' Bradley recalled. 'Some said he had little choice as he had such a high-maintenance wife who then went around spreading her legs to all and sundry,' he exaggerated.

'I think he came back because he missed it, as we all will when our time comes,' I predicted.

Bradley thought about it and sighed. 'Well, whatever the reason, he was never the people's favourite and hated being the centre of attention. He once slapped a press guy who got well under his skin at Ascot, which was a bit out of order even if the arsehole deserved it at the time. And what about when he appeared on that sporting panel show and barely said a fucking word and got his specialist question wrong into the bargain? He did racing no favours that day.'

'He's facing problems of a different sort now, so there's no telling how he's going to react to things happening around him,' I contributed.

'Needs to sort himself out for sure. And that goes for his missus too, she's taken him for a mug for far too long. Mind you, I wouldn't turn up the chance of giving her a poke myself, know what I mean,' he said crudely, gesticulating with his fist.

'We all make mistakes, I think Paul would be first to admit to that,' I said, not overstating the obvious.

'You don't suppose he's done her in, do you, or harmed her in some way? Jealousy can bring out the worst in people,' he speculated.

'Not likely,' I said, disguising my nagging concerns brought about by Paul confessing to the shotgun incident with his wife's new lover.

'Wouldn't think he's ever picked up a parking ticket in the past, he's so squeaky clean,' Bradley prattled on. Then he had a rethink and remembered something. 'Come to think of it I did once see him lay out another jockey over by the stable block at Chepstow. Must have been ... ten years ago, not long after he married Connie. I think this young apprentice made some innuendo towards Paul's new bride and got a broken jaw for his bravado. There was a bit of a fuss made but it was all brushed under the carpet and he got away with it, jammy sod.'

I sat squarely on the fence and said, 'I'm sure he's no angel, we all have our moments. You said yourself he had got annoyed with a reporter a while back, enough to make him want to strike out. I've felt like that myself on many occasions.'

Bradley stopped to think again, then slowly nodded his head. 'I had an incident once with an arsehole of a steward at a point-to-point in Worcester. He ended up with a bloody nose and I got a long suspension. But I'd do the same again, only probably hit him harder next time.'

'I rest my case,' I said smugly. 'None of us are perfect.'

'No we're not, we shouldn't judge others,' Bradley conceded. 'And we should stick together because there are a lot of clowns involved in racing determined to make our jobs ten times harder they should be. Take that idiot who banned you on Friday for instance, what fucking planet did he come from? Somewhere they don't teach common sense for sure.'

Bradley's face was reddened and his hackles were up. He might have been one of the top jockeys on the National Hunt circuit but it didn't make him feel any less vulnerable. He knew he might be next in line and I wondered, if it happened, how he'd take it.

I resisted a strong urge to slag off Curtis Fielding and instead pointed to the nearest TV monitor. It seemed Eddie Gifford's racing day was over. He had pulled his horse up two fences from home after a miserable ride and was cantering back in his own time. We both imagined he would be pretty glum on the homeward journey.

'Poor sod, he'd have been quicker on a donkey,' Bradley summed up.

'That's racing for you,' I agreed.

8

The next time I saw Tristan Jolly was as we waited for Eddie next to Bradley's car. He was pacing about nervously a few feet from his metallic silver Range Rover, talking and then listening on his mobile. Trudy Jolly was sitting in the passenger seat checking her hair and make-up in the sun visor's vanity mirror, impervious to anyone around her. I took several slow-motion steps towards Tristan, waiting until he had finished on the phone before calling across to ask for news of Paul.

He took a step backwards and shrugged his square shoulders. 'Not much to tell,' he responded without raising his voice. 'All I know is he's being held in custody in Gloucester on assault charges. I've been ringing round to anybody who might know more but I've drawn a complete blank.'

Behind me Bradley was muttering something about Paul teaching his wife a lesson, a thought I tried not to dwell on.

'Will you ring me if you find out more?' I asked Tristan. 'It's very important that I know what's gone on.'

The expression on Tristan's face changed as if he was taken aback by my sudden interest and the unconvincing nod he delivered in reply left me somewhat in limbo wondering whether he would or wouldn't comply with my request.

'Call me when you can,' I repeated, not at all sure if he still had his receptors switched on or was in the mood to listen.

76

'Didn't know you cared so much,' Bradley commented, his eyebrows twitching.

'Paul needs all the friends he can get at the moment. Talking to him at Cheltenham on Saturday made me realise winning races isn't everything, the guy's life is in turmoil away from the racecourse. We should look after our own when adversity strikes.'

Bradley's eyebrows ceased moving and he just seemed to accept what I had said, taking a long look at his watch and cursing Eddie for holding him up. As if his ears were burning Eddie arrived in a rush and we joined the mass exodus of cars departing the course with the Jollys about three vehicles ahead of us.

'What's the latest on Paul Eddison?' Eddie asked, prompted by catching sight of the personalised plate on the Range Rover.

Bradley was quick off the mark. 'I bet he's been trying to rearrange Connie's looks. He's been done for assault.'

I gave him a curt, sideways look and told Eddie that as yet no one knew the truth.

'Stands to reason,' Eddie presumed, ignoring me. 'It's what a lot of blokes in his situation would do. Hardly a crime in my book, she's bloody well asked for it.'

Eddie Gifford, as always, looked untidy which matched his general casual approach to life and noticeably held him back from getting more regular rides though he never showed whether that bothered him or not. He was thirty, single and supposedly dating a female apprentice jockey who lived way out in the Lincolnshire countryside. His blinkered attitude to Paul and Connie Eddison's problems hardly made him good boyfriend material in my estimation but he was entitled to his opinion.

'The longer he's banged up the better for you eh, Sam? Especially now you're on the Jollys' radar and you've rode a winner for them,' he said, making huge assumptions. 'You could even get to ride Spice It Up at Liverpool on Saturday in the big chase there. Some buggers get all the luck.'

'That's never going to happen, my ban starts at the weekend,' I reminded him.

Both Bradley's and Eddie's eyes lit up at the same time. There was a lot of combined wishful thinking. Spice It Up was one of the best young chasers around and another that David Miles was grooming towards stardom thanks to the generosity of the owners who packed a powerful punch when they bid for likely candidates at the auctions.

'Pity about that,' Bradley piped up. 'Still say you were hard done by, Sam, the stewards must have ganged up on you. Most of them have probably never sat on a horse and don't have a clue what we have to deal with during the course of a race. I gather Nathan's put together another strong letter to the BHA about the whip guidelines but it'll be a miracle if they see sense over that one.'

We were all in agreement and Eddie even mentioned a boycott, which for me was like serving a double punishment. But he did have a point with so many jockeys having their hard-earned income cut or cancelled out by fines and periods of inactivity due to the length of the bans.

'One thing's for sure it needs sorting out and pretty damned quick,' Bradley went on. 'How can the powers that be sleep at night knowing everybody's suffering because of their bloody rash decisions and incompetence? Maybe we should all turn up at their headquarters one day and knock a few heads together.'

Eddie loved the suggestion. 'I'd vote for that, it would send a few feathers flying mind you, but it might show them we're fed up of being taken for mugs.'

After the two of them had finished griping and putting the racing world to rights I made some guarded calls to Father and Tamara, and took one from Dominic who wanted the lowdown on Bookends. I gave him a favourable report to match that of the head lad's and after he had told me about his plans for the horse I asked him what he had heard about Paul Eddison's arrest. He knew little more than me but stated categorically that Connie was not the victim of his crime, understanding Paul had been picked up by the police at a house in Swindon this morning where a man had been injured and needed hospital treatment.

The news had three journeying jockeys literally pulling names out of a hat to identify the man, with me unable to get Bruce Fielding out of my head on the back of Paul's confession and in spite of Chief Superintendent Southgate's warnings.

On a family note Father had briefly told me Big Dave was on the mend and had now given the police a full statement and vague description of his assailant which they said they would act upon accordingly. There had been no more sightings of dead fish and the man from the Environment Agency was pretty sure no permanent damage had been done by what he described as 'an act of unprovoked sabotage', which the police had now been made aware of and would investigate alongside the attack on Big Dave. Father said he wouldn't hold his breath on there being a quick result in either case, adding he felt uncomfortable around the law now that he was chief suspect in a criminal damage enquiry and having been grudgingly logged into the police computer system.

As for Tamara, her displeasure had waned and she even congratulated me on my victory in the Jollys' colours. Like every racing connection, she was aware of Paul Eddison's unfortunate incarceration. She also asked me how my bruised ribs were, but stopped short of agreeing to see me whenever I got back, citing spending time with her daughter and a nagging migraine as legitimate excuses. She said she was also due back in London tomorrow and it might not be until the weekend that I saw her again, which made me think maybe picking up a ban covering Saturday to Tuesday wasn't so bad after all. Sometimes life brought worthwhile compensations.

Once reunited with my car I drove straight to Cricklade and found Sam Woodall Senior in reflective mood. He was surrounded by paperwork – so much it made finding somewhere to sit a challenge, so I settled for the wing of an old armchair that he should have put to rest a long time ago. Suddenly my ribs were complaining and testing my pain threshold again but I steered clear of giving him an injuries update.

'Something I can help you with?' I offered, secretly hoping he'd decline my help, paperwork having never agreed with me. He was wearing narrow-framed reading spectacles which he curiously took off to speak to me.

'I think I've found a way out of this mess,' he said mysteriously, leaving me in suspense.

'Go on, I'm all ears,' I urged.

Father sucked hard on his teeth and grimaced as he straightened his back, which he had probably had bent double for too long.

'I'll have to get it checked out of course but I think it's worth pursuing. The previous owner of the land once told me Sloane Farm was restricted to arable and livestock farming with the exception of the land on which the lakes are sited, so unless our mutual friend Fielding has made a successful application for a change of use he has no right to build his precious caravan park and make it residential. I'm buggered as to why I didn't think of it before. I could be pissing in the dark, Sammy boy, but wouldn't it be just champion if my hunch is right.'

'And does any of this relate to the land Fielding owns?'

I asked, fingering a couple of pages that were closest to me.

'All this came attached to the lease, it's mainly the do's and don'ts and a maintenance schedule which only covers the fishery. I would need to see the pre-registration deeds to the land and any amendments made at the time Fielding purchased the farm. I'll get on to Mann and Co. tomorrow to tell them there's a dispute with the owner and ask them how much it'll cost me to get them to examine the title deeds fully. I suddenly feel a whole lot better even if it proves to be a long shot.'

There was colour back in his cheeks and his pessimism subsided. With the vigour of a much younger man he raked up the papers and shuffled them into some semblance of order.

'Wish I'd known about this on Friday when we tried talking sense into the man,' I lamented. 'I might not have pissed him off quite so much and antagonised him into giving me a ban I can ill afford.'

Father shook his head. 'He'd have screwed you over no matter what, he takes pleasure from it. He can do his talking through a solicitor in future, I won't take any more of his shit.'

We drank to it and I brought up the subject of Paul Eddison and Fielding's half-brother which he theorised about as though he had already given it some thought. 'What if this half-brother is putting the squeeze on Curtis for money? It would explain why he pulled the rug from under the Thompsons and is trying to force me out. It could be a long-term plan to dispense with the fishery, fill in the lakes and put his infernal mobile homes there instead. Providing he could get permission he'd be on a money spinner though it might not give him much in way of instant liquidity.'

Call it telepathy but I'd been having similar thoughts,

and what Father said about Fielding appearing desperate to raise cash seemed to ring true although it could be argued he needed it to purchase Sloane Farm. Without exact dates and more info we were simply speculating. But at least it was good to see Father smiling again and back in the land of optimism. And it was encouraging that he was talking about taking on Curtis Fielding through legal channels instead of resorting to criminal behaviour which for him had been merely a cry for help. I decided it was best to try and keep the positive vibes going and do some impromptu sleuthing.

'Unless I get a late call I have no rides tomorrow and thought I might pay Anthony Thompson a visit as well as trying to find out exactly what Paul's been up to,' I told him.

He didn't argue. 'Never had you down as a detective, but even crumbs could make a difference. I'd even go a step further and try to track down Bruce Fielding, he's more than just Paul's wife's lover, I'd bet on him playing a big part in what's been going on.'

There was logic in what he was saying but in truth I knew nothing about the man nor what he looked like. There was still a chance, of course, that he had been the assault victim. I was already signed up to find out. 'Get on to your solicitor first thing and I'll deal with the rest, and pass on my best wishes to Big Dave. Tell him I always thought he had a thick skull but make sure he knows I'm only joking,' I said, smiling.

Father kept up the optimistic theme. 'He's being let out tomorrow and it'll take wild horses to keep him away from the lakes but I'll try. When I told him about the dead fish he cried. I won't tell you what he said he will do to the culprit if he's found but as a clue it involves two spherical shaped objects and a sharp knife.'

I smiled again and didn't rule out such an eventuality at

all. Even gentle giants have their tipping points. 'Sounds painful, remind me to buy a ticket for the spectators' gallery,' I said, acting out a pretend wince.

I could tell that Father was thinking Curtis Fielding should be on the receiving end of something similar but he stopped short of saying it out loud.

Having accepted a bed for the night and risked mixing painkillers with a tot of medicinal brandy, I batted away questions from Father about Tamara that were born out of his desire to see me settled down into family life again. Failed marriages and jockeys were like cheese and wine so far as I was concerned and no one typified the theory better than me. Like many young jockeys, thoughts of serious relationships and marriage had been kept off the radar until I had established myself and had a pretty steady income. There were girlfriends and the occasional one-night stands that now pricked at my conscience, and then there was Janice Jones, who I met at Hereford racecourse almost twelve years ago on a bitter, cold and bleak January afternoon. She was five years older than me, single and worked for her father's catering company, which had just won the contract to rejuvenate several poorly organised racecourse restaurants. After only the second race of the day the stewards sensibly pulled the plug on the meeting due to the freezing conditions and a shroud of persistent fog that made it far too much of a lottery.

With an awful lot of food potentially going to waste a generous sponsor donated the bulk of it to trainers, owners, jockeys and grooms whose day had been ended abruptly. Some declined, deciding to travel back whence they came before the weather got worse, but I joined a bunch of jockeys who for once forgot their strict diets to partake in a complimentary feast. That's when our eyes met over a plate of sausage rolls, Janice later giving me her phone number, which led to a date followed by a whirlwind courtship and a wedding in the summer.

To say I rushed into things and ended up marrying the wrong woman is too simplistic because the few days after the birth of Grace three years later were probably the happiest of my life and I revelled in the whole repertoire of good emotions that went with the territory of new parenthood. That Janice then suffered badly from an acute version of post-natal depression and went cold on me was a cruel twist, and within eighteen months came an inevitable separation that not even a counselling medium could resolve, as mutual despising set in from both sides of an ever increasing divide.

At the time Father was always philosophising, having gone through a similar experience with Mother, but his was a voice from another era which didn't ultimately help me or my ailing marriage. Now I gave my ex-wife a wide berth and had to be content with seeing Grace once a month, drumming it into my head that my very much loved daughter would one day find happiness for herself and thrive in a loving relationship.

Such thoughts I took to bed with me, comforted that Father hadn't dragged up the past or dwelled on our combined mistakes, nor delved too deeply into what my real feelings for Tamara were. The Blackwoods were a close family and she had already been physically and mentally scarred. Even though I had somehow fallen in love with her and wanted a life with her, it didn't mean for a single minute it might happen. But I knew I would do whatever was needed to turn wishful thinking into reality.

9

Tuesday morning went more quickly than I wanted it to. There was no news about Paul Eddison, not even via the racing press, and Anthony Thompson was too busy to see me having a full day of surgery although I had reluctantly agreed to meet his mother at her home where she had insisted on me joining her for a light lunch.

Castle Moat Lodge was a Victorian country house that Henry Thompson had inherited long before he had been found dead there by his son when he suffered a heart attack and fell from a ladder. That was fifteen years ago and not something Lavender ever talked about. Needless to say the property was hers to do with as she pleased, which included mortgaging it up to the hilt to bail Anthony out and offering it as sanctuary to over twenty cats. The house and grounds were at a midway point between Chippenham and Wootton Bassett and overlooked the M4 motorway to the north and Marlborough Downs to the south-east. I imagined long before the motorway was built it enjoyed peace and serenity.

Lavender reminded me of my own mother in some of her overbearing mannerisms, but not in looks as she was infinitely taller and thicker set and dark instead of natural blonde. Sadly her home was no longer as salubrious a place as it used to be, which made her a nervous host and always at pains to point out that she was just too busy to get around to rectifying anything in need of repair.

We took lunch in a modern conservatory that had been added to the original building and looked out on neat lawns and modest shrubbery that partially hid a rather run-down, overgrown area where there was a large dilapidated greenhouse, a slowly rotting tool shed and what I imagined used to be a well-stocked vegetable patch. Two of the resident felines sat motionless on a weed-strewn patio rather like statues carved out of coloured stone, whilst another which was totally black seemed to be stalking something that had attracted its attention on an overgrown lawn.

Keeping her rekindled friendship with Father for another day I purposely asked Lavender about what Tamara had told me, and after fighting away an isolated tear from her eye she was quite forthcoming.

'It's all complete lies, Sam, but there are certificates missing and the thing's an unmitigated mess,' she said with an icy shudder. 'Anthony is a brilliant vet, though by his own admission not such a great businessman but he's sure his records were in order. He strongly believes Curtis Fielding has coerced somebody into removing important paperwork from his files just to make it look like he has been cutting corners and failing in his duties. The implications are serious and this has come right out of the blue. We thought our troubles with the man were long since over. Seems they are not.'

'What's Anthony proposing to do about it?' I asked.

She sighed heavily. 'He's stubborn, Sam, just like his father was. I suggested he ought to involve the police if he felt his confidential files had been tampered with but he's hoping the powers that be will just turn a blind eye this time or at the worst just reprimand him.'

'Who has access to the files apart from your son?'

She struggled to think and then generalised. 'Several staff, full-time and part-timers. Nobody Anthony wouldn't trust...' she hesitated. 'Well he did have to dismiss a young lad he took on as a favour to a friend, he was totally unsuitable. But I doubt it was down to him, he was simply useless and couldn't do anything right.'

'Not likely then but he can't be entirely discounted,' I considered. 'I suppose no one's above suspicion.'

Lavender sipped tea from a china cup and took stock. 'It doesn't bear thinking about that somebody could do such a thing to Anthony given the way he looks after the people who work for him. It's really quite upsetting.'

I watched her delicately pick at a tuna salad sandwich and bided my time.

'What can you tell me about Anthony's invention, the one Fielding wanted a share in?'

Her face shrivelled up and her eyes became even more intent. 'He's still hoping one day to patent it but these things take a lot of time and money. The latter we don't have at the moment thanks to that poor excuse of a man. I can't tell you how much I despise him.'

'Is it true Anthony made him a partner in the business on the strength of Fielding stumping up the money to pursue the patent?'

'That was how I understood it, but quite soon after they shook hands on a deal Curtis rang Anthony and said there had been a hiccup and demanded the money back. Some of the money had already been paid out on legal fees and other expenses so it just wasn't possible to pay him back in full.'

'So that's when you had to intervene to raise the cash?' I surmised.

Her jaw dropped slightly at the mention of the money and she stared back at me. 'I did what any mother would have done in the circumstances,' she said, guardedly. 'My son had been hoodwinked by a very clever man, but that said, my late husband would never have entertained him. He would have seen right through him.'

'Did Fielding ever say what the hiccup was?' I quizzed her.

She shook her head empathically so I moved on. 'Can I

ask you about Fielding's half-brother, Bruce? Have you ever
met him?'

'Oh yes,' she replied immediately. 'Another distinctly
disagreeable character. A bit of a charmer with the women
I gather, but I found him profoundly arrogant. Rumour
has it he went to Eton and he certainly speaks with a plum
in his mouth. Must have been a real shock to Curtis when
he suddenly turned up claiming to be his brother. Why he
kept himself hidden for so long is a mystery. But if you ask
me just like his older sibling the man's a born troublemaker.'

I wanted to know more. 'When and where did you meet
him?'

A harassed-looking Lavender searched her memory bank
and recalled with disdain the two occasions of being in the
close proximity of Bruce Fielding.

'I met him at a charity dinner about three weeks ago and
he was brazenly parading Paul Eddison's wife on his arm
like some prized trophy,' she said disapprovingly. 'And then
again a fortnight ago at the Andoversford point-to-point
meeting but he was with another man then and they seemed
to be handing over a large sum of money to a bookmaker,'
she recollected.

'How would you describe him,' I asked her. 'What I mean
is, does he bear a resemblance to half-brother Curtis?'

'Not much doubt about it, Sam,' she conceded. 'He's
much younger of course but if they were horses you'd
definitely say they were from the same stable, similar in
build and yes, very much a chip off the old block.'

'So quite a big man, about my age and well spoken?'

'Sums him up,' she sighed.

Lavender was now looking at me with an inquisitive smile
and perhaps expecting me to reveal the reason for my
interest. But I hadn't finished with the questions yet. 'How
well do you know Paul Eddison and would you say he was
capable of assaulting someone?'

She stirred a little in her chair and poured herself some more tea, offering me some which I declined. 'Paul's been an acquaintance for many years and he's a very tactile and generous man. Always dips into his pocket at charitable events and finds time for others. When I heard about the problems he was having at home I really felt for him and to see Connie arm in arm with another man, well ... I was lost for words. What will happen to those poor children? I don't know what she's thinking, taking up with a man like that.'

There was genuine sadness in her eyes and she had to pause a while before carrying on. 'Anthony and Paul used to play golf together with a few other jockeys but it's become increasingly hard with work commitments and they don't play any more. He's no more capable of assault than me so I just won't accept what people are saying about him.'

I agreed with her. 'That was my immediate reaction too but he has had a bit of an altercation with Bruce over Connie already which he has reluctantly admitted to me and, of course wouldn't want made common knowledge.'

'Altercation?' Lavender puzzled.

'He confronted him and threatened him,' I replied, economising on the truth.

'Hardly surprising I suppose, stealing another man's wife could turn even the mildest-mannered person. But I still think Paul's incapable of actually physically harming someone.'

I didn't disagree. 'My sentiment too but it remains to be seen if he did or didn't overstep the mark. I thought I might try the Jollys later today to see if they've heard any more.'

'And I'll make enquiries too,' she assured me.

The rest of our conversation at her instigation revolved around Father and his ongoing troubles. She warned me about complacency where Curtis Fielding was concerned and even offered to give sanctuary to my harassed parent if he needed, in her words 'moral support and a bit of old-fashioned TLC'. The idea of Father literally spending time in the bosom of Lavender Thompson amused me and I would be sure to flag it up with him when I caught up with him sometime later. I would wait with bated breath for his reaction and hope he could keep a lid on his enthusiasm.

The call to Tristan Jolly was made from my car after Lavender had escorted me to it and wished both Father and me luck. The voicemail tone kicked in straight away and I left a message that brought me a response within ten minutes. With no hesitation he told me Paul had been released on bail and was currently in a hurriedly convened meeting with a top law firm in Charlton Kings who he had himself recommended. He also told me Paul would be back in the saddle tomorrow and riding one of his horses at Worcester in the two-thirty race but he stopped at further information when I tried to press him.

Assuming Paul would afterwards head for his Malmesbury home where I had several times previously played poker, I drove there and waited outside until his unmistakeable canary yellow Alfa Romeo pulled up next to my Ford Focus. His face told me I was unwelcome but it didn't stop him inviting me in and pointing me in the direction of one of two leather sofas in a traditionally furnished living room liberally decorated with photographs chronicling his sporting career. He poured us both a small whisky, adding soda water to mine but not his own, and stood with arms folded.

'I suppose the grapevine's been working overtime and painting me as a villain?' he asked me, battling to stay as calm as any man in his position could.

'Not something you hear of every day,' I said, holding

back on anything that might be misconstrued as flippancy. 'Some of us care what happens to our peers and don't speculate until they know the hard facts. I think you know me well enough to know which camp I favour. In view of what you told me at Cheltenham on Saturday and what's been happening with my father recently I felt I had to come, although it would have been your prerogative to send me away.'

Paul pressed his unshaven chin into his chest and sighed. 'I've nothing to hide, Sam, but proving my innocence won't be easy. Like the naïve fool I am I walked straight into the spider's web and got well and truly caught. Even a criminal lawyer with many years' experience thinks he's going to have his work cut out to build a good defence for me. Right now I feel like every of bit of shit from the fan has been aimed in my direction.'

Rather as my father had last week, he seemed to be seeking consolation from the whisky glass he held to his lips, already much of its contents gone.

'Are you at liberty to tell me exactly what happened to you?' I asked him, deliberately sounding as contrite as I could for badgering him.

Keeping the glass inches from his mouth and, figuring I knew more than most already, he willingly parked his bottom on the edge of the second sofa and took in a big, deep breath.

'Late Sunday I got a phone call from a man called Stan who I vaguely knew to be a bookies' runner. He said he was down on his luck and needed money and asked me if I was interested in purchasing some incriminating information about Bruce Fielding,' Paul divulged. 'At first I thought I shouldn't even entertain the idea and was of a mind to put the phone down on him but then again I thought it might be worthwhile to find out more even if it was going to cost me, so I went to a couple of cashpoints to draw enough out on the way to meeting him at the address he gave me, arriving there around midnight.'

'Where was the house?' I asked.

'In a pretty grotty part of Swindon not too far from the M4, it looked like one of those ex-council maisonettes and was right in the middle of an estate. He had told me earlier to let myself in as he was nursing a broken leg but when I got in I found him sitting in a chair clutching a wet tea towel to quite a nasty head wound. There was a lot of blood and of course I tried to help him best I could although he wouldn't say what had happened. Foolishly as it turns out, I got his blood on me and touched things I shouldn't have and before I knew it there were sirens and the place was swarming with cops and this Stan was insisting I had tried to kill him.'

'What about the phone call he made to you, surely that could be traced back to prove he lured you there to set you up?'

Paul grimaced. 'The man's admitted he phoned me to try to sell me information but he's told the police when I got there I got angry and tried to beat the information out of him and it didn't help when they found over five hundred pounds stuffed in my wallet.'

I sighed inwardly and could see the fix he was in and why any representing lawyer might think they were taking on a hopeless case. Although I was no super sleuth it was obvious to me that Stan was just the cog in a none too elaborate plan to stitch Paul up and have him charged with a serious crime.

'There are plenty of people ready to vouch for you, Paul, myself included,' I said, trying to raise his spirits. 'Anyone who knows you well would testify that you were incapable of assaulting somebody. We need to break this Stan's story and find out who paid him to set the whole thing up. This has to be the work of Bruce Fielding or...' I paused to think, 'even the policeman who threatened you. Or maybe both of them acting together. You must pass on every scrap of information to the law firm, if they're clever enough they're bound to be able to dig something up to discredit those who are quite blatantly attempting to frame you for something you didn't do.'

He listened and then reminded me of something. 'But I did threaten a man with a shotgun, Sam, remember? If I admit to that I'm in the deep stuff. What's that well-worn saying about the fat and the fire? You do see the mess I'm in. That's what comes of trying to deal with things on my own.'

'Anybody could have done the same,' I tried to pacify him. 'So what happens next?'

'The police said they needed time to investigate further and I'm due back at the station next Monday for another interview when I expect they'll officially charge me. Do you know anybody with a fast boat, Sam? I think I'm going to need one. I don't think I could face prison.'

'It won't come to that,' I reassured him, with no real grounds to believe it wouldn't happen other than a deep sense of injustice.

Paul stood up and closely considered his now empty glass. The age lines on his face had grown and he looked like a man much in need of the sleep already denied him.

'That might help in the short term,' I said, gesturing to the glass. 'But it's sleep you need more than anything else. Tristan's told me he's expecting you at Worcester tomorrow. In the racing world nothing gets in the way and the cogs keep turning. Focus on the undeniable fact that you are innocent and there will be many people out there rooting for you.'

Almost like a best friend might he put the glass down and shook me warmly by the hand, seemingly reluctant to release it again.

'Thanks Sam, don't know how I'll ever thank you, what a star you are,' he said with no false sincerity.

'By letting me win the big race tomorrow,' I told him with an unconvincing and poorly executed wink.

He gave it no real consideration. 'Over my dead body,' he quipped, not a bit perturbed by what he had said, which seemed like a good omen to me.

I drove through Cirencester just before rush hour and on into the depths of the Cotswolds out towards Burford where Sloane Farm lay in a narrow valley running along the course of the river Windrush. The first person I saw as I parked was Big Dave Burrows who was endeavouring to put some fuel in the tank of a quad bike and sporting a nifty head bandage which resembled a Mexican bandana. He waved to me and with Father nowhere to be seen I thought I'd take the opportunity to interrogate him.

'You should be putting your feet up not slaving away for my old man,' I humoured him, drawing a heavy shrug and toothy grin from a man who was literally twice my size and liberally covered in tattoos on chest and both arms.

'Seriously I'm glad to see you back and was hoping to find out more from you about the attack you suffered. Dad was pretty vague as usual so if it's not too painful to relive it again perhaps you could spare me a few minutes.'

As the words tripped off my tongue I saw Father homing in on us carrying a full rubbish sack in one hand and a broken bottle in the other.

'Dad, I've asked Dave to help me out, providing you can manage without him. Maybe we could start at the place the attack took place,' I said quickly before Father had time to intervene or object.

'OK by me, boss,' Big Dave replied obligingly.

Father seemed put out. 'Why don't I come along too?

94

After all we're all in this together,' he huffed, appearing out of breath.

'Don't let me stop you doing what you're doing,' I said, trying to deter him.

Big Dave, now standing stock-still with petrol can in hand did a good impression of a tennis spectator rolling his eyes swiftly between us before I conceded ground and muttered the word 'whatever', allowing Dave time to finish topping up the quad bike's tank.

In the time it took him I briefly told Father I had found out what had happened to Paul Eddison and also that I had been to see Lavender Thompson and she had sent him her love. I was sure that he went slightly red when I mentioned her name and he seemed visibly relieved that Big Dave was now purposely striding down towards the match lake to revisit the scene of the crime, not even looking behind him to check that we were following.

I had, of course been close to the spot where Big Dave led us before, but it was dark then and it looked so different in the last glimmers of evening light. I asked Dave to re-enact what had happened, still in wonderment at how anyone could have got the better of such a big man, and he sensed my unease.

'Like I said to the coppers, I 'eard this noise and was thinking it'd be a stray horse as we've 'ad a few in 'ere before,' he remembered. 'Then this bloke came from nowhere and bashed me with a piece of broken slab. I think I tried to grab hold of the bastard but he must have hit me again.'

'He took you by surprise then?' I assumed.

'That's pretty obvious,' Father piped up. 'Would you take him on without the element of surprise?'

Although he had a valid point I ignored him and secretly wished he'd go back to his tidying up. 'Did you see the man who hit you? What sort of build was he?' I asked Dave, pressing on.

It took him some time to answer. 'Never saw him, well not his face anyway 'cos it was too dark you see ... he was quite big, as tall as me but thinner.'

I thought straight away that narrowed it down to a few million suspects and carried on. 'A big man and obviously strong? Did he speak or was there anyone with him?'

Big Dave shook his head to both questions and looked forlorn.

Father was welling up in anger. 'Not much you can do if somebody jumps out on you wielding a fucking concrete slab. Had it been you or me we've had been dead and there would have been a murderer on the loose.'

'Quite,' I agreed. This was serious and somebody needed to be stopped sooner rather than later. 'Did you notice what the man who hit you was wearing?' I persevered.

'I think he was all in black and his jacket had a hood. If only I'd seen him coming, the bastard would've needed a hospital not me.'

As I took in the thickness of his forearms and biceps from close quarters I never for a minute doubted his hypothetical claim.

'Can you remember anything else about the man?' I asked him, expecting nothing in return.

'He was driving a Mercedes,' he shrugged with certainty.

'How can you be so sure of the make?'

He looked ever so slightly smug and repeated the shrug. ''Cos I know one when I hear one, I've got a good ear for that sort of thing.'

'So you heard a car driving away after the attack,' I presumed.

Big Dave looked back at me with a hint of annoyance as if I hadn't been paying attention and nodded.

'So he didn't knock you out then?' I said surprised.

'When I found him he was practically unconscious,' Father clarified. 'It must have been delayed reaction.'

'I see, so we're not looking at a regular punter with a grudge then. I thought most of your clientele drove battered old vans or ten-year-old hatchbacks. Don't suppose you know if it was a new or old Merc, or do they all sound the same?' I turned back to Dave.

Father agonised. 'Bloody hell, son, isn't it enough to know he's pinpointed the make of car? A Mercedes is a Mercedes.'

The cogs in Dave's brain were now working overtime despite Father's remonstrations. It was clear the man with the looks of a night club bouncer had an exceptional gift and who was I to break or punctuate his line of thought.

'Presumably the police know all this?' I asked after a lengthy pause.

Big Dave hunched his broad shoulders and sounded vague. 'Well ... I think I told them everything.'

'We all know who's behind this,' Father said with accusing eyes. 'Had I thought it would have done any good I would have gone bleating to them long before they showed up at the hospital but after what happened last week I doubt they'd even have listened to me. Perhaps you can persuade somebody that the two incidents are related. It's safe to assume they were not coincidences.'

'I can try. I'll call somebody tomorrow, time permitting,' I pacified him.

From where we stood it was just possible to make out the unfinished area of excavation which according to the landowner had invalidated Father's lease. A short row of metal stakes covering an area of no more than ten feet had yellow tape stretched between them to mark clearly the offending strip of land my father was being accused of encroaching onto. It was right at the outer edge of the horseshoe shape which was to give the new lake its rather predictable new name, and from my vantage point I could not see why the excavation could not have been moved to satisfy both parties. I made the mistake of bringing it up with Father who had now sent Big Dave off looking for more litter.

'Do you have any idea how much it costs to hire a JCB to do stuff like that? We are only talking about a few feet of what was hedgerow and scrubland. When all the soil that's been piled up has been shifted I don't even think the edge of the lake would touch Fielding's land but it suits him to leave things as they are because it strengthens his case the way it looks now. He will stick to his story and accuse me of trying to deliberately move the line of the border to my advantage.'

'And as we already know,' I conceded, 'the man's in no mood to negotiate with us.'

Father looked like a man in an imaginary headlock pondering which way to twist and turn to get free. I told him to pursue the change of use angle and said I'd speak to him after racing tomorrow. Knowing that Worcester, like Cheltenham, wasn't my happiest hunting ground he wished me luck with perhaps less verve than normal but it was still appreciated.

10

Worcester's skyline was littered with low, marauding cloud and its cathedral spire was barely visible from the starting point of the meeting's second race, which saw Paul Eddison back in the saddle and up against all the usual suspects including me aboard a Dominic Ingles trained hurdler called Harry Houdini. As the predictable rain lashed down it noticeably slowed the pace of the race but my mount had no intention of progressing from the rear of the field. It was all I could do to coax him home last of the finishers with Paul triumphant, though in no mood to milk his victory, on a horse owned by a Warwickshire syndicate.

He had received a somewhat cool reception in the weighing room an hour ago with some still coming to terms with the reason for his two-day absence and others, already not fans of his, keeping acknowledgements to the absolute bare minimum. With the exception of myself, only the usually loud Nathan talked to him as though nothing had happened, which might have been a help on another day but only seemed to show others in an unforgiving bad light. 'Getting on with it', as he had told a reporter from a racing tabloid, was what it was all about and he was certainly getting the thumbs up from a bawdy group of syndicate members who had shoehorned themselves into the small winner's enclosure and would no doubt be dining out on their winnings tonight.

Unlike Cheltenham I had frequented the winner's enclosure at Worcester several times before so I knew how Paul really felt inside, but for me it seemed so long ago I was beginning to feel jinxed. My next race, the fourth of the day, did nothing to alleviate the feeling, with a local owner and trainer looking as forlorn as me at the end of it as their horse trailed in amongst the also-rans despite my persistent promptings. And a young Dominic-trained novice chaser fared little better in the last race to fold up a miserable and unforgettable day.

On the relatively short journey home I fielded a call from Tamara from her agency's office in London. She asked about my health and my day in general but I didn't bore her with the details. Then almost immediately came another call, this time from the police, and it left me in a cold sweat. It was from a Gloucestershire Constabulary DCI, reporting a fire at my father's lock-up near Stonehouse and, worryingly, to notify me he was in a hospital ward suffering from smoke inhalation, his condition unknown. I did a rapid detour and was at his bedside in less than an hour as dusk closed in.

Apart from being wired up and breathing through a mask he looked in reasonable shape given his ordeal and in between taking in gulps of rejuvenating oxygen his language was straight out of the gutter.

'Fucking hell,' he spluttered and spat. 'The bastard's gone too far this time. The cars have gone son, they've been destroyed for sure. I feel like somebody's torn my heart out.'

The cars he referred to were the six classics he kept there in mothballs, including the prized Bugatti. The remainder of his treasures were hopefully still safe in their other hideaway several miles away. I had never shared his enthusiasm for them and imagined they could be rebuilt despite his gloomy forecast, so I paid them no great heed compared to his own welfare which he had foolishly put at risk by disobeying orders.

'Why did you have to go into the building against the

fire fighters' wishes?' I reprimanded him, having been briefed on his actions by a doctor on the way into the side ward where he was now being closely monitored.

'What the fuck do you think, son? How could I just stand there and watch them go up in smoke?' he croaked. 'Do you have any idea how much they were worth?'

I did know and didn't think it wise to remind him how well they were insured. It would have been scant consolation to any fanatical classic car collector. 'It was still an act of stupidity,' I lectured him. 'You could have put other lives at risk, they had a job to do and rescuing you wasn't on their agenda.'

Father re-employed the oxygen mask and seemed to be at odds with me for my apparent lack of sympathy. 'Couldn't stop myself, son ... I had to go in,' he wheezed whilst fighting back tears.

I was sitting next to him and resting my hand on his forearm. I waited for him to settle into a less frantic breathing pattern.

'So, we need to find out for sure that the fire was deliberate,' I said in an unquestioning tone, keeping my hand where it was if only to reassure him I really was on his side.

There was no uncertainty in his eyes despite the vagueness of his reply. 'Fires like that don't start themselves. You don't have to be an expert to know that.'

He sat up now with the mask held away from his face as if he wanted to see if he could breathe freely without it, which he clearly couldn't. I waited again for him to take in more oxygen before testing his memory.

'How on earth did you get there so quickly and who alerted you?' I asked.

He raised himself up and stubbornly waved away my outstretched hand which I had instinctively moved from his arm to offer his torso extra support. Even in his current predicament there was to be no let-up in the trademark Woodall defiance whether uncalled for or not, but at least he came back with an immediate response.

'I had not long left there after doing my weekly check when the owner of the lock-ups rang me to say the detectors had gone off and he had called out the fire brigade,' he recalled painfully. 'I rushed back and when I got there the fire was practically out and everything was...' He couldn't bring himself to say it. He was close to tears again.

'Was everything in order when you left and are you sure you locked up properly?' I badgered him.

'Of course,' he snapped back, agitated. 'Everything was secure and the shutters were in place. I've done it a million times before.'

'And did you notice anyone hanging around, maybe somebody watching you?'

He needed more oxygen and thought hard whilst drawing air through the mask. 'Didn't notice anyone,' he wheezed. 'Are you saying you think I was followed and then whoever it was broke in and set fire to the place?'

'I'm trying to piece together in my mind what happened. You can't be sure that it wasn't just some kind of accident. Only the experts can determine the cause. You should have stayed well away and not had to have been dragged out like that. It was sheer lunacy.'

He was now sitting bolt upright and trying to swing his legs around as if intending to get up. I used both hands to stop him and he crumpled awkwardly into a heap, almost losing hold of the face mask before using it to draw in another lungful of reviving air and managing to manoeuvre his body into a sitting position again. Even then he still seemed to be wilting in front of my eyes as the onset of exhaustion took its toll, accelerated I imagined by my questions which had only intensified his terrible ordeal.

Deciding he'd been through enough and consciously

raising my voice, I forcibly made him listen. 'Dad, you mustn't ... you need as much rest as possible. You have to stay here until they say it's safe for you to go. It's outrageous what's happened to you but the damage has been done. We need to let the police deal with it.'

Undeterred, Father was doubly determined to regain his composure, forcing his head up from his pillow and holding the mask away from his mouth to speak. 'So we might as well expect another unsolved crime then,' he groaned cynically. 'What the fuck am I going to do, son?'

It was my turn to breathe uneasily and search for an answer. But there wasn't one that readily came to mind and all I could do was concede how unbearable his plight had become and that this was the lowest I had ever seen him during my adult life.

'Look, get yourself right and don't you dare discharge yourself. Some of the nurses here are pretty damned fit,' I quipped, trying to inject some urgently needed humour which failed to register with him. 'Dave can cope on his own,' I went on. 'I'll make arrangements for you to stay somewhere safe when you are released. I'm sure Lavender Thompson will take you in for as long as necessary if I ask her. I'll also do whatever I can to convince the police there's a serious vendetta being waged against you,' I stopped for breath. 'This has become too personal now, Dad, and it's imperative that I speak to Fielding again to tell him it has to stop before someone gets killed. I will also chase the fire officer in charge of the blaze at the lock-up to establish for sure the cause of today's fire.'

In no real position to argue, Father lay back and kept his oxygen supply line hovering inches above his gaunt, shock-riddled face. There was not even a shift of his eyes in my direction and, disturbingly, for a man well known for his boundless energy and vigour he looked desolate.

I gripped his hand and felt only modest warmth from

within him. It convinced me he had nothing more to give and no capacity to take either. But tomorrow I felt sure he would be flirting with the nursing staff, doing what men of his age do all too well to embarrass his peers and making me feel inadequate in the kindest sense of the word. But for now it was all I could do to hold back the tears as our emotions intertwined. This was a journey neither of us had ever planned or wanted to take.

Finding logic and using it to guide me, I immediately phoned Tamara to tell her about the fire and Father's smoke inhalation. I waited for my ears to burn, which was an ironic analogy but one I was prepared for and deserving of, and with some hard-hitting words she admonished me. Mostly for not taking the threat made to me seriously enough, and also for indirectly toying with my father's life by hiding behind a misplaced loyalty to him. Though I said something lame about jumping to conclusions it did lay bare my guilt and I did feel inadequate. I offered her no defence. She said she was sorry for what had happened to my father, and I simply said sorry. I think she knew I meant it. But it didn't stop me thinking the Woodall stubbornness was not something anyone could find a cure for.

Later I made a cluster of calls beginning with one to my father's nemesis and following it up with calls to the police, fire service, an anxious Lavender Thompson, Big Dave Burrows, who was back home in his caravan, and Father's solicitor via his twenty-four-hour voicemail.

My initial call didn't get past Curtis Fielding's mobile paging service but when he did phone back soon after he announced he was shocked on two counts, first that I had actually accessed his number and second that I had the temerity to phone him so late in the day. He reminded me what he had told me and my father at Cheltenham on

Friday and said there was no point in talking to him again on the subject.

I told him frankly a herd of cows and a couple of broken door mirrors were minor inconveniences compared to physical assaults, poisoned fish stocks and arson at which he merely laughed and called me delusional. But when I brought up Christopher Southgate's name and mentioned I knew about the Chief Superintendent's interest in Paul Eddison he appeared momentarily hesitant, before reverting to type, rendering me more predictable bluster and flatly refusing to my demands for a meeting tomorrow.

The setback did not deter me and another call secured Father a relative safe haven, with an audibly shocked Lavender insistent that he stay with her for the foreseeable future and adding that she would call on her many contacts inside and outside racing to rally round and help in any way they could. Like Father I sensed she too would feel outraged and would surely shed a tear or two over the burnt-out cars as a proud classic car owner herself and someone who took the modern mass-produced equivalents for granted. Despite her overbearing nature, which might or might not yet annoy Father to distraction, it felt good to have somebody like her in our corner and I found myself heaping praise upon her that came from a desire to believe she was the one person I could depend on, at a time when friends seemed scarce and emotions were running high.

Once convinced of Father's safety in her hands I made several more calls with three goals in mind: to put an end to my father's troubles for good, to show Curtis Fielding to be a manipulative and vindictive bully, and to ultimately expose him as such and bring him to account. Far from easy but achievable. Lady Luck, I conceded, might play her part. Being a jockey I knew all about that.

The call I made to the police beforehand had certainly not convinced the same DCI who had reported the fire to me that foul play was the cause, and a senior fire investigator had said it was still too early to draw such conclusions, although he did concede it appeared an accelerant was highly likely to have been involved and that would explain the speed at which the initial fire took hold of the building. But he emphasised that such things were always to be found in a garage, and remained uncommitted, adding that it might be several days before the cause could be positively confirmed.

Worryingly for me, and with a high level of frankness, he said he had not totally ruled out my father's visit to the lock-up as being connected to the fire which I took to mean a possible insurance swindle. When I reminded him what he had said about the speed of the fire and that my father was twenty minutes away when he had been alerted he seemed to back off and instead brought up the subject of enemies who might want to harm him. I told him about the current feud with Fielding and in a routine voice he promised he would liaise with the police to undertake the fullest of investigations.

As for Big Dave, who was not known for being articulate, I got plenty of grunts and groans and supportive sounds which for a man still bearing the scars of war following his attack was all I could ask for in such trying circumstances. Like Lavender Thompson he was an ally and a brave soul to boot. With a simple mind like Dave's it was a case of unquestionable loyalty reigning over self-interest, which perhaps made him a saint in the eyes of those who knew him and richly deserving of such an accolade. That didn't stop me giving him clear instructions and asking him to rein back on his bravery however; there was no point in taking unnecessary risks. He appeared happy to oblige.

With an early start and two fancied rides at Ludlow the next day I summoned an uneven but revitalising pattern of sleep that at least put me in the right frame of mind as well as restoring my adrenalin levels. The Shropshire course was one of my favourite places and my win ratio there was impressive by anybody's standards. Some racing venues were like that, and whereas for me courses like Cheltenham and Worcester filled me with apprehension, the manicured turf of the busy market town's picturesque course held no such fears and, if anything, inspired me.

The opening race on a cool, dry and virtually windless day was evidence if such proof were needed to back my case. A fairly novice trainer based in Shrewsbury against whom I rode many times when he was jockey had engaged me to ride his most successful horse to date. The bold jumping chaser named Pitcairn quite simply cantered home in some style without me ever having to ask him for more than a moderate effort from start to finish.

I was allowed no time to congratulate myself or bask in any semblance of glory however, due to the late arrival of a much more relaxed-looking Paul Eddison who hastily urged me to leave the noise of the weighing room and follow him to an area of lush grass which he considered far enough away from eavesdroppers.

'What's going on, Paul, what's so damned urgent?' I asked him.

He answered me with an almost lyrical tone to his voice and a rediscovered glint in his eye. 'The charges against me have been dropped, thank God,' he said with great relief. 'And following another meeting with Chief Superintendent Southgate yesterday everything's sorted regarding that business with Bruce Fielding. I've even made my peace with Connie for the sake of the children. Thought you should know as you were being so supportive.'

I was shocked, not pleased. What he had told me was too clinical.

'But somebody tried to frame you for a serious crime you didn't commit,' I reminded him. 'Don't you want to know who that person was?'

He shrugged as if it didn't bother him. 'All I know is that there was some sort of misunderstanding which the police owned up to and have apologised for so that's the end of the matter for me.'

My eyes questioned his but they gave nothing away. 'Misunderstanding?' I said, puzzled. 'Paul, you need to explain what they mean by the word misunderstanding.'

He didn't feel there was need for an explanation. 'What does it matter, I'm an innocent man, wrongly accused. Must happen all the time.'

Hardly the time for flippancy, I thought. 'Paul, the other day you were in serious bother with the law, now you tell me it was due to a misunderstanding. That doesn't make much sense.'

His earlier sparkle was slowly deteriorating and it was as if he wanted to draw too convenient a line under what now appeared to be bogus assault charges made against him. He tried making his point again.

'Look, as far as I'm concerned I'm off the hook and that's all that matters. I can get on with life, move on, make plans. By the way, Sam, sorry to hear about what's happened to your dad.'

It felt as though the soft grass below his feet was cushioning him from the harsh realities of life and helping him ignore the cold stare I had purposely levelled at him. I thought about my father struggling to breathe without assistance in a hospital bed and a twenty-stone man having a portion of concrete slab slammed down onto his temple. Sensing my unease and wanting the conversation over, Paul tried friendly persuasion.

'Sam, you're a good mate, I understand your concern. Delving further into what went on doesn't interest me, it's over. But thanks anyway, nobody else gave me the time of day but I can cope with unpopularity, it's nothing new. All I want is to get on with what I do best and try to build up a decent retirement fund and look after my kids. The clock's ticking, Sam, and none of us really know how long we've got left in the saddle. Everything else is unimportant.'

He had begun to sound like a salesman but I wasn't buying anything he had on offer.

'You can't seriously sweep what's happened to you in the last couple of weeks under some imaginary carpet,' I argued, challenging his apathy. 'The very reason I became involved was the belief we were up against the same enemy and by showing a united front we could stand up to those who took us to be easy targets. Unlike you I don't see a backdown is any reason for letting them off the hook; if anything it's a disturbing sign of weakness. I won't let you allow them to get away with it.'

Paul looked visibly shocked. Any friendship between us was teetering on the brink. In his eyes I had clearly gone too far by calling him weak and making demands on him. But he gave it one last try. 'Look Sam, all I care about is getting my life back on track. Sometimes you just have to forgive and forget. My advice to you is not to go seeking any kind of retribution because I think that could end badly for you and your father.'

It felt like he was somebody's messenger warning me off. Like he had been given the role of devil's advocate.

'So that's it, you're saying we roll over and play dead,' I replied cynically.

He shrugged and studied his watch, looking up at the clock on the main stand for assurance. Then he trained his eyes on the ground. 'I must go. Good luck in the third race, Sam, you'll need it. I'm on the favourite, see you in the weighing room. And think about what I said.'

He brushed past me and practically jogged back to the row of buildings that housed the jockeys' changing room as an announcer ran through the runners and riders for the second race.

It now felt as though Paul Eddison was no longer a man I could calmly converse with. For whatever reason he had sold himself to whoever had been playing dangerous games with him and there was no point even trying to make him reconsider. Less than a week ago he was confiding in me like a trusted brother and now he had alienated himself from me as though I was some kind of social pariah. I wondered if he would still be a good opponent out on the course or whether I had made us sworn enemies by challenging him off it. I would find out either way soon enough.

The Ludlow faithful meanwhile witnessed a competitive amateur-jockeys-only contest which I watched on a TV monitor alongside Irish rival Liam Dowdy. I hadn't ridden against him since Cheltenham on Saturday. He had heard on the grapevine about my father's latest ordeal and with typical Irish blarney told me if I needed time off he'd gladly take on some of my forthcoming rides, trainers and owners permitting. I reminded him that I was banned for three days from Saturday onwards and he shrank back a little at not being approached already but then turned it into a joke at his own expense.

In the changing room soon after I watched him feel his way around Paul as they mingled with others and was relieved when we had all weighed out and were inside the parade ring to meet the owners and mount up. The same Shropshire trainer had paired me with a novice hurdler called Duck Down Donald with strict instructions to stay in contention for as long as possible, as though just getting to the end of the race unscathed was the ultimate goal. The dark grey horse had failed to make the grade on the flat as a three-year-old, but two years on I was assured it had the stamina to get today's two-mile trip. Coupled with its real prowess over the obstacles, my chances grew as the race developed until suddenly we moved up through the field into second place approaching the last half mile. Paul, I assumed, was some way behind me but Liam was six lengths ahead and looking well in control as he kicked on into the last bend. With the trainer's instructions ringing in my ears I followed Liam's lead and whilst his horse might have looked full of running, mine was the one in ascendancy, quickly reducing the deficit before overtaking and easily clearing the last hurdle to romp home by a comfortable margin. A good result for the bookmakers, an amazing one for the trainer and a pleasant shock for its laid-back local owner.

Good for me too but not so the wealthy owner of the short-priced favourite that Paul Eddison had coaxed home sixth of the eight finishers. The look of indignation on Paul's face as we were led back said it all, but my attempt at eye contact afterwards failed to breach the divide. In a very short space of time he had become a bad loser and undignified in his post-race reaction. And his uncomplimentary body language did him no favours.

Liam, who had no axe to grind with Paul, said as much only a short while after the weigh in, his words summing up what some might call an awkward situation. 'Bloody hell Sam, what's his problem? Nobody has the divine right to think they will win just because they get to ride favourites all of the time. Miserable bastard. I'll never figure the guy out. He's living the life of a celeb but has a face like a wet Monday morning when things don't go right for him. He ran a fucking bad race and has nobody else to blame but himself.'

'He has high expectations for sure,' I commented. 'I don't envy him if the winners dry up, and I wouldn't want to be in his shoes.'

Liam observed Paul from a safe distance as we got changed and endorsed what I had said from his own perspective.

'When I rode for one nameless trainer as an apprentice in Ireland he bollocked me for winning a race, claiming I had tried to break the horse. That stayed with me from there on and I never forgot it. Mister High and Mighty Eddison should count his blessings. It's not all about winning. Finishing second ain't so bad,' he said with an animated wink.

'But sixth ain't so good,' I japed, unable to resist the temptation.

Liam disguised his horror and shrugged. 'Coming from someone who's won both his races that sounds cruel. You're no better than him, you callous bugger,' he joked. We both figured Paul's skin was thick enough to absorb such rhetoric. It made us feel like backstabbing, envious schoolboys and not highly trained professional jockeys.

What Paul's skin did have to absorb was a dramatic fall in the next race when he seemed to have every chance approaching the second from last fence. I took no satisfaction from seeing him walk dejectedly back, nor from the fact he appeared to be having an off day at a course that had been kind to him in the past. But I was genuinely pleased for Liam who had benefited from Paul's demise and steered his horse home to take the honours. If finishing second wasn't so bad, winning was pretty good too and the Irishman's smile was almost as wide as the margin of his victory and remained so long after the finish of the race.

I had, of course declined the invitation to celebratory drinks from the local owner for whom I had succeeded in the previous race, demonstrating both my professional side and a sense of duty to trainer Heath Coultard whose only entry for the day I was due to ride in the last race. He had arrived late with the horse's female owner and when he learned of my double success his eyes lit up and his eyebrows did a dance of their own.

'No pressure then,' I said as he congratulated me and

the owner smiled at me hopefully. She seemed very young for an owner, slim, stunningly attractive, a definite head-turner. And when Heath introduced me properly her name resonated on me, though I managed to disguise any element of shock.

'This is Gabrielle Southgate,' he said. 'Christopher Southgate's daughter, assuming you know who he is.'

I struggled to see a family resemblance and imagined she took after her mother in looks.

She touched the tip of my fingers with a gloved hand, licked her bright pink lips and widened her smile. 'The horse was a birthday present from Daddy, and such a nice surprise. I do hope you can get the best out of him, Sam, he's an absolute smasher. Heath thinks he's got a real chance,' she said optimistically.

'Sam's your man,' Heath flattered me. 'Your horse could not be in better hands.'

'Win for me, Sam, I know you can do it,' her eyes flashed at me.

I was left speechless and just smiled back at her.

11

Gabrielle Southgate's twenty-first birthday present was a small, unremarkable-looking chestnut chaser with an exotic-sounding name, Sultan of Somalia, who boasted a reasonable track record as a novice jumper. Her father, only an infrequent racegoer due to his other commitments, had turned up at Heath's stable three months ago and asked him to purchase a suitable horse at the right price that would give his riding enthusiast daughter a thrill or two and hopefully win her some rosettes. Presumably Sultan of Somalia fitted both the racing profile and the suggested price range, though his size would have been a concern for me.

Why Heath had been the favoured one I did not know, he was one of several trainers operating in and around Gloucester and no better judge of a horse than any of the others. But Gabrielle seemed happy enough with her extravagant gift and when I entered the parade ring for the last race of the day the proud owner was depositing some of her pink lipstick onto the horse's nostrils for good luck and not looking at all out of place amid the usual throng of legitimate racing connections. In addition she was also attracting plenty of admiring glances and her choice of black and white polka dots and complimentary pillbox hat would easily have graced the enclosure at Royal Ascot or Cheltenham on Gold Cup day.

Heath was there of course, in favourite dark-green waxed jacket, waiting to give me my final instructions. So too was the man Paul Eddison had called 'an intimidating bastard'

114

at Cheltenham last Saturday. Seeing the man made me check my stride but Christopher Southgate, in plain grey suit and canary yellow tie, spotted me before the others and was first to move towards me to wish me luck and shake my hand.

'Sam, so glad to meet you, hope you can do Gabby proud,' he said, gripping my hand like his daughter's life was dependent on me.

'I'll try my best, sir,' I stuttered back, unable to get the words out as I would have liked which I felt for sure wouldn't endear me to him.

'I'm sure you will,' he said, looking slightly less nervous than his daughter. 'We have every faith in you.'

His powerful stare and steely smile made me shrink back and I couldn't help but think of what Paul had originally said about him after I had seen them together.

'That's comforting to know,' I thanked him, hurriedly refocusing my thoughts.

Behind us Sultan of Somalia was sweating up noticeably but the trainer shrugged it off before giving me a leg up and delivering his precise instructions for the race which I later hoped to be able to transmit to the horse once the starter had dropped his flag. Once I was settled a bubbling Gabrielle gave me an animated wave but as I got out onto the course I couldn't bring myself to share her optimism, due to the repetitive habit the horse had of turning on a full one hundred and eighty degree axis and its determination to pull my arms from their sockets.

Once the race began my worst fears were mostly alleviated as the horse responded to my promptings but although there were only five other runners to compete against, two of them looked too strong and I knew at half distance, barring jumping disasters by both of them, there would be no winning hat-trick for me.

Third place and a bit of a spurt on at the end as the

fourth-placed horse made a late charge wasn't such a bad result, I thought, and both father and daughter looked relatively content despite Heath giving me the third degree as I dismounted. I think he was probably doing it for the Southgates' benefit, letting them know he was on his mettle and that they had nothing to worry about, the horse would improve next time out.

As it was the last race there was an invite from the off-duty Chief Superintendent to join him and Gabrielle in the bar afterwards which I would have sidestepped had it not been for the trainer accepting on my behalf.

'Wouldn't be polite to turn him down,' Heath said to me as I turned to leave the unsaddling enclosure. 'Besides how many times do you get the offer of a free drink from a copper? Must be a first for me.'

I mustered a grin, headed back to weigh in, showered and changed. No part of me felt comfortable and when I entered the hospitality bar fifteen minutes later I was the last of the invited guests who were now both sitting and standing evenly spread around a corner table that was almost obliterated by food and drink.

Heath had been joined by his wife Felicity and his daughter, who was about Gabrielle's age, together with the horse's groom and another man I assumed to be the horsebox driver. Christopher Southgate had his broad back resting against the end of the bar and he was talking to two jockeys, one of them Paul Eddison who, for once, looked entirely relaxed. The other jockey was an apprentice named Simon Mendes who was half Spanish. He seemed to have one eye permanently trained on Gabrielle Southgate's shapely legs, which were probably being amply displayed from where she sat with the deliberate intention of reeling him in. She had removed her hat and had let her naturally blonde hair cascade down around the padded shoulders of her designer dress. Next to her was another less attractive girl in a

116

shapeless blue dress who was downing a glass of sparkling wine as though she was in Ibiza and it was a drinking contest. Another owner and a couple of other trainers I had occasionally ridden for over the years made up the motley crew, who were making as much noise as the whole of the rest of the busy room.

'Sam, what will you have?' Chief Superintendent Southgate asked upon seeing me edge tentatively into his eye line. 'We've got plenty of the fizzy stuff, not quite champagne but that's on ice for next time,' he said, sounding confident.

'Just a Coke please,' I replied.

'You jockeys eh? Tonic water and Coke, when do you ever let your hair down?' he nodded towards the other two jockeys.

'When the trainer's not looking,' Paul joked, looking at me and then Heath Coultard who didn't hear his attempt at bad humour.

'Or when we're laid off,' I joined in.

Paul grimaced. 'The curse of the poor, unfortunate blokes who go out there and put their lives on the line for the rich and famous.'

The Chief Super didn't sympathise. 'My heart bleeds, you should have to deal with the crap that lands on my desk every day. Some of it you wouldn't believe.'

I was now standing next to Simon Mendes whose jet black hair was twice as long as mine and heavily slicked back. He seemed to be mentally undressing Gabrielle Southgate with his big, bluish-black eyes, which was either an act of bravado or sheer stupidity given her father was within cuffing distance of him. But even Paul, who had once married a much younger woman, was partially occupied with her thighs which were well exposed by the side split of her dress and not in any great hurry to be covered up. She was laughing at her friend's antics and enjoying the trappings of racehorse ownership, a privileged position for one so young and welcoming contrast to the many owners whose age was now heavily weighted against them.

To my surprise Gabrielle called me over. Her tipsy friend moved onto an adjacent chair and just leered at me.

'Sam meet Susie, Susie this is Sam,' she introduced us.

Susie straightened her back and pulled at the ringlets in her complicated-looking hair which was mostly brunette but had been tinted with red and blue streaks. 'I love jockeys,' she slurred. 'I bet you have lots of fun when the racing's finished.'

Gabrielle laughed and put a hand on my arm. 'He's mine, hands off. Get your father to buy you a horse and then you can have a jockey all to yourself.'

She saw me blush but kept her hand attached to me. It was hard for me not to stare at her legs and she was revelling in my awkwardness. 'One day I'm going to have a string of horses and Sam can ride them for me. The mere thought of it turns me on,' she flirted with me, flashing her bright blue eyes again.

Beside me Susie was giggling loudly but nobody seemed surprised. Maybe they had seen and heard it all before.

'And what if he's spoken for already,' Susie teased her, when the giggling subsided.

'We would just have to work around it. Nothing's impossible.'

Gabrielle loosened her grip on my arm but still kept her hand there. I wondered how many men she had moulded into putty with her forward behaviour.

Susie was now reacquainting herself with her glass and swigging back some more wine. 'God, this is so good,' she said, stopping for breath.

'Susie's the ultimate party girl, never a dull moment when she's around,' Gabrielle filled me in.

I looked around to see her father locked in a deep conversation with Paul, and a frustrated half Spaniard not quite knowing what was going on between Gabrielle and me. Then she enlightened me about why Simon Mendes was there in the first place.

'Daddy's brilliant but he does go about things the wrong way,' she revealed. 'He's a bit of a control freak, probably because of his job. Likes to think he can vet who I see and don't see. He's been like it since I reached puberty and doesn't seem to want to let go. Simon's a nice enough chap but he's too young and immature, and also a bit too greasy for me if you understand my meaning but I pretend for my father's sake that his attempts at matchmaking aren't so disastrous. If it keeps him happy and stops him organising the whole of my life then it's a minor inconvenience I can live with.'

'Fathers are a law unto themselves sometimes,' I agreed with her, thinking of my own.

Her hand was still feathering my arm and her eyes were looking straight into mine. 'So Sam Woodall, are you spoken for or is Susie wrong about you?' she asked, putting me very much on the spot.

'I'm sort of seeing somebody,' I said, confusing her. 'It's early days yet.'

She didn't look too disappointed and her confusion was soon gone. 'The early stages of a relationship can be a wonderful time,' she said, sounding twice her age.

I didn't argue or pass a comment. Was her father such a control freak that he monitored all her movements when it came to men, I thought? After knowing her for practically a whole hour I doubted it strongly. Just like the horse I had ridden for her earlier, she was headstrong. And, contrary to what she said about her father, I quickly surmised whether right or wrong that no one told her what to do or who to do it with.

The hand that she had so delicately poised on my arm had now been removed but she hadn't given up on me.

TOM BUTLER

'If things don't work out with whoever she or he is you must give me a call, Sam, it's always worthwhile to have options,' she said as if she meant it.

'Indeed,' I said, stuck for words.

Gabrielle sighed before taking a drink and smiling back at me. 'I find jockeys fascinating,' she said, as if she had known a lot.

'So Simon's still in with a chance then?' I glanced over towards him. He seemed to be sulking.

She gave him a sly, sideways look and shrugged. 'Not so sure about that but...' she reconsidered. 'It might be amusing to let him try to entertain me.' She threw Simon a smile and I suggested to her that he change places with me, which she deliberated over.

'OK by me,' she smiled across at him again. 'But remember what I said.'

Not since he had won a race I rode against him last season had I seen Simon smile so broadly. Once installed on the chair he began with some classic chat-up lines straight out of Casanova as his quarry lowered her defences.

Paul and Christopher were now standing apart as the Chief Super took an incoming call on his mobile. It didn't seem too cynical of me to bring up the turnabout in Paul's demeanour where the policeman was concerned.

'Look, like I told you, everything's fine now, Sam,' he swiftly replied. 'I wouldn't say we're best of buddies but I know when somebody's being sincere. We didn't see eye to eye before but his bark is definitely worse than his bite. Let him convince you himself, talk to him, ask him about us, you'll see I'm right.'

'I might do that,' I said, none too sure.

'Go on,' Paul pressed me. 'Just ask him, do it, Sam.'

'Ask me what?' Christopher Southgate intervened, switching off his phone.

'Sam's unconvinced my troubles are over,' Paul told him.

'Ever since he saw us talking at Cheltenham he's got it in his head that I'm in need of a nursemaid. But seriously, we are in the same jockeys' union and we do tend to look out for each other,' he said, throwing me a backhanded compliment.

'Gratifying to know that,' the Chief Super said, his eyes travelling between us.

'Paul exaggerates,' I shrugged. 'We do what we can.'

Keen to escape, Paul left us to join an ongoing conversation with the owner and two trainers who he knew as well as anybody. The police chief offered me a word of advice.

'If I were you I wouldn't worry too much about him, I find him an altogether complex character and not one to waste too much sympathy on. Like a lot of men who suffer because of the infidelity of a partner he let his emotions rule his head and was hell-bent on revenge. But I got him to see there was no sense to his actions and I'm pleased to say he's come to terms with it. Just let him work it out of his system and don't get too involved, concentrate on your own troubles, Sam, I would have thought they should take priority.'

He had turned to lean on the bar and was gazing up at the ceiling. I was keen to know how much he knew about me even if it meant not being able to coerce him into talking about Bruce Fielding.

'What exactly have you heard?' I asked him, struggling to conceal my unease.

His bottom lip extended over his top lip and he gave it a lot of thought before sounding vague. 'Oh, this and that, you know. One doesn't hold down a job like mine without having an ear constantly to the ground.'

I made a swift assumption. 'So you know what been happening with my father and our mutual friend Curtis Fielding then?'

'I know about the dispute and the damage your father did to one of Fielding's vehicles which led to his arrest and possible criminal charges,' he confessed, his eyes still raised upwards.

'And the fire at the lock-up?' I went on.

He didn't flicker an eyelid. 'Terrible thing, I trust he was insured.'

Still there was no eye contact and I sensed no great sympathy either.

'I made sure some years ago that he didn't keep his cars in one place and got them fully covered. But they are still irreplaceable,' I shrugged.

'Quite. It's a bad business but fires happen. At least there was nobody seriously hurt, I take it your father's OK?' he inquired.

'He's in hospital, probably chasing nurses around, there's no permanent damage.'

'What about his friend? The one who got hit over the head?' he asked.

'Luckily Dave's got a thick crust around his skull, otherwise it could have been a lot worse.'

'I'll get an update and see if I can chivvy somebody along. We can't have local thugs going around carrying slabs and using them as baseball bats. We'll catch the people responsible and I'll personally see they're put away for as long as the law permits,' he said, posturing a little.

'What makes you think there's more than one and they're local?' I asked him, without making it sound too much like an interrogation.

'It's just a figure of speech, Sam,' he clarified. 'Whoever it was they did it on my patch and I won't tolerate that.' He turned sideways to me. 'Since I moved here the crime detection rate has shot up. I intend to see that trend continue no matter what it takes.'

'My father's convinced, like me, that the crimes are connected,' I informed him, watching him closely to gauge his reaction.

CAUGHT

For a man with a lot to say for himself he suddenly became reticent and picked at his words. 'It might look that way but ... I would keep an open mind.'

It made him sound like a junior detective with too few leads to follow and I wondered if I had touched a nerve.

Christopher Southgate raised himself to full height so that I was now staring at his partially open jaw. His dark green eyes looked right through me. 'I don't know your father, Sam, and I quite understand how upset he is, but I've known Curtis Fielding for quite some time. We even attended the same college way back in the early eighties and I would know if he was up to anything illegal. People get envious of him and I'll admit he does have an uneven temper at times but he's not dishonest. You and your father should remember that and not jump to hasty conclusions. I ask you to apply some common sense and allow my officers and the fire investigators to do what they have to do.'

He lubricated his throat with a glass of wine and took a long look around the room, settling his eyes on his daughter and Simon Mendes. 'I understand you have a young daughter, Sam, so you have all this to come,' he said as though reading from an file marked with my name.

'She's eight, that's a long way off,' I said, not sure of the direction he was heading.

'Gabby's precious to me, and woe betide anybody who hurts her or lets her down. I watch her flirting with men and see the looks she gets and sometimes I forget she's not my baby any more. Maybe secretly we never want them to grow up,' he said, suddenly becoming far too self-indulgent.

'Every child's a worry,' I replied, joining in.

'Goes with the job of a parent, it's what we happily sign up for,' he chimed in profoundly.

A raucous laugh from Susie broke his concentration and he smiled. She was nudging Simon and winding Gabrielle up. They both seemed to be blushing.

'Look Sam,' the Chief Super sighed. 'Leave the detective work to me and my lot. I'll see what I can do to help. Don't put yourself in danger again, next time you might not be so lucky.'

I masked a joint feeling of surprise and horror at his concern for my safety, given that the assault on me at the cottage had not been reported. He had played a card he should have kept in his hand. But he didn't look worried or put out. I felt that he had made his point and I was the one with decisions to make in the wake of his coldheartedness towards me.

Though we had exhausted everything that needed to be said, I forced myself to smile back at him and thank him in advance for his efforts. It left a bitter taste in my mouth and a knot in the pit of my stomach.

12

Whilst the National Hunt racing circus moved on to Norfolk, and Fakenham racecourse, I spent the early part of Friday at Dominic Ingles' yard near Cirencester in exercise and schooling mode. Though sending no horses eastwards that day, he had two strong prospects gracing Aintree the next, and had booked me to put them through their pre-race-day routine prior to them being loaded up and transported to the track twenty-four hours in advance.

It was a bittersweet feeling for me to be riding out on the gallops that Dominic shared with another local trainer knowing I couldn't be at Liverpool tomorrow for the start of a two-day meeting, due entirely to the overzealousness and just plain vindictiveness of Curtis Fielding. But there was no time for feeling sorry for myself. I had a job to do and the early start was vital to the preparation required to give both horses the best possible chance of winning or at least achieving credibility for their owners who would judge their trainer accordingly.

Dawn had barely broken when I accompanied five of Dominic's early risers out onto the mist-strewn moor overlooking Lower Churn Stable, just prior to breaking into a canter down a steady slope fittingly nicknamed the Glide by racing connections. Halfway along the slightly undulating sand-covered track I peered through the mist to where Dominic was standing with his head lad, and two owners who had given up their lie-ins and were both holding binoculars close to their faces almost as if hiding themselves from view. All four men wore waxed jackets of varying colours and condition, Dominic being easily identified by his usual headwear and one of the owners sporting a large deerstalker.

On my return canter up the hill he called for me to ease up on the pedal and I let the others go on, catching them again when they slowed at the brow of the hill in readiness to turn and make a second downward sweep. This was repeated twice more before we all wound our way back onto the specially built dirt road that took us alongside a twisting tarmac road and back to the stable gate. Once back inside I handed the horse back to its girl who had readied the second of tomorrow's runners and saw me safely mounted. The whole exercise procedure was repeated until, with every swirl of mist now gone I returned again to face questions from the trainer regarding how I felt about them for tomorrow.

Dominic had engaged a young professional jockey in only his second full season since turning pro to fill my boots, and although not local I could not fault his selection, though like any laid-off jockey I felt slightly insecure. Aintree was one of the courses you didn't want to miss out on. Frustratingly I had good recent memories of the place, having three years in succession finished the nation's favourite race, the Grand National, on supposed 'no hopers' and won several minor but still worthwhile races there over the past few meetings. It was simply one of National Hunt's flagship venues and an occasion that I would rue not being available for despite ex-jockey Dominic's philosophical take on what had happened to me at Cheltenham.

'I said at the time you were unlucky and I stick by that, and so does the owner, but bans are an occupational hazard we all face in this bloody game. I once picked up a seven day ban for taking the wrong course in thick fog and no amount of complaining would make the stewards listen,' he reminisced.

'I didn't do a thing I wouldn't do again in the same circumstances,' I moaned. 'Sometimes I wish we could swap places with them and see how they get on with half a ton of horse beneath them. They might not be so quick to hand out punishments that don't always fit the crime, if indeed any has been committed.'

We had already assessed prospects for tomorrow and were sitting in an office and food store at the first of three defined stable blocks which had a capacity to house up to forty-eight horses in identical boxes. It was usual for us to have a bonding session at the end of the morning ride-outs where we would have a candid exchange of words whether it put the racing world to rights or not.

Dominic knew about Father and the supposed goings-on with Curtis Fielding, who he felt was just trying to lay the law down in the quest for total obedience and unreserved respect. He also knew that I didn't have much in the way of the latter when it came to Fielding, that it was too plainly obvious in my strained body language and had been intensified by the tinge of sourness that had crept into my voice.

'Holding a grudge isn't wise,' he said, shuffling papers around the edges of a relatively tidy desk. 'Nor is coming to conclusions about the man just because you sense he's trying to get one over on you and make a point. Most decisions made by stewards are for the good of the sport and it goes without saying that they're bound to upset somebody when they make a bad call especially when there's so much at stake. Generally they do a good job and get taken for granted but as the saying goes "Nobody's perfect". Mistakes, or let's say errors of judgement, happen,' he finished.

I stood leaning against the strong supports of a wooden shelf a few feet away from him and couldn't argue. Dominic was one of the most sensible men I knew and though his racing career had been cut short by injury in his late twenties he knew what it was like to feel aggrieved with officialdom and how to absorb the shock of the disappointment that often followed on from short-lived euphoria. Trainers felt it too and so did owners. Perhaps it was worse for them, what with months of focused training and preparation in the run-up to a race not to mention the heavy costs involved which many owners never got back.

Only recently in an interview I had been asked what I wanted to do when I retired from the saddle, and I mentioned wanting to stay in racing in some capacity without ever considering becoming a trainer. Maybe Dominic had his mind made up for him when a seriously busted shoulder forced him to quit riding at an age most jockey's careers were flourishing. Holding on to that thought made me feel privileged but I still had unfinished business with Fielding on behalf of my father and not even Dominic's unselfish assessment and a head full of advice could derail me from a track I knew I had to go down.

For no other reason than curiosity I asked him if he knew about Curtis's half-brother Bruce. He gave me a vague answer as if it was of no consequence but assured me anything he did hear about the sibling that was reportable would come my way.

With that in mind I left him to his paperwork, wished him luck for tomorrow and headed for Chippenham with two hours of the morning still left, arriving at Castle Moat Lodge within minutes of the taxi I had booked to collect Father from the hospital upon his inevitable discharge. I found him wandering around the conservatory looking lost and cursing me under his breath for bullying him into staying there under the watchful eyes and overbearing attentiveness of Lavender who, true to form, was already trying to organise his life.

'Haven't had a man, apart from Anthony, stay here for

years,' she said, sounding strangely excited. 'You'll have to bring his things over later of course but I've plenty of towels and toiletries and can even run to a bath robe, but not pyjamas I'm afraid. But then I don't see that to be a problem.'

There was the playful glint of a much younger woman in her eyes as she said it, and I watched as Father's dreary eyes pleaded with mine before he was distracted and looked outside with horror to see a large cat roaming the garden with the remains of a bird in its mouth.

'That's Monty, he seems to live most of his life up trees at the moment,' Lavender informed us. 'Hope you don't have allergies where pets are concerned,' she addressed Father. 'Didn't Sam warn you I had several generations of felines living here? They come and go and are no trouble at all.'

Now was the perfect time for Sam Senior to invent an allergy to cats, but he just kept staring at the backcloth of trees beyond the garden and flexing his fists which was a giveaway that he was angry.

'Dad loves all sorts of animals but his speciality is fish,' I reminded her.

'Oh yes, of course,' she responded immediately. 'How is the fishery doing after all that nasty business with our mutual enemy and how is that poor man who was so savagely attacked?'

'Business is slow but should recover and Big Dave's OK. He's made of pretty strong stuff, thank God,' I replied, seeing as Father had lost his tongue.

Lavender raised a hand in relief but the thought of somebody going around breaking skulls incensed her. 'What are the police saying about his attack? Surely they must catch whoever it was?'

'Feedback isn't forthcoming, I aim to chase them when I call about the fire,' I said, watching Father grimace and take to the chair Lavender was pointing him towards.

'Just awful, what is the world coming to,' she generalised.

'It's not the one I was brought up in for sure,' Father joined in suddenly, trying to get comfortable. 'Too much greed and envy and far too many devious bastards about now.'

Lavender, a devote churchgoer, didn't flinch. It was better he say the word than beat about the bush and she was soon nodding her head. 'Devious, callous, scheming, just plain dishonest. You know who I'm talking about?' she thought aloud.

Sitting on the larger of two sofas on the side nearest Father, she wrinkled her already wrinkled face and tore another strip off Curtis Fielding, the unofficial bane of her life. 'Anthony had a phone call yesterday from an official in Newbury working at the head office of the EVA; that's the Equine Veterinary Authority to the uninitiated. Seems he is looking at a hefty fine if the misplaced certificates don't turn up, which could tip the scales back against us as we simply couldn't afford to pay.'

Her mood had switched from melancholy to bitterness in not much time at all and it made me feel bad about burdening her with a man whose mood matched hers but for a different reason. It didn't help that I was also burdening her with questions. 'How long has he got to find what's missing? Doesn't he keep back up records on his computer like hospitals and doctors do?' How much of a fine are we talking about?'

Lavender took a big breath and sighed again. 'Not sure, many hundreds if not thousands of pounds. Anthony was vague, as usual. As for duplicate records I think he just thought a paper trail was enough. He does use a computer of course and I'll suggest he does something about it to prevent this happening again. But honestly he thought nothing like this could ever happen. He has good reliable people working for him, people who wouldn't want to jeopardise their own jobs by getting him into bother with the authorities.'

That got my father thinking. 'But Fielding is a very persuasive man. If he greased somebody's palm they might do his dirty work for him. It's as plain as daylight he has no scruples whatsoever,' he piped up, suddenly looking more at ease with his surroundings.

'Well we can't assume it was down to him,' I tempered, careful not to sound as if I was defending the accused man. 'Maybe there's another explanation. Surely Anthony would have been on his guard after what happened over the money Fielding lent him and even more so after the business with the patent on that invention of his?'

Anthony's long suffering mother shook her head. 'Pains me to say it, Sam, but the boy is gullible,' she said as though he was a naïve teenager and not a forty-five-year-old man. 'He excels with animals, horses especially, but is a bit of a disaster when it comes to dealing with humans.'

Father scoffed aloud. 'That man's hardly human, he's the lowest form of mankind.'

We all looked at each other and concurred unreservedly.

After a pregnant pause our hostess muttered something about tea and quietly disappeared, which was Father's cue to chastise me for suggesting a period of convalescence under her close supervision. I quickly reminded him it was more for his safety than for his health, and as Lavender and her son had so much in common with him he ought to relish the prospect of putting on a united front against the person responsible for making them miserable. But even the acceptance of the point I had so convincingly put across didn't make him look any more at home, despite the fact he was now settled in his chair and had his shoulders slouching and his legs crossed.

It seemed as good a time as any to tell him about Paul Eddison's exoneration and my conversation with Christopher

Southgate, and the latter became the focus of attention when Lavender returned with tea and digestive biscuits.

She had met the Chief Super several times and didn't believe he was in any way involved in shady goings-on with his golfing pal Curtis Fielding. It was wrong, she said, to tarnish him because of their association; he was one of the most generous men she had ever encountered, doing an awful lot for charity, he was well respected, much liked and wouldn't jeopardise the reputation he had built up by doing anything remotely dodgy. It perhaps told me where her son might have picked up some of his gullibility from, but it would have been so wrong of me to make an issue of it bearing in mind she was so well connected and had already offered her help to expose Fielding, which might yet prove invaluable.

Changing tack, I asked her if she had heard of a man called Stan, who might once have been a bookie's runner and lived on a council estate in Swindon. It sent her memory into overdrive.

'Stan, you say, and he worked for a bookmaker? Lives in Swindon?' she repeated. 'Nobody I know but I will ask someone who might. Why are you so interested in him?'

'Paul Eddison told me he went to meet the man at his house and found him nursing a nasty head wound. Next thing he knew the place was alive with police and this Stan was making a statement claiming Paul had viciously assaulted him. Paul was arrested and then bailed. Now it appears charges have been entirely dropped which I find extraordinary.'

Lavender shared my disbelief. 'Very strange. Have you spoken to Paul about it since?'

'He played the whole thing down and said he just wanted to get on with his life. He wasn't interested in any kind of retribution. That makes little sense in view of what he must have been put through.'

132

'Indeed,' Lavender puzzled. 'Do you think Paul and this Stan had history and perhaps they harboured a grudge against each other?'

'No, I think Stan, if that's his real name, was paid by somebody to frame Paul, it's the only logical explanation.'

'The police could identify him,' Father piped up. 'They took a statement from him. Might even have prosecuted him for wasting police time and making false allegations. Get on to the Swindon nick and question them, lad.'

It did seem the obvious thing to do so despite reservations I said I would.

I then tackled the thorny problem of what clothes and belongings to get from Father's house. He shrugged back at me as if it really didn't matter, as I sensed another round of hostilities to come whenever Lavender chose to return to the kitchen and was audibly out of range.

The cosy scenario I had hoped for would take a little longer than I had planned, but I still lived in hope of harmony between them. One thing they did have in common was their love of classic and vintage cars, but with recent events likely to make them emotional I broached the topic with cold trepidation and no real stomach for it.

'Do you want me to contact the insurers and if I do will they send somebody out?' I asked.

His top lip quivered but he dug deep to find the bravest face available. 'I should be there now, God knows what a mess the firemen have made. Go to the bottom drawer of my bureau and bring me the box file. There's a name and number, you'll need to notify them. The company are based in Manchester but they may have a local agency or team of assessors. This is going to knock them sideways for sure. The Bugatti alone was insured for . . .' he paused, unable to bring himself to name the amount.

Lavender stared down at the floor and I thought momentarily she was about to be sick. 'The restorers can do wonderful things,' she rallied, almost mishandling a china cup before reuniting it with its saucer.

'Of course they can,' I agreed, without knowing whether it was true or not.

The fire chief I had already spoken to had said not all the cars had been badly damaged, especially those at the front of the building which his crews had reached first. The Bugatti, I understood, was somewhere in the middle covered by quite a heavy protective synthetic shield that Father had spent wise money on for such an occasion. There was perhaps reason for him not to be so glum and I knew I had to rally him.

'Look, before I go to your place I'll make a detour to the lock-up, even take some photos with my phone, well, the borrowed phone,' I corrected myself. I had almost forgotten that I had salvaged the SIM card from my smashed phone and put it into Tamara's handset. It was just something else I needed to sort out, adding to the growing list that circulated in my head.

'Thanks, son,' Father nodded back. 'And badger the fire people about the cause, although I think I know what their answer will be.'

Lavender offered us top-ups of tea and we polished off the digestives. And encouragingly, when she left us to return to the kitchen my father sat looking at several cats he had not noticed before and not once did he complain to me about his enforced living arrangements. Maybe he was just getting tired.

Conveniently, Gloucester's Assistant Chief Fire Officer met me at the lock-up an hour later and he walked me slowly through the debris, which looked worse than it was. Father had rented the brick-built building which had been a car body repair shop for many years; it boasted a strong security grille as well as an electronic shutter door, a small side door that was normally kept bolted and a skylight in the roof. That might have seemed the most vulnerable area, seeing as the roof was flat and accessible from other similar buildings on what was a fairly modern and well-maintained site.

The stench of smoke and charred remains was almost overpowering but I was relieved to see that the expensive cover shield had done its job in restricting damage to the most costly item in the garage, although the car still looked in need of serious restoration work. Two vehicles, a fully restored Triumph Dolomite and a Sunbeam Alpine, which had been at the rear of the building were both burnt-out shells. The sight and smell of them made me heave a little as I took photographs and then edited them on screen. A black Ford Consul next to the Bugatti had paint and upholstery damage but the two rare specimens nearest the doors, a Scimitar and a TVR, had only water damage as far as I could ascertain. Somebody up there must have quite liked Father after all; the overall picture wasn't as bad as we or the fire service first thought, though to many it would still have been a heartbreaking scene to endure.

The Fire Officer, who looked far too young to be in officialdom gave me his best early assessment based on his initial findings. 'We think, and I emphasise the word think, that somebody forced open the single door at the side of the building and once inside poured paraffin over one of the cars at the back and quite simply put a match to it,' he said. 'Obviously the fire spread but because the cars aren't grouped together too tightly we think it didn't spread as quickly as it might have done. Those two vehicles at the back took the brunt of it, and it's just lucky that the fire detectors sounded and somebody raised the alarm when they did to allow us to get a tender here so quickly. A sprinkler system would have put out the fire for sure and I implore you to consider installing one in the future.

Hindsight is a wonderful thing, Mr Woodall, but in my experience these things do work and are worth every penny spent on them.'

'What are the chances, in your experience, of catching the person or persons who did this?' I asked him straight.

'Depends on how well he or they covered their tracks. Scene of Crime officers have been down to do a sweep in the hope of something, but as with most fires evidence can be obliterated. So I would say we only have a slim chance of finding out who did this. But we will liaise with the police and you never know, arsonists do regularly get caught. A fingerprint or a footprint or hopefully a passer-by noticing something. And of course DNA, which has revolutionised crime detection. We never give up until all avenues have been exhausted.'

'My father and I have already given a name to the police of someone who might have a motive,' I informed him. 'Beyond that we have no theories.'

He looked at me with sympathetic eyes and drew on his own experiences. 'Arsonists come in all shapes and sizes and from all walks of life. Some people are obsessed by fire and are indiscriminate. This might be the work of someone with a grudge against your father and that in itself should, in theory, make him or her easier to track down. It could be somebody with a fixation for fires who likes to watch the aftermath, and then again somebody who simply has no real explanation for their actions. We see it all and on the positive side our detection ratio is high. So tell your father we'll carry on with our investigations and submit our final report to the police as quickly as possible.'

I thanked him in advance for his diligence and he talked me through what was needed of my father before he left me for another ongoing investigation.

Was Gloucester home to many arsonists, I thought? Or were they spread around, waiting to heap misery on the next unsuspecting soul? I didn't envy him his job, but then I thought about what I did for a living and the risks I took in the saddle and it didn't seem so bad. At least he had a career path and a solid goal to aim for, whereas all I had was the next big race to look forward to, and hopefully, the next one beyond that.

After another look around and more photos I spoke to Father on Lavender's landline and gave him the best description that I could, which he took remarkably well. He was talkative again and bearing up. He and Lavender had spent an hour or more chatting about the past and swapping experiences, which I actually thought he might hate. She had shown an interest in Sloane Farm too, and Father had promised to take her there when he was ready and able to do so. They had walked around the grounds with Father consciously ignoring all the cats he encountered, genuinely admiring the many rose bushes her late husband had nurtured when he was alive and taking in the views across the valley that stretched beyond the motorway.

Within another hour I had bundled everything I considered he needed into two suitcases and was on my way back with the promise of shepherd's pie and apple strudel for tea, though for me it would be half portions. And afterwards my suggestion of a brainstorming session aimed at Curtis Fielding and anyone else we could think of who might be considered the enemy was received favourably. It lasted most of the evening and was punctuated only by a twenty-minute phone call I made to Tamara in London who was waiting to board a train bound for Swindon which would arrive before midnight. Optimistically I said I would meet her and see her safely home, secretly praying she hadn't given up on me. I was encouraged when she said how much she had missed me, and shocked to be asked to stay over. I said I would, and faced the inquiring eyes of both Lavender and my father when I said I would have to leave them before eleven.

'Such a lovely girl is Tamara,' Lavender said with genuine warmth. 'Being such close neighbours I've known the Blackwoods for a long time, though I do think Olivia can be incredibly stuffy at times and has certainly let her visit to the Palace go to her head.' She grimaced. 'But I do like Joe, he's such a card and the other daughter's just about bearable. For me Tamara follows her father and has brains and beauty too. I'm sure you make the perfect couple and I wish you all the luck in the world.'

With eyebrows aloft, Father didn't spare our blushes. 'Go for it son, you're only young once and the clock's ticking. Don't do anything I wouldn't do.'

I wondered, in view of Lavender's fondness for him, if he would live to regret saying something that might be misconstrued as giving her false hope. After all, pretty soon she would have him all to herself again and there would be no interruptions, what with son Anthony staying with friends in Chepstow overnight. I wondered what Father's mood would be like in the morning and smiled to myself. Sometimes through adversity there was nothing else to do but smile and get on with it. So all the way to the station I held that thought.

13

Whilst I felt awkward in view of the previous night's telephone conversation, Tamara knew there was no point in dwelling on things that were outside her immediate control, nor did she think it worthwhile to punish me further for having been born so stubborn. Somewhat relieved, I told her enthusiastically what Lavender Thompson had said about her a couple of hours ago and she didn't blush too much. I also remembered what I had told a flirty Gabrielle Southgate after racing at Ludlow and decided there was no point in hiding my true feelings. It was with that in mind I now revelled in my good fortune, watching as Tamara stood combing out her damp hair a few feet away from me, and savouring her every move as her overactive mind wandered.

'You don't really think your father and Lavender will ... you know ... get to know each other better?' she said, her voice edged with mischief. 'I imagine that would set tongues wagging and raise a few eyebrows among her so-called chums on the fund-raising circuit.'

My eyes remained focused on her whilst I contemplated the absurdity of what she had said.

'Sam Woodall Senior and Mrs Thompson, eh? Now that's a match made in bedlam, not heaven,' I said, deadpan.

'Opposites attract,' she suggested, looking back at me through her dressing table mirror, her face a study of human eccentricities.

After some thought I said, 'Well, it's got its merits I suppose. Both of them are on their own, albeit Anthony's

139

still on the scene, coming and going as he pleases. But stranger things have happened.'

Tamara shut her eyes and shook her head. 'Anthony's too much of a mommy's boy for me. Good with horses and rabbits, but not so people. I doubt she'll ever be shot of him.'

It wasn't something anyone could seriously level at me, although my ex-wife did once say I preferred horses to her, which at the time she said it was probably true. Not something to be proud of, but long since consigned to history.

I offered my own take on Anthony and his relationship issues. 'He'll find somebody if he bothers to look and Lavender doesn't smother him,' I convinced myself. 'But until that happens I can only envisage problems should Father stay longer than intended. That big old house of hers would become a war zone as they fought over the toothpaste and who got the last of the cornflakes. It's too comical to think about.'

Tamara smiled then giggled. 'That happens here all the time, so I hope you've brought your own. Mornings can be mayhem in the Blackwood house sometimes so be warned.'

I smiled back. 'I'll remember that for future reference. Sadly I don't have anything with me, except the clothes I've just hung up.'

She had finished combing and was taking off her robe. 'Clothes can get in the way,' she teased. 'And I'm sure I can rustle you up a toothbrush. If I recall rightly I never got a chance to find you one last week, remember?'

I hadn't forgotten my sudden desertion. 'And this is where I make it up to you and pray no one calls before daybreak,' I said, turning down the sheet for her.

Tamara pointed to my phone beside the bed and didn't mince her words. 'So turn the damn thing off, Sam Woodall Junior, that way there'll be no danger of you rushing off before it's light. We have some serious catching up to do.' She made it sound like a military order.

The change in the tone of her voice and the first touch of her skin on mine soon had me searching for the off button in an act of submission.

'I once read somewhere that jockeys have boundless energy and stamina,' she said inquisitively.

'No pressure then,' I replied, having no way of knowing if she was making it up. I felt sure I would rise to the challenge.

Autumn rain heralded another Saturday but this wasn't the normal start to a weekend for me – waking up next to a radiant Tamara and the leisurely pace of a languid morning made it seem totally surreal. I should have been journeying north to Aintree and looking forward to drinking in the atmosphere there, not eating lightly buttered toast and reading a tabloid newspaper in Dame Olivia Blackwood's sitting room, listening to Joe Blackwood's opinion of the racing world from his somewhat blinkered standpoint as he set about a breakfast of sausage, egg and mushrooms.

'If I had my way I'd take the whips off jockeys altogether and that way we'd have a level playing field,' he said, after I'd reminded him I was banned and not allowed to ride again till Wednesday.

'But Daddy,' Tamara admonished him, 'Sam's ban has nothing to do with the whip. He was unfairly adjudged to have stopped another horse from winning. I did tell you, remember? Do try to remember,' she repeated.

'Yes, but I'm sure Sam agrees with me,' Joe prattled on regardless, waving the last sausage on the end of his fork. 'Stands to reason if you stop jockeys from striking a horse you'd get much fairer and closer matched races.'

Saying nothing, I let his daughter do my talking, guessing it was something she relished when her somewhat demonstrative mother wasn't around.

'Surely the better horses would still win and the winning margins wouldn't change,' she challenged him. 'Sam says some horses are naturally lazy and the whip is just used to chivvy them along, otherwise they wouldn't perform and the punters who backed them would demand their money back. The modern whips are so much more animal-friendly than the old type anyway and in some instances merely used to correct horses and keep them running straight,' she summarised.

Joe Blackwood looked like a man used to family arguments and, though I suspected he hadn't won one in his life, he didn't back down, strangely waiting for her to finish her grapefruit before wading back in.

'Horses can be trained without the aid of a whip. I don't subscribe to all that correction nonsense. A bloody good jockey will steer a well-trained horse in a straight line and position it exactly where he wants it. Am I right, Sam? It's not rocket science is it?'

Looking across at Tamara I decided on some diplomacy. 'Well, the unfortunate thing is, Joe – and I've been in the situation many times myself – that even the best-trained animal can decide it doesn't want to cooperate with you. Then it becomes a bit of a war of minds and still some horses make you look like a bungling amateur. Not so long ago Hologram hated the parade ring and once practically refused to let me mount him. He's a highly intelligent animal and expertly trained, but he's also got a temperament that means he can be either a joy to ride or just plain hard work. But it's his temperament that makes him so special, that makes him stand out from the rest and ultimately makes him a winner.'

I took a breath, and an admiring look from Tamara, but Joe wasn't entirely on my wavelength, though I think I had him floundering a little. 'Lots of racehorses have naughty streaks I know but I'm pretty sure they know who's boss and just need a strong hand to guide them. Whips will be gone in five years, they serve no purpose. If I were a betting man I'd put a bundle of cash on it. Just remember who said it first.'

It was unlike Joe to be quite so bullish, he had never been so opinionated on the subject of whips before, but then it was the talk of the sport in general and maybe the natural aftermath of the foxhunting ban and associated taboos. It also had something to do with his wife not being around to hog the conversation – I felt for sure that she would have clipped his wings and forced him back inside his shell.

'It could happen,' I conceded. 'For now there needs to be some tinkering with the rules, otherwise you'll have too few jockeys available to ride as they serve out their bans, and owners and trainers having to withdraw horses from races, imagine that.'

My poor attempt at sarcasm at least left him speechless for thirty seconds. Then he hunched his considerable shoulders and moved the subject on to my father and the woman who lived close enough to be considered a neighbour, but only after condemning the callous actions of an arsonist.

'Couldn't believe it when Tammy said what had happened. Awful business, and on top of everything else that's been happening too, it puts all this niggling that's going on in racing into perspective and makes you shudder. Somebody could have got killed, and for your dad to end up in hospital in addition to the damage done by the fire well … it's utterly beyond me.'

Joe had known my father only briefly but his sincerity was genuine. His eyes had temporarily glazed over and the hand holding his large coffee mug appeared to be shaking.

'It could have been worse,' I confirmed. 'Father is a law unto himself and profoundly stubborn. What he did when he got there was wrong, but it was instinctive. He did put others at risk and I think he would admit that now.'

Joe shrugged. 'Well, we all do things we're not proud of,' he thought aloud. 'Who can really say they wouldn't have reacted the same way? The impulse must have dulled his senses for a split second, that's all the time it needed.'

'Well he'll be fighting fit soon. All I'm concerned about is his future welfare, that's why he is where he is at the moment,' I said, underplaying my relief.

Joe looked at Tamara and their eyebrows flickered in unison. I was well aware from what Lavender had already said that she and Dame Olivia did not get on. Theirs was a clash of personalities, not helped by one of them being famous, having a title and obviously having met the Queen.

I assumed Joe echoed Tamara's less extreme feelings about Lavender Thompson as he had no reason to dislike the woman, even if I had heard him refer to her as both 'Catwoman' and 'the strange widow up the road' which was undeniably harsh, and unmerited. That aside, it was my opinion that mattered most and, no matter what anybody else thought, Castle Moat Lodge was the safest short-term haven on offer. If I had to force Father into making it longer term until the dust settled, then so be it. Other options simply weren't on my radar and anyway, what real harm could he come to, lodging with an ageing, feline-friendly widow for a few days and sharing classic car stories?

Reading Joe like a well-thumbed novel I could tell he was thinking it would be the last place on earth for him to go if circumstances were different, and he was probably itching to say so but didn't want to hurt my feelings or disappoint his daughter who had already said her piece on the matter, with her tongue very much in cheek.

'So how long has your dad known Anthony's mother?' Joe inquired, his urge to ask too great to ignore.

'Years. Quite a few I think,' I shrugged my indifference. 'They meet up at Classic Car conventions, that's what they really have in common. Her late husband owned a classic

Bentley which she obviously inherited, and it's so precious it's kept in a museum and is brought out only for very special shows. It's a one-off, not another like it. I gather she once turned down a fortune from an American film director who wanted to buy it, ship it back to the States and drive around Hollywood in it.'

'Fascinating,' Joe said, pretending. 'Nice that they have something in common. They must be a comfort for each other.'

I ignored the hidden meaning, threw Tamara a look of exasperation and tried changing the subject without making it seem too obvious. 'When's Emilia due?' I asked, feeling strangely nervous.

'The minder said ten to ten thirty and she's usually on time,' she replied.

Joe rerouted his brain and poured praise on his granddaughter. 'That little girl's going to be a star, and a damned clever one too. Takes after me and Tammy of course, but don't let Olivia know I said it.'

Tamara scowled a little at him. 'She'll be what she wants to be; fame and a high IQ aren't everything. She'll find her own way and I'll never see her pressured.'

'But talent and intelligence shouldn't be suppressed,' Joe said, sounding suddenly pompous and making it seem as though his wife was there in the room with us.

Tamara gestured to me with her eyes, as if she'd heard it all before and that Joe had said it for my benefit. The sound of a car on the gravel outside made her spring off the arm of the chair she'd been perched on and, after a swift peck on my cheek which Joe didn't see, she went outside with him not far behind her.

I flicked through the racing page of the newspaper and waited. Emilia, her hair tied up with ribbons, skipped past the sitting room door and headed for the back garden with Joe in hot pursuit and with the promise of a push once she was seated on a swing there. It reminded me of Father and Grace on her last school break, when he unknowingly monopolised her for an hour or more as they played in a sandpit I had hurriedly installed. I was never going to be anything but a temporary dad with limited access but at least I could hope that one day she'd fully understand why it had to be that way. I prayed that she'd never hold it against me in later life.

When Tamara returned we stood by the sitting room window and watched her daughter and Joe play piggyback rides and tag. We both had our arms crossed and thoughts entwined. There was a kind of telepathy that came with parenthood, a belief that no matter what life threw at you, your children came first and that could never be compromised. The coincidence of our lives came with our own daughters, and that could never be taken for granted or undermined either. Whether that bonded us or not, we would still have to deal with the inevitable fall-out that came with dysfunctional life. It made me feel warm and cold at the same time, and I imagined Tamara felt the same.

'So, Monday, are you up for a walk in the park, ice creams by the lake and a sneaky turn on the roundabout?' I asked her in advance. 'The great British weather permitting, of course.'

'I would love that, Sam. Emmy will too. If it rains we can go to yours or come here. Yours I think. Less competition.'

'That's settled. And a pub with a play area for lunch naturally,' I added.

Tamara gave me another covert peck on my cheek. 'Can't wait,' she smiled.

I left three generations of Blackwoods to their games and pointed my car in an easterly direction to descend quickly upon the less-impressive Thompson domain unannounced.

I found Father and Lavender both talking on their mobiles at opposite ends of her huge but sparsely furnished living room. Lavender had let me in but continued talking, quite happy for me to listen in, as the call was very much for my benefit. When she finished she preened herself like a prized hen entertaining a cockerel, and made my visit worthwhile.

'I think I've tracked down your mystery Stan,' she said, applauding herself and overdoing the smugness. 'And I have his last known address too, well the name of the road, at least.'

'Marvellous, who gave you the info?' I asked.

She tapped her nose and then wrinkled it. 'Call it intuition. I asked an old friend to contact the bookmakers he used to lose money to before his wife put a stop to it. One of them remembered using a runner named Stan many years ago before he became unreliable, and they reckoned he lived in a rented house in Swindon, near the station.'

'Could be our man,' I said looking at my watch.

Lavender gloated. 'I thought we'd go there this afternoon and see if he's in and he's the one who got Paul into trouble.'

'We? What do you mean, we?'

'More of us the better, it might be a very long street. I'm not too old to go knocking on doors, you know,' she said sharply. 'And besides I thought we could pretend to be canvassing for a charity, that way this Stan won't suspect a thing and he'll probably let us in.'

I thought of Agatha Christie and Miss Marple in the bat of an eyelid, but declined her help. 'This Stan might not be a very nice character, I couldn't put you at risk.'

'Nonsense, I can look after myself and so can your father, the fresh air will do him good.'

'But...'

'There's no buts, if I don't go you don't get the address,' she said, standing firm.

My father had finished talking to Big Dave at the fishery and was now all ears. 'What's this about? Whose address are you talking about?' he badgered us.

'Father, stay out of this. The whole thing's preposterous. Just let me deal with it on my own. I can't risk somebody else getting hurt.'

Lavender wasn't listening. 'We can look out for each other, and save a lot of time. Strength in numbers.'

'Sammy, what are you talking about? Will somebody please tell me?' Father remonstrated.

Lavender told him and they both turned on me, with Father nominating himself as spokesman. 'Look son, Lavender's right. The three of us can cover the ground quicker, it'll be broad daylight so what harm can any of us come to? I'm in this up to my armpits whether you like it or not, neither of us are invalids and we're going with you. No more arguments.'

They were forming a united front and it was akin to getting an uncooperative horse to run when all he wanted to do was graze.

'What's the address?' I stared at Lavender. 'This is very important.'

She wavered a little, looking unsure.

'Don't give it him,' Father ordered her.

She chewed on her top lip. 'I won't,' she agreed.

'Jesus Christ!' I exclaimed loudly, Lavender's eyes scolding me. 'I'll knock on every door in every street within two miles of Swindon station if I have to. Please just give it to me.'

The 'strange widow up the road' looked pensive, but my dad rallied around her. 'What if something were to happen to you, son? You've already had somebody in your house and you had to fight him off. At least let us come and watch your back. Don't be so stubborn. Cemeteries are full of dead heroes. Don't become another.'

I thought about it. It was crazy. Everything in the world had suddenly gone mad. A jockey and two old-age pensioners pretending to be super sleuths. Then, in the interests of harmony, I backed down and watched the two of them simultaneously grin from ear to ear as though they had just won the lottery.

'Unbelievable,' I said out loud. They were too excited to hear me.

'Let's have an early lunch first then we have a mission to accomplish,' I heard Father say as the two of them headed, not quite arm in arm, towards the kitchen.

'Unbelievable,' I repeated to myself. 'How on earth did I let that happen?'

14

Musgrave Road was indeed close to the station and painfully long. There was a mix of council, ex-council and housing association properties both sides of the road, with a small row of shops a third of the way along on one side and a two-storey, modern-looking health clinic halfway along the other. Cars were parked on both sides which made it difficult for two vehicles going in opposite directions to pass each other, but that apart it seemed like a pretty ordinary urban street in a mundanely average setting.

On the way I had listened to several strategies courtesy of my travelling companions who were treating the whole thing like a Darby and Joan outing and making me scream inwardly. Lavender used logic and suggested we knock on doors in chronological order which made the most sense, then Father said we should approach the houses from opposite ends until we met in the middle. She reminded him there were three of us and he then conceded that, as I could probably walk more quickly, why didn't I do all the odd numbers and they tackle the evens? That brought some derision from her and another brainstorm, which resulted in nothing but more complicated plans and objections as to why they wouldn't work.

None of them were necessary, however, because as I slowed to search for a parking space an eagle-eyed Lavender spotted someone standing outside an off licence whom she said she had seen before. The man was puffing on a cigarette, and wore the clothes of someone down on his luck. She squinted hard and then said she wasn't sure. When the

150

man moved off and began walking down the road she
noticed his limp and said for definite it was him.

'Who? Who is he?' Father asked impatiently.

'The man I told you about,' she turned to me. 'He was
with Bruce Fielding at the point-to-point meeting in
Andoversford. I remember now that he was dragging his
leg and having trouble keeping up. It's him, I'm sure.'

'You said they were handing a bundle of cash to a bookie?'

'Well that's what it looked like. I was manning a charity
stall for a friend but I did get a pretty good look at him.'

Father was keen to speak to the man and was opening
his door whilst the car was still in motion.

'Wait, don't scare him off,' I stopped him. 'I want you
both to stay here while I follow him. I'll offer him money
for information and see where that gets me.'

For once they did what I asked. I left the car running
and told Father to drive if I suddenly disappeared from
view. He seemed happy enough with that.

From much closer it looked like the man had one leg
shorter than the other, which accounted for his limp. He
seemed in no great hurry to go anywhere. As he paused to
light up another cigarette he put down a plastic carrier bag
that clearly had cans inside and gave out a raucous cough as
if his lungs were protesting. It was then I noticed the narrow
piece of sticking plaster on one side of his forehead, partially
covered by his uncombed and matted frizzy grey hair.

I pretended to read the advertising board in a newsagent's
window before following him as he started to walk again. He
crossed the road when it was clear and put one foot on the
step up to a poorly painted door with number 33 on it.
Checking for traffic and breaking into a trot I crossed over,
reaching him before he had chance to put his key in the door.

'Excuse me,' I said trying not to alarm him. 'I think you
dropped this.'

He turned on a pretty tight axis considering his

troublesome leg and looked straight at the twenty-pound note I was holding out towards him.

'Er, ... very careless of me,' he said, not hesitating to take it. When his eyes met mine some recognition registered in his. He blinked a couple of times and stubbed out his cigarette. 'Aren't you a jockey? Never forget a face. Sam ... Sam Woodall, well blow me down.'

'Sorry, I don't remember you, remind me?' I said. There was a distinct smell of booze on his breath.

'Me and Piggy Harris used to run for bookie Doug Hoolahan at Cheltenham and half a dozen other courses. You must remember Doug, the poor sod, he was killed by a train a couple of years ago not a mile from here. Mind you, they say he did walk in front of it 'cos he was depressed at the time.'

'I still can't quite remember your name?'

'Stan, I'm Stan Abbots,' he slurred.

I shrugged for effect as he swayed slightly, his key still in his hand. He looked surprisingly unruffled by my sudden appearance so I took advantage. 'Can I help? Why don't I let you in? Maybe we could have a coffee and a quiet chat. I bet you've got loads of tales to tell. I love racing stories.'

Stan Abbots rocked a little on his heels and refocused. Then he looked at the money which he'd scrunched up in the palm of his hand.

'I don't think this is mine after all,' he backtracked. 'Why did you think it was mine? What brings Sam Woodall to my door? Why are you here?'

'Do I need a reason to help somebody out?' I said evasively. 'What happened to your head? That must have hurt.'

He rattled the key in the door and became agitated for the first time. His body language told me there was unlikely to be the quiet chat or any kind of hospitality. The door sprang open causing him to stumble on the top step but he snubbed my attempt to steady him. 'Whatever you've come for you're wasting your time. Just leave me be. I'm in no mood for a chat.'

'Look,' I said. 'I'm not the police and I'm not here to cause you any harm. I just wanted to talk to you about Bruce Fielding and Paul Eddison. There's more money in it for you if you tell me what I want to know. You know who I am and you know what I do for a living. Five minutes of your time and let's call it another hundred for the right information. That's one hell of an hourly rate. Call it a contribution to your retirement fund. Five minutes, a few questions, where's the harm?'

Stan was now halfway through the door but he was thinking about the money. It would buy a lot of cigarettes and lager. Talk of a retirement fund hadn't won him over but instant liquidity might.

'A hundred pounds, how do I know you've got it? Show me and pay me in advance. I'm not being taken for a mug. The money up front or you can forget it,' he insisted.

I panicked momentarily and reached inside my windcheater jacket. Thankfully I had just enough so as not to bother my two assistant sleuths, and I quickly showed it to Stan, praying that he wouldn't shut the door in my face.

'Perhaps we can go inside,' I prompted, virtually ushering him through the door and following on behind. 'The cash is guaranteed, trust me.'

He wasn't sure – the word trust didn't sway him. But he was now inside a tiny hallway and for sure his previously jaded-looking eyes were alive with talk of a financial boost, even if his half-drunken brain was still putting up some resistance based on his survival instincts.

My wallet was highly visible and my eyes turned towards a partially open door, so he relented, backing himself onto the arm of a chunky sofa and allowing me to sit opposite him on a matching armchair. The room was in semi-darkness, on account of the dark-brown curtains not being fully pulled back and the windows being partly obscured by grotesquely shabby net curtains. It was hard not to inhale the stench of stale air and cigarette smoke which rapidly reached the back of my throat as I got down to business.

'So, Stan, this must be the spider's web Paul Eddison was lured into before somebody called in the law?' I presumed, the stench leaving a nasty taste in my mouth.

I could tell he was listening but the money was more important to him.

'I seem to remember you promised me the money first,' he reminded me, staring intently at my wallet. 'A hundred smackers.'

With some resentment I plucked the money from my wallet and handed it over. He didn't count it, shoving it into the same pocket of his tatty jeans that he had stashed the twenty pounds.

'Who got you to frame Paul Eddison?' I asked him directly, my throat uncomfortably dry.

He shrugged and was evasive. 'I didn't frame anybody. It's true Paul came here and he got taken away by the police but it was all a misunderstanding. Ask Paul, he'll tell you the same.'

'A misunderstanding?' I said, baffled. 'You accused him of assault. If he didn't give you that bump on the head then who did?'

Stan started shaking like he was cold. I repeated the question. He fumbled about in his other trouser pocket for his cigarettes, taking one out and putting it between his lips, then lighting it. He blew smoke in my face and I could now barely see him. Then as if the cigarette had magic properties he began to talk, although what he said was straight out of a fairy story.

'Look, when I drink I get confused. Don't even remember what bloody day it is or what month we're in. That's what happened when that other jockey came to see me. I must have fallen on the way home from the pub and then passed out. Paul found me and when the police arrived they assumed that I'd been attacked and in the confusion I told them it was Paul.'

He took a long pause to draw heavily on the cigarette and disappeared behind smoke again. Then he waved the hand holding the cigarette about and carried on story telling. 'When I came to my senses I was in hospital and when the police came to see me I told them I was sorry, that I had made a mistake and that it wasn't Paul who attacked me. So that's when they released him. Like I said, everything got jumbled in my head. Too much alcohol numbs the brain.'

Although he was sounding just about plausible, his version had too many flaws in it compared to Paul's and I wasn't about to let him bamboozle me. 'According to Paul you didn't phone the police before they descended on the house, so who did?'

He waved the cigarette-bearing hand around as if swatting flies. 'Don't remember. I must have called them. It must have been me.'

Even through his dull, inattentive eyes I think he could see I wasn't buying his version of events.

'Look, I want the truth.' I became impatient. 'Who paid you to set Paul Eddison up? Was it Bruce Fielding?' I asked him.

He puffed on the cigarette like it was a rare source of inspiration and amended his story. 'Look Sam, OK, so Bruce did ask me to help him out and get his own back on Paul,' he admitted. 'Them two, they hate each other, not surprising really as Bruce had been shagging Paul's missus behind his back before he found out and threatened to kill Bruce. Pointed a shotgun at him no less, so he says.'

'So you set Paul up by getting him here under false pretences and Bruce called the police, right?'

He nodded from behind another smokescreen. 'Well, yes,

Bruce said it was just a game he was playing to make Paul sweat. He didn't like having a gun thrust in his face and he said he wanted to teach the arsehole a lesson. Bruce ain't the sort of bloke to go upsetting like that. No one crosses him and gets away with it. What kind of dickhead goes around pointing a gun at somebody and thinks he can get away with it?'

'How long have you known Bruce Fielding?' I inquired.

Stan thought hard. 'Not that long, he ain't been around here long, less than a year. Rumours say he suddenly turned up and not even his older brother knew he existed. That really pissed Curtis off 'cos he found out he wasn't an only child, know what I mean.'

I asked him about the day Lavender saw him and Bruce together at Andoversford point-to-point and he thought back again.

'Oh, that. That was the day Bruce wanted to lay a big bet on a horse and I helped him 'cos I knew just the bookie to see. Bruce needed someone to vouch for him you see, some bookies get twitchy if they get a punter they don't know trying to lay really big bets. There are some devious professional gamblers about and most bookies get shit scared of taking a big hit and getting wiped out.'

'How much money? How big a bet?'

Stan blew out his cheeks to indicate it was a lot. 'A shit load, two grand, all in readies,' he said eventually, accentuating it with a deep sigh.

'Did Bruce say where he got the money?'

Stan shrugged. 'He said it was part of what he was owed and there was plenty more where it came from. That it was the tip of the iceberg.'

'His brother, Curtis. The most likely source?' I suggested.

The same shrug preceded his laboured response. 'Your guess is as good as mine,' he said vaguely. 'It wasn't my place to ask.'

'What about the bet? Did Bruce win?'

Stan shook his head and looked a little sour. 'He picked a wrong 'un. The fucking horse was pulled up before the last fence. Two grand down the shit hole, what a waste. As a punter Bruce is a total disaster.'

'How did he take it, losing all that money?'

'He just smiled, said "Easy come, easy go", stuck another five hundred on the next race and lost that too. He just laughed. Two and a half grand up in smoke and he just fucking laughs. What a tosser.'

Stan stubbed out the remains of his cigarette in a smoked-glass ashtray on the cheap teak-effect coffee table between us, the thought of the money Bruce Fielding had lost on a whim clearly playing on his mind.

I wondered what the going rate for setting someone up for serious assault was, but didn't pursue it. I also thought about the cash I had just handed over and whether I had received value for money from a man who clearly had few if any scruples at all. Although he looked pretty spent so far as answers were concerned, I put just one more question to him.

'Do you know a man called Christopher Southgate, Chief Superintendent Southgate? Or had any kind of contact with him?'

Resisting the temptation to light up another cigarette Stan looked back at me through sheepish eyes. 'He's the one Bruce told me about, the one he said would sort out the bogus charges and make everything sweet so I didn't get charged with anything. A good friend of the family he called him, a man well worth having on your side and not up against you.'

As soon as he said this he stood up, still unsteady on his feet, and after avoiding the coffee table he came in close as if about to confide in me. 'Listen Sam, everything I've told you is between you and me, right? Bruce doesn't have

157

to know about this, does he? Why you want to know is your business, but a word of warning, don't cross the man, he's as hard as nails and he knows a few people, understand my meaning?'

'Loud and clear,' I replied, deciding I'd had enough of his bad breath and starting to move towards the door before I remembered something else. 'I'll need Bruce's phone number. You must have one for him. He won't know it came from you, I promise.'

He began shaking his head but I fixed him with a determined stare and reminded him about the money he had fleeced from me.

'He'll know, nothing gets by him,' he remonstrated.

'A risk you'll have to take. Let me have the number. Don't piss me about.' My composure was deserting me, the man was becoming tiresome.

He sidled across to an old-fashioned wall unit with mirrored recesses and produced a piece of paper from a drawer which he squinted at before jotting down a mobile number on it.

'Try this, but don't come knocking my door down if he doesn't answer,' he sighed, passing me the number and looking relieved as I headed for the hallway.

'This better not be the number of the nearest Chinese takeaway,' I told him, which he ignored.

'Let yourself out and remember, this conversation never happened,' he said backing off and standing aside.

'Try not to drink yourself to death,' I told him, unsure if I meant it or not.

Outside I savoured the fresh air, but not the sight that greeted me. Father had parked my car right opposite the house and Lavender Thompson was waving and shouting to me through the open back window. Not the covert operation I had favoured, but the best I could expect given how anxious they said they were when I climbed back into the driver's seat.

'Hadn't a clue what was going on and thought you might need help and a quick getaway,' Father smiled, as I drove off. 'You should've took one of us inside with you just in case,' he said annoyingly.

'I coped,' I said sarcastically. 'I found out what I wanted to know.'

What I intended to do with it, however, was another thing. There were two eager people in the car itching to ask me and I simply didn't know.

Back in Lavender's kitchen we drank coffee and ate date and walnut cake, three conspirators desperately searching for inspiration. Lavender was of the opinion that we should now confront the Fielding brothers head on in the quest to expose them for what they were. Father wasn't so far behind her in wanting Curtis, for sure, to be brought to book for his contemptuous intimidation of vulnerable people. I reminded them that there was a senior policeman implicated too, by association, and if he was under the Fieldings' thumb it might be difficult to prove any acts of bullying and deceit by either man.

'If as I suspect Bruce is sponging off his brother there's no telling what lengths Curtis will go to,' Lavender said with a heavy heart. 'Anthony and I curse the day we set eyes on him.'

'I could try talking to him again,' I said unenthusiastically. 'Had I been racing at Aintree today I could have approached him because he was stewarding there. The last time we tackled him we didn't know what we know now, and in view of that he might back down and call off the hounds – that's assuming he's the one orchestrating things.'

'Oh, he's behind it all right,' Father mouthed off. 'I think we should pay both brothers a visit and watch them squirm. I'd dare them to say it's got nothing to do with them. It's time they had the tables turned.'

'Yes but I think it's best you stay here. The doctor said rest and recuperation, remember?' I cut him short.

'I'm fine, they always say stuff like that. I've never felt better.'

An unconvinced Lavender scrutinised him closely and looked back in my direction, doubting his speed of recovery. I was glad she saw sense and sided with me. Without patronising Father she turned to him and smiled. 'Sam Junior's right, I think we should let him deal with them but,' she turned to me, 'I think you should take somebody with you to be on the safe side. What about that Dave your father employs? I gather he's the right build to be a minder.'

Size didn't make much difference when Big Dave was knocked unconscious last week, I thought, but she did have a point and Father wasn't against the idea, making all the right noises. 'I'll offer him a bonus if I have to,' he said, nodding. 'He's bound to relish the role.'

Lavender looked at both of us contentedly. 'That's sorted then. I only wish Anthony and I had thought about enlisting help when we took on Curtis. I love my son but he's a wimp when it comes to standing up for himself.'

'Some men are just born bullies. Fielding's done it all his life, he knows no other way,' Father said bitterly.

'I'll make some calls to track him down and arrange a meeting,' I said, hiding my own wimpish tendencies and sounding ultra positive.

'And I'll give Lavender a tour of Sloane Farm and speak to Dave before it gets dark,' Father replied, looking at his watch. 'Why not drive us there and make your calls while you are waiting for us? Then you can take me to pick up my car. The police took it to a holding pound in Gloucester, I feel really lost without it.'

I shook my head. 'So much for taking it easy. What about your stress levels?'

He dismissed me the way he always did when he sensed

an imminent lecture. 'Look at me, son, am I not a picture of health? Stop worrying, sometimes you cluck like a mother hen.'

He looked to Lavender for support and she gave it in abundance. 'Perhaps I could get you to teach me to fish as well,' she said, sounding deadly serious.

Father rose to the challenge. 'It will be my pleasure. Call it a favour returned for looking after me.'

I just smiled to myself and imagined that anything was possible.

15

I watched as an inquisitive Lavender Thompson picked her way slowly past some die-hard anglers who were liberally spaced around the match lake savouring a break in the cloud above as evening closed in. With wholly inappropriate footwear and tentative steps she did her best to keep up with Father, who had spied Big Dave on litter-picking duty over on the far side and was primed to effect an introduction. It was almost comical to watch the three of them together: Dave wiping his grubby hands together in a hurry before leaning forward to shake hands with Lavender who, despite not being at all short, still seemed only half his size; Father looking slightly unsure of himself and obviously trying to impress on Dave that he and the woman in tow were just good friends and not anything approaching an item.

I was standing in a large wooden shed-like building that doubled as a café and general office, where one wall was plastered with photographs of memorable catches. My eyes were drawn as always to one taken last year by Father of me holding a sixteen-pound mirror carp and trying every which way not to drop it. Though never sharing my dad's enthusiasm, I had fished as a boy and hadn't forgotten the basics so when he challenged me on that particular day to break my personal best I was up for it, and perseverance was rewarded.

Big Dave was instrumental in my success of course, he being a master at pinpointing areas where fish were at any given time, almost as if he possessed psychic powers. But I still had to land the fish once I'd hooked it and that, as I

162

recall, was no picnic. The fish stripped line off the reel in one last run for freedom and made me literally follow it round a section of the lake before I gained the upper hand.

I concluded at the time that it wasn't that different to getting a headstrong horse with a dubious temperament to do exactly what you wanted and go where you pointed it. Many a time such an unwilling mount had got the better of me and either dumped me on the turf or finished a race too far behind the others before reverting back to impeccable behaviour when reunited with its groom. So perhaps fishing and racing weren't so unalike after all. The principles were the same. The determined angler fighting for supremacy over the fish that does not want to be caught and subsequently netted, and the belligerent jockey likewise sometimes having to battle to get a horse over obstacles and past the winning post before similarly-minded opponents. But despite the falls, broken bones, disappointments and heartache I knew which I preferred – although the photograph, my genuinely broad grin in it and the overall sense of pride were there for all to see and admire.

Also there, but not in such pride of place, were random photos of me in jockey's colours that I had passed on to Father. He had at least displayed them as any proud parent would, which was gratifying even if they were beginning to curl up and turn brown at the edges. Maybe, I thought selfishly, I would be able to replace them with more up-to-date snaps, especially of recent successes and those yet to come – the sort of wishful thinking, I assumed, that kept fishermen and jockeys all over the world focused and forever optimistic.

As several anglers acknowledged the fading light and called it a day, I watched in opened-mouthed amazement. Father now had Lavender riding pillion on one of the two quad bikes he had invested in, her long skirt tucked in around her knees and blowing in the breeze and one hand holding her beret-style hat in place. And there was a slightly nonplussed Dave, standing with hands on hips probably thinking if this woman wasn't going to be a permanent in Father's life, this was hardly the way to prove it, especially the way they laughed and smiled and carelessly churned up the mud to further soil her already heavily stained shoes.

At least Father was wearing a smile and his glow had returned. Not even being told he couldn't collect his car until Monday morning had phased him as I'd expected it might. Given everything that had happened to him recently, I had to admit his collaboration with the woman also known as Catwoman was a welcome diversion, even if I had endured the worst of them when they put their collective heads together. Perversely this had been akin to two argumentative and scheming teenagers pitting their wits against an under pressure and weak-minded parent, something my father knew only too well from being manipulated by my sister and me when we wouldn't take no for an answer or agree to a compromise. I imagined he wouldn't want reminding of it, and refocused on other more urgent issues.

Apart from calling the number my father had been given by Gloucester police, only to be told they were closed for vehicle recoveries, I had left short and pertinent messages on both of Curtis Fielding's answerphones and got only constant engaged tones from the number Stan Abbots had reluctantly supplied me for half-brother Bruce.

Tamara, too, was unobtainable, and as I stood and watched the bizarre spectacle unfolding in front of me while dusk crept in and the day-ticket patrons drifted away, I felt somewhat ignored and helpless, so I resorted to reading some of the letters Father had received and displayed from appreciative customers before his troubles began.

One of them was from the secretary of the very same angling club that had now withdrawn its patronage following the cow invasion debacle, during which several of its members had been scared witless and had had expensive tackle trampled on by the four-legged invaders. Another from somebody signing themselves Jeff praised the fishery for having the foresight to cater for disabled anglers, reliving a memorable day spent there last May and promising another visit soon. Next to the letters, hanging from a white board, was the café's limited menu, and on the other side of a wood-panelled counter which had a primitive serving hatch were further endorsements from satisfied clients and even more photos, including one of Father shaking hands with an ex-England team angler who had spent a day at the fishery last year accompanied by a film crew.

On another wall, almost hidden by a soft drinks cabinet, was a detailed plan and artist's impression of Horseshoe Lake – the lake which had caused all the aggro between landlord and tenant. Given that the area was previously an eyesore with dilapidated wooden shacks and brick outbuildings that the previous tenant had both neglected and failed to utilise, its conversion into a third lake should be a major improvement, although closer inspection of a nearby map highlighted its strategic position in relationship to Curtis Fielding's proposed caravan park extension.

Quite simply, from the northern perimeter of the part-excavated lake a straight line southwards connected to the nearest main road that had links with major trunk roads and eventually the motorway network. To bring a road through from the existing caravan park was an option but it would be like negotiating a maze, which Fielding clearly had doubts about, particularly as it would mean him losing a number of mobile home pitches to accommodate any revised road infrastructure. As Father had been at pains to point out, he was in the way. Seeing it so clearly on paper made me feel a compromise plan wasn't so viable.

Under the artist's impression in black marker pen and Father's unmistakeable writing were the words 'Opening

Soon, Watch This Space', to which somebody with a bad sense of humour had added the words 'Why are we waiting'. Controversially another scribe had written the words 'Cows Rule' which had understandably been partially obliterated. Adjacent to the plan there was a photo of Father in a hard hat, sitting aboard a JCB earth digger, with an attached newspaper cutting reporting the then new venture. He was quoted as saying the new lake would give keen anglers and beginners alike their dream venue, and subtle landscaping would beautify the site to give it a much-needed makeover which would be beneficial to local wildlife. Honest words from a genuine man. And a vision that was so near and yet so far.

Almost on cue, the man who was delaying the project and allegedly acting like a rural Hitler came on the phone and his voice sounded creepily friendly and unemotional. He politely asked me what I wanted, and when I told him and suggested an urgent meeting he paused as if it might upset his busy diary.

'Tomorrow's out, I won't be back from Liverpool till late,' Fielding deliberated. 'So shall we say Monday, preferably late afternoon? About four would suit. Come to the house, assuming you know where it is, and bring your father along.'

There was no variation in his voice. It was as though our run-in at Cheltenham the previous week had never occurred.

I immediately had second thoughts about Lavender's suggestion of taking Big Dave with me, sensing my father should be there after all to witness whatever Fielding had to say for himself.

'Yours, Monday, at four?' I replied, shocked at the ease of engagement.

'With your father,' he repeated, his tone unchanged.

'Of course, I'll make sure of it,' I assured him, almost casually enquiring whether half-brother Bruce would be joining us.

'Why would I need him there? This doesn't concern him,' he said, ice cool. 'We can settle the dispute without anybody else's involvement. I have a very sensible compromise to put to your father, I rather think he'll like it.'

'But what about the impending charges for damages to your property?' I reminded him. 'What are you going to do about them? And what's this about a compromise?'

He remained unshaken and became dismissive. 'I may have been a little harsh on him, but Sam knows what he did. Tell him I'll instruct the police to drop the charges and we'll deal with the other matter like grown-ups.'

But I instantly brought up the attack on Dave Burrows and the poisoned fish, and for the first time he sounded vexed, vehemently denying any involvement and refuting any allegations likely to come his way. I backed down strategically, telling him I would pass on his message to my father and immediately asking him to deliver one to his half-brother. He huffed and sounded greatly put out as though being treated as a go-between was beneath him, but I carried on regardless.

'Tell Bruce I've spoken to Stan Abbots about the stunt that got Paul Eddison arrested and the later retraction of Stan's original statement to the police. Tell him I know it was his idea.'

Silence followed, before Fielding sighed and grudgingly said he would let Bruce know, hanging up before I had a chance to thank him.

I went looking for Father to pass on the good news and found him showing Lavender the spot where Big Dave had been laid low by the intruder the previous Saturday and the area of the match lake that had been targeted close to where the dead fish were discovered. With simultaneously pricked ears they shared the same intrigue when I told them about the call and the impending meeting that might yet bring an end to the dispute. Unexpectedly, Curtis

Fielding's climbdown over the criminal damage charges didn't draw an immediate reaction from Father but Lavender was quick to condemn it.

'Bloody nerve. Don't be taken in by him, Sam, he's clearly up to something. The man's a rat. What did he have to say about the attack on poor Dave and the fire? Denied all knowledge of them, no doubt.'

Father looked at her and then at me.

'We'll listen to what he has to say,' I shrugged. 'He won't want this thing dragging on any longer than necessary; time is money to a man like him.'

Lavender scowled and bit her bottom lip. 'And money is all he thinks about. Don't let him hoodwink you, Sam.'

Father looked down, noticing the bad state of both his and her shoes, and skirted around the subject. 'Best we leave all that till Monday,' he said resignedly. 'Let's get you cleaned up. Next time we come better prepared. Wellington boots or something like.'

She shrugged off the inconvenience and gratifyingly raised a smile again. 'I've been in muddy fields before, loads of them. Some far worse. Charity organisers have sadistic tendencies. They think you'll put up with anything if it's in aid of a good cause. This is nothing, just a bit of dirt, and at our age I think we should be allowed to live dangerously once in a while.'

Father winced at the word 'age' as usual, especially as he was keen to promote the modern belief that sixty-five was the new forty. I went back forty-eight hours to how he had looked wired up in a hospital bed and shuddered, secretly hoping I'd have the same powers of recovery and the same attitude to adversity that had seemingly sustained him in later years.

Similarly it occurred to me then that, despite her senior years, Lavender Thompson was a formidable opponent. That made it even more surprising that Curtis Fielding had got the better of her, although I imagined him homing in on her son's vulnerability first and keeping the pressure on him, so much so that even his mother's strongest resistance was to prove futile. It was akin to a one-sided power struggle.

It was now nearing darkness and there was mist shrouding the water as cold air nudged in, making the trees in the distance partially disappear. But there was still enough light left for me to check out the area I had identified on the map as the key to Curtis Fielding's plans and its apparent prime location in terms of accessibility to the land he had begun to develop, which snaked around a natural slope and was being terraced for accommodating caravans. There was also evidence of trunking for electrical wiring being installed and gravel had been laid to enable access for heavy vehicles, one of which, a bright orange earth digger, was parked across the entrance to the site as if to stop any trespassing vehicles and hinder prying eyes.

Back at the shed, or hut as Father preferred to call it, I witnessed the spectacle of Father and Big Dave jointly trying to clean up Lavender's shoes with kitchen roll and some kind of brush. The lady in question was secretly enjoying the attention and sitting with her stockinged feet up on a chair just inside the door.

'Make us a brew when the kettle boils, son,' Father said, gesturing towards the small kitchen where an electric kettle was beginning to hiss.

'Four teas coming up,' I humoured him, not bothering to argue.

'Milk in the fridge, sugar and biscuits in one of them cupboards,' he gave out his orders, examining one of Lavender's shoes which was now looking relatively spotless.

'I think you've found your calling, Father, you should take it up for a living. Used to find shoe shiners on every street corner once,' I teased him, banging cupboard doors.

'Mock all you want, son, rich coming from somebody

who gets a valet to do for him on race days,' he retaliated. 'Jockeys are such idle beggars.'

I let him gloat and then watched him reunite the shoe with Lavender's foot – a scene from Cinderella springing to mind. He then examined Big Dave's handiwork and pulled a face, giving the second shoe another polish before getting the lady in waiting to step back into it. He then asked me if I had found what I was looking for on my short walkabout, and after dishing out the tea I shared my thoughts with him.

'Building an access road across land that you lease will save him much time and, above all, considerable expense,' I said, not really telling him anything he didn't already know. 'My guess is that instead of trying to force you to leave he'll try and persuade you to agree to him having a right of way, which will mean you will get your lake finished and he will get his precious road, providing there are no traffic complications.'

Father huffed and puffed. 'So he gets what he wants and I'm stuck with a bloody ugly road running alongside the far end of the lake once I've revised the length and shape of it. Why should I be the one to be put out? I won't agree to it, I'll fight him all the way.'

Lavender clenched her fists in approval and shuffled about as if she was supporting a political campaign, the heels of her extremely clean shoes clicking together under the hem of her skirt. She took a breath to say something but I got in first.

'Have you considered you might profit from this?' I suggested. 'I presume there are people who like caravans and fishing. What better than having a day-ticket fishery on your doorstep? This might be a business opportunity and not the time to carry over a feud with a neighbour. Much as I also dislike the man and know what he's put you through, you could both capitalise and at least rub along together as best you can.'

Whilst Dave sat sipping tea and looking a little confused, the two others were aghast at my take on what might or might not happen and my bizarre notion that Curtis Fielding could indirectly help Father make money whilst raking it in himself. Not for the first time they looked at each other and all I could see in their combined eyes was defiance.

Lavender showed her colours first. 'I think you should tread carefully, Sam. That man has form, remember? He will suck you in and spit you out if you let him. Personally I wouldn't agree to anything he says. He knew he didn't have legitimate grounds to evict you and tried bully boy tactics instead – that sums him up and tells you how low he's prepared to sink.'

Pulled in opposite directions Father chose to sit uneasily on the fence. 'All this is just speculation, let's wait and see. I won't be forced into doing anything I don't want to. I'll tell him where to stick his compromise if I have to, that's the only dialogue he knows.'

'Good for you,' Lavender responded, her heels clicking again.

They drank tea in synchrony as if they had done it all their lives and in spite of everything I smiled to myself, wondering what pleasures life had in store for me, should I reach retirement age.

Big Dave still wore a face that told me he wasn't sure about Lavender, although knowing how subservient he could be I imagined he might accept her as a friend, especially given the fervent way she had supported my father. Beyond that I couldn't tell what he would think or how he would react. For sure Lavender would clash with his wife who I gather came originally from an itinerant family in the Bristol area and tended to view anyone she didn't know well with suspicion. Dave himself wasn't the most sociable of men, speaking only when he was spoken to and never using long words when he did, though he was prone to tell rude jokes and sing crude songs after a drink or two. Churchgoer Lavender would most certainly not approve.

With the light fading quickly I joined Dave on his late rounds of the fishery, asking him to retrace the steps he took exactly a week ago and coaxing him to mention anything that came to mind about his attacker. At the point where the attack took place he stopped and slowly talked me through it. Then he mentioned the Mercedes car again and I asked him if he was sure, bearing in mind he had just been hit over the head with a chunk of paving slab.

'I heard it all right, as clear as day. I know my cars, it was a Merc,' he said, unfazed.

'But you never saw it or who was driving it?'

He shook his head. 'Nah, I was seeing stars...' he paused. 'I think the car was grey, maybe silver.'

'So you did see it then?' I persevered.

Dave didn't seem too sure and took some time to think, processing everything inside his fuddled head as if now, a week on, he was getting his memory back. It was as though the re-enactment had jogged it into recollection mode and he was suddenly remembering much more than he had told the police in his statement.

Looking up at the sheer size of him I still found it bewildering that somebody had managed to overpower him and leave him concussed. It made me think that either his attacker was a big man too or it was someone who just got lucky, bearing in mind the assault had taken place in a fairly open place and in pitch darkness. The man who attacked me, I recalled, was tall and reasonably strong but surely no match for Dave although I hadn't entirely ruled him out, whoever he was.

After enough of a pause Dave went on. 'The bloke who hit me must have scarpered pretty quick. His car must have been on the other side of that hedge. I heard it start up and there was this flash of grey through the bushes, that's how I remember it.'

'So even though it was pitch black you saw a grey flash?'

'It weren't that dark,' he corrected me. 'It was a clear sky and the moon was out. Not murky like it is now.'

I could see as he said it that it wouldn't have been so difficult for him to see something, even though he was also dealing with stars in his head at the time.

I tried coming from another angle. 'Did your attacker say anything or make any noises?'

Straight away he said, 'He was breathing heavy, he came out of nowhere, I wasn't ready for him.'

'From behind so you had no idea of his height or size?'

'More from the side ... I was stood here and he came from over there.' He demonstrated. Again he stopped as if wracking his brain for answers. Then he let out a big sigh of frustration and knocked the fist of one hand against his head as if banging on a door.

'You were unable to give the police a description but the bloke who hit you must have been at least as tall as you, would you say?' I led him, trying to help him remember.

From his reaction I could tell he liked the idea whether true or not. Being downed by a much smaller man was not good for his ego but I sensed now he genuinely believed it must have been someone more his own size just from the nature of the attack and the weapon used.

'He had to be strong to hit me so hard,' he said, sounding less frustrated.

'And you are a hundred per cent sure about the car?' I backtracked.

'Damn well certain,' he said back immediately.

'So we're looking for an above average-sized man who drives a greyish Merc then,' I summed up, sounding too much like a policeman. 'Anyone you know come to mind?'

We both thought about Curtis Fielding at the same time. His wife owned a Merc of that description and he was often seen driving it. But I also thought the man who attacked

173

Dave was likely to be much younger, fitter and nimble of foot.

'I wished I'd remembered sooner,' Dave said, guiltily.

'Things become clearer in time,' I placated him. 'Sorry you had to be reminded of something you'd probably rather forget.'

After another pause he carried on with his clearing-up duties and I helped him the best I could, doing a sweep around both lakes for angler's litter as moonlight at last broke through and shone a path for us.

Back at the shed Father was briefing Lavender on the photograph library I had studied earlier and I saw her shudder with the onset of cold air despite her unflagging interest in the subject matter.

'Best get you home and back to the warmth,' I said, deciding not to tell either of them about Big Dave's memory boost until later.

Lavender nodded and said, 'Tomorrow Sam's going help me catch my first carp. Hopefully bigger than that one of yours,' she teased me.

'Here's to beginner's luck,' I encouraged her, seeing for real in her eyes that the challenge was on.

Father shrugged at me and decided to remain silent, not knowing what tomorrow would bring, and I thought how rare it was for him to allow me the last word.

16

Soon after I had delivered my human cargo to Castle Moat Lodge Tamara phoned me to say Emilia was running a temperature and that she thought it best I didn't spend the night at the Willows. I hid my disappointment and asked Lavender for a loan of the sofa bed in her lounge, which drew disapproving looks from Father and a complaint from him when she was out of earshot.

'Checking up on me is really not necessary, son, you really do have some cheek,' he grumbled.

'A bit sensitive aren't we?' I retorted, seeing I'd struck a nerve.

Although he appeared to ignore me I was sure he swore at me under his breath. 'What's up? Has her stuck-up mother decided you're not good enough for her precious daughter?' he retaliated, raising his voice so Lavender could hear from the kitchen where she was making coffee.

'Emilia's ill, children come first,' I said with a distinct edge.

He pulled a face. 'Young children can be a convenient excuse when you want them to be. Your mother was famous for it when you and Heather were that age,' he recalled.

It was my turn for facial distortions. 'She had a lot to put up with. It was a struggle for her as well you know, and you weren't always around to support her.'

He reacted. 'What's that supposed to mean? I think you're in no position to lecture me. How often do you see your own daughter?'

The word 'ouch' came to mind, but he had said it before as part of an inbuilt defence mechanism, though it still

175

hurt. 'Your granddaughter will be spending most of Monday with me,' I informed him, trying to defuse a ticking bomb. 'Even thought I could bring her over here at some stage, assuming Lavender's OK with it.'

Father paused and looked a little sheepish, by which time Lavender was back in the room carrying the coffee and smiling. 'Of course you must bring her, Sam's told me all about her, says she's a little princess. Bring her and I'll buy something nice, a little spoiling won't hurt her.'

'You're very kind,' I thanked her.

Father let his mind wander and did some reminiscing. 'Grace is the spit of Heather when she was that age and she never failed to tie me around her little finger. She once had me pushing her dollies in her pram and singing lullabies to them in a park with everyone staring at me as I went past thinking I must be mental. And she could be a real tomboy too, forever wanting to climb trees or play cricket. Happy days.'

'There is a likeness,' I conceded.

'I could make fairy cakes,' Lavender enthused, sounding excited.

'Heather once told her primary school teacher I was a spy who worked for the government and I got some strange looks from other parents after that,' Father rambled on.

'She could stay for tea, I could get some of those chicken things that children seem to eat these days,' Lavender persisted.

'That all sounds brilliant, I'm sure she'll enjoy that,' I thanked her again.

It was like being at the fulcrum of two separate conversations, with me stumbling to say something wholly relevant to either of them and deciding it was best to let them carry on until they exhausted themselves. Father rarely ever spoke about Heather, so it was heart-warming to hear him compare her to Grace who had indeed inherited my sister's good looks and a few of her mannerisms too. As for Lavender, though not blessed with grandchildren herself she had catered for seven nephews and nieces in her time and had also later played host to their children, so entertaining youngsters was nothing new for her and no real challenge.

Father regaled us with several more tales from the scrap-book in his head before his memory gave up, and likewise Lavender spoke of her disappointment with Anthony for never settling down, in addition to suggesting more food items she could obtain before Monday to tempt Grace. Then inevitably the conversation turned to Curtis Fielding again and I mentioned Big Dave's recollections from a week ago which were now becoming clearer.

The spectre of an allegedly tall and strongly-built man driving a grey or silver Mercedes away from the scene of a vicious assault after attempting to contaminate a section of the lake dominated our thoughts, and Father was quick to throw another name into the mix given he believed Fielding would never do his own dirty work.

Neville Truman was Fielding's estate manager, responsible for the day-to-day running and maintenance of the three adjoining farms that Fielding owned plus the original caravan park site which was the centre of the dispute. It was his pick-up on which Father had taken out his retribution, and there was little love lost between them. They had clashed over relatively minor issues in the past and exchanged four-letter expletives.

'He's well capable of putting somebody the size of Dave in hospital. Don't know why I didn't suspect him before. In truth he's all mouth and trousers but he is built like a brick shithouse and I've seen him chauffeuring Fielding's missus around in that swanky car of hers so he'd probably have access to it.'

'But would he risk going to prison for his boss?' I asked, not wanting to jump too quickly to conclusions.

'Curtis Fielding is a crook and he employs crooks,' Lavender interjected, her agitation showing.

'She's not wrong,' Father nodded.

I felt disadvantaged by not knowing the man who had suddenly become prime suspect, but I kept an open mind. After all, the man who had jumped me at home might have fitted his profile and could well be the arsonist who went on the rampage at Father's lock-up, the location of which would not be known to many.

'If Fielding did get this Neville character to do his dirty work he'd hardly employ him in a day job looking after his estate?' I questioned, looking doubtful.

Father disagreed. 'What better cover? Neville's a lap dog and he'd do practically anything he was asked to do especially if Fielding made it worth his while.'

Then Lavender added her weight to his argument. 'Around the time Curtis was hounding Anthony for his money back that man came round twice shouting the odds and threatening us. He looked and sounded like a charmer on the outside when I first met him, but behind the façade he's a mean bully just like his boss.'

Again I questioned it. 'But is he capable of serious crime? Assault and arson isn't the same as picking up a parking ticket or using a mobile whilst driving, and would he stoop so low as to almost commit murder?'

'He would do what needed to be done,' Lavender answered smugly as she turned to Father and got his silent support.

'Perhaps the police might like to interview him then,' I said without too much conviction. 'At least to see what kind of alibi he has for the various crimes. They should at least know about Big Dave's sudden memory gain, given he told them virtually nothing in his original statement.'

Two heads nodded in agreement and I said I would speak to Dave on the subject in the morning. Father then turned his attention to fishing, with an early start in mind, only to

178

be met by resistance from Lavender who reminded him her carp-catching exploits would have to wait for God as tomorrow was Sunday. He looked at me, shrugged and puffed out his cheeks. The lady, she then told him, was well worth waiting for and as he was a guest in her house he was in no position to argue.

Soon after dawn as rain threatened I went for a walk to clear my mind and exercise the body. On my return Lavender was waiting with the offer of coffee, toast and homemade marmalade which we consumed together in her kitchen, the conversation monopolised by the monotonies of life. She happily spoke of her love of cats, her varied charity work and the pride she felt for her son Anthony. I told her more about my daughter Grace and she went all soppy on me like a stereotypical, goggle-eyed granny, reminding me of the promise I'd made yesterday to bring her over on Monday, which was now shaping up to be a busy day and not the one I'd originally planned solely around my daughter.

When Father materialised, Lavender said good morning and left us to get ready for church, confirming that she would change into the scruffiest clothes she could find on her return ready to tackle the great carp challenge. He raised one eyebrow as if a night's sleep had dulled his memory, somehow managing to summon up a courteous smile even though she had already disappeared through the door.

'Why don't you go with her and sing a few hymns?' I teased him, remembering how he and Mother had forced me to join the local church choir when I was too young to protest.

'Behave,' he grizzled back, still annoyed with me for staying the night and cursing me under his breath again. 'I ought to be helping Dave but I'm rather stuck without a bloody car. Make yourself useful, son, I'm gagging for a drink and a couple of rounds of toast wouldn't go amiss either.'

Making himself at home on a pine stool and digging his elbows into the marble-effect breakfast bar that looked out on the side gardens of the house, I watched as his eyes tracked the movements of two of the resident cats.

'Two rounds of toast coming up but don't expect me to spread the marmalade as well,' I said sarcastically.

He made a two-fingered salute and meant it.

'Charming,' I muttered under my breath. He just sat watching the cats.

'Bloody hell,' he exclaimed after a long pause. 'Why did you let her talk me into it? I don't carry a magic wand. I can't make the fish take the bait for God's sake. This could end in tears and tantrums.'

'If anyone can, you can. I'd put money on it. In a few hours she'll be smiling from ear to ear. She might not be able to convert you to religion but you might convert her to rod and line. Wasn't Jesus a fisherman of sorts?'

Father turned and looked at me as if I'd taken an insanity pill. 'Sometimes I really wonder about you, son, the things you say are priceless.'

'I must get it from somewhere,' I shrugged.

We heard the noise of tyres on gravel as Lavender left for church, and with slightly burnt toast in hand Father sounded understandably down when I moved the subject on to the fire at the lock-up and asked him what he intended to do about it.

'I still feel numb, like it's all been a bad dream. Things like that just don't happen in the real world. Having people around me has certainly made things more bearable. For all her faults Lavender has a heart of gold – and before you state the obvious there's nothing going on between us and there never will be, so you can stop winding me up.'

'I would never do that,' I lied, camouflaging a smile.

Father talked as he chewed, as if good manners had deserted him. 'I fear I'm going to lose a small fortune on those cars destroyed in the fire,' he grimaced, trying to put on a brave face. 'Insurers never pay out the true value of collectable vehicles and classic cars are hardly fetching good money at the auctions at the moment especially with the current state of the economy. Whatever they offer won't be enough.'

'Insurers always try to wriggle off the hook. There might be some room for negotiation, wait and see what they offer,' I said, endeavouring to raise his spirits.

'It's a mess son, a God-damn mess,' he sighed, still chewing the toast.

I didn't disagree but dared not say it. Rarely had I seen him look so deflated, but those cars, like his other pastime, were the love of his life and the thought of losing them was worse for him than any marriage break-up. He picked at crumbs on the plate like a condemned man and stared aimlessly out of the window. Two cats were pawing at each other, though whether it was play or acrimony I couldn't tell.

'Lavender's nickname is well suited,' I said, tactfully changing the subject.

Father slowly shook his head. 'Never saw the fascination with domesticated animals myself, although you and Heather did keep rabbits and hamsters which your mother tended to look after.'

'But you do like fish,' I patronised him. 'Well, catching them at least.'

'And keeping them too,' he corrected me.

'Each to his own,' I said.

'Suppose so,' he conceded.

Now all he had to do was magic one of his wily old carp on to Lavender's hook and everything would be heading in the right direction again,

We exchanged more thoughts and dissected a Sunday newspaper before I caught up with Tamara for an update on Emilia, who was much improved. By midday Lavender was back and decked out in her gardening clothes which still looked pretty spotless and which she topped off with an old wax jacket and deerstalker hat. We drove in two cars; she followed me in her Peugeot with Father sitting beside her no doubt talking in terminology that I hoped wouldn't put her off. Within an hour he was settling her down on a comfy chair adjusted to her liking not too close to the edge of the lake, in front of her two appropriately baited rods secured on their metal rests which he had already cast over a central gravel bar that attracted fish, his words of advice and encouragement ringing in her ears.

Not far away, I was trying to convince Dave he should go back to the police with the additional info following the return of his memory. This didn't go down too well with the gentle giant who preferred a quiet, uncomplicated life which obviously didn't include conversing with the law. Worn down by my persistence, and providing Father gave him the time off, he promised he would go the next day. I told him I would be checking up on him, like some overbearing teacher mentoring a wayward child, before watching him climb back aboard his quad bike to complete his rounds of the complex.

On the opposite side of the match lake to where Father and Lavender were seated there were about a dozen anglers competing against each other in a contest Dave had helped to arrange. These were the defiant ones not put off by the marauding cows, an attempt to poison the water, and recent bad blood between landlord and tenant. Careful not to break their concentration I wandered around and spoke to some of them about what had happened. Not one of them had a bad word to say about Father and indeed complimented him on the facilities he had installed at the fishery, which included easily accessible and defined fishing pegs, clean toilets, and hot and cold fast food. One elderly angler with a shock of grey, unkempt hair was clearly not a fan of Curtis Fielding and happily talked about the day the cows were let on to the fishery.

'That weren't no accident,' he recalled as if he knew for sure. 'They were herded up and driven across the land away from their usual grazing pasture and when they saw the water they headed straight for it to drink. No one will convince me otherwise.'

I told him who I was and thanked him, but he thanked me also as he had already recognised me. 'I had a tenner on Sir Matt at Newbury last week and thanks to you I won a nice bundle. My son's named Matt you see, so I had to didn't I, and a bloody good job I did too. Thanks again,' he said, his eyes aglow.

I asked him about the new, as yet unfinished, lake and he raised both thumbs at once. 'Bring it on, the more places to fish the better but don't tell my wife I said it,' he chuckled.

I walked on and spoke to the last angler of the competitive bunch who seemed to be having most success, having netted three sizeable fish since my arrival. With an economy of words he also bigged-up my father and said wild horses wouldn't keep him away. So cows, I assumed, were not a problem.

Raised voices and a controlled scream of excitement shattered the tranquillity. Everybody's eyes trained on Lavender, who was now on her feet at the water's edge with Father doing his utmost to calm her. Big Dave was rushing towards them on his bike, kicking up mud and grass, and I was breaking into a frenzied jog to reach them with mobile phone in hand primed for a photo.

Then everything went quiet and whatever had feasted on Lavender's bait was gone. Father was consoling her, convincing her that it happened to the best and like buses

there would be another one along in no time. There was
gentle laughter from the other side of the lake that certainly
wasn't mischief or fun making, and when I added my
consolation Lavender was outwardly philosophical about
her near miss.

'Well at least I know what it feels like. My heart was racing
but I was all fingers and thumbs too, I never imagined it
would be so hard.'

'Plenty more fish in the lake,' I said, inadvertently sounding
corny and making Father cringe.

I fetched bacon sandwiches and mugs of coffee for all
of us and sat on a chair Dave had provided whilst he perched
on the bike and devoured his food in no more than four
exaggerated bites. Lavender, in complete contrast, ate
demurely, her deerstalker and jacket now dispensed with
as the late afternoon sun broke through to warm us and
hopefully stir the fish into a feeding frenzy. Opposite us
the match men were now weighing in their individual catches
and exchanging opinions on the day's events, a couple of
them lighting up cigarettes and looking anxious as the
contents of their nets were put on the portable scales and
duly recorded.

Father then placed one of his baits only a few feet from
the bank, having noted the tell-tale disturbance of a fish
grubbing about on the bottom for food, and reeled in the
other line to try another area approximately midway between
the bank and a small man-made island which was virtually
in the centre of the lake and home to quite a number of
resident ducks.

I had watched Father many times and knew that he never
let frustration get the better of him when fishing, but even
I sensed the pressure as the clock ticked and the sun started
to disappear behind trees in the distance.

Then the reel of the left-hand rod which carried the
close-in bait was stripped of line at a rate of knots. A startled

Lavender was up on her feet with Father guiding her every move, trying manfully to make sure she didn't let the fish run too far or retrieve the line too quickly.

The fish surfaced about ten feet from where I stood and Big Dave, not prone to excitement suddenly shouted out, 'That's a bloody double for sure, would you bleeding believe it.'

A far too preoccupied Lavender ignored his choice of vocabulary and listened as Father, looking increasingly nervous, barked out his instructions.

'Keep the rod high, apply some side strain, steady now, stay calm,' he said amongst other things.

Careful not to spook the fish so close to the bank, Big Dave slowly positioned the landing net so that with Father's help Lavender could steer the fish over it. There was a chorus of whoops and hollers as it was safely and swiftly captured.

'Bloody hell,' Father exclaimed, not caring much about anything he was saying. 'That was nerve-racking. For a while back there I didn't think it was going to happen.'

'But it did happen, Sam, and I'm absolutely exhausted,' Lavender thanked him, regaining her composure.

'You did great, well done,' I congratulated her.

'You're a natural at it,' Father exaggerated.

The fully scaled common carp was now lifted carefully onto the bank and after Father removed the hook from its mouth he hazarded a guess at its weight which conflicted with Dave's earlier prediction.

'It's eight to nine pounds, closer to nine. Not bad for a first fish, in fact it's pretty damned good. Sammy's first was a tiddler in comparison but then he was only six years old and it was in the pouring rain on the local canal.'

'As if I needed reminding,' I shrugged, trying not to sound too envious.

'Please say it will come to no harm, it looks so helpless,'

Lavender said, taking a closer look at her catch and growing concerned.

Father reassured her with a hand on her upper arm. 'It will be fine, it will swim away none the worse for its experience. First we need to get some photos to show your friends, I'll even put one on the wall of fame in the hut.'

He then organised the impromptu photo shoot, with me taking several snaps on my phone and also on the digital camera he just happened to have ready for the occasion. He took a few more as if not fully trusting me to get the light right and then Dave released the fish to swim slowly away.

Lavender could not hide her euphoria and if the light hadn't been fading and clouds rolling in I believe she would have wanted to do it all over again.

'I think this merits some kind of celebration,' she turned to all of us. 'A meal at mine perhaps, I'm sure I have some steaks in my freezer.'

Dave's ears twitched and his mouth was watering. I told her I had other plans, and Dave's hopes were quickly extinguished by my father saying, 'Just us two then, sounds like a good idea to me.'

Dave didn't let the disappointment last very long and was quickly back on the bike roaring around on yet another search for litter.

'Are you sure you won't join us?' Lavender asked me as Father set about the rods and began to break them down.

'Quite sure,' I replied. 'Three's a crowd.'

17

In a fit of rage, and for no logical reason, my ex-wife once told me I would never see my daughter again. So every hour I spent with her now was precious. The taxi had delivered her at eight-thirty as arranged. She had noticeably grown another inch and had had her hair restyled; the usual curls were gone and it was combed out straight and nestled like smooth silk around her shoulders. She wore bright but functional clothes and carried a small holdall that presumably held her favourite possessions. She was quick to show me a new bracelet that her stepfather had bought her following one of his business trips abroad.

When I told her we were meeting up with Tamara and Emilia later her eyes lit up and from then on it was a case of her asking me when every five minutes, as if nothing else mattered. Like so many part-time fathers I found it hard to communicate with an eight-year-old who, whilst always looking at ease in my presence, said little that made me feel totally relaxed and answered questions with an economy of words or sometimes just a nod or shake of the head.

If I was honest it was just enough for me to watch her and retrospectively savour memories of her childhood before things between her mother and me came to a head and careered out of control. And though it was akin to staring at a goldfish bowl from the outside I knew this was the best I could expect, given my ex's hurtful ultimatum of five years ago before we settled on a reasonable access compromise that for me still sometimes felt like picking the shortest straw.

Days like today would become the memories of tomorrow,

so I had decided it couldn't be wasted, having already persuaded Lavender to take Father to pick up his car and asked Dominic for a favour. For the second time since her arrival Grace's eyes shone bright at my proposal and she skipped about as any excited child might in anticipation of a treat, so my nagging doubts about being able to keep her fully entertained were soon put aside.

The suggestion of a visit to the stables had been Tamara's not mine, but it had been quite inspirational and both girls, in her words, would simply adore it. I had gone to The Willows the previous night and made up a bridge foursome with Tamara's parents whilst Emilia slept off the dregs of a chill that had given her a slight temperature. The prospect of seeing Grace tomorrow was motive enough to put her to rights and doubly ensure a sound night's sleep.

During the game, with Dame Olivia concentrating hard, Joe Blackwood tactfully grilled me about up and coming races with me back in the saddle on Wednesday, tipping his nose with his finger as he was prone to do when in search of inside information.

'Caper Sol Mio is well handicapped at Haydock on Wednesday,' I told him, making him plainly aware I wasn't contravening any trade secrets act.

He chewed on his bottom lip and pulled a face at the hand he'd been dealt. 'What's the gossip on Metal Mountain? Is he still bound for Ascot on Saturday or will Dominic hold him back?' he went on, much to Olivia's annoyance as she waited for him to play a card.

'Not sure, I'll find out tomorrow if I can. You know Dominic, never one to give much away, keeps his owners in the dark sometimes. I'll keep you posted.'

Tamara joined her mother with a slight disapproving look and I rolled my eyes back at her pleading for sympathy. I could hardly ignore her father and it wasn't as if the game was a matter of life or death.

CAUGHT

'Yes, please let me know,' Joe sighed, a hesitant hand hovering as if he was in two minds which card to play.

'I will,' I promised, not so sure I would remember to find out.

With three pairs of impatient eyes trained on him Joe put down a card and his wife tossed her head like a restless mare in the parade ring and whispered under her breath.

'No pressure then,' I said to Tamara as she looked to me to follow on. This might be a long game, I thought.

We played on until half past ten when Tamara's mother muttered something about her beauty sleep and an early start, wishing us a good day tomorrow. Joe poured himself a last whisky and I had a ginger beer. He did some more unsubtle probing before Tamara told him bluntly he looked tired and he took the hint and left us alone.

'Parents get worse as they get older,' she suggested, one eye focused on the sitting room clock. We sat and kissed and planned the forthcoming day which was to be temporarily usurped by the meeting with Curtis Fielding in the afternoon.

Tamara had it all under some sort of control. 'You can leave me and the girls with Lavender whilst you sort your father out, I'm sure she'll look after us. Personally I never listen to the gossips.'

'She's a real softy, honest,' I reassured her, tongue in cheek. 'Father would never put up with her if he felt uncomfortable around her,' I added, lending myself to the idea.

'I'm already kind of looking forward to it,' Tamara said contentedly.

The hugs and kisses Tamara had given me then to pass on to Grace this morning had long since been delivered, and my daughter and I were now loosely engaged in a game of I Spy which challenged the alphabet as well as my powers of logic and made me laugh out loud like a child again. Luckily, with the game disintegrating into silliness, Tamara's car arrived on the stroke of ten and the mid-morning peace and quiet of a Stroud suburb was shattered as the girls squealed at each other in a pent-up show of sheer excitement and anticipation.

'A complete recovery I see,' I observed from a safe distance as they danced around flowers bordering my neat front lawn.

Tamara kissed me and smiled. 'She's been up for hours and hasn't stopped. Batteries fully recharged.'

'Brilliant to see them together again. It's like they've never been apart.'

'Hope your neighbours have good sound insulation. Listen to them, it's pure mayhem.'

In reality it was like music to my ears and not a bit annoying. It was a sound I had missed and felt deprived of. As sweet as birdsong during a summer's dawn chorus. I wished for the moment to continue and said so. 'They can make as much noise as they want, let them complain, just let them try.'

We watched on as our daughters formulated a game of their own, the rules to which were typically vague and altered as they went along until a minor argument erupted regarding the score, with Grace the main protagonist.

'Takes after somebody I know,' Tamara teased me as the dispute was quickly defused.

'Competitive right to the end, it's what the Woodalls are well known for,' I smiled back.

We took the girls inside. I fed them crisps and cheese puffs and they drank fresh orange juice whilst looking through a racing scrapbook I had started some years ago and added to only infrequently since. And when it was time to leave for Lower Churn they literally stumbled over each other in their haste to get to my car, with Emilia marginally in pole position having been told by her grandmother that Dominic had agreed for her to sit on Hologram in the prep yard as a very special half-term treat. It explained why she wore jodhpur-style trousers and a green padded jacket.

'It's a bit like the start of the Grand National,' I commented as we were told to hurry.

Tamara puffed out her cheeks and moaned ever so slightly. 'Emmy's pretty insufferable when she wants to go somewhere and twice as bad when she doesn't. Blame my mother for this. As soon as she overheard our plans she was on to Dominic and I don't think he had the balls to turn her down.'

Not many would, I thought to myself, Dame Olivia was used to getting her own way. 'I'm sure he knows there's no harm to be done, it'll be a photo opportunity and a chance to add to the scrapbook,' I acknowledged.

Just because it was a rare blank day in the National Hunt diary didn't mean a holiday for the staff at Lower Churn, and Dominic had already been out on the exercise gallops for several hours and barked out his daily orders to his minions on his return. When we arrived he was sitting at his desk behind a pile of important-looking paperwork talking to an owner on the phone and waving at us to sit down. Our chatterbox daughters had already been taken off by the head lad and a stable girl to visit Hologram's box and to help her saddle him up ready to be brought out into the yard.

'This is very good of you, Dominic,' Tamara told him when at long last he finished his call.

'You should be thanking your mother,' he said with a gracious smile. 'I'm just here to make people happy. Well, people who pay me of course.'

He quickly switched his attention to me and asked me how things were progressing where my father was concerned, which was a veiled attempt at assessing my state of mind with some important racing to come over the winter months.

I told him about the meeting with Curtis Fielding later and he couldn't resist offering his opinion and passing on some gossip he had heard. 'If you ask me it's that half-brother of his you have to be wary of. Did you know Bruce Fielding had threatened a Cheltenham bookmaker after some kind of dispute and the police were called? And he's been seen knocking around with some pretty low life too.'

I acted surprised, which in truth I was. It was the police involvement that interested me. 'What did the police do exactly?'

Dominic hunched his shoulders. 'They sent somebody round to get Bruce's side of the story so I'm told, but further than that I don't know.'

'No arrest or anything?'

'Not that I know of. The grapevine only stretches so far. Such a lot goes on behind the scenes and people like that are always trying to drag the good name of racing down. Curtis himself is making himself unpopular with jockeys as we know and that has to have a knock-on effect with implications for both owners and trainers.'

'Worth mentioning when I see him, I suppose,' I thought out loud.

With a wide grimace Dominic questioned my motives. 'What good would that do your father? You need to get them to resolve their differences and move on. Bruce is probably an embarrassment to Curtis so I wouldn't remind him. I only brought it up because you mentioned Bruce to me and I'm just telling you what I've heard.'

I thanked him and without trying to bore Tamara too much he quickly briefed me on forthcoming events, including the inclusion of Metal Mountain at Ascot on Saturday which I made a mental note to remember to pass on to Tamara's father. Briefing over and happily ignoring the paperwork, the trainer joined us outside to watch the joy on the faces of Emilia and Grace as they stood in awe of Hologram. He was led into the yard all tacked up and looking every inch the star he was hopefully destined to become.

'Did I tell you Emmy wants to be a jockey although Mother's already grooming her for the Olympics?' Tamara told Dominic as her daughter waited to be helped aboard.

'Tricky,' he said. 'Glad it's not my problem. Wish you luck with that one.'

We all smiled and thought today wasn't the time for decisions to be made. Then it dawned on me I had no idea what life held in store for Grace, though riding horses for a living would not be encouraged. That was in no way putting the profession down, but just me showing a hint of the chauvinistic side of my nature. It went without saying that whatever she decided to do I would support her. And even if I was to be shoehorned into the role of a part-time father my love for her would never diminish or fade.

With Emilia posing like a seasoned model for photographs I watched Grace as she looked up enviously but without any hint of resentment, awestruck by the sheer size, magnificence and surefootedness of the horse who was the real star of the show. It was as if he had deliberately suppressed his temperamental side for the time being, to revel in the attention he was receiving, though sensibly he still had two handlers in position ready and primed in case he reverted back to form and his usual mischievous ways.

He responded to my voice with flared nostrils and a knowing dip of his statuesque head and I stroked his neck and shoulders as I always did before riding him in a race or schooling him at the stable. I lifted Grace up so that she could do the same and she tentatively ran her hand down the length of his wide neck before giving him several soft pats as if she believed hard ones might hurt him.

'He feels like he's made of leather,' she said when I put her down.

193

'Well he has to be tough to jump all those fences,' I told her.

'And his breath tickles my hand. It feels funny.'

I smiled and imagined I might have said the same thing nearly thirty years ago. 'Would you like to see Daddy ride Hologram in a race if I can arrange it?' I asked her.

She nodded. 'But you mustn't fall off, Daddy. You might get hurt.'

Tamara overheard her and smiled at me. 'No, you mustn't get hurt,' she shared Grace's concerns.

'Not likely. But then not impossible. Best not to think about it,' I said.

Emilia was now being helped down and her little round eyes were agog.

Both girls waved simultaneously as Hologram was led away. One of the stable hands assigned to us by Dominic was urging them to follow him for a guided tour of the other stable boxes that were occupied, and Tamara and I tagged along.

'Brilliant idea, beats pushing them on a swing any day,' I commented.

'Not such hard work you mean,' she teased me.

Pretty soon after that a mobile catering van delivered pre-ordered sandwiches and snacks and we all sat where we could on bales of hay and upturned buckets to eat our impromptu picnic. Half-term days when I was a boy were never like this, nowhere near such fun. Before I had time to reminisce some more, Father called my mobile to tell me he had heard from the police who confirmed that criminal damage charges against him had been dropped. The relief in his voice was tangible and I took it as a good sign in the run-up to our business with Fielding later. It was a step in the right direction and Tamara could tell from my face that I too was a relieved man.

By one thirty we said our goodbyes and were heading for Castle Moat Lodge where Lavender had laid on afternoon tea and a warm and loud greeting for the girls. Grace hugged her grandfather and looked puzzled as to why he was there with the lady of the house. I didn't bother explaining and luckily she didn't ask. Lavender took Emilia and Grace for a walk around her grounds and watched as they tried unsuccessfully to befriend some of the cats they spotted en route.

With no shame Father flirted with Tamara, and she with him, but when he started asking questions that I'd rather him not know the answers to I diverted the conversation back onto the children. That's where it remained until they reappeared with tales of shy cats, dead birds and one brave grey squirrel which ran the feline gauntlet and survived.

Lavender Thompson was a big hit with the girls, and for sure she was well on the way to becoming an honorary aunt long before they ventured into her kitchen to re-emerge laden with dishes and plates carrying hot and cold food of all descriptions. I looked at my watch and reminded Father it was time to go, and he hurriedly reached out to grab a slice of pizza and a chicken wing.

'Here Sam,' Lavender intervened. 'Take a couple of serviettes and eat it on the way, we'll leave some for when you return. And the best of luck.'

Father already had his mouth full and a hand now hovering over a neat pile of salmon sandwiches.

'Go on,' I urged him. 'Don't let me stop you. I'll have something later.'

'A leaf of lettuce or a piece of cucumber no doubt,' he poked fun at me and my jockey's dietary needs.

'Scoff all you want. It goes with the job. Be glad you don't have to watch your waistline.'

It was said with subtle sarcasm but hit very stony ground. Tamara smiled and Father just kept munching. Missing out on food was an occupational hazard. You did it for a reason, not least the pay cheque at the end of the month.

'Good luck, both of you,' Lavender repeated herself.
The word luck grated on me, but it was well intended
and needed to be said.

18

Curtis Fielding lived two miles from Cheltenham town centre and his house, a lavish, modern barn conversion, was only a third of the size of the one he'd inherited and sold off to developers several years ago. But it was still what an estate agent would call imposing, substantial and sought after, and in addition he was thought to own another large property in central London as well as a holiday apartment near Malaga.

From the courtyard entrance at the head of several similar properties we paused momentarily to take in the stunning view from the rear that encompassed the westernmost tip of the stunning Cleeve Hills, famed for their backdrop to the racecourse at Prestbury Park. Unsurprisingly, Fielding owned the largest of the completely refurbished plots, next to which there was a large detached garage resembling a stable block which looked big enough to house at least three cars and also boasted an upstairs games room and gymnasium.

'Not somebody so short of money he had to hound the Thompsons like he did,' Father said, the bitterness I'd hoped he'd keep under wraps already threatening his karma.

'A house isn't the same as ready cash,' I reminded him. 'And ninety per cent of it could be owned by a bank.'

'Not likely,' Father groaned back, his eyes now focused on a familiar charcoal-grey pick-up with the words 'Fielding Estates' on the side that we passed on the driveway.

'Is that the one you ... attacked?' I asked him, watching him smile to himself as he smugly nodded back.

After parking in front of the garage next to a silver

Mercedes and red Porsche, I told Father to let me do the talking and immediately spotted the owner already waiting for us in a doorway which had colourful hanging baskets on either side. There were no handshakes on offer, but the greeting we received was civil.

He wore plain, casual clothes and led us through a wide hallway into a vast room in which there was a man sitting facing us on one of three leather sofas. The man made no attempt to stand as we entered.

'You know Neville of course,' Fielding said to Father, who looked across the room with contempt but said nothing.

Fielding then looked at me. 'This is Sam Woodall Junior, the jockey. Sam, this is Neville Truman my estate manager. I felt he needed to be here to listen to what I have to say.'

We exercised our eyes and saved on wasted vocabulary.

Although unable to assess his true height I could tell Neville Truman was a big man. He had wide shoulders, a substantial upper torso and long legs which were crossed in front of him. His head was practically bald except for two clumps of reddish brown hair on either side of it from which grew thick bushy sideburns. He had a dark moustache and half beard, and I guessed he was about thirty-five to forty years old. My first overpowering impression was that he resembled a nightclub bouncer.

If this was the man who had hit Big Dave over the head with a piece of slab he was very cool about it and he seemed far too smug, as well as appearing much too at home on his boss's sofa to be a hired hand for my liking.

It was all too apparent that Fielding had a well rehearsed speech prepared. As we sat on one of the other sofas he took to a leather armchair which had been angled towards the three of us and he smoothly dispensed with further pleasantries.

'Right then, gentlemen,' he began. 'We have bridges to build and as you are probably already aware, as promised

I have instructed the police to drop the charges I made and to close the case which they have obligingly done.'

Father went to say something but stopped when I glared at him.

'That's a very good start,' I conceded, speaking on his behalf.

'Quite,' Fielding said, pushing his back hard against the chair and trying to look relaxed. 'This unfortunate business got too personal, things were said, we both went a bit too far. Neighbours fall out. It's inevitable. But we needn't be enemies, in fact I'd like to think we can work together and both get something out of it. A bit of mutual back-scratching, so to speak.'

I glared again at my father. He was already on the edge of his seat.

He stared straight back at Fielding. 'You've changed your tune, what's this all about? Why are you suddenly being nice to us?' he asked, his suspicions aroused.

Fielding, fighting back his usual impulse to react to confrontation, ran a hand through his dark, slightly greying hair. He grimaced slightly but plodded on regardless. 'As you know, I have plans for the land adjoining the newly excavated lake and need easy access to the site from existing roads without causing a traffic hazard. Having had preliminary talks with the planning people I think I have found a way around the problem and therefore I have a proposition to put to you that I hope you will like, which means benefits to both sides.'

I could see my father welling up inside and remembering Lavender's last words to him about not trusting a man she politely described as a weasel. If I didn't intervene quickly I felt the proposition would never see the light of day.

'You want to build an access road through land currently leased to my father, right?' I surmised. 'And make a reasonable adjustment to the rent he pays perhaps,' I guessed.

It was a pretty good assumption based on what I had seen of the site, and Fielding wasn't shaking his head or looking the least bit uncomfortable, which contrasted with my father, whose cheeks were turning pink.

'Back scratching. It's what business thrives on. It helps to oil the wheels of commerce,' Fielding shrugged, hoping my father wouldn't implode in front of him.

'Bloody incredible,' Father said, ignoring my existence in the room. He had saliva foaming at the corners of his mouth and was shouting. 'How you have the nerve to sit there and assume you can do and say as you like and get away with manipulating people and hoodwinking them into believing you're doing it for their benefit. Back-scratching my arse, there's only one person having his back scratched here and that's you. You can whistle for your access road, it won't be coming through land that I'm leasing. You will have to find another way.'

The man incurring my father's wrath did not seem perturbed. I imagined he was expecting me to intervene. That might involve pulling a rabbit from a hat judging from the irate expression on Father's face. Neville Truman just sat in silence, taking it all in and not so much as blinking an eye or moving a muscle. That might have come across as being intimidating but I had to put aside such things to concentrate on Father.

'It's quite clear after what's gone on that my father's reluctant to agree to any compromises. An access road where you suggest makes sense on paper but it mustn't affect the day-to-day running of the fishery in practice. Many people who come to fish want peace and quiet, it's what makes that place so special.'

I looked at Father but his expression hadn't altered. It said there would be no concessions. No compromises.

'You're right to call the place special,' Fielding agreed in a patronising tone. 'When I first clapped eyes on it I said the same and if I'm honest it's the lakes that make it so special. I know how popular the place is and from the business side of things most fishery owners would relish the thought of having caravans sited nearby. It's a potential goldmine. The way I see it, it's a win-win situation for everyone concerned.'

It was a convincing argument and he knew it.

And despite his reticence, deep down I knew Sam Woodall Senior knew it too – but still all I got from his body language was rage and unbending defiance. There just weren't enough rabbits or hats in the world to change the way he felt.

Curtis Fielding was showing the unflappable, patient side of his character and, though now sitting forward in his chair, he appeared perfectly at ease with the stand-off, as though he had scripted it himself and was mulling over his next move.

'It would be no trouble to get my solicitor to draft a new lease with terms heavily in your father's favour,' he addressed me. 'Further to that I'll guarantee that the new lake gets finished without further delay and any additional landscaping is prioritised and at my expense. The benefits for both of us from a new access route onto the respective sites will be colossal and to cap it all you will be paying out substantially less in overheads. And there'll be no more arguments, and no more lost revenue,' he summed up, looking at both of us. 'Think about it, Sam, that's all I ask.'

'And no more stray cows?' I added for good measure, trying to lighten the mood a little.

'Or attempts to poison my fish,' Father piped up, pouring scorn on my sudden flippancy.

Remaining seated, Fielding became defensive. After denying all knowledge of either event he made eye contact with me and virtually blanked my father who was now on the brink of baring his teeth like a wounded dog. With my insistence on doing all the talking already usurped, all I could think to do was plead with my eyes again and hope Father got the message I was trying to convey.

Gratifyingly and after some deliberation he made the effort to engage the eyes of the man he still considered the enemy, and without too much volume and bad language he said his piece. 'Why of all people on this planet should I bloody well trust you, Mister High and Mighty Fielding? You have something of a reputation for being ruthless in business and making people's lives a misery. The one person making the most out of this is you. Last week you wanted me out and now you're offering me a rent reduction plus other inducements to stay. It doesn't add up. So you see my dilemma.'

Fielding shrugged at the conjecture and attempted to set the record straight. 'My land, my rules,' he said without fear of contradiction. 'The problem with you, Sam Woodall, is you are gullible and believe everything that certain people have said about me. Now let me guess...' he paused for effect. 'The Thompsons for example, poor dear old Lavender and that scheming son of hers. If I told you the truth about him I fear things would not be so harmonious in the Thompson household and you would not be so quick to judge me.'

Even more contempt registered in Father's eyes and inevitably he raised his voice. 'There you go, making out it had nothing to do with you when you virtually ruined them. Now you think you can do the same to me. Well I won't let it happen, I'll fight you all the way,' he growled.

Instead of inducing anger all he received back was an exaggerated shake of the head and the peculiar hint of a smile. 'Look Sam, I don't know exactly what you were told but I can guess. Most of it is pure fiction on behalf of Anthony, who portrays himself as the dutiful son but goes crying to his mother whenever he's in trouble and blames everyone but himself. I have nothing against the old lady, in fact she's a veritable angel compared to that brat of hers. Take it from me I did not try to ruin them – contrary to popular belief I tried to help them and I can honestly say everything that went on was for a reason. I'm not the villain Lavender Thompson has painted me to be, far from it.'

He seemed far too sincere to be inventing a storyline designed to wriggle off the hook and even Father looked intrigued enough to want to know some more. 'You can prove all this of course,' he said with some scepticism. 'Are you telling me Anthony lied to his mother?'

Fielding shrugged. 'All children lie to their parents, only some lies are bigger than others.'

'Why should I believe a thing you say?' Father backtracked.

He got a look of indignation back for daring to go there again. 'Because it's the truth. Let Anthony Thompson deny it. Don't expect me to take more flak from his mother. I happen to think a lot of the woman for the charitable events she helps organise and she doesn't deserve a son like him. Go and ask him, see which version of the truth you get from the snivelling little bastard. And tell his mother from me that her so-perfect son is heading for an almighty fall.'

The question of whether Anthony Thompson was lying or not had inadvertently undermined the real reason for the meeting, but at least it had taken Father aback somewhat, taking wind from his sails. If Curtis Fielding hadn't stitched up the Thompsons in his business dealings with them it wouldn't necessarily make him look like Mister Integrity, but it would surely change Father's perception of a man he had down as a sworn enemy based jointly on hearsay and personal experience.

It was left to me to bring the conversation back to current events. I asked for twenty-four hours to think the proposition over, glancing at Father for some sort of agreement in principle which he gave with a long-awaited shrug.

At this point Neville Truman stood up, towering over all

of us including Fielding, who was himself above average height. And although the man didn't at all strike a menacing pose I couldn't help myself but think about Dave and the bungled attempt to contaminate the lakes.

As I was thinking this was not the time to bring it up or trade on speculation, Father stood up too and faced the man, pointing a finger at him. 'Don't think I don't know what you did,' he snarled accusingly. 'And if I find either of you were behind the fire at my lock-up I'll make sure you rot in prison for a very long time.'

Neville had inched forward to face the verbal barrage head on but Fielding was quick to stand between them and deny them any form of toe-to-toe combat. 'Not us, Sam, you need to look elsewhere. Don't for a minute think I will just sit back and allow you to make these wild allegations.'

I stood up and gripped my father's forearm and he tried to wrestle with me. 'Leave it, Dad, another time maybe,' I tightened my hold. With strength and persuasion I manoeuvred him towards the door and manhandled him through it into the hall. Then I sent him outside with my car keys and told him to wait. He swore at me, but did as I asked.

Fielding met me in the hall and reiterated what he had said about false allegations, looking straight at me as he said it. I made no promise to him that I could convince Father otherwise although I said I would try. Then when I thought he had his guard down I mentioned half-brother Bruce as a strategic afterthought and the older sibling shook his head vigorously.

'He's got nothing to do with any of this. You can't pick your relatives and I'm not responsible for him. If he's making enemies then that's his lookout not mine. I'm not his keeper.'

'So there's no truth in the rumour he's trying to bleed you dry?' I asked him. There was no rising to the bait or reaction to hearsay.

'I think you know my answer to that, Sam. Rumours bear no relationship to the truth. You should stick to what you do best and steer clear of the gossipmongers. Whatever Bruce has been up to has no bearing on any of this. I can't and won't be responsible for his bad behaviour. If the truth be known I barely ever see the man, he comes and goes as he pleases. I have no hold over him whatsoever.'

I gave up leaning on him over Bruce as there seemed to be nothing to gain by it, and told him likewise I had no hold over my father. I also said that I shared some of the scepticism about the sudden u-turn that now saw him practically falling over backwards to reach an amicable solution, when a week ago there seemed none available.

'I'm not a man to bear grudges,' he said, completely out of character. 'If your father has a problem with me in my capacity as a landlord he knows what he can do. If not I think we can rub along nicely together and I think you're intelligent enough to spot a good thing when you see one. But I accept your father may be coming at it from a different angle and that might cloud his judgement.'

'I'll talk to him,' I repeated, making no promises.

He thanked me in anticipation, making me feel like some sort of deal broker. There would be, I imagined, an awful lot of soul searching to be done before a decision could be reached. But I assured him I would do as much as I could.

It meant a heated debate on the return journey, with Father resisting any of my attempts to get him to admit Fielding's proposal had its merits. All he kept repeating under his breath at annoyingly frequent intervals were words containing only four letters and not ones recognisable as the Queen's English. And although I suspected he was just letting off steam it sounded like he meant every one of them.

Back at Castle Moat Lodge Lavender sat us down with

tea and cake whilst the children carried on as if we were invisible, Tamara keeping a watchful eye on them. Our hostess wanted to know how we had got on, and I could tell Father was itching to ask her about Anthony in light of what Fielding had told us.

'We're going to think things over and give him a decision tomorrow,' I said, not giving Father time to respond. 'His proposal seems fair and from a financial point of view it makes a lot of sense.'

'You mean he tried to bribe you?' Lavender asked with distaste.

'Not exactly, but he would be in a pickle if he couldn't build his precious access road where he wants to. It would rather scupper his plans if he had to put it somewhere else.'

'The man's obsessed with money. Promise me you'll get everything checked out properly and keep a close eye on him,' she said, undeniably worried.

'We will,' I assured her, looking over at Father who seemed ready to explode all over again.

Putting Fielding to one side I thanked her for entertaining Tamara and the girls while we were away and she said it had been her pleasure.

'They've been out on a cat search and found eight so far and I've been trying to teach them their names,' she informed me. 'Such bright children and a credit to both of you. I can see them both becoming charming young ladies and making you oh so proud.'

The envy in her eyes and tone of her voice hinted that not having grandchildren of her own to fuss over was her one regret in life, but the role of honorary aunt was a big consolation prize for sure and I found myself promising her a repeat prescription.

Emilia and Grace were keen for me to meet their new feline friends so the four of us went outside and left Father and Lavender to chat about things, with son Anthony no doubt on his agenda. And while our daughters resumed their search for well-camouflaged felines I told Tamara what Fielding had said about Lavender's son. She didn't take sides.

'To be honest I think Anthony is a bit weird. An excellent vet according to Mother but I find him, well, weird. Creepy, if you understand what I mean.'

'You mean eccentric like his mother,' I suggested. 'Perhaps a legacy of still living at home with her?'

'Maybe, but nevertheless not someone you want to be stuck in a lift with for very long if you get my drift.'

I thought about it. As far as I was concerned Anthony was Anthony, a well-respected veterinary surgeon who knew more about horseflesh than most and who, to me, always seemed quite pleasant, if occasionally abrupt.

'Although you say he lives here, Lavender's told me he sleeps at the surgery most of the time mainly so he can keep a close eye on his patients. Perhaps he spends too much time around horses and not enough with humans, that might explain a lot,' Tamara went on.

'The same could be said about me. Next thing you'll say is I smell like a horse and neigh in my sleep.'

She laughed aloud and the girls turned around to see what was so funny. 'You ride them for a living but you don't sleep in the next room to them, that would be weird. And besides you use a strong deodorant.' She laughed again but not so loudly.

I gave her a pretend punch and we played an impromptu game of chase as she started to run away from me, the girls both standing with their hands on hips puzzled by our unexpected childish behaviour.

'Mummy, what are you doing?' Emilia asked her, not knowing whether to disapprove or not.

'Just horsing around,' she replied, half under her breath.

'What?'

207

'Emmy, quick come and look,' Grace interrupted, and the great cat search thankfully resumed to save our blushes.

Their attention was drawn by two cats climbing the same tree and Tamara had now stopped running. I caught up with her, put my arm discreetly around her waist and said, 'Meow.'

'Steady Tiger, not in front of the children,' she scolded playfully.

'They'll have to get used to it. Can't keep pretending.'

'No, suppose not.'

My arm remained where I had put it and we watched our daughters as they strained their eyes to see upwards into the lower branches of a particularly old and accommodating oak tree.

As dusk closed in and we returned indoors, Father had his head buried in an evening newspaper that a boy on a bike had delivered earlier. Lavender sat quietly away from him, suddenly finding a smile from somewhere to greet us like all good 'aunts' do. I could tell she had been crying and as Father was hiding from all of us, I knew straight away he had been the cause of her upset.

Tactfully Tamara got Lavender to join her and the children in the kitchen, on the pretence they were thirsty, whilst I tackled Father who had clearly gone down in somebody's estimation. He appeared crestfallen, having inadvertently dug a hole for himself and put a slowly blossoming friendship in jeopardy. Things, I feared, might never be the same between them.

'What the hell did you say to her?' I asked him bluntly.

'Just told her what Fielding had said. Well not everything of course, she got the watered down version.'

'And she took it badly?'

'Worse than that,' he moaned. 'She wouldn't even listen and accused me of being taken in by Fielding. You heard her say something about him bribing me. Virtually accused me of crossing over to his side which is ridiculous because I haven't made a decision yet. Obviously she knows her son is no angel but she swears he would never lie to her.'

'Well, we need to find out the truth and soon. We're going to have to ask Anthony about it. I'll phone him tomorrow when I've finished at the stables and in the meantime I'll try talking to his mother and do my damnedest to get you off the hook, you silly man.'

Father sighed a thank you and breathed a little easier. A few days ago the thought of upsetting her wouldn't have bothered him very much but now despite his protestations that they were merely good friends he seemed gutted to have brought her to tears by questioning her son's dealings with a man she despised so much.

'Convince her I'm not taking sides or doubting Anthony. I only repeated what Curtis Fielding said earlier and you were there and heard him say it so you can back me up,' he urged me. 'I never imagined she would react like she did. It's a long time since I made a woman cry.'

'Mother, I assume?'

'She cried all the time when she didn't get her own way.'

I didn't remember and I didn't want to. It was all an irrelevance anyway, just something that perhaps in hindsight shouldn't have been mentioned at all. One of those all too forgivable moments in time.

The next time I got Lavender far enough away from the others to make it count I did bring up Father's genuine dismay over antagonising her and she rather played it down, insisting that any conversation involving Fielding wound her up so much she became naturally emotional and let it dictate her mood.

'Like everyone else,' she remembered, 'I was taken in by Curtis, by his charm, his ideas and his energy. But pretty soon after Anthony entered into business with him he was coming home and telling me he'd wished he'd never set eyes on the man. That all he was out to do was make money as quickly as possible and move it around so that he could make some more. That's why he demanded back the cash he'd loaned to Anthony to expand the business and why I had to come up with the money to bail my son out.'

'Were you ever party to any business meetings your son had with Curtis or did you see any paperwork relating to this loan that you say he called in early?' I asked her.

We were standing in the doorway to her vast farmhouse-style kitchen and I was deliberately talking to her as quietly as I could. I could see there was no danger of any more tears and that she had guessed I was only trying to set things right between her and my father. I could also see she was itching to get back to making a fuss of the children, so her reply was understandably short and to the point.

'Anthony dealt with all business matters, I'm his mother not his secretary. Why would I get more involved?'

'No reason,' I agreed. 'Just thought I'd ask.'

I gave her my best made-up smile and thanked her again for entertaining the children and she said she hoped it was the first of many such occasions. Undoubtedly Lavender had been a big hit with Emilia and Grace. There was a chorus of groans when time was called on their visit and a familiar look of resignation on the face of my daughter when the private taxi that had been booked and subsequently rerouted to chaperone her back to her mother arrived uncannily on cue.

And it was with a lump in my throat that I hugged her and said my goodbyes, before waving her off with memories of her day hopefully stored and not forgotten. Like all part-time parents I felt sad, and a little empty inside.

19

Seas The Moment was a big dapple-grey gelding owned by a newly formed Cotswold syndicate comprising relatives and close friends of Dominic Ingles. Though obviously no thoroughbred, to me he still looked the real deal.

On a cloudless, mild October morning I had been given a leg-up and had begun exercising the horse under the trainer's watchful eye. Dominic had high hopes for the former novice chaser despite its dubious history and lack of form from a previous owner/trainer regime that, in his words, 'chose all the wrong options and tried to run before they could walk'. What he meant was the horse was overrated as a novice and entered into races it had no little or no chance of winning, which is why it ended up at the sales three years later and barely put a dent in the syndicate's budget.

Like most of the better trainers, Dominic had a shrewd eye and was a good judge of character in a horse and, as I had already found out soon after taking the reins, Seas The Moment had character in abundance and was not afraid to show it. And if anyone could iron out the rough edges and improve the horse it was Dominic. He was renowned for such a challenge.

Back in his stable office an hour and a half later I stood toe to toe with the trainer and I told him what I thought. For once he seemed in a mood to listen.

'His stamina's unquestionable but he ambles rather than gallops and he stands way off his fences. I would school him over slightly bigger jumps and make him put in that

211

extra stride. Getting the height isn't a problem, you need to shorten the time he spends in the air and get him to pick up his stride quicker.'

'You mean flatter jumps and more speed?' Dominic asked, making it sound the same.

'That's about it. He's big and bold and though now seven he's still got plenty of time to learn. He could become a star performer.'

'Not so sure the owners will agree with you, but we'll do what we can with him in the limited time we have before they'll expect to see him out on the track. Might aim him for Hereford in December rather than hold him back till the new year. What do you think to that, Sam?'

It was rare for a trainer to ask for my opinion on where to send a horse but I could see the dilemma he was in, half of him wanting to please the owners and the other wanting to get the horse in better shape before committing him into a race.

I gave it serious thought. 'He'll be suited to Hereford. And it's still six or seven weeks away. Sounds OK to me.'

We went on to discuss the following day's meeting at Haydock Park and when it seemed right I levered the conversation around to Anthony Thompson. I told him enough of what Curtis Fielding had said about him to stir his intrigue and show an interest.

'Apart from being a top-notch vet I would have thought Anthony's too smart to get himself in a financial pickle,' Dominic said. 'Although like everyone else I did hear he had money problems a while back. Anthony does like a flutter and I'm not talking about a few pounds on the tote. He used to pester my stable lads for inside info and occasionally ask me for tips. But then there are hundreds of others that do the same, it goes with the job.'

He was confirming what I was beginning to believe and adding meat to the bones.

'So he gambles large amounts?' I quizzed him.

'He's been known to,' he nodded. 'Vets make a lot of money. Well, the good ones do and he's amongst the best there is and with a few rich clients too.'

'Hundreds, or thousands?' I persisted.

'Can't help you,' he shrugged. 'You know as much as me now. I let him get on with his job and he generally lets me do mine. That's what makes the world go round.'

'Would any of the staff here know whether he bets regularly on races and what sort of amounts he risks?' I asked.

He shrugged again. 'Don't see any harm in asking them, feel free, they may know something. Just don't keep them from their work for too long, Sam, or I'll be docking your fees,' he smiled sarcastically.

Dominic looked at his watch, conscious he had to be at Taunton in a couple of hours for the day's meeting there, to oversee the two horses he had running with a leading amateur jockey in the saddle covering for me. So he left me to get ready and, with nothing to lose, I toured the stable chatting to anyone who wanted to talk and asking all and sundry what if anything they knew about Anthony Thompson from his infrequent visits there to tend to the horses.

One stable girl, Melissa, said she thought he was strange and had dishonest eyes, and a talkative lad named Robbie admitted to bumping into Anthony in a Cirencester bookmakers' several times though he never saw him place a bet.

I would make a point of asking Father if Lavender ever mentioned her son placing bets or gambling money on the animals I was more used to seeing him take a stethoscope to. His occupation didn't preclude him from such behaviour and I once knew of a very reputable horse doctor who was an obsessive gambler and usually won more than he lost.

Robbie was a likeable sort who had ambitions to be a

jockey and was always asking me for tips of the trade, which I gave without favour knowing how hard it was to make it in my chosen profession. The clock was ticking for him and the lack of encouragement from Dominic probably summed up Robbie's chances of ever making the grade as slim, but it wouldn't stop me from letting him think he could still live his dream as I did and prove Dominic wrong.

Somebody else with an opinion on Anthony Thompson, and an unlikely source of gossip, was Clare Ingles, Dominic's usually sombre-looking wife who spent some mornings at the stables doing what she called 'admin' work and general tidying up any mess he left in his wake, rather like today. I was heading back to my car when she sauntered over to me waving a piece of paper which she quite openly showed me as she muttered under her breath. It was an invoice from Anthony for carrying out routine vaccinations and one emergency call out which Clare clearly did not approve of and said as much.

'I keep telling Dom there are cheaper vets who do perfectly acceptable work but because he's been pals with Anthony for ages he doesn't listen. This is an extortionate amount of money to shell out for a couple of hours' work but because he knows he can charge it to the owners' accounts Dom just pays up without giving it a minute's thought.'

Clare was a thin, straight-backed lady in her early forties who didn't share her husband's interest in horses but loved him nevertheless and was the dedicated mother to three bright, school-aged children. She went on to say she'd found out I was asking questions about Anthony and appeared somewhat astounded that her husband hadn't filled me in fully about the man and his lifestyle, especially his gambling addiction.

'Dominic said Anthony likes a flutter and Robbie's seen him in a local bookmakers'. Does that constitute an addiction?' I queried.

214

Clare thought about it and became guarded about what she said next. 'If you bet on the horses, lose money, but just carry on betting again and again ... well, that's the next best thing to addiction in my eyes.'

I made some sort of eye contact with her and pressed on. 'I asked Dominic if it was hundreds or thousands and all he said was Anthony made a lot of money. So are we talking the latter here, assuming you know?'

Clare's sombre cheeks puffed out and her eyes darted between me and the invoice she was still holding out in front of me. 'Well he makes a lot of money out of us for sure, but I don't suppose my bleating about it will change things. Habits die hard and Anthony Thompson, for all his sins, is a bloody good vet and knows his stuff, that's why so many keep going back to him, there's nothing he doesn't know about horses.'

I stared back at her looking a little puzzled and went off at a tangent. 'According to his mother, not so very long ago Anthony was struggling to stay in business because of his dealings with and some bad-mouthing by Curtis Fielding. That, in a way, brings me around to the reason for all my questions about her son's gambling or at least his money problems.'

Clare seemed pensive, which sort of mirrored the way she always looked. 'I thought Anthony and Curtis were OK with one another. News to me they had a falling-out. Anthony's not one for chat but I used to have a bit of a chin wag with him over a cup of tea occasionally.'

'So Anthony gambles and his mother's none the wiser, perhaps?' I thought aloud.

'Lavender's a bit odd, Sam,' Clare reminded me. 'It wouldn't be difficult for him to keep things from her. After all, he practically lives at that surgery of his, or Equine Hospital as he prefers to call it. Not what you'd expect of a doting son.'

'Well, that's not the impression she gives,' I argued.

'Probably a mother thing. Deep down she must be proud of him but I always get the impression they're not as close as she would have you believe.'

I thought about it. 'Well, you may be right, I can't say that I've seen much of them together.'

Anthony Thompson had certainly not slept at Moat House Lodge since Father had moved in and neither of us had bumped into him there. Maybe it was just a temporary arrangement to give Father and his mother some space, or more likely a matter of convenience as Anthony's surgery was only minutes from Cheltenham.

Clare Ingles then brought into play another likely and highly believable reason for Anthony sleeping over at the surgery. 'Did you know Anthony dislikes cats?' she said as if dropping a major bombshell. 'A vet who can't stand the most common of domestic animals, a bit weird that.'

'Not unheard of, I suppose, lucky that he specialises in horses then.'

'Very convenient, I'd say.'

So it was unlikely Father had made Anthony leave home at all; much more likely that his mother preferring cats had done the trick.

With a less serious face Clare asked me how my father was after his recent ordeal and I sarcastically mentioned that he had a guardian angel who had taken him in and that Father didn't object to cats, which almost made her smile. Then she frowned. 'Dom told me he was staying with her. It was an awful thing to happen, will you send him my regards.'

I said I would and thanked her for filling in a few blanks. The shrug she gave me was accompanied by another frown as if she didn't envy my next move.

Getting hold of Anthony Thompson to have what I wanted to be an informal chat was difficult in the extreme. His second in command at the practice told me he was somewhere on an emergency where mobile phone reception was dictated by the hills around the farm he had rushed to. So when I didn't get a call back in an hour I took pot luck and drove to the surgery, an immaculate-looking, white-painted, much-extended building at the end of a long driveway bordered by a field and a row of purpose-built stables. Cheltenham racecourse was a mile to the north and the town centre a similar distance to the west. A mile in an easterly direction would get you somewhere near to where Curtis Fielding lived. Very convenient, I thought if only from a geographical point of view.

To complement the large, new-looking sign that I had already passed there was another smaller one to greet visitors on one side of the main entrance, and through some wide wrought-iron gates there was good access to a yard which led to the stables and a paddock beyond. A newly-built, square-shaped construction with a flat roof was next to the stable block and this I assumed to be the hydro pool Lavender had told Father about. Like the rest of the impressive buildings it was appropriately clinical in design, smelling of emulsion paint and disinfectant. Collectively the whole place was strangely palatial compared to Moat House Lodge. And there was not a cat in sight.

I had used a small amount of deceit on the phone to broker a meeting with Anthony upon his return, concocting a story that a friend who owned several horses was looking to switch allegiance to a new vet and had asked me to have a chat and a look around. How the man would respond when I peppered him with questions about alleged gambling and financial dealings with Curtis Fielding I had no idea, but the longer I sat in the plush leatherette seat of the waiting area the more nervous I became.

Around the walls there were framed certificates and photographs showing Anthony and his staff with satisfied customers and their horses, and everywhere there were printed flyers advertising the business with Anthony's smiling face on them. I read through one and then secreted it away in my pocket thinking it might come in handy. I tried to relax.

Two cups of complimentary cups of coffee and an hour and a half later the in-demand vet breezed through the door with apologies galore and a hearty handshake to accompany them.

'Great to see you, Sam, but shouldn't you be riding winners somewhere?' he said, putting down his essential surgeon's briefcase and several loose folders.

'Would if I could, but this is the last day of a ban I picked up on the day we last spoke,' I reminded him.

He raised his eyebrows. 'Ah, yes. Unlucky that. Angus Gunnell was in the steward's room that day. He's got a reputation for being a bit harsh. Well let's just say he's not on many jockeys' Christmas card lists.'

I agreed, smiled back and resisted the temptation to criticise or condemn. Anthony's hair was getting long and was curling up around the edges, he was unshaven and his eyes looked heavy as if in need of urgent sleep. The dark-blue suit he wore was in need of pressing and the grey buttondown shirt underneath it certainly hadn't been clean on today.

We reconvened in his office which was a few yards down a corridor from the waiting area and carried on the plush theme with real leather furniture and a glass-topped desk.

'Nice,' I said, not expecting such luxury.

He made no comment and looked somehow different from normal once he had seated himself, a legacy I presumed of my never having seen him off his feet before.

Almost slouching and without waiting for me to sit he asked, 'So Sam, how can I help, or more to the point who can I help? You mentioned a friend.'

I took the biggest breath I could find and told him the truth. 'Well, forgive me for misleading you, but I'm really here to talk to you about something else. Something that's been bothering me,' I replied, feeling slightly less apprehensive now I had unveiled my deception.

His optimistic expression changed to one of confusion and his eyebrows merged with the loose hairs of an unkempt fringe. 'What's this about, Sam?' he asked me.

I was now sitting at his level and gathering my thoughts. It was akin to the start of a race, with strategy uppermost in my mind and antagonising Anthony so soon after walking into his office hadn't been my intention.

'Did you know my father and Curtis Fielding were waging a war over land at Sloane Farm?' I asked him in a calm voice. 'And Dave Burrows who works for my dad was attacked by somebody hell-bent on poisoning his stock of fish?'

I could tell from his reaction he knew about both but bemusement was stopping him from saying so.

I went on. 'Then last week Father's lock-up was broken into and set on fire, destroying several classic cars and he ended up in hospital with smoke inhalation.'

There was no sympathy in his eyes at all, only confusion. Then he broke his silence.

'Sam. I already know about these things. I'm sorry for what's happened to him and I was deeply saddened when I discovered that lovely Bugatti of his got damaged. Cars like that are irreplaceable. But that said, I'm at a loss to understand why what has happened to your father has got anything to do with me.'

The unexpected comment about the fire-damaged Bugatti shook me, momentarily knocking me off course. It was not so much what he knew as how he knew that worried me, as I was unaware such information had been made common knowledge.

Eager to get back on track I chose my next words carefully.

'Your mother's been brilliant. I was sorry to burden her with my dad but I didn't want him at home on his own when he came out of hospital and I'm sorry if that put you out. She's told us about your trials and tribulations with Curtis Fielding and how he nearly ruined your business, and she's been as keen as anybody to find out if Fielding was behind everything that been going on.'

'My mother hates the man for what he put us through,' he said with a huge amount of bitterness. 'And she's got a heart of gold. Always taking in waifs and strays, not that your father is either of those, of course.' An unexpected smile redesigned his mouth as if he was suddenly desperate to lighten the mood.

'I gather your mother raised a considerable amount of money to pay back what you owed Fielding. Money initially spent on this place I presume and a lot by the looks of it?'

Anthony gaped and his eyes visibly grew in size. 'Mother shouldn't be discussing things like that with you; she's usually more circumspect than that. Your father's obviously got a way with her.'

'She told both of us and was quite open about it. I think she was merely trying to convince us what a rogue Fielding was and the lengths to which he would go. She believed it might help us.'

'Well, there's nothing I can do about it now though I would have preferred it not to be made common knowledge. I will be having a quiet word with her just the same.'

He was leaning forward in his chair looking mightily uncomfortable. It was clear he felt he was in an awkward place because of her indiscretion. I saw no reason to make it any easier for him.

'According to the man himself, Fielding that is, your money troubles were not down to him. Father and I were round his place yesterday and he was most insistent that he had nothing to do with you almost becoming bankrupt. Why do you suppose he said that?'

'Not a clue. The man would say anything that wasn't true.'

'So he's lying?'

'Obviously.'

'Did he lend you money to spend on this place like your mother says he did?'

'If that's what she said then he did.'

'But is that really the way it happened?'

Anthony had visibly begun to shake, like somebody on the edge of a precipice when there was no going back. He picked up a pen and began tapping it nervously on the edge of the desk as though the distraction would help him and, at the same time distract me.

'Mother gets things wrong. She doesn't always listen. She will have got herself into a muddle,' he shrugged unconvincingly.

'I find that hard to believe. Her words were so precise,' I told him.

'This is becoming tedious, Sam. Why are you doubting me and accepting everything she says as gospel? And anyway, what's it got to do with you? Why are you so interested in what goes on in other people's lives?'

For a second it looked as if he was going to stand up and show me the door. Instead he tried reasoning with me.

'Look Sam, your dad's fallen foul of Curtis Fielding. He's a man full of his own importance and a pain in the backside. I did once think me and him could be business partners but then that bloody awful brother of his came on the scene and ruined everything.'

'How?' I asked, naively.

'By claiming half of Curtis's inheritance, of course. There's no secret. Bruce made sure people knew what he was after. That's how he managed to get to screw Paul Eddison's wife.

Why else would she choose him over an impoverished, ageing jockey? A younger model with potentially a million pounds owing to him. Some women can't resist that.'

It felt like Anthony was buying himself some time and trying to put me off the scent. Although I held some affection for his mother I carried none for him and was about to let it show. 'A few people I've spoken to tell me you gamble. Anthony, is that true?'

He stayed seated and clenched both fists. 'You mean do I have a bet on a horse like millions of others? Doesn't everybody enjoy a flutter now and again?' he replied, flippantly.

I shook my head. 'I'm talking serious amounts of money. I'm talking about an addiction. And I'm guessing your mother didn't have an inkling as to where all the money she raised for you really went. Am I right?'

Wild horses would not have stopped Anthony Thompson from getting to his feet then and aiming his wrath at me. The pen he had been holding became a projectile and only just missed me. My eyes were attracted to it as it bounced on the carpeted floor and I instinctively reached to pick it up just as his raised voice echoed around the room.

'So that's why you're here. You want to discredit me, to humiliate me. This is your father's doing. I knew he was up to no good when I saw him sniffing around Mother like a stallion at a stud farm. And who the fuck are these people you have spoken to behind my back, they know nothing about me. You have no right to come here and say such slanderous things about me. If I was not such a civilised person I would wipe that smug expression off your face for good, Sam Woodall.'

I was glad of the desk between us and the fact I had been able to stand up quickly and retreat towards the door. There were voices in the corridor outside and the sound of footsteps to accompany them. Anthony had saliva around his mouth and his eyes appeared to have grown in size yet again .

'Best that I leave,' I said, producing the understatement to beat all others, 'before you do something you'll regret.'

Anthony bared his teeth and said something incoherent. Somebody outside the room was calling to him, asking if he was all right which I found odd as I was the one being threatened. This was the exact scenario I had wanted to avoid and the intensity of his angry reaction towards both me and more noticeably my father was frightening. In his own words he had said my father was up to no good where his mother was concerned and that concerned me deeply. As did the threat to wipe the smug look off my face for good, which had been said with genuine malice by a man who suddenly looked out of control.

Outside there were two female colleagues of his, one young, the other much older, barring my way. They parted like the red sea when they saw how determined I was to get away. I heard Anthony feeding them some cock and bull story about me to explain his fit of temper. The young receptionist I had seen on my arrival stood at the reception desk not quite knowing what to do. When I reached the exit immediately in front of her I turned back to see Anthony being fussed over like royalty, and from a safe distance I shouted down the whole length of the reception area and into the corridor.

'I'll find out the truth about you, so you better be ready for when I come back,' I yelled, pretty certain no one could help but hear. There was a distinct echo to accompany my message and I had left four shocked faces in my wake. The pen I had picked up was still in my right hand so on my way back to my car I carefully wrapped it in a tissue I had in one of my pockets and stowed it safely away.

A mile from the surgery I pulled over to call Father to warn him that Anthony Thompson might be on the warpath.

He told me he had worse things to think about than an irate vet. There had been more trouble at Sloane Farm and it was all to do with Big Dave and Neville Truman.

20

'He either remembered something or overheard us talking about our suspicions and put two and two together,' Father said, sounding breathless.

'So what actually happened?' I asked, knowing only that there had been some kind of fight and both men were in police custody.

Father didn't rush himself as there was a lot to tell. 'Around lunchtime Dave shot off on the quad saying he had something to do. About ten minutes later an angler came running up to warn me something was kicking off in the field behind the Specimen Lake. It took me about another five minutes before I got there. Dave had Neville Truman pinned up against a hedge with the quad bike and there was a lot of shouting.'

'Did you hear what was being said?'

'Neville was making most of the noise because he was clearly in some pain but Dave was telling him it was nothing to what was in store for him. He kept revving the bike and threatening to break the man's legs. I don't think Dave even heard me calling to him to back off but I reckon nothing would have stopped him from reaping his revenge. I've never seen anything like that before. If he wasn't scaring the shit out of that bastard Truman he was certainly putting the fear of God into me. Dave's normally such a gentle bloke.'

'That was until somebody tried to cave in his skull with a piece of concrete,' I interrupted.

'Quite,' Father acknowledged.

'So, what then?'

'Well, I don't exactly know how he got himself free but Neville managed it and ran, well limped, back towards his pick-up with Dave in pursuit. At one point I thought the silly sod was going to end up in the lake with the bike on top of him but he was eventually forced to jump off and give chase on foot. Then he caught up with Neville and after literally rugby-tackling him to the ground they fought like cat and dog until Dave gained the upper hand and poleaxed him with sweetest right hook you'll ever see.'

His description of events left me flabbergasted. The two men were well matched in size for sure and, bizarrely, I almost felt disappointment that I had missed it, especially the knockout punch.

'So when did the police arrive?'

Father pondered a bit. 'Not for some time. Somebody who knew first aid sorted Neville out and soon had him sitting propped up against that pick-up of his. His face looked a mess but as it was bloody ugly to start with I don't suppose it made much difference. Dave suffered some damage too, mostly to his knuckles, but that was a small price to pay for getting even with that sewer rat. When he'd calmed down I asked him why he didn't just go to the police and turn Neville in, but he said he needed to be sure it was him and that's what spurred him to do what he did. It certainly worked because while Neville was backed up in the hedge he as good as admitted it was him who whacked Dave over the head and tried to contaminate the lake.'

'As long as he says the same in court we'll have Fielding by the balls,' I said with smug satisfaction,

'I've thought that myself but I won't get carried away. We need to get Dave out of jail and back here. He shouldn't be locked up.'

'Do you know if they've charged him with anything?'

'I phoned half an hour ago and they just said the standard thing. He's helping them with their inquiries. His wife drove up there shortly after they carted him off to make sure he's OK. As far as I know Neville's still at the hospital being checked out. Let's hope he's in a lot of pain for what he did. The man's an animal.'

There were only a few anglers scattered around the match lake in front of us as we stood outside the shed on what had been a mainly dull but dry day. Afternoon was becoming evening, and I told Father I would fill in for Dave and help with the daily ritual of clearing up and locking up. I also got him to sit on a bench that was nearby to tell him about my run-in with Lavender's son.

His mood soon changed and his face lost the warm glow it had gained when he relayed Dave's earlier actions to me. 'So what am I supposed to say to Lavender now? Will she have already thrown my clothes and overnight bag onto her front lawn?' he reacted.

'We don't know for sure that he will go running to her to bad-mouth the Woodalls. He might think about the awkward position I've put him in before he decides what to do about it.'

'She will be livid. She got quite cross yesterday when you were asking her about him. Best I phone her now and gauge the mood she's in.'

'Whatever you think best, it doesn't sound a bad idea,' I conceded.

The only two things I didn't tell Father about my explosive meeting with Anthony were the obvious disdain the man held towards him for his growing friendship with his mother, and that I had pocketed the pen Anthony had thrown at me with the intention of handing it in at Gloucestershire Police HQ as possible evidence in an arson case. It was a straw worth clutching, even if I rarely believed in hunches unless they were racing related.

Father was now talking to Lavender on his mobile, winking at me to tell me all was quiet at Castle Moat Lodge and continuing to have a pretty aimless chat. It was obvious things between them were not as before due to me, but at least she was not putting the phone down on him or verbally blasting him which was encouraging, even though for him I knew it would mean walking on eggshells around her for some time. Unexpectedly she then asked about me and all he said was, 'Never better,' which of course was a profound lie.

He wisely didn't broach the subject of the fight between Dave and Neville on the phone but did leave her in suspense by revealing he had something important to tell her later on. I thought how at ease he seemed talking to her and wondered, if only for a microsecond, if there was indeed something behind Anthony's theory that he was in his words 'Sniffing around' the eligible widow. To an uneducated observer it might easily have looked that way. I remembered Father once telling me he would gladly sell some of his prized cars to get his hands on her rare Bentley, which I assumed would eventually pass to Anthony in time-honoured fashion as it first belonged to his great-grandfather who no doubt bought it for a relative song at the time. It had been purchased originally by a duchess who had certain unique modifications done before it left the factory and it was truly 'a one-off'. If what Lavender had told us was true, about the house being heavily mortgaged and her savings withdrawn, the car was her only major asset, and as Father had many times called vehicles like that 'priceless' I began to understand Anthony's concerns, though I could not condone his behaviour.

With all that in mind I transferred the pen from a tissue to a small plastic bag I had found on the office desk at Sloane Farm. After seeing Father safely off to Lavender's I travelled to Gloucester to submit it as possible evidence, trusting a bright-eyed young desk sergeant to pass it on to the forensic team working on the arson case and asking for any relevant updates in due course.

Whilst there I read an 'Obligatory Mission Statement' signed by Chief Super Christopher Southgate, stating his force's determination to see that no crime went unpunished and his personal pledge that victims of crime would be vanquished. Brave words and supposedly said with honest intent. But they left me feeling cold and ever so slightly cynical. And thinking maybe it was OK for him to think it didn't apply to him. That he was above the law.

From Gloucester I drove to the Willows where Tamara conjured me a jockey-sized meal which I ate on my lap as we watched TV. I told her about my run-in with Anthony and the heavyweight contest at Sloane Farm and she seemed amazed at my almost casual demeanour.

'I've calmed down a lot from the way I was earlier, and I can't change what's gone on,' I shrugged, feeling safe by her side. 'I think it would be wise not to say anything to your mother about Anthony yet. He looked like a much-troubled man this afternoon and I've no idea what his next move will be. Good vets are hard to find so let's hope he sorts himself out for the sake of his clients.'

The last bit was said tongue in cheek with my suspicions hard to ignore. I knew Tamara would never forgive me if I was pretending or suppressing the real seriousness of the situation. If we had a future together as a family I couldn't make the mistake of being a hero, nor could I choose the wrong route and end up taking her too much for granted just because I felt it was for her own protection.

For sure she wouldn't be worrying over anything remotely to do with her mother and especially the precious horses she owned. Significantly, Dame Olivia still prided herself on dealing with every eventuality head on and noticeably without mountains of fuss or deliberation, at the same time striving to disprove the theory that advanced years might be something of a hindrance to a smooth-running operation like hers.

Tamara readily remarked, 'My mother thinks Anthony is OK but as she knows so many people in the equine world, finding another vet wouldn't lose her any sleep. She'd be shocked of course because up until now his mother is the one she would describe as mad, having never really felt the need to get on with the woman despite her close proximity in geographical terms.'

Having warmed to Lavender over the past week and seen her bewitch the children in the nicest sense of the word the previous day, I could only come out in favour of her and say it as I saw it. 'That's a great shame because having been wary of her myself at the outset I find her nothing more than eccentric – and there's not a thing wrong with eccentricity in my book. Sometimes I think it's an advantage.'

Tamara nodded, but knew her mother's opinion was set in stone. 'Even when her husband was alive and to most people they came across as a normal, well-to-do couple, Mother chose to steer clear of her and would lambaste Daddy for even acknowledging either of them, which made it awfully difficult for him. Henry Thompson used to be a member at the same golf club as Father and they even paired up a few times, though he kept it quiet from Mother of course. He would tell Ann Marie and me things and swear us to secrecy all the time. I think he rather enjoyed defying her, it was all a bit of a game to him and he loved ducking and diving – still does.'

'Sounds familiar,' I sighed. 'My dad did that a lot, but the difference was he was never very discreet and Mother felt totally insecure because of it, but then she was a complex person anyway which didn't help their relationship one bit.'

Tamara stopped reminiscing and turned to the present. 'My parents are solid as a rock, thank God. I couldn't imagine them apart. Lavender hasn't been so fortunate and maybe her relationship with Anthony has suffered because of it. He certainly doesn't appear to spend that much time with her and perhaps she finds the cats are better company. Nevertheless she's in for a nasty surprise if what you tell me is true. I really think you should put your father fully in the picture before there's some kind of showdown.'

She was right, but for me it wasn't so clear-cut, not knowing which way Father would react.

'Inadvertently I made things worse for Anthony by dumping Father on his mother after the fire and God knows what's been going on in his head since. And if he does have a gambling addiction that he's so far hidden from his mother, there's no telling how that might affect her, especially if he's conned her out of money that she believed was for something else.'

'Perhaps she's known all along but is just in denial. Parents tend to know everything. Mine can read me like a book.'

Again she might have been right, and I was the one showing too much gullibility. Lavender's reactions had said differently, but family matters are sacred and emotions can gather people up and sweep them away into alien places.

'Well, I'm just a humble jockey not a psychologist,' I offered. 'I don't suppose anything I do now will alter the course of history.'

She looked at me through concerned eyes and I cupped her hand in mine. 'Let's not have secrets and skeletons in cupboards. They weigh too heavy and can destroy you,' I said, surprised at my own profundity.

'A clean slate,' she replied, as if we were about to embark on something special.

Although seduced by temptation she knew I needed to be as close to Father as I could get, so I left her around midnight and drove the short distance between houses as heavy rain drew in from the west. Lavender had retired but

Father was sitting in the dark of the conservatory watching an angling programme on a satellite channel. He shushed me a few times and then in the commercial break informed me he had told Lavender about the fight, saying she was both horrified by the violence and delighted Fielding's henchman Neville Truman was under arrest. His ongoing efforts to speak to Dave had been frustrated by the police but they did concede he was due to be released on bail with further inquiries pending.

Further to that, Lavender had spoken to her son on the phone and there seemed nothing out of the ordinary from what he could hear of the relatively short conversation.

'It sounded like any mother/son chat and I don't think she suspects a thing,' he said, mightily relieved. 'It's up to Anthony now. He may not do a thing, try and tough it out. How was Tamara and why aren't you with her? I think I'll be quite safe in my bed.'

'She's fine and I think it best I stay here. I'll be leaving to cadge a lift to Haydock pretty early in the morning. I think you should leave at the same time and head back to Sloane Farm. Hopefully Dave will be back, his wounds permitting, and he might well get a few cheers from the regulars for his heroics. Not many men would have put Neville Truman in hospital but he did and that's worth a free drink or two.'

'Lavender says he deserves a medal and she's going to make him a special steak and kidney pie.'

'Hope it's a big one,' I said with predictability.

Father smiled from ear to ear and went back to his programme. Worn out by the day's events I headed for the sanctity of the lounge sofa, shut my eyes and hoped the next day would be eventful for all the right reasons.

21

The autumn rain that had been unrelenting ever since I woke gave way to a mixture of light grey and pale blue skies by mid-morning. Dominic had picked me up from just outside Cirencester at eight and we had a late breakfast at Stafford Services on the M6 at around ten thirty. Well, Dominic ate heartily as many trainers do, but I merely nibbled on toast with a thin scraping of butter as it was imperative I made the weight for the feature race of the day on Caper Sol Mio. Woe betide me if I didn't.

As I had already divulged to Joe Blackwood on Monday the race handicapper had been kind and the eight-year-old three-mile chaser wasn't burdened too heavily, having won twice last season and finished second at Leopardstown in Ireland a month ago on its first seasonal outing. Dominic was banking on a big winter for the horse with a major race at Kempton on Boxing Day his priority target, then the Cheltenham festival in March if all went to plan.

Haydock Park on a Wednesday in October with plenty of competitive fields expected seemed like a treat to me after four days of inactivity, and I received handshakes and back slaps from early-arriving jockeys and an especially warm reception from Paul Eddison who couldn't wait to tell me his news. Pulling me over and away from a bunch who were trading the gossip he looked like a man with a winning lottery ticket in his hand.

'Me and Connie are back on, we're going to try again. She moved back in yesterday and Bruce Fielding is history.'

I tried not to look too surprised and just smiled back at him.

He was so full of himself he just carried on. 'It's the kids I'm more happy for, they were stuck in the middle of a war zone but now everything should go back to the way it was before. Just goes to show if you wish for something hard enough what can happen.'

'I'm very pleased for you both,' I said. 'It's great news.'

He did the jockey's version of an Irish jig and reeled away happier than I had ever seen him. Even winning races didn't compare.

A cynical-looking Nathan Scully caught my eye and came across the dressing room to enlighten me further.

'How insufferable is he going to be? And how gullible can a person be?' he groaned, making sure Paul was out of earshot.

I knew what he was getting at. Connie Eddison was hardly a candidate for the 'Faithful Wife of the Year' award. 'Perhaps he'll stop winning races now,' I said sarcastically.

'It'll end in tears. Marriages like theirs always do,' Nathan prattled on, as if it was his expert subject. 'She had her fun, made a laughing stock of him and sauntered back as if nothing had gone on. And to cap it all that bloke who was knocking her off is now shagging some high-ranking policeman's daughter. He must have bollocks of steel.'

If my jaw gaped open Nathan didn't notice. He was scouring the room, making sure Paul wasn't back in range.

'The name of this policeman, do you know it? Well?' I pressed him, raising my voice suddenly and inviting quizzical stares.

He obviously didn't and shook his head. 'Who cares? What does it matter?'

It mattered a lot because all I could see in my mind was temptress Gabrielle Southgate being courted by a much older man purporting to be Curtis Fielding's half-brother.

And her father, his face a distinct shade of purple, pacing up and down his office and contemplating whether to call out Gloucestershire's equivalent of the National Guard.

Paul would know for sure who his ex-wife's lover was now seeing, but I had neither the heart nor the inclination to ask him given his newfound state of euphoria. I doubted anybody had ever seen him in such high spirits or so animated before, not even when winning a Gold Cup as he had done twice in his long and chequered career. It was a struggle for me to take my eyes off him despite the fact my concentration had already been sabotaged by two interlinked revelations and I sensed it would be a while before I could settle and focus on the task in hand.

Besides riding for Dominic in the third race I was booked by a Derbyshire-based trainer for the second, and there was a likely spare ride or two later as several jockeys were inevitably unavailable through injuries and suspension. And it wasn't long before I was summoned by a trainer who had brought a horse down from Cumbria, and asked to stand in for a jockey nursing a broken collarbone from a fall at Taunton the day before. That meant I had three back-to-back races and the capacity for more if called upon.

Such spare rides are invaluable to a jockey not assigned to one of the bigger yards and if I'm honest it was somewhat refreshing not to have someone as pragmatic as Dominic bending my ear or doubting my ability, which was a bad habit he was never likely to find a cure for. Nathan had come to Haydock with no pre-booked rides and already he had picked up two and was touting for more. I had done the same myself on occasions and rarely been disappointed. The nature of the sport and the strict rules regarding jockeys involved in falls open up many avenues for those waiting in the wings and although there's no substitute for performing out on the track sometimes just watching others made you a better opponent next time round.

For a mid-week meeting there was a big crowd, helped
I supposed by the fact it was half-term for many. On a
walkabout whilst the competing jockeys readied themselves
for the first race I noted several bouncy-castle-type attractions
for children and even a young couple offering donkey rides.
All the bookmakers from the north-west were lined up in
the betting ring, cagily displaying their odds in the hope
of not giving anything away – and standing fairly central to
the row of pitches with his back to me was a man I had
already given some thought to that day.

Senior policemen had just as much right to bet on horse
races as did butchers and double-glazing salesmen, so he was
doing nothing illegal or career threatening. Half of me
wanted to stride boldly up to Christopher Southgate and ask
him what he fancied, whilst the other half told me to steer
well clear. Then I watched while, as if suddenly inspired, he
thrust a few notes at a bookie who barely acknowledged him
apart from giving him a betting slip. With the inquisitive half
of me winning the imaginary contest inside my head I walked
towards him at precisely the same time as he swivelled around
to face me. He wore a sober grey suit and no tie.

'Small world,' I said hurriedly, looking up at him as he
tried desperately to summon a smile.

'Indeed it is, Sam,' he agreed. 'But then again this is
where you earn your money week in week out so it's not
so surprising.'

'Day off?' I asked, not making it sound like an interrogation.

'For good behaviour,' he said, deadpan.

We walked slowly away from the noise of the bookmaker's
trademark bellowing, with the Chief Super showing signs
of nervousness and looking around as though he was
expecting somebody else.

'I've just seen Paul Eddison walking on the ceiling of the
changing room so if I were you I'd put some money on
him,' I advised him. 'Never seen him looking so happy.'

He registered some sort of acknowledgement and said, 'Already have and at those odds he'd better win.'

I decided to play games with him. 'Why do you suppose he's looking so pleased with himself?' I asked him.

The policeman had extra-sensitive receptors and knew I knew. 'Good news,' he shrugged. 'The sort that travels fast.'

'A bit of a turn-up that, not so long ago he was in deep despair and nearly blew a man's brains out with a shotgun.'

The reaction I got was pure theatre and his eyebrows spoke for him. If he was going to say something on the subject it wasn't going to be in such a public place. He did a one hundred and eighty degree pirouette and gave away the fact that he was meeting someone.

I hastily changed the subject. 'How's Sultan of Somalia shaping up after Ludlow? Fit and raring to go I hope?'

'Never better,' he replied, indifferently.

'And how's that lovely daughter of yours?'

He stopped scouring the immediate area in front of him with his eyes and fixed them on me. 'She's very well, why so interested?'

'No reason,' I lied.

He just stared back at me.

With the weighed-out announcement ringing in my ears I thought it best to try to excuse myself before I did any real harm. 'Must get back, I'm due out in the second race. Nice to have met you again.'

'And you. Good luck,' he replied swiftly.

Whether he meant it or not I didn't know, nor did I care. I thought to myself as I headed back towards the weighing room that race days used to be boring and uneventful. Since I had arrived at the course today however it had been both taxing and informative, with an element of surprise added for good measure, sending my head into a spin.

Not a lot felt right about having the Chief Superintendent

of an area's police force stalking bookmakers for their best prices and acting as though he was due to meet somebody unlikely to be a law enforcer. The last time I spotted him deeply entrenched with someone at a race meeting was at Cheltenham with Paul, and I couldn't get the idea out of my overworked brain that this was no social visit.

In my allotted space in a remarkably quiet changing room I sat and wondered why any self-respecting racehorse owner would burden its jockey with pink spots on a purple background and complement it with a yellow cap. An ageing valet who was nearby and saw me staring at the colours hanging on my peg seemed to echo my own thoughts before smiling to himself and thinking no more of it. Nobody could accuse racing of being drab and colourless from a spectator's point of view and I knew it was up to me to wear the ensemble with pride and not act like a wimp.

From where I was now sitting I could keep tabs via a monitor on the first race that threw eleven novice chasers together and which had Paul sitting astride the favourite, who seemed too one-paced for me in the early stages to be a serious contender. Paul, as everybody knew, had rediscovered the knack of riding winners and showed no real concern when three fences from home his horse remained last of a leading bunch of five and ten lengths behind the long-time leader. Jumping the second last his placing was the same, and it was only by virtue of the fact that the second-placed horse fell at the last that he finished fourth and the bookmakers said thank you to God.

Five minutes later he was back to change into his colours for the second race, looking more like he had won, with the earlier smile still tattooed on his face and a demon glint in his eye.

'Don't you get thinking you might win today, Sam,' he teased. 'Can't think why you bothered turning up.'

'I need the money,' I said, which as it happens was true.

'Should've took another day off, you'll be wasting your time today.'

It transpired that we both wasted our time in the two-thirty novice hurdle race, neither of our horses even crossing the finishing line due to Paul being unshipped at the third obstacle and me pulling up a quarter of a mile from home with the horse completely spent. It was a memory quickly to be forgotten.

For Paul, who took a pretty hard knock to his body, his racing day was over and there was talk of precautionary scans and x-rays to see what lay under the bruising. Suddenly not having him in the weighing room to rub shoulders with disappointed me, and not having him down at the start for the next race strangely didn't raise my confidence.

By a quirk of fate amateur Simon Mendes, who I last remembered ogling Gabrielle Southgate at Ludlow, took over Paul's ride and as the race developed he seemed my main threat. Caper Sol Mio was pure class and Dominic had him in fine fettle. He loved nothing less than a fast pace and took his fences so clinically you barely noticed them on your travels. With no other horse willing to kick on after the first circuit I let him go, and with half of the back straight and the final bend and run in to go we had stretched our lead to twenty lengths. I could hear Dominic's voice ringing in my ears not to push the horse out too early and sensed those behind me might be thinking it a foolhardy tactic given this was a testing three miles. But Caper Sol Mio wasn't yet in top gear and when I asked for more I got it in abundance. Only Simon on a smart chaser owned by the Jollys could match my pace over the last quarter mile but because I had built up such a lead I cruised home unchallenged at least twenty-five lengths clear.

When I was being led back in I thought perhaps I had made it look too easy, and wondered if Dominic and the horse's wealthy industrialist owner might think the same thing. Certainly the handicapper wouldn't be so lenient next time around but I felt the sheer ability of the horse would counterbalance any penalty imposed upon him, and if I was lucky enough to be aboard him again I would probably adopt the same tactics in an effort to win the race.

Thankfully trainer, owner and a posse of well-wishers were thrilled with such a convincing victory and the look of envy I got from other jockeys back in the weighing room spoke volumes for the overall performance. Even a quite satisfied Simon Mendes, whose horse had put up a game show, looked at me through envious eyes and said my horse was in another league. I in turn praised him for sticking to the tactics that on another day would have paid him handsome dividends.

Typically I was brought back down to earth in more ways than one when the relatively experienced chaser I was paired with in the fourth race decided to deposit me on the turf at the first fence, in the one racing scenario that jump jockeys dread. Simply he put in an extra stride that wasn't needed, and sent me and numerous birch twigs flying. Luckily I took a soft landing and got up none the worse for wear. Some might point the finger and call it pilot error; others less critical would say when half a ton of horse has a mind of its own, falls like that are inevitable and in the main unavoidable.

Having been checked over by a St John Ambulance nurse I got a lift back via a course official and had already showered and changed before the other competing jockeys got back, to find I had been the only faller in the race. Such anonymity – the shame after the euphoria.

My riding duties over, I beat a hasty retreat, finding the quietest spot I could to phone Father to get an update on Big Dave who, as I very much expected, had brushed aside his injuries from yesterday to put in a full shift at the fishery. There was no news of Neville nor whether his boss had been implicated, and so far as Father was concerned normal service had been resumed at Sloane Farm which must have been an anti-climax for some given the wild events of the day before.

With Dominic busy somewhere socialising with other trainers and presumably due to check out future opposition in the remaining two races, I ventured back into the boisterous betting ring where early prices for the fifth race were beginning to change as some of the hardcore punters moved in. And though Paul was ruled out it wasn't stopping every bookie from offering evens or less on Chez La Fur, fresh from its fortuitous victory with him aboard at Cheltenham, showing faith in Simon Mendes who was again benefiting from Paul's absence.

From where I stood I could see across to the finishing post. Despite the crowds it wasn't too difficult to make out Christopher Southgate, who was standing with his legs spread far apart and talking to a man in a smart suit whose back was turned towards me, making it impossible for me to see his face. Like a bloodhound on a mission I made ground quickly so that in what seemed seconds I had manoeuvred around people and was just a matter of yards from them. They were huddled very closely together but my instincts told me this was no last-minute deliberation over the race card to find the winner of the forthcoming contest.

I paused and watched, confident they were too engrossed to notice me, and after about two minutes of discussion and with all eyes trained on the track or the strategically placed monitors, the Chief Super took a bulky envelope from the inside pocket of his jacket and passed it to the man who virtually snatched it from his hand. To get an idea of what the man looked like I shifted to my left so that I was at an angle to them, and it was then I felt for my borrowed phone, switched it on and set up the camera. I could feel sweat on the palms of my hands as I positioned

241

the mobile and took what I hoped was as clear a photo as I could.

If nothing else it would surely confirm to me that the second man was on a par with the policeman in the height department and that he was a good bit younger. It was clear that he also possessed an all-too-familiar jaw line, plus well-groomed hair, and stood with a confident gait that was a definite giveaway. Although there was much noise and excitement around me I was still near enough to pick out the clarity and tone of his voice, which had been temporarily raised by a decibel or two to make it audible. A kind of madness overcame me, prompting me to edge as close as I dared and utilise the camera again, if only to confirm my fears that I had met him once before but in completely different and more harrowing circumstances.

In unison they both spotted me. I had no choice but to smile stupidly and pretend I was aiming the camera at the track beyond them, at the same time stepping backwards to distance myself from them. Christopher Southgate's face scowled at me and the other man, turning fully towards me, focused his eyes on one thing only, the phone in my hand. And I could tell from his whole demeanour that he would go to any lengths to take it from me.

22

Instinct told me I should stow the phone away safely and run, but making a clean escape was ludicrous as there was a sudden rush of people around me clambering to get vantage points to watch the race. Nobody, not even a desperate man, would make a scene in such a public place, or so I thought. Then it dawned on me that the man launching himself into panic mode and scattering the innocent in his wake was with a top-ranking policeman who, if he joined in the impromptu chase, could not only wave a warrant card about to make the pursuit more plausible but also arrest me and read me my rights.

The headlines in the next day's racing journals flashed before my eyes and made pretty poor reading. 'Jockey Sam Woodall held for Serious Affray at Haydock' or something equally depressing. Encouragingly it didn't seem that Chief Superintendent Southgate was in any mood to give chase or get publicly involved, but any complacency was wrestled from me by a strong hand that had clamped onto the sleeve of my leather jacket and was trying to swing me round.

'Pickpocket,' shouted the man, grasping me for all he was worth. 'He's nicked my mobile phone.'

It felt like I had the eyes of many on me and that his quick thinking would reward him, with every likelihood of somebody helping him to restrain me. But the smooth material of my jacket aided me and the vice-like grip he had was under threat from my intensity to shake him off.

'You've smashed one already, I won't let it happen again,' I yelled at him, prising myself free.

243

Although the help he had banked on hadn't been forthcoming, there were plenty who might still baulk me or make a citizen's arrest, and despite losing his hold on me the man was in no mood to give up. The words 'stop' and 'thief' boomed across the enclosure as he again sought assistance from the masses for whom this was an unwelcome and unexpected distraction to the main event.

In the corner of my eye I spotted the bright-yellow jacket of a member of the security staff and, though stumbling and making little headway, I knew that if I could reach him I would be safe. It so happened that he was heading my way to investigate a commotion in the crowd and got to me in double quick time, immediately recognising who I was.

'Mr Woodall, are you all right?' he asked anxiously, surprised to see me.

A look over my shoulder told me the pursuit was over as the man purporting to be the victim had pulled up and now stood with his hands on hips, no longer posing a physical threat to me despite an icy glare that cut through me like a knife.

'Yes, I'm fine, thanks for your concern, it was nothing,' I told the bearded security officer who, though not fully believing me, seemed to accept it.

'Just doing my job,' he said matter-of-factly, his hand raised as though he was about to salute me when in truth I should have been the one signalling my gratitude.

Almost every eye was trained on the ensuing race but all I could think of was to get back to the sanctuary of the hospitality area and eventually the weighing room. By flashing my official pass I slipped through two heavily guarded security barriers, which at least allowed me to relax enough to watch a replay of the climax of the race on a monitor and see Simon Mendes's mount hold off a strong late challenge to win by a length and record yet another success for the Jolly conveyor belt, albeit without Paul's help.

It was only then on the approach to the parade ring that I noticed a tear in the arm of my jacket as well as some broken stitching around the shoulder seam which had endured the weight of a man hell-bent on apprehending me. A man whose identity was of little doubt, endorsed by the distinctive tone of his voice, the chiselled bone structure, his physical strength and unquestionable nerve.

Somebody else who immediately spotted the material damage inflicted on me was Dominic, who was now conversing with me in sign language and looking mightily puzzled as he did. He was a few yards away with a clutch of owners and trainers, readying himself for the last race in which he had entered a young hurdler for the first time, a contest strictly for amateur jockeys. He had reluctantly employed a female amateur who just so happened to be a niece of the horse's owner, and was obviously gearing up to meet her and give her some constructive advice.

I had no idea how I would explain away my ripped jacket other than to tell him I had been mobbed by my fans, which was absurd wishful thinking on my behalf. I didn't know as yet whether he would ever get the truth out of me regarding my on-course fracas and subsequent rescue by a security guard.

To remove further attention and hide the evidence I took off my jacket and slung it haphazardly over one shoulder, film star mode. Then when the jockeys began to arrive I left and went in search of Paul Eddison, mobile phone held tightly in hand. He had not long got back from seeing a physio with the next day's racing in mind and was naked but for a towel around his waist. I waited for him to shower and dry off and as the changing room began to clear again I sat down beside him, commiserating with him on his rotten luck and switching on the phone.

'I need you to look at something and answer a few questions,' I said, becoming serious.

245

Both his eyebrows lifted and he seemed genuinely intrigued. 'What's this, more detective work?' he guessed, reading me like a book.

'Sort of,' I replied, teeing up the photo I had taken ten minutes ago. 'Recognise anybody?' I showed it to him.

He screwed up his eyes a little and stared at it for quite some time. 'It looks like two men talking to me,' he shrugged.

'But I think you know who they are?'

He stopped looking at the screen of the phone and ran a comb through his damp hair.

'Well?' I urged him.

'What does it matter if I do know them, what's it got to do with me?'

He rubbed cleansing cream into the ageing skin of his cheeks and forehead and became standoffish.

'Paul, just before I took that photo I saw the man on the right hand over a thick envelope to the man on the left, who when he spotted me gave chase. Had it not been for some security guy's intervention who knows what he might have done to me. The man is Bruce Fielding, right?'

'It bears a resemblance to him,' he shrugged again.

'And the other man is Chief Superintendent Christopher Southgate, no less?'

'If you know, why ask?'

'So what do you suppose was in the envelope?'

Paul became flippant. 'Holiday snaps perhaps?'

'Look, I'm really chuffed for you that you're back with Connie,' I changed the subject. 'And that Bruce Fielding has moved on to somebody else. When I heard the rumour that he was seeing someone and that person was the daughter of a top-ranking policeman I immediately thought about Gabrielle Southgate who I met at Ludlow last week. Am I right to think that?'

Paul sighed heavily. He sat down next to me and after a lengthy pause he spoke from the corner of his mouth. 'Who he sees is his business, suffice to say I'm glad he is no longer with Connie and she had the good sense to ditch him. I just want things to go back to how they were, and so does she.'

'So it was Connie who ended it then?'

'What does it matter who did what?' Paul was beginning to get annoyed. But I needed answers.

'Did Bruce cheat on Connie with Gabrielle?' I went on, regardless.

'That's the gist of it,' he admitted. 'He's that sort, he'll cheat on her with somebody else too. And he's not bothered how many lives he wrecks on the way.'

Underlying bitterness surfaced and Paul then offered me both stark reality and a serious warning. 'You say you saw an envelope change hands and Bruce came after you. That means he probably thinks you have clear evidence on that phone of yours. I would have thought it would have been Southgate chasing you with handcuffs, as he's got more to lose if whatever was inside that envelope could incriminate him. But then again he practically runs Gloucestershire's police force and I've heard he is bound to make Chief Constable. So Sam, take heed, ruffling his feathers is not an option I'd take in your shoes.'

Suddenly the bigger picture lumbered me with two desperate men and very few places to hide. Paul had seen at close quarters how manipulative Christopher Southgate could be when he intervened on behalf of Curtis Fielding to end the feud between an enraged, shotgun-waving husband and his wife's cold-hearted lover. The very same philanderer he appeared to be paying off to leave his daughter alone. Assuming that's what I saw.

It was bad enough that Bruce Fielding had manhandled me twice now and for differing reasons, but at least I felt he would have no ally in the other man in the photo who surely only had his daughter's welfare in mind and wouldn't therefore be coming after me from the same angle.

Paul could see his words had resonated with me. 'What are you planning, Sam?

Where's all this leading?'

'It was a spontaneous thing,' I shrugged. 'With everything that's happened to my father and the Fieldings' involvement, I suppose I'm looking for anything that might help his cause and bring people to book. It was never my intention to open up such a bad can of worms.'

It felt like every cliché in the world was ruling my life and dragging me down. Thankfully I think Paul had just enough sympathy for me to try to lift my spirits.

'Although I don't envy you, Sam, maybe the worst is over. Bruce might not hang around here for much longer if he's now made an enemy of the Chief Super, whether he's a mate of his half-brother or not. Equally Southgate may feel you are no threat to him because he will have covered every angle and not left himself too exposed. He's both clever and ambitious.'

I thought about it, but nothing he said eased my vulnerability, and to go along with his theory wasn't going to help me sleep or feel any safer at night. But perversely I didn't reproach myself for anything I had done and it still felt that I had right on my side.

'Do you know where Bruce Fielding lives, or where he's staying?' I asked, sure he would know.

He looked back at me surprised but saw no point in withholding anything. 'Sometimes he stops over at Curtis's place but you're more likely to find him at Dockham Green. He's renting a house there off another of his brother's golfing pals and that's where he took...' He stopped in mid-sentence.

'Connie?'

'Yes.'

'Do you know the number of the house?'

'It's called Sunny Ridge and you can't miss it. A large

white house on the left as you enter the village, next to an old vicarage.'

'Sounds idyllic.'

He passed no comment but after a short pause became deadly serious. 'Meddle with Bruce at your peril, Sam. He's got Fielding genes, remember. The day I held a shotgun to his head and looked straight into his eyes he never flinched. Thinks he's one of the untouchables and mixes with all the wrong sorts which makes him dangerous.'

I knew that already but it was generous of him to share his concerns. It was food for thought and I thanked him then rose to my feet, confirming I would see him at Stratford the next day where I assumed we would resume our rivalry. There was no reason to believe it wouldn't be anything but service as usual, just a different venue with slightly less prize money to be won.

Outside the changing rooms and in a safe enough place, I belatedly caught up with the numerous texts that had gone ignored through pressure of work and worrying distractions. One from Tamara wishing me luck, another much longer one from her father congratulating me and at the same time thanking me for making him richer via my win on Caper Sol Mio, and a third from my own father to tell me Neville Truman had now been officially charged with grievous bodily harm and had been bailed to appear before magistrates next week. A follow-up text from the same sender timed an hour later then informed me Curtis Fielding had phoned him to say how shocked he was to hear of Neville's alleged crime, adding that he believed there was a logical explanation and the police were barking up the wrong tree.

Alarmingly there was a further text sent only minutes ago from a mobile number I did not recognise, which made simple reading. 'Kings Hotel, the foyer, 8.30 pm. Be there,' it said anonymously.

It sent my imagination into overload and I looked up at a clock to note the time. Dominic would want to stop for a meal somewhere on the way back and might be in no hurry to leave the course to avoid traffic delays. Getting back to Cheltenham for half past eight was pretty nigh impossible but despite already having palpitations I knew I had to be there. Thinking quickly, I ran back to the jockeys' changing room only to find Paul had left, so I made inroads to the privileged car park and easily spotted his distinctive yellow car making its way to the exit.

He looked perplexed when I flagged him down and unsure when I asked him for a lift. 'Just as long as you don't ask me any more questions on the way and we stick to talking shop,' he agreed.

I said I was happy to comply, sliding in beside him and thinking I must phone Dominic.

'What happened to the jacket?' Paul asked me, noticing the damage as I threw it onto the back seat.

'Don't ask,' I grimaced.

'Just pretend I didn't,' he replied, before repeating himself about the subject matter of any further conversation. 'Racing only, nothing else, understand?'

'Understood,' I said, engaging my phone and waiting to hear Dominic's voice so that I could advise him of my revised travel arrangements.

With Paul anxious to get back home to Connie and the kids and the next phase of his life, he dropped me off on Cheltenham's busy ring road shortly after seven. I walked towards the town centre, investing in a strong cup of tea on route from a bar more famed for its coffee, and chomping on some awful-tasting chewy health snack for meagre fortification.

The receptionist at the hotel was polite but uninterested when I told her I was meeting somebody there, completing the onerous task of filing her fingernails and looking at them through critical eyes. As the time approached I could feel the sweat rising through my pores and I paid a nervous visit to the toilet before pacing about in front of the reception desk which didn't seem to bother the girl in the least.

Precisely on time Christopher Southgate breezed in through the revolving door and pointed with his eyes to where he thought we would be least conspicuous, a small table in a narrow alcove. The kind of setting I imagined he felt comfortable with. He was still in the same suit which had picked up a few extra creases and his hair had that windswept look that seemed of no great concern to him.

'You seemed pretty certain that I'd turn up, some might have kept well away,' I told him, taking to a chair facing away from the body of the main foyer.

'Not you, Sam, I figure there are questions you need answers to,' he shrugged.

Though I didn't nod my head in agreement my face gave me away. 'Am I that transparent? I could never be a spy for the government.'

Nerves were fighting the need for composure but at least my curiosity had been laid to rest by his prompt arrival and I sensed in him too some mild apprehension. Easing himself into the chair directly opposite me and keeping his legs uncrossed he started what I hoped wouldn't turn out to be a long saga based on the facts as I saw them nor an attempt to blind me with science.

'I'll give it to you straight, Sam, no bullshit, no hidden agenda,' he said in a measured and determined tone. 'There would be no point denying what you saw, especially as you have it on film I presume. And any attempt to abuse my position with somebody so well known as you in a place where I am also well known would be foolish. Besides it was never an option, as I'm as keen for you to continue riding my daughter's horse as she is. You have a fan there,

251

Sam, and if that sounds like I'm trying to patronise you I assure you I'm not.'

His sincerity seemed genuine but the habit he had of staring beyond me still left me feeling on edge. Looking down, he appeared to sigh as if whatever he was about to get off his chest would rid him of any guilt and make me the recipient of the contents of his inner soul. I folded my arms and tried to make myself look unshockable.

'I would do anything for my daughter within reason, as would you for yours, I'm sure,' he began. 'Inadvertently I suppose I'm partially to blame as it was me who introduced her to Bruce at a function. I ought to have read the signs, the way he looked at her in an almost predatory way. But he had Connie Eddison on his arm at the time and I never thought any more about it. Lots of men have drooled over Gabby and not even knowing who her father is has stopped them from ... well you know what I'm trying to say.'

I fully understood and nodded.

He went on. 'Of course I know she's no innocent child any more and draws in men like flies, but when I found out she was seeing Bruce I reacted the way any parent would and did everything to put a stop to it.'

'Naturally,' I said, understanding his dilemma.

'Think ahead a few years, Sam. What would you do if a man like that who is fifteen years older than your daughter and who has just broken up somebody else's marriage came on to the scene and took up with her the way he did? All the nasty gossip behind your back and blank stares you get when people know, not to mention the torture and strain it puts on a close family unit like the one I've tried to nurture.'

I listened and knew exactly where he was going.

'Gabby's still young and it goes without saying I would never want to see her unhappy. But men like Bruce are only out for what they can get and I could hardly throw him in jail for what he did, though believe me I did think in my position it wouldn't be hard to arrange something.'

I immediately thought about the framing of Paul by Bruce and the intervention of the Chief Super to resolve the matter, and then also about Southgate's friendship with Bruce's half-brother and whether that had dissuaded him from putting Bruce behind bars. I listened some more.

'Though not a particularly wealthy man I'm not poorly paid and didn't have to think twice about asking him to name his price for leaving Gabby alone. I was pretty sure him dumping her wouldn't break her heart. After rejecting what he told me out of hand I made him an offer and added an ultimatum, as well as enlisting some help from his older and wiser half-brother, and finally we reached a satisfactory settlement. What you saw was the first of two payments and he knows there will be no more 'after the second one.'

'Why in such a public place, why not behind closed doors?' I asked, intrigued.

He hunched his broad shoulders. 'For the very same reason I chose this place to meet you. Not so long ago you used the word "transparent" and I can't afford to be anything else. And where Bruce Fielding is concerned I have nothing to hide. He hasn't blackmailed me and I haven't bribed him. It's a financial arrangement that suits all parties, you do see that don't you, Sam?'

For once his deep-set eyes sought mine and, though not convinced about the blackmail/bribe speech, I didn't question his ethics. 'From what I know of Bruce, which doesn't amount to much, I do know he likes money,' I said thinking about what Lavender had reported to me.

'Like is an understatement. Ever since he found out he was Curtis's illegitimate half-brother he's been on a quest to make up for lost time and who, to some extent, could blame him, it must have been quite a shock.'

'For Curtis too,' I added. 'It's influenced his dealings with my father and caused a lot of grief. But we seem to be sorting that out, though Curtis still has some explaining to do regarding the actions of his estate manager.'

Chief Superintendent Southgate switched to an official role in an instant and wasn't entirely on my side. 'Ah, yes the GBH charges against Neville Truman. I have a copy of the file on my desk and it's not such an open and shut case as you think.'

I frowned at him and sensed he was about to demonstrate the manipulative powers of his nature. 'I thought the evidence was pretty damning; the victim now remembers who hit him from behind with a lethal weapon,' I pondered.

A thoughtful Chief Superintendent inhaled and puffed out his cheeks. 'According to Neville's statement he says he went to investigate noises next to one of the lakes and chased somebody off although it was too dark to see who it was. Next thing he knew the victim, as you described him, was trying to grab Mr Truman from behind and he claims all he did was try to defend himself against an unknown attacker which resulted in him picking up a piece of concrete and striking out with it like any man might in fear of his life.'

I sat open-mouthed and astounded. This story I knew to be pure fiction. There was worse to come.

'Mr Truman was infinitely wrong in not reporting the original incident of course but he has now filed a complaint against the supposed victim for a subsequent incident involving the two men which might well undermine the prosecution's case.'

'That's absurd,' I found my voice. 'It's quite ridiculous. The man left Dave Burrows for dead.'

Southgate looked surprised. 'It was hardly life-threatening, Sam. He was just a little dazed according to my sources.'

'My father found him unconscious,' I corrected him but he just shrugged back impassively.

'Well it's up the courts to decide now,' the Chief Super said, trying to sound unbiased. 'The police have put a case to the CPS and if it goes to Crown Court then it's down to a jury. I'm only telling you what I know. I assure you my colleagues will make Mr Truman aware of his error of judgement in not coming forward sooner but I'm sure he had his reasons.'

I didn't speculate or argue. Nothing seemed fair.

The thought of Neville Truman walking free naturally troubled me, as did Curtis Fielding being exonerated. It meant no justice for Big Dave. And certainly no great satisfaction for my father.

With nothing to lose I asked the policeman what he knew of the arson attack on Father's lock-up in Stonehouse. Although full of sympathy he admitted it had not crossed his radar yet, but said he would seriously do what he could to solve it, reaffirming his mission statement to me. I told him briefly of my suspicions and about the pen I had dropped off as potential evidence.

Further to that and for reasons of self-preservation I checked with him on the mood of Bruce Fielding following my escape from his clutches a few hours earlier, and though he didn't sound overly worried he did warn me against unnecessary confrontations. The kind that resulted in bruised ribs and torn jackets I assumed, ending any notion I had of visiting the address I had extracted from Paul. At that the Chief Super stood up, and as quickly as he had arrived he was gone, rather like a whirlwind. When eventually my head had stopped spinning I phoned for a taxi, enabling me to return to Cirencester and retrieve my car.

23

When Father found out about what Neville Truman had said in his defence to the police he turned the air blue and groaned about injustice.

'I wish Dave had hit the bastard harder, maybe then he'd really know what pain was,' he moaned.

'That wouldn't solve anything,' I suggested, 'only make matters worse.'

'It would make me feel better. If he gets away with what he did I'll do more than smash his door mirrors, I'll...'

'You'll go nowhere near him,' I interrupted. 'Think about your blood pressure.'

'If I were twenty years younger,' he went on.

'Well you're not, so don't go there.'

Father prattled on regardless as I knew he would and I indulged him, allowing him time to let off steam. In a bizarre fishing analogy he went on about the biggest worms wriggling off the smallest hooks, and said we shouldn't just sit back and let it happen. It was our duty to see justice prevail. Neville Truman was just a puppet and the one pulling his strings should be ultimately accountable for his criminal actions.

His mood hadn't been helped by his inability to talk Lavender round to our way of thinking over Anthony, which resulted in the cold shoulder treatment from her that other people tended to use on her when she was in close proximity. I could tell that it had got under his skin, as he was not a man who made friends easily and had precious few to boast of, especially ones he could turn to in times of crisis.

Although her son was now a major concern to me, I genuinely believed Lavender was nothing more than a likeable eccentric whose unpredictability was an important trait in her character, not a reason for people to ridicule her. But it still remained to be seen how far she would go to protect Anthony and to what lengths he would go to continue to deceive her, as I was now sure he had done frequently and without any hint of a conscience.

Having phoned ahead I drove to the Willows and despite the lateness of my visit the Blackwoods welcomed me like a hero back from the trenches. Kisses from Tamara, a bear hug from Joe and a warmer than usual smile from Dame Olivia said it all. They had all benefited from my win on Caper Sol Mio, Dame Olivia having broken her golden rule and wagered what she called 'a small amount', which I took to be a week's wages for most.

'I think she's getting used to the idea and no longer trying to pair me off with a millionaire,' Tamara said later as we sat together drinking coffee in the lounge.

'I'll never be that for sure. I'll just have to win on Hologram next time to clinch it. Nothing like putting yourself under pressure.'

'So it's dependent on a race then, whether we move on,' she teased.

I took it on the chin and reminded her of the first time I took her out on a date and what her mother had said upon meeting me.

'As an equestrian I thought she'd have an affinity with jockeys but that soon went out the window when she asked me if I was any good, prior to letting me ride for her, remember?'

She laughed. 'Up until then she had that dreadful jockey who Dominic never rated. I think she chose him because she secretly fancied the breeches off him but don't tell her or Daddy I said that.'

'So are you telling me she doesn't fancy me? I'm crestfallen,' I faked my disappointment.

'Don't flatter yourself. Sometimes I wonder why I bother with you myself,' she teased again.

'Sometimes I ask myself that. I still pinch myself.'

She could see I meant it, and blushed a little, embarrassed by her flippancy. 'Joking apart, Sam, I'm with you because I want to be and I love you. And yes I fancy the breeches off you. There I've said it. But I would hope you already knew.'

I wanted somebody to pinch me again, and just basked for a few seconds. 'Pity, wish I was wearing them now. And before you ask I feel the same way. I think about you all the time. I love you too.'

Tamara flashed her big, beautiful eyes at me and we sat together in silence, hands locked together as if this was a pivotal moment in our lives. She rested her head on my shoulder, whispering the words again, making them sound so real that they resonated on both of us, our emotions merging as one.

Rarely had I felt as I did at that moment. There was a calm and a real sense of purpose about life ahead, and though I knew the peace inside would soon be disturbed by the return of normality I had no qualms about letting my mind meander and bask a little longer.

'How's Emilia?' I asked suddenly, breaking the moment.

'Looking forward to tomorrow,' she said. 'She's off to Thorpe Park with some school friends and parents. I would've gone but there's a bit of a crisis at the agency so I'll be in London, back here on Friday.'

'Shame. I'll call you from Stratford after the racing, OK?'

We wished each other luck and just sat for a while before I left, the taste of her lips lingering on mine, reminding me of what I was missing.

* * *

258

I drove myself to Stratford next morning, pulling over barely five miles into my journey to field a call from Father who had news of Anthony Thompson. Well, news of his disappearance more like.

As he and Lavender were exchanging understandably subdued pleasantries over breakfast, he said, two policemen, one in plain clothes, had arrived hoping to speak to Anthony, thinking they would find him at his home address. When Lavender told them he had a habit of sleeping at his surgery they asked to see the room he slept in when he stayed with her, which she flatly refused to allow, demanding to know what it was all about. All they would say was that they were conducting enquiries into a crime and were hoping he might be able to help them. When Lavender badgered them about the alleged crime they said next to nothing, asked her to confirm his surgery's address, and left.

Shocked and concerned, Lavender then called her son to tell him to expect visitors, keen to know why the police might want to interview him. From her reaction, Father said, Anthony took the news badly and quickly hung up on her. Not long after she phoned the landline at the surgery again, only to be told her son had left in a hurry after instructing staff to cancel his appointments for the day. Soon after that the two policemen arrived, taking a quick and unchallenged look around, concentrating on his office and upstairs living quarters and leaving a number for Anthony to call them on his return.

His mother had subsequently called his mobile numerous times but it was permanently unobtainable. An hour and a half later no one knew where Anthony was and Lavender was beside herself with worry.

It sent my imagination into overdrive again. From the lay-by I phoned Gloucestershire police and asked for the desk sergeant or anyone familiar with the ongoing arson investigations. After a long wait I got through to a detective constable who cagily informed me they were just following up a line of enquiry and that he was not at liberty to discuss the finer details. He understood my anxiety and was sorry for what my father had been put through following the fire, promising me some feedback in due course.

It was a crumb of comfort but the burning questions were where was Anthony now and what was going through his head after our curtailed meeting on Tuesday? I tried to put that aside, and after tedious traffic delays arrived at the racecourse an hour before the first race in which I was partnering a Heath Coultard trained novice hurdler named Blind Summit that had run all of its previous races on the flat and with no great distinction. For once Dominic had no runners at the meeting and from all accounts he was deserting the stable to take his wife shopping, which must have been a first. Clare, I assumed, had put her foot down or they had drawn straws and he had lost. Either way it was a groundhog day in the Ingles household and I wondered how he would cope with all the sarcasm that was bound to be heading his way. Such was his dedication and loyalty to the sport.

Even without his horses on show there was good crowd for a Thursday and the picturesque track was bathed in autumn sunlight which together with a stiff breeze helped dry the turf after heavy overnight rain. Stratford had been reasonably kind to me over the years and with three scheduled rides I felt optimistic rather than confident, though secretly uncertain about the first. Sometimes intuition kicks in when you get on an animal's back and the vibes I got when I finally got sole control of Blind Summit out on the course were not ones I much cared for. The race was over two miles, and for a good mile and a half of it the horse fought with me rather than cooperating, almost sending me to the turf twice with dodgy jumping and only settling when it was too late, picking up several places to finish fourth. Work in progress I told the trainer and he knew straight away what I meant. It didn't need much of a post mortem from him after that, just more fine tuning until the training mentality bore fruit. I wished him luck. With no late calls to action I was to sit out the next two races and used the time to gather information. Well before the next race was due off I joined punters in the betting ring, spying all the usual faces of the bookies on their rostrums and listening to them bellow out the odds. Taking something of a liberty I went up and down the rows talking to them about Anthony Thompson and displaying the flyer with his photo on it. All of them recognised me but not the photo and shared a puzzled look – except one. He was a well-known Cheltenham bookmaker working his usual pitch at Stratford and though not one hundred per cent sure he said the man in the photo seemed familiar.

'Perhaps you've seen him at a Cheltenham meeting where he's one of the official vets on duty?' I suggested.

He seemed unsure but said he thought he had met him somewhere else.

'Has he ever placed a bet with you?' I asked.

He thought hard but his mind was distracted by a sudden swarm of punters bearing cash and all I got in the end was an uncommitted shrug of his broad shoulders.

After the race I mingled with jockeys, owners, trainers and hard-working grooms, choosing my words carefully and not making it out to be anything of major importance. Many of them knew Anthony, quite a few owners employed him and nobody had a bad word to say about him.

I sent a brief text to Father and got a much longer one back saying he'd heard nothing more from Lavender, imagining she was still gobsmacked by her son's behaviour, and that Big Dave was still understandably hopping mad about Neville Truman's counter claim against him. He also told me the fishery was dead quiet except for the noise of the diggers down at the far end of the new lake and that he might head back to Castle Moat Lodge early and risk leaving a moody Dave in charge at Sloane Farm to tidy up.

In the fourth race of the day I was working for a Warwickshire trainer who owned half shares in a three-mile chaser called Sober Judge that I had ridden at the course twice before, finishing second and third. To go one better I had to beat seven others including a fit-again Paul. He had arrived late to ride yet another Jolly-owned horse with the imaginative name of Totally Tropical that, because of a run of good form to match the jockey's, was likely to be short-priced favourite.

Despite sporting a few bruises from the previous day, Paul looked completely at peace with the world and annoyingly smug, winking at me as he searched for the peg with his colours hanging from it and getting a valet to fuss around him like royalty. Coincidently we were both in blue; mine light blue with white chevrons and his a much darker shade with tangerine sleeves, not the usual Jolly colours.

He briefly explained to those with puzzled faces that Tristan and Trudy's daughter Lorna had been gifted the horse as a twenty-first birthday present and that she was now the proud new owner, hence the change of colour scheme. I immediately thought about Gabrielle Southgate and her generous parents and hoped that one day I could do the same for Grace, a thought I held all the way to the parade ring and one I promised myself I'd rigorously pursue.

What went through my head after that was to become a blur as, despite his jumping pedigree, Sober Judge inexplicably slipped on landing over the third fence. One of his hind legs caught me somewhere around the ribcage as I parted company with him. Another horse, taking evasive action, swerved but still managed to kick me in the head as I desperately tried to roll myself into a ball in time-honoured fashion. With the noise of hooves fading fast I lay perfectly still for a few seconds, but upon trying instinctively to raise my head the sky above was spinning at a million miles an hour and a voice was giving me strict instructions to stay where I was.

Exactly how long I lay there I wasn't sure. The fence behind me was being taped off to be excluded on the second circuit and an angel from St John's was talking to me, telling me not to be in any kind of hurry to get up again. When at last I did move my limbs it was at a snail's pace and I felt for sure I was going to be sick. Gradually my senses returned and after waving away a stretcher bearer I rose to my knees, then stood upright and was helped onto the steps of an ambulance and made to sit while a nurse checked me over. It had happened before and the law of averages said it would happen again. I had signed up to the hazards of an occupation I loved a long time ago and nothing would convince me I was in the wrong job, even though mild concussion was bound to play havoc with my mind.

Assured by an official that my horse was unharmed, I felt better and as the blood began coursing through my veins once more the light-headedness rapidly left me and I was asking questions instead of answering them. The obvious one about whether I would ride again that day was met with negativity in general and a definite shake of his wise old head by the course doctor, who gave me a second check over inside a small annex next to the changing rooms. That meant Heath quickly having to engage a replacement jockey for the next race and Paul picking up a bonus ride at my expense, which reminded me of what had happened at Plumpton when he was otherwise engaged by the police. What goes around comes around, I thought, cursing my bad luck.

Fifteen minutes later I was left to count the cost in monetary terms as Paul prevailed to win by a short margin, to add to his convincing victory in the previous race. It would send the Coultard stable home happy and chalk another one up for Paul who was now a serious contender for champion jockey, a mere three wins behind leader Nathan Scully, though there was still a long way to go. A whole winter in fact; so far too early to predict.

With more rides I might have considered myself amongst those vying for the title, but in truth it had never been my goal; I never once thought like the machine you had to be to keep racking up the win-to-ride ratio. Dedicated and enthusiastic I might be; a workaholic I was not.

Not for the first time I looked at my helmet and body protector and said a brief prayer. Without them I might not be walking and talking and listening to Paul, who was becoming a tiny bit obnoxious though quite entertaining at the same time. Contrast that to how he had been two weeks ago and he had come full circle, winning more races than ever, having his gorgeous if adulterous wife back by his side and becoming popular with his peers instead of boring and unsociable. He raised a tumbler of water to me as if it was vintage wine and wished me a speedy recovery, then he was putting on the familiar green and white again ready for the last race and looking single-minded, pursuing a race day hat-trick and another notch on his well-used saddle. I found myself wishing him luck too and almost wanting him to succeed, which was unfair on the others now queuing to be weighed in. These were people I knew well, some who needed the luck that Paul seemed to have to compliment his undoubted ability, some who might secretly be modelling themselves on the likes of him and Nathan and maybe even me. And those much younger than the three of us who might or might not make the grade in years to come.

In the doctor's opinion it was unwise for me to drive so I accepted Heath's offer of a lift back to the Cotswolds. On the way back he poked fun at Dominic for going shopping when he ought to have been checking out the opposition out on the track.

'Felicity knows she won't get me within a mile of Debenhams,' he said, scoffing a little. 'And anyway she does most of hers on line now like the rest of the nation.'

'Progress,' I said, struggling for conversation, a faint headache still dogging me despite taking aspirin.

'I gather in Ireland breeders advertise horses on the internet, and buy and sell them too without seeing them in the flesh. Ruddy stupid if you ask me but enough said about the Irish.'

'Madness,' I agreed.

'There's something similar in America because of the long distances between buyers and sellers, but the bids are conditional upon the buyer examining the horse before the money is finally handed over.'

'Still, risky and open to abuse.'

'Quite,' Heath concurred. 'It'll never happen here, hopefully.'

'Perish the thought,' I said for good measure.

We were little more than ten minutes into the return journey. My eyes felt heavy and my brain numb. Heath recognised the signs and tried keeping me awake with racing chat, occasionally asking me questions that I struggled to find answers to. When he moved on to the subject of my father and his recent troubles I told him things appeared to be resolving themselves, not entirely satisfactorily I added, but edging slowly in the right direction. I was drawn to ask him his opinion of Anthony Thompson, letting him know of his sudden disappearance though not the reason behind it.

Heath, a man in his late forties and with a wealth of equine knowledge, was one of several trainers who had heard via sources that the vet was unreliable and had therefore employed another vet from further afield to look after his string of horses. 'When word like that gets around you sit up and take notice because owners continually worry about the welfare of the horses they have invested in. They don't like to think their precious beasts are missing out on the best treatment available,' he said by way of explanation, without appearing to condemn the vet for being the target of rumours.

'From what I know, Curtis Fielding was the man laying the poison after having some dealings with Anthony that didn't run smoothly and causing the two of them to fall out,' I responded, my head still at the mercy of a very light but persistent hammer.

Heath thought back. 'Curtis certainly knew a lot of people in racing and could well have been responsible. But Anthony didn't help himself with his irrational behaviour at the time which included some pretty bad language as I recall.'

'Bad language? Irrational behaviour?' I repeated.

'Probably due to frustration at the thought of losing business more than anything else, though I always found him to be slightly weird, certainly not the easiest person in the world to talk to,' Heath replied.

'So a man capable of anything, would you say?'

'Depends what you mean.'

'Breaking the law to get back at somebody maybe?'

He took in what I said and made certain assumptions. 'Has that got something to do with him going missing, Sam? What the hell is he supposed to have done?'

I gave no answer, only a look that might have hinted he was on the right track.

'Some of my lads used to say he was a nuisance when he came into the yard,' he said. 'A real pest when it came to asking about certain horses and how well they looked in training. If ever he asked me I would just humour him a bit and make sure he didn't try to overcharge me for services rendered like he'd done before.'

'Did you think he might be trying to gain inside info and then betting on your horses when they raced?'

'The thought occurred, yes,' he nodded. 'Everybody's after an edge. As a jockey you must know that. It's not a very professional thing to do in Anthony's job, but he wouldn't be breaking any laws by hunting out snippets that he believed would give him an advantage. I would never have dispensed with him for something like that. If I'm honest I ought to be flattered that he should have such faith in my horses.'

By way of thanking him for being so candid I told him in confidence that Anthony might have some sort of addiction to gambling and that he was wanted by the police for questioning. He didn't flicker an eyelid as far as I could tell. Some trainers never gave their innermost thoughts away and Heath was no exception. Additionally I then thanked him for keeping me awake with conversation which made his day, because usually he was accused of sending people to sleep or boring them senseless. I only hoped he wouldn't ask me to repeat anything he'd said that was of any importance. The filing system in my head was temporarily suspended.

24

Falls in racing are a painful inconvenience. No matter how well prepared and protected you are, every jockey in the sport knows their next fall could be their last. Even if you feel one day that you will recover from a particularly bad fall and be fit to ride again, it might never happen. This time I knew my aching body would mend quickly as per usual and my head had already cleared by the time Heath dropped me off in Stroud. Pessimistic thoughts I did not need, but they materialised sometimes when you least expected them to and today was one of those days.

I lingered for a long time in a remedial hot shower, put on clean clothes and caught up with Tamara who had decided to stay over in London, having not fully sorted out her problems. After playing down the extent of my racing injuries she passed some remark about me living far too dangerously out on the track and bemoaned the fact she couldn't nurse me as she had done after somebody had taken a swipe at my ribs. It seemed poignant to confirm to her now that Bruce Fielding had been responsible for that, and following a pause she swore and then used a further period of silence to show me her displeasure.

With less than perfect timing my father arrived, phone in hand and with a troubled look on his face. He had already been briefed on my fall and my temporary lack of transport but his expression bore no relation to either and for sure it had nothing to do with him getting to me later than planned.

'What's wrong? Do we have a problem?' I asked him.

'It's Lavender and that wayward son of hers,' he said, puffing out his cheeks.

'What about them? Has Anthony showed up?'

He waved his phone by way of a partial explanation and nodded. 'As soon as I left to come here by the sound of it. He must have been watching and waiting, itching to get her on her own.'

'So he's with her now at the house?'

He shook his head and fiddled with the phone before putting it away in a trouser pocket. 'He was there, but she says he's left again, he came to collect some things.'

'What things, did she say?'

'Clothes and belongings I assume, she wasn't sure.'

'So where has he gone now, does she know what he's planning to do?'

Like somebody swatting a summer swarm of midges he looked at me exasperated. 'I don't know, she asked but he wouldn't tell her. He just said he had things to do and people to see.'

'Things? People?' I repeated.

He ignored me. 'We must get back over there and quick. No telling what state she'll be in. I didn't want to leave her on her own but she insisted I come. She's been muttering a lot to herself ever since Anthony made himself scarce. I can't imagine what's going on in his head and what's behind his insane behaviour.'

I still didn't inform him of my suspicions and after stretching his imagination he did his own speculating.

'This has Curtis Fielding written all over it,' he pontificated. 'The slimy git sat there in his house more or less saying Anthony was lying about their business dealings and making out he was pulling the wool over his mother's eyes by letting her think he was some kind of angel. That's the depth to which Fielding will go to make people think he never does anything wrong.'

I listened and made noises that let him think everything he was saying was true but there was no gloating from him, only an impatient glance at his watch and a reminder that Lavender ought not to be left alone.

When I should have been switching my brain to standby mode I was now heading back to Castle Moat Lodge with Father at the wheel staring out every red light. I sat beside him praying for safe passage rather as I did subconsciously every time I climbed on a horse. And never before had I wanted a journey to end so much, albeit that my father was normally a driver who left nothing to chance despite a 'need for speed' obsession when he was younger.

We found Lavender in a dither, somewhere between confusion at her son's irrational behaviour and her long-held belief that he was the perfect example of the male species. Straight away I usurped Father and asked her if she had any idea where Anthony was now. She sighed heavily and said no.

'I couldn't get much sense out of him. He said I shouldn't worry, that everything would be taken care of. He said he would speak to the police when he was good and ready but he had things to do first, whatever that meant.'

For once the hair that was usually neatly lacquered into place was hanging loose. She kept sweeping it away from her pale, colourless face only for it to end up back where it started much to her obvious annoyance. I had made her sit but she kept fidgeting like a restless child and when she stood again and began pacing around her lounge I knew there was no point in trying to get her to settle in one place. But I needed answers, so I began to interrogate her, mindful of the delicacy of her situation and the thin line I had almost crossed previously.

'How would you describe Anthony's mood, especially at the time that he left you?'

Peering at me through strands of hair and still pacing up and down she thought hard about it and shrugged.

270

'If anything he seemed to be in a world of his own, going on and on about things being put right and telling me I mustn't fret. He said he didn't have much time and pleaded with me not to tell anyone I'd seen him. I'm afraid I've let him down in that respect but I just didn't know who to turn to.'

'You did the right thing,' Father told her. 'We're here to help and Anthony needs to know he can trust us.'

I didn't totally agree with that, and judging from Lavender's reaction I think she still harboured doubts about me where Anthony was concerned. It made my next question even harder for me to ask.

'Did he mention me or my father at all during the time he was here?'

She shook her head at once and asked, puzzled, 'No, why should he?' To which I offered no reply.

Moving on I asked her about the things he had supposedly come to collect from the house. She stared straight back in my direction and looked pretty clueless.

'He never said what and I didn't ask. He did leave with a large holdall that he kept at the back of his wardrobe but what was in it I couldn't tell you,' she said impassively.

'So he went to his room to get the holdall and anything else he needed?'

'Yes.'

'So, clothes perhaps would you say?'

'Quite possibly. I'm not sure. I didn't like to ask him.'

'So just whatever it was from his room, is that it?'

Lavender started to get agitated. 'I think so, yes ... oh and whatever it was he went looking for in the cellar.'

'The cellar?' I repeated.

She looked at me as though I was hard of hearing and suddenly stopped pacing. Father too seemed to be getting exasperated with me.

'What do you keep in the cellar?' I asked regardless.

TOM BUTLER

'Sam, what does it matter what's kept down there?' Father intervened.

I ignored him and waited for Lavender to answer.

'Lots of things. Anthony called it his den when he was younger. He and his father used to spend hours down there. I don't go down there myself, too many spiders for me I'm afraid.'

Summoning up a paltry, sympathetic smile I asked her if I could take a look, which drew disapproval from Father. 'Sam,' he admonished me. 'Is that really necessary?'

'Just a quick look, it might be important.'

Lavender didn't raise an objection. 'I don't see why not.'

'Perhaps we could all go down,' I said, suddenly sounding a little like a child who was ever so slightly scared.

Father shook his head, still bemused by my request. 'Bloody hell son, you do pick your moments.'

I shrugged his conjecture away and waited for Lavender to lead the way after having to search for and find the correct bunch of keys. The cellar, once we had negotiated the well-lit steps opened up into a huge room that had plenty of cobwebs and no doubt as many memories.

There were odd bits of furniture scattered about and an old-fashioned wooden school desk, behind which was a large, mostly empty bookcase and a modern-looking filing cabinet. Over on one side, running the whole length of the wall, was a purpose-built platform containing some disconnected Scalextric track and associated accessories including bridges, crash barriers and a canopied grandstand. Other toys of varying descriptions were strewn about in boxes and on the floor, and fixed to the wall furthest from the steps was a large, but not very deep, locked wooden cabinet.

'What's kept in there?' I asked Lavender who seemed to be on spider alert and looking nervous.

She muttered her reply as though it meant revealing a family secret.

272

'It's where Henry kept his collection of guns. He always kept it locked. I've no idea what's in there now.'

Father looked at me and I looked back, simultaneously pretending the discovery of a gun cabinet in a cellar room was an everyday occurrence. Lavender saw no great significance in it despite the lack of decibels in her voice, and wasn't even focusing on the cabinet as she took a look around, as if reacquainting herself with things she hadn't seen for some time.

'Do you have a key to the cabinet? Is it on the same bunch you used to get us in here?' I asked.

'Yes, there should be a key for everything on here, just let me find the right one,' she replied, holding them up close and straining her eyes.

Whilst she deliberated I got much closer to the cabinet and noticed fresh fingermarks around the doors where a thin layer of dust had been disturbed. As I did so Father inched over towards me. With Lavender preoccupied he nudged me and in a whisper asked me what I was thinking.

'I'm thinking Anthony didn't come down here earlier to pick up his favourite teddy bear. Let's hope I'm wrong.'

There was no time to gauge his reaction as Lavender was now passing me what she believed to be the key to the cabinet before returning to the spot she seemed most comfortable with, which was only a short stride from the bottom step. I was ultra-careful in unlocking the cabinet and eased open both doors with growing apprehension.

In days gone by I imagined the purpose-built container held an arsenal of weapons, but all that remained now was an old, sorry-looking air rifle with heavily scratched butt and rusted barrel. Next to it lay a half-used open box of pellets. There were also some oddments that I took to be spare gun parts and, worryingly, several shotgun cartridges that were obviously unused. More worryingly for me there were ominous spaces in the middle of the cabinet where I assumed shotguns could be stowed out of harm's way and lots of empty compartments for the storage of ammunition. Pinned to the back of the cabinet was a dog-eared owner's manual clearly showing make and model. It read, 'Winchester 23 Magnum 12 Bore'. My heart skipped a beat.

Lavender, standing quite some way from us, did a quick tour of the inside of the cabinet with her unsurprised eyes and for no reason other than nostalgia started to reminisce.

'We used to be plagued with crows and starlings here and Henry hated them. They would decimate his vegetables if he didn't either shoot them or fire a few shots to scare them away. Sometimes he would sit in his shed and wait for them to come, and very often Anthony would sit there with him. His father got him that air rifle and he used to be quite a good shot, taking great pride in showing me the remains of the birds he had killed. Not many birds venture into the gardens now because of the cats but Henry had an allergy so he would never have allowed me to keep them then.'

I couldn't help but fear the worst. Father too wore a worried frown.

'Think back to earlier,' I looked across at Lavender. 'Did Anthony emerge from the cellar carrying anything? He must have come down here for something. Think hard.'

She shrugged and bit on her lower lip. 'The holdall. The one I told you about which he kept in his room.'

'So he took it down to the cellar with him and had it with him when he left?'

'Yes.'

'We're talking about a big holdall, not some small overnight bag, right?'

She nodded. 'It was the one he used to carry all his cricket gear in when he used to play. It had built-in wheels because it used to be too heavy sometimes to lift. It was threadbare and battered but was still usable.'

Still a tired-looking Lavender had no idea what I or my father were thinking. Although deeply concerned for her son's welfare she hadn't made any connection between the holdall and what might or might not have been kept in the cabinet. And though Anthony was in effect a fugitive running from the police, I could tell she was of a mind that there was some rational explanation for his behaviour and he would eventually sort things out, albeit in his own time.

I relocked the cabinet without touching any of its contents and passed the bunch of keys to Father to give to Lavender. He did so with a forced smile and she took it as a cue to turn tail and take to the steps. We followed on, waited for her to lock the cellar door and accepted her offer of tea and cake, though the slice I had was little more than a sliver.

The time was now approaching ten o'clock; it had been over two hours since Anthony had left Castle Moat Lodge. At my suggestion Lavender called his number again but once more found it unobtainable. And though not wanting to bombard her with more questions I did ask her if there was anywhere else apart from his surgery and home that Anthony might stay. Friends, family etc.

She wracked her brain and drew a blank. 'Not that I can think of,' she admitted. 'But in times of need he has been known to sleep in his car or book into a hotel.'

I thought about his Audi estate car. I assumed the police were on the look-out for it so Anthony was unlikely to park it in a lay-by overnight as that might draw attention to it. More likely, I thought, was the hotel option. He could easily book into one where no one would know who he was and conceal his car relatively well alongside others.

Although she seemed less on edge and valued our growing concern for her son, Lavender hadn't sat down since I had arrived, even drinking her tea and nibbling fruit cake whilst standing up and occasionally going on a pretty pointless walkabout, stopping to say something of next to no relevance as if hiding from reality. The melodic ring tone of my phone broke everybody's train of thought. Inevitably it was Dominic wanting to know how I was feeling and whether I felt fit enough to ride a race for him at Uttoxeter the next day. Heath had reported my fall to him, saying it had been a particularly bad one, adding that for sure I would be sore for a few days and casting some doubts over my availability for the next day's meeting.

I had almost forgotten about my physical state but told him categorically I wouldn't let him down, though I would be needing transport to get there with my car stranded in Stratford.

'You're a glutton for punishment,' Father commented after overhearing me.

'The show must go on,' I replied with profundity. 'I have a high pain threshold.'

Lavender, discovering a smile from somewhere, asked me if I was sure I wouldn't like some more fruit cake as if it had medical powers as well as tasting quite good. 'I made this for a charity do on Saturday but I'm afraid your father and I decided to sample it, and before we knew it was half gone. I hadn't felt like eating before then what with worrying about Anthony,' she suddenly sighed. 'Oh Sam, what do you think he's playing at? Do you really think he could be in some kind of bother?'

'It's lovely cake,' I complimented her, avoiding an answer.

Deep down I sensed she knew Anthony wouldn't walk in any time soon wearing a halo above his head and a reassuringly broad smile. Our efforts to protect her from the truth had probably worked too well and I wondered what she would think of us later on. Indulging her with the cake was fine for now, but when the real facts emerged I feared there would be no such sweet offerings to help soothe the pain and heartache away.

'Tomorrow I'll make another,' she said, planning ahead. Father, only half paying attention, smiled and muttered something about a jam sandwich. She pretended she hadn't heard him.

I was facing another night on Lavender's surprisingly comfortable couch, together with another early start, and my body was beginning to feel somewhat fragile. But the urgent rest I needed was going to be denied me as my phone sounded again. A remotely familiar voice that evoked nothing but trouble requested my presence.

A distressed-sounding Curtis Fielding took a long time to say what I hadn't wanted to hear, but I had no reason to believe he was anything other than genuine. Although feeling infinitely weak I knew I had no other course of action. Putting on a façade I asked to borrow Father's car keys, which alerted his and Lavender's inquiring eyes.

'Something I must do. Don't wait up for me,' I said.

It was nearly half past ten and they both looked mystified. But thankfully neither of them made it difficult for me to leave.

25

Not even approaching the most notorious of fences in heavy ground made my heart pound quite as much as when I drove on relatively quiet roads towards Cheltenham. Many thoughts interacted inside my head, and the most powerful one of all was asking me whether I should be going it alone in view of Paul Eddison's Swindon experience. But a desperate sounding Curtis Fielding had told me to come on my own or I would have the blood of someone precious to him on my hands. It was the ultimate Catch-22.

It helped that I had the layout of his house stored in my mind. I consciously parked Father's Toyota in an adjoining street approximately a hundred metres from the turn in to the barn conversion development. There seemed nothing unusual upon entering the block-paved road except that, when I got closer, Fielding's abode at the far end was in complete darkness, in contrast to the others I had already passed. The red Porsche and silver Mercedes were parked where they were last time and the only noticeable noise was a dog barking in the distance from across a farmer's field at the rear of the house. When it stopped there was barely a sound except for a faint drone of traffic coming, I assumed, from the Cheltenham ring road.

As instructed by Fielding an hour before I shakily rang his mobile number and let it sound out three times before cancelling. He had been insistent I come alone and tell no one where I was going, to stand away from the house so that I could be seen and to wait outside until invited in. Facing the front door which was shadowed in half moonlight

I felt more vulnerable than at any time in my life, the words 'sitting duck' coming frighteningly to mind. When I expected something to happen nothing did. In panic I checked my phone to ensure I had dialled correctly. The temptation to go to the door and listen was translated into forward movement which at least confirmed that all the front windows of the property were obliterated by curtains, the downstairs ones probably heavy-duty drapes.

As if by remote control the front door now slowly opened, which made me find reverse gear and back off. Whoever had released the catch had no intention of showing themselves and now my dilemma was clear. Be brave and go in or stay out, retreat and call for help. The consequences for somebody if Fielding wasn't lying to me were dire if I did turn tail and run. And for me to go in not knowing what might confront me was bordering on madness.

In racing you take your chances when you genuinely believe it's the right move to make. Other times you just sit tight and let the horse take the strain. Then there are those occasions when you play safe and later wish you had been a little bit bolder. With pure gut feeling and instinct I made my move, terrified eyes fighting to find something to focus on as I entered the hallway.

I knew that the large lounge where Father and I had met the owner and Neville Truman had double doors to the left and the spiral staircase was directly opposite on the right, with the luxurious state-of-the-art kitchen diner straight ahead. The doors to the lounge were partially open. It was then that I decided to call out. I went unanswered but there was the merest hint of movement coming from inside. That's when I drew parallel with the doors and peered in.

The room I remembered was approximately thirty feet by twenty feet with a massive open fireplace to the left, over which there was a huge plasma screen television. There was artwork on the three remaining walls with one large painting dominating the wall to the right, along which there was bespoke carved wooden furniture consisting of two small bookcases and a glass-fronted display cabinet.

From where I stood I could tell the nearest of the three leather sofas was unoccupied, but not so the others. To my right I could make out the shape of a woman I assumed to be Caroline Fielding lying across the whole length of the second sofa and not too far away in the middle of the room someone sat bolt upright on the third. The woman wasn't moving at all, but the other person was and he was breathing unevenly.

From the shape of the head and shoulders I knew it was Curtis Fielding. When I ventured up close to him, despite the darkness I saw the whites of his eyes and the fear in them. I also saw that they were looking beyond me. In an instant I felt cold and knew what they were trying to tell me. But it was too late and the back of my skull, still not totally recovered from the kick by a horse, was inconvenienced further by something heavy, a blow that brought back the stars I had seen at Stratford and sent me, via my knees, to the hard wooden floor.

The impulse to roll myself into a ball and stay there until pounding hooves had gone was immense, but it would have meant folding my body around a solid wood coffee table that I had landed beside. There was suddenly subdued light from a table lamp and I managed to turn my head enough to see the shoeless feet of my attacker.

'Glad you could make it, Sam,' an echoing voice said. 'Now the party can really begin.'

I twisted my torso and slouched my back against the sofa Fielding was sitting on, my left shoulder brushing against his right leg. I could now see there was a trickle of blood on his forehead and blood stains on his pale-blue polo shirt. More significantly he had a necktie pulled tightly around his mouth and knotted at the side. The look he gave me was born out of both sheer terror and deepest concern for his wife, who for all I knew was already dead. I strained my eyes in her direction and she certainly looked bereft of life. She appeared to be wearing nothing more than a pink towelling bathrobe with flower motifs on the pockets, and if she was still alive she certainly wasn't moving. Then I glanced up at Anthony Thompson. He was cradling a double-barrelled shotgun under one arm as if it was suddenly his one and only friend, and he stared back at me, his mouth on the brink of a sickly smile.

'Curtis says he didn't shop me to the police so it must have been you, Sam,' he said eventually. 'Why did you want to go and do something like that? You're just a fucking jockey for Christ's sake and your old man's a sad bastard who likes fishing and old cars. Perhaps I should have got him over here as well. Maybe I will.'

He certainly fitted the profile of a man on the run from the law, decked out all in black with the zip of his flak jacket pulled high and a woollen hat concealing his hair.

'My father's done nothing to hurt you,' I told him, my head clearing. 'And I genuinely believe the police would have come looking for you with or without my help. It was just a matter of time.'

Anthony nervously fingered around the twin triggers of the shotgun. Fielding nudged my shoulder with his knee as if to tell me not to antagonise the man further but it was plain to see he was already wound up.

'You're so bloody cocksure of yourself, Woodall. I knew when you came to the surgery you were out to get me. And don't pretend that dear old Daddy hasn't got designs on my mother just so that he can get his hands on her prized asset,' he snapped. 'You're both as bad as each other. Why couldn't you have left us alone?'

There were more panicky leg movements from Fielding and fidgeting from Anthony. Then a murmur that appeared to come from where Fielding's wife was lying.

'Don't worry,' Anthony said, not even bothering to look at her. 'She's only asleep but one more jab of the needle and I wouldn't rate her chances of ever waking up again.'

With that Fielding became frantic, virtually screaming though the sounds were obviously muffled. Although his limbs weren't restrained in any way I noted his movements were slow and cumbersome. It was as though his strength had been sapped. But he still tried to stand up, before Anthony strode forward and used the business end of the gun to push hard against his chest making him slump backwards.

I fought my impulse to grab Anthony by his legs, knowing that if the gun went off Fielding would be blown to bits. All I could do was stay where I was and pray Fielding didn't try to stand up again. Sensibly he didn't and Anthony went back to where he stood before. I half expected him to beat his chest like King Kong, but he just manoeuvred the shotgun so that it fitted snug under his armpit again and educated me with a lecture on the merits of anaesthesia.

'I gave his missus a good dose so she wouldn't go round screaming the place down, but he only got a pinprick, just enough to make him drowsy and easy to handle. Horses are different of course. You can never be a hundred per cent sure you've used the right amount,' he expanded. 'Some come out of it quickly and before you want them to, but others take a lot longer. I treated a horse once that took twice the prescribed time to recover from the anaesthetic and I was sweating I can tell you. That bloody horse was from a top-notch stud and easily worth a million. Imagine what would have been said if that had gone wrong.'

The irrelevance of the tale he was telling gave me time to think, steering me towards an attempt to both distract him with flattery and to stall him by engaging him in conversation.

'I think we have one great thing in common, Anthony,' I said, trying not to make my ulterior motive obvious.

After a pause he humoured me. 'Oh yes? So enlighten me.'

'Our love of horses and horse racing, of course. The noble sport of kings.'

He looked back at me blankly and shrugged.

I soldiered on. 'And it's dedicated people like you who make a jockey's job so much easier. Not having a horse in prime condition to race is rather like asking a Formula One driver to compete in a grand prix with three wheels instead of four. I have nothing but admiration for your profession. We should be on the same side, not fighting each other.'

There was no arguing from him but he saw right through me. 'Clever Sam. Pay me a few compliments, gain my confidence, hope I drop my guard. You are so transparent. You and I have nothing in common.'

Anthony widened his stance a little and tried making himself look even more fearsome.

I reverted to persuasion. 'All I was trying to do was talk you out of something you'll regret for the rest of your life. Think about what it will do to your mother, she's already beside herself with worry.'

'And whose fault's that?' he raised his voice. 'You had to go poking around, why couldn't you just leave it alone?'

'Because I felt I had no choice. My father could have died in the fire at his lock-up,' I snapped back, riskily. 'As I've already said it was only a matter of time before the police caught up with you. I've no idea if what I provided them with has had any bearing on them coming after you.'

I could barely see his eyes through the dimness of the room but his body language wasn't good given the predicament he had me in. There was nothing but contempt for me in his coarse reply.

'You're an interfering bastard, Sam Woodall, and I wish your old man had ended up as toast. At least that would have evened things up and perhaps you'd have understood.'

'Understood what?' I asked.

'Nothing,' he said abruptly, more agitation showing.

I guessed what he was thinking and took a gamble. One I might regret.

'Henry Thompson would not have liked to see you like this, Anthony. He would have been shocked by your behaviour. Why don't you put the gun down and save face? That way the law won't be so hard on you.'

He was not for giving up. Mentioning his father had been a grave mistake. Fielding sensed it too, and I could tell he was about to find the strength from somewhere to do something foolish. But I beat him to it.

It perhaps helped that I was trained to have quick reflexes when parting company with a horse, which meant launching myself in a forward, slightly sideways direction. With still aching limbs I was able to surprise Anthony and knock him off balance. Trouble was, in spite of my speed and agility, Anthony still managed to fire off an almighty deafening shot from the ageing shotgun and then another immediately afterwards. Although I knew for sure they had missed me, I had no idea who or what had been hit. For sure there had been an explosion somewhere directly behind me, and the combined smell of smoke and dust was almost overwhelming, making me feel physically sick. I thought the ringing in my ears would never stop.

Thankfully an unscathed Curtis Fielding, having summoned up what little strength he had left, was now alongside me minus the necktie, shouting and cursing. He helped me win the battle as we pooled our resources to both sit on the man thrashing about beneath us.

'The gun,' I shouted to Fielding, not even sure he could hear me.

'I have it,' he shouted back.

'No you don't,' corrected Anthony who had obtained superhuman strength from somewhere. He kicked out at both of us in a frantic attempt to break free.

'Bollocks!' exclaimed Fielding in blind panic.

'You bastards,' Anthony retorted, the hat he had been wearing slipping from his head. Suddenly Fielding yelled out in agony as a flailing Anthony managed to stamp down hard on his right hand which he had tried to grab the gun with. The same expletive ripped from Fielding's mouth several times and all of a sudden two against one didn't look such favourable odds. Anthony seemed to have mustered the strength of two men.

My knowledge of weaponry was practically nil so, although both barrels of the shotgun had been discharged, I just wasn't sure exactly how much danger I was in should Anthony triumph in his frenzied attempts to get it back. I sensed for sure he had spare cartridges in the pockets of his jacket and would have no hesitation in reloading and using them. So in sheer desperation I tried to tear his hands away from it, which meant pulling so hard on the fingers of one of them I felt sure they would snap in two. They were practically bent double and I was still applying pressure. Not even when wrenching hard on a horse's rein had I ever used such brute force. But slowly it seemed to work.

He yelled out in pain and voiced loud obscenities. But eventually and reluctantly he let go and, with a huge sigh of relief, whilst I continued grappling with Anthony a bloodied Fielding got a good grip of the shotgun with both of his hands. That in itself then became a major worry as he pulled it free and pointed its menacing twin barrels towards Anthony who just happened to be partially concealed by me. Unloaded or not, it made him look an immediate threat to life and limb.

'You bastard Thompson, look what you've done to my wife,' Fielding raged, staggering about and waving the gun dangerously inches from my face. 'Give me one good reason why I don't shoot you dead.'

I could think of a hundred and one reasons but I was too preoccupied with restraining Anthony to air them.

Fortunately for all of us, at that precise moment Caroline Fielding moaned, only faintly but loud enough to grab her husband's attention. The gun was still pointing at me but Fielding was looking over at his wife, not sure exactly what to do.

'Make the gun safe for God's sake,' I instructed him through gritted teeth. 'Go on, make sure it's disarmed. Do it,' I urged.

'But we have him where we want him,' he argued.

I began to rant. 'The gun, break it in two and check it, then put it somewhere safe before it kills all of us. Do it!' I repeated.

He obeyed me but only in slow motion which didn't help my already inflated blood pressure. As I had hoped, it was empty, but I had no time to sigh with relief as Anthony had gained himself both second and third winds and was near to escaping my grasp.

I could not now rely upon Curtis Fielding's help. He was on his knees cradling his wife's head in his hands, trying to get her to understand what he was saying and to respond. Although we were relatively well matched in weight and overall size, Anthony had one great advantage over me – his insane determination not to have me hand him over to someone who had the means to lock him away for a very long time. That in itself was too powerful for me to counteract. With his hair sticking out in all directions and saliva around his mouth he punched and kicked out, looking forlornly over at the gun, no longer easily accessible where it lay once Fielding had decided to drop it. I instinctively put myself between the two and was ready to meet blows with blows if I had to. No way could I allow him to rearm himself. I think if he had been allowed to do that he would have killed me for sure and anyone else who got in his way. And he would have enjoyed it. For him there was no going back, no compromises.

CAUGHT

He was nearest the door and therefore an escape route, and although the ideal scenario would have been to overpower him and make a citizen's arrest, I knew from the dark madness in his hate-filled eyes it was never going to happen. With his options cut right down he swore again, turned tail and fled out into the night like a fox hearing the call of the hounds. Once he was gone there was an eerie silence, broken only by Caroline's irregular breathing that told me what to do next.

The emergency services took brief details over the phone and I told them to hurry. There was a knock on the open door from an elderly neighbour disturbed by the gunshot who seemed to be shaking as much as me as I met him in the unlit hallway. I told him everything was under control although he would be disturbed again very shortly. More noise, blue flashing lights, comings and goings, etc. His inquisitive eyes looked back at me and he asked if it was anything to do with the man he had seen running away from the houses a couple of minutes ago.

Probably, I answered him, suggesting he go back indoors and to expect a visit from the police at some stage. He seemed strangely excited at that prospect and kept trying to look beyond me to gauge what on earth had happened. When he asked if somebody had been shot I ushered him away and told him he'd read all about it in the newspapers. He looked a little put out by my evasive answer but then trolled off back to his house to await developments and hopefully a knock on his door.

Returning to the lounge where Fielding was now becoming frantic in his efforts to revive his wife I searched feverishly for a light switch. A large ornate chandelier illuminated the central part of the room and my eyes were drawn to something above the elaborate stone mantelpiece of an expensive-looking feature fireplace. Well, not so much something as nothing at all. A hole about three inches in diameter had been punched through inch-thick plasterboard right the way to solid brickwork. It had missed the giant television screen by centimetres and I was amazed that the force of the blast at such short range hadn't caused more damage. Easily repairable but nevertheless a sickening sight given how close the gun had been to both Fielding and me when it went off.

There were more pressing matters, not least the welfare of Caroline Fielding whose ordeal had perhaps been so much worse and might still prove life-threatening. Her eyes were heavily glazed over as if she was in a hypnotic trance, but at least there was significant movement in her limbs. Curtis said he was sure she could hear him but just couldn't snap out of whatever she was under enough to render a reply.

'Just keep trying, keep talking to her, someone will be here to look after her soon,' I encouraged him.

He took the time to thank me and said I had probably saved her life and possibly his too.

'I did what had to be done. Hopefully Anthony will be caught quickly and we can all rest in our beds a lot easier.'

Fielding raised his head a little and sighed.

'I never set the police on him, Sam, though I could have done some time ago,' he informed me, no doubt wishing he had.

'For what exactly?' I asked him.

'Fraud, well a kind of fraud.'

'What do you mean?'

He seemed reluctant to tell me, then suddenly did so. 'I found out he was treating horses illegally, using equipment he had invented and boasting about it when all along it hadn't been approved for use.'

'The heat wrap, right?'

'Yes,' he sighed again. 'He got the idea from a similar one in America that he saw in use when he went over there.

He duped me by saying he had perfected an even better system and I foolishly lent him the money he said he needed to register a patent for it, on the understanding I'd get a healthy return on my money. Little did I know that he then gambled all the money away just like he did with the loan for the building work and that bloody pool he had installed.'

'So what stopped you from exposing him after you got all your money back?'

The question grated on him and he went quiet, turning his attention back to his wife who looked like she was beginning to stir, though her eyes still looked the same as before. I decided not to press him. 'Another time then.'

He nodded resignedly and tightened his grip on Caroline's hand.

'When are they coming?' he asked. 'Why are they taking so long?'

'Soon,' I said, sharing his impatience. 'They will be here soon.'

I left everything as it was and just sat and waited. The only thing I did was answer a call from Father who naturally wanted to know what was going on. I told him enough to stop him worrying but said nothing about Anthony for fear he would tell Lavender, other than to remind him he was still at large and not to be meddled with. Poor misguided Lavender would learn of her son's atrocities soon I thought, but not now. I imagined it might break her in two rather like the discarded shotgun I now sat staring at. The notion made my bruised body shiver. All I wanted was sleep but I had a feeling I wouldn't get much of it.

The sound of a siren grew louder and another coming from the opposite direction only stopped when I clearly heard the screech of tyres outside and the subsequent hurrying footsteps. It had been a virtual dead heat between the police and the paramedics, and that made me smile inwardly. The latter dealt with Caroline after establishing what had happened to her from her animated husband whilst I briefed the uniformed officer who relayed some of what I said over his radio, activating an immediate search for Anthony Thompson and even scrambling a police helicopter in an attempt to trace his whereabouts.

The neighbour up the road I assumed would be watching and waiting along with others who couldn't have failed to hear the late night commotion. The suburbs of Cheltenham rarely attracted such excitement. It would keep the locals busy for some time. Gossip-mongers would have a field day tomorrow.

More vehicles arrived in due course and after I had given my initial statement to the same policeman in his patrol car I went for a short walk, sat in the passenger seat of Father's car and shut my eyes. I opened them again to watch an ambulance drive past me with blue lights flashing but no siren sounding. I shut them again and subconsciously prayed. Unsurprisingly I fell asleep.

26

I was awoken by the sound of a policeman drumming his fingers on the windscreen at a quarter past one. He asked me if I was sure I didn't need hospital treatment, and when I said I didn't he checked that I was fit enough to drive, informing me that scene of crime officers were still working in the house and one of his colleagues would therefore secure the property and get the relevant keys back to the owner.

For all his faults and the bullyboy tactics that he had strenuously denied using on my father, I bore Curtis Fielding no real malice. Although I barely knew his wife I drove straight to Cheltenham General and located them in a side ward at A&E, finding Caroline now fully conscious and Curtis at her bedside mightily relieved. He had a piece of sticking plaster covering the area on his forehead where I had noted blood earlier and his right hand which Anthony had maliciously stamped on was heavily bandaged. The recovering Fieldings were both extremely happy to see me. Caroline shuffled and sat up straight, insisting she shake my hand as well as thanking me for being so brave.

She was quite a small lady with short dark hair that was turning grey and a pale complexion. If anything she looked older than her husband but I suppose I was not seeing her at her best, having just woken from an coma induced by somebody clearly no longer of sound mind. Only rarely could I remember seeing her out and about with Curtis, usually at race meetings or horse racing functions; she was not a person who stood out in a crowd or dressed to impress.

She even apologised to me for how she looked now. Although I didn't dare say it, I thought she looked a damned sight better than when I first saw her about three hours before when I seriously thought she might be dead. But for some good fortune and no little endeavour by her unlikely saviour she might well have ended up that way.

As quickly as she had sat up to greet me she was now back with head on pillow, her eyes looking heavy and her husband insisting she rest. He reluctantly told her he was going to leave her for a short while to chat with me. I think she was asleep as soon as we left the room and headed to where he had been told there was a drinks machine. We sat in a waiting area next to the vending machine sipping black coffee from plastic cups. A thoughtful Curtis Fielding seemed overly keen to talk.

'Pretty dire stuff this but it's just about palatable,' he said, holding his cup to his lips. 'Shouldn't complain, not after what we've all been through.'

'A nightmare comes to mind,' I replied, keeping my voice low.

He didn't seem to hear me. 'Thirty years we've been together, twenty-five of them married,' he carried on. 'We met at university and have been inseparable ever since. My son's even at the same uni in Durham studying medicine and my daughter's hoping to switch to there too after her gap year. She's travelling the world, last postcard we had was from China of all places, you wouldn't catch me going there but then kids today can go where they wish. There are no barriers.'

For a few seconds he sat looking into his cup and then sighed. 'I've been a fool, Sam, and that's not something I ever thought I'd hear myself say. As you get older you're supposed to get wiser but in my case I think the opposite applies. What's happened to Caroline is down solely to me and my stupidity.' He repeated the sigh, took a drink and tried to explain.

'I truly believed I could deal with things without them escalating as they have done. Even when I found Anthony at my door a few hours ago and saw the anger and hatred in his face I thought I could invite him in and talk him round to my way of thinking. But no. Within seconds he produced that infernal gun and said he was going to teach me a lesson I would never forget, and though I tried to reason with him I knew he had completely flipped. That's when he lashed out at me with the butt of the gun and stormed past me into the house and did what he did to my wife.'

'Frightening,' I said, struggling for words.

There were tears welling up in the corners of his eyes and the man who had a reputation for being as hard as nails suddenly looked both human and vulnerable.

'Hindsight is a wonderful thing,' he grimaced, regaining his composure.

'What I should have done is called Anthony's bluff a long time ago and simply reported him for what he'd done, instead of taking some of the blame for the predicament he found himself in. I had his mother bleating in one ear and Anthony painting me as the man who was trying to ruin him when he was doing it all by himself.'

'I don't fully understand,' I said in bemusement. 'What was the hold he had over you? What stopped you from turning him in?'

Fielding discarded his now empty cup and dropped his head as though in shame. He left it there and I had to listen hard to hear him.

'The first time I got wind that Anthony was a secretive gambler was in a casino in London about five years ago. He had only just split from a practice in Gloucester and had set himself up. He was the last person I was expecting to find propping up a blackjack table and leering at a pretty blonde croupier. He had a huge pile of chips and I assumed he was in credit. Although I tried to avoid him he saw me and he obviously saw who I was with, and that's when my problems began,' he paused. After a slow, exaggerated shake of his head he went on with his story. 'Problems isn't perhaps the best word to use because Anthony was very convincing and had a lot of bright ideas as well as interesting business propositions. What he needed was someone to invest in him and to my cost that person was me, seduced by the thought of having a stake in something that would make money and plenty of it. A partnership I honestly believed would work but one I now deeply regret. It proved nothing more than a foolish notion.'

'You mentioned being with someone at the casino,' I backtracked, needing him to fill in the blanks.

He raised his head and turned it towards me. 'Let's just say it wasn't Caroline and leave it at that,' he stared at me with pleading eyes. 'Some things happen in life that you later wish hadn't. I was a man on the wrong side of forty staying in the big city for a meeting and with a full wallet, if you know what I mean. Need I say more?'

'I get the picture,' I muttered back. 'No one will hear it from me.'

'Good, thanks Sam, it's appreciated,' he looked relieved.

For a man who wanted nothing to rock his marital boat I could see what a powerful hold Anthony would have over him. Whether he willingly helped the vet establish his business and branch out into other things or not it was still there in the background, giving Anthony the kind of insurance that was as watertight as any could be.

'So in effect Anthony blackmailed you?' I asked, wanting to move on.

'In a way yes,' he shrugged. 'I had no idea how addicted to gambling Anthony was, and he swore me to secrecy and somehow managed to keep it from his mother. Most of the money I loaned him to rebuild and extend the surgery was used for that, though I found out he was cutting corners with the builder and siphoning off money to fritter away on his addiction. Repayments into my bank were made for a few months and then stopped, and he also lied to me about the heat-wrap system he claimed would revolutionise the industry after I'd supplied him with more cash to invest in it. I later found out he'd never obtained a patent on it but was using it on his clients' horses, which could have seriously harmed them. That's when he took it upon himself to lose or destroy some of his customers' files to cover his tracks, and again he gave everybody the impression I'd arranged it as sour grapes after we fell out and he'd paid me back all monies owing to me.'

He stopped for breath and I asked him about Bruce.

'Lavender Thompson thinks you pulled the plug on Anthony because you needed as much money as possible to give to your half-brother. Was there any truth in that, in view of Bruce's involvement in what was happening at Sloane Farm?'

Curtis blew out his cheeks and was full of apologies for someone he clearly wasn't close to despite the blood ties.

'Bruce is an embarrassment to me, Sam. What he has done he's done on his own. What he did to you was out of order, he had got it into his head that it would help me and, yes, he wanted a share in my future plans for the caravan park. He thinks I still owe him and he can do as he pleases. Of course I'm somewhat obliged to look after him but he must understand he can't go round upsetting people as he does. He's not been back in the country long and he's made himself far too many enemies.'

Straight away I nodded. 'I had him in the frame for trying to poison Father's fish, attempting to break Dave Burrows' skull and the fire at the lock-up,' I told him.

He shook his head. 'That's not Bruce's style. He prefers to confront people head on and intimidate them. OK, so he got into your house uninvited and used a bit of muscle to get his message across and also tried to frame Paul Eddison, but generally I would never have thought he had it in him to physically hurt somebody and as for those other things they were completely out of the question.'

'He didn't have to confront Paul to wind him up,' I argued.

The older half-brother winced as I reminded him of it. 'Stealing a man's wife is something different altogether,' he said. 'Who knows how anyone might react to that. But Bruce did rather flaunt Paul's wife around like she was a trophy won in a contest. Paul didn't like that and he at least gave Bruce brown trousers in threatening him the way he did.'

I read his mind and wasn't tactless enough to pursue images of a shotgun whether it had been loaded or not. But I did bring up the name of Chief Superintendent Christopher Southgate, and waited.

It didn't grate on him as I expected, and he was quite philosophical about it.

'It's as well that I asked Christopher to intervene otherwise things might have gone too far,' he said, sounding particularly satisfied. 'All that was required was a proper threat from someone with the clout to deliver it and follow through if need be. I didn't see that as exceeding his authority and it certainly did the trick.'

I wanted to tell him about what I had witnessed between Southgate and Bruce at Haydock on Wednesday afternoon, and my subsequent meeting with the Chief Super in Cheltenham, and gauge his response, but I could see he was beginning to look weary as was I and I left it. There was still, however, a prickly question for him to answer relating to Neville Truman. This time his composure waned and he showed some frustration.

'Ever since I appointed him as my estate manager he's

overstepped the mark and done things without consulting me,' he confessed. 'The cow stampede I'm sure was down to him but he's strongly denied it and without proof there's not much I can do. I rent out land for grazing and the owner of the herd swears it was probably vandals who left gates open. Who am I to question it?'

On the subject of the attempt to poison the fish he seemed keen to sing from the same hymn sheet as Christopher Southgate and said his estate manager's story was perhaps hard to swallow but undeniably plausible. 'It was dark, there were no witnesses, confusion reigned. I've no reason to think Neville was committing any crime.'

I looked back at him disbelievingly and at least he granted me one concession. 'Look Sam, if the police prosecute Neville and he's found guilty I will make sure he never sets foot on my land again, is that fair?'

It seemed the best outcome and I was too tired to argue. He went quiet so I suggested he go back to his wife's bedside and I cleared my head to drive back to Lavender's to catch some sleep. Only three hours at the most I thought, but some small offering that might be enough to sustain me for later on.

Over early morning toast and stimulating coffee I briefly told Father what had happened at Curtis Fielding's house and his jaw dropped further than I thought was physically possible. With Lavender out of earshot upstairs stripping beds and waging war on the dust mites, Father listened and his anxiety for her grew. It was more apparent than ever that she had blanked out her son's misdemeanours, still expecting him to walk in, smile at her and tell her not to worry.

Then I told him that Anthony had set fire to the lock-up, stood back and waited for him to implode. Predictably the profanities came thick and fast. When they subsided he somehow suppressed his outrage and just sat looking incredulous, trying to understand the reason why.

'What did I do to him? I can't believe he would do such a thing.'

'Call it insane jealousy and leave it at that for now,' I said vaguely.

'But what have I ever done...'

'Later, I'll explain everything then,' I cut him short.

More bad language followed and as he stood up with fists clenched, his whole body shook. It was a scene I was used to of late but not what was needed now. Level-headedness was a must.

Reading my frustration he returned to the events of the previous night, focusing on the ferocity and evil intent Anthony had shown towards three innocent people which led him to one swift and indisputable conclusion.

'She has to be told, Sam,' he said with a resounding sigh. 'She simply can't hear it from anyone else and certainly not the police. Then there's the radio, TV and newspapers. We have to say something and soon. Now's as good a time as any.'

I could tell from the tone of his voice he wasn't offering to tell her and was looking for me to do it. But there wasn't much time as I had to be somewhere by nine if I was to get to Uttoxeter on time. For sure Dominic wouldn't be at all amused if I got to my pick-up point late.

'I'll need your car to get to Cirencester, so get Lavender to drive you to Sloane Farm and suggest she stays so she's not on her own. We can't rule out Anthony being a threat to her. In fact we can't rule anything out.'

'Will you speak to her first?' he asked coyly.

'I'll do it now,' I replied.

He threw me a tell-tale smile that had relief written all over it and wished me luck. Then re-immersing himself in the reality of what Anthony had done to him he gave it more agonising thought.

The upstairs cleaning had stopped momentarily and I found Lavender outside wandering the patio as she was prone to do, talking to three cats who bizarrely appeared to be listening to and understanding everything she was saying. They dispersed when they saw me and with time of the essence I didn't spare her feelings with sugar-coated words.

'Anthony's got himself into serious trouble,' I said warily, trying to look deep into her eyes. 'And I'm sorry to tell you he went to Curtis Fielding's house last night armed with a shotgun, one I suspect he took from that cabinet in the cellar. As a result Caroline Fielding ended up in hospital and the police have had to launch a full-scale man hunt.'

She already looked pale with worry but the news took every shred of colour from her face. She sensibly took to a nearby wrought-iron patio chair, sinking herself heavily onto it and making it scrape noisily against a moss-infested flagstone. It mattered not that there had been a recent shower of rain and the chair was wet. She slowly absorbed the information.

'Are you saying he shot her, Sam? Is she...'

'He injected her with a syringe, one of those meant to be used on horses.'

'Oh dear,' she exclaimed. 'So is she all right?'

'She's fine now, but it was still a crazy thing for him to do.'

The word 'crazy' immediately resonated with her as if it had switched on a light at the back of her brain.

'When Anthony's father died he went a bit that way,' she recollected. 'It was the shock you see, but six months later he was as right as rain. He's been under a lot of stress. I'm glad Caroline's all right, I bear the woman no malice at all. It was wrong what Anthony did. I shall be having strong words with him.'

She was talking as if in a trance and treating Anthony like a naughty schoolboy. But this was no playground prank.

'Your son threatened both Curtis Fielding and me with a loaded double-barrelled shotgun and I fear he would have killed us both if we hadn't prevented it,' I told her, my voice unequivocally edged with emotion.

She repeated the words 'Oh dear' several times and she wouldn't look at me, as though she felt she was in some way to blame. 'I never thought about the guns, they were old and when Henry died I just never bothered with them, in fact I rarely ever go down to that cellar, I hate spiders you see, always have done.'

'Well Anthony knew they were there for sure. Do you know exactly how many guns were kept in there?'

Lavender didn't hesitate with her answer. 'Three I believe, the one you described and two air rifles.'

'That's not good,' I panicked. 'There's every chance he's out there somewhere and he's armed.'

'Oh dear,' she said again matter-of-factly. 'If only I could talk to him I'm sure I could help clear this up. Anthony's such a gentle person normally, he's really quite shy as a rule.'

I gave her a reality check. 'I think he's pretty unapproachable. He has committed serious crimes. He may feel he has nothing to lose now, so I fear a bad outcome to all this. I hope I'm wrong.'

It wasn't hard to see she still thought I was being over-pessimistic.

'Whatever he's done he can put it right surely,' she argued. 'He's a brilliant vet and I will support him all the way.'

Her loyalty was unbounding but I felt it was misplaced. 'I would suggest that he hasn't been honest with you about things for quite some time and now it's all come to a head.

Did you know, for instance, that he was addicted to gambling and that was the real reason he had to raise all that money you found for him? He just used Curtis as a decoy, knowing how upset you would be if you found out the truth.'

She shook her head to the gambling losses theory. 'If you mean poker I doubt very much that he lost money at it. My late husband taught him well. When he was fifteen he was red-hot. Henry and some of his friends used to let him sit in on a Saturday night session and he could beat them all. Henry said he had real keen eye for the game and was the best bluffer he knew.'

I didn't doubt it, but I felt Anthony's problems lay elsewhere if Curtis Fielding discovering him in a casino was anything to go by.

'I do actually think he ran up gambling debts and led you to believe he needed the money to pay Curtis back. I also believe he was using his so-called invention illegally and when Curtis found out the real trouble between them began.'

'That man's a liar and a cheat. I'm surprised at you, Sam. How could you possibly believe anything he says?'

'I also believe,' I went on, 'that having Father stay here with you has pushed Anthony over the edge and that's why he poured paraffin over some of Father's cars and set them alight. He thought my father was after the Bentley, you see.'

'Nonsense,' she raised her voice.

'He's as much as admitted it to me. I'm afraid it's the truth.'

She stood up as light drizzle began to fall. 'So why hasn't Sam said something to me? Why is he still here?'

'Because I only told him ten minutes ago and he didn't want to be the one to tell you.'

A cat reappeared, and uncharacteristically she shooed it away.

'Tell him I'm sorry about the cars. Never for a minute

did I think Anthony would be capable of such a thing. Your father must despise me, as must you.'

I was quick to exonerate her for any blame. 'None of this is your fault. We will both try to help but I really feel Anthony has gone past the stage where he will listen to anybody, even his own mother.'

She looked woefully sad and when I suggested we go in out of the rain she shook her head and said she wanted to walk. That's exactly what she did, wandering off, probably in search of something I felt she would never find.

Father saw her from the kitchen window and came out to me, itching to know.

'How did she take it?' he asked me.

'Not well, but at least she knows we are on her side. Give her some time and space. And keep a very close eye on her.'

'I will,' he said. 'What a mess.'

'It could get a whole lot messier,' I told him. 'Anthony's almost certainly got another gun, an air rifle. Certainly not as lethal as the one he aimed at me, but still a dangerous weapon.'

'Shit!' Father exclaimed. 'For God's sake. Nobody is safe if last night is anything to go by.'

I agreed with him, looked at my watch and left him to make the best of more bad news. I had the feeling it was going to be a very long day.

27

I had the presence of mind to telephone the police to notify them of the possibility of a second gun, but when I asked for an update on Anthony and his whereabouts I got the standard reply which was polite but unrelentingly vague. The fugitive veterinarian's behaviour, when it became common knowledge, would dumbfound those who knew him well and send shock waves around the Cotswolds where he earned his living. I wondered how Dame Olivia Blackwood might react and how the many other owners, trainers and dedicated horse lovers would receive the news.

For the meantime I only scratched the surface with Dominic, who was more concerned with the way I looked and my riding abilities than anything else when he picked me up at ten minutes past the prescribed time and set off north.

'You look bloody awful, Sam, do me a favour and have a doctor check you out soon after we get there. We can't let Grant think you're not fully fit and raring to go,' he groaned within a matter of seconds.

Grant Ibbotson sat in the front passenger seat, looking at me worriedly from over his shoulder and readying himself to listen to what was about to be said. I was due to ride another of his small string that Dominic had been painstakingly knocking into shape and I knew he wouldn't settle for having a half-fit jockey aboard one of his investments.

'I'll be fine,' I said in reply, trying to sound nonchalant for the benefit of the owner who I could tell was having trouble believing me.

'Still, best to be on the safe side eh? We have to give the horse every chance,' the trainer insisted, thus making it compulsory.

I knew deep down he was right because many parts of my body ached and the trauma and lack of sleep had stripped me of my usual lustre. Besides he didn't want any incriminations from Grant who just happened to be a criminal lawyer based in Trowbridge.

With that in mind I told them both briefly about Anthony and the crimes he might be facing when caught and got two differing views. A quietly stunned Dominic prattled on about Anthony being a fool to throw away the career he had worked so hard for in the past. Grant, reverting to type and now looking at me with far more interest, went into a summary of what Anthony's legal options were without committing himself to a likely outcome. I was almost sure he was going to produce a business card and ask me to somehow get it to Anthony at some stage but thankfully he didn't, though for the rest of the journey he sat there looking pensive as though his intrigue was nagging at his senses and asking all the relevant questions inside his head.

The novice hurdler in which the lawyer had invested modest money had ridden out well for me on the gallops a couple of weeks before, but if Dominic was truthful it was very much work in progress and expectations were modest too. Its only other race so far with me on board had been early in September on a bone-hard track at Newton Abbott, where a quick early pace had me playing catch-up all the way to the line, making up a few minor places to finish sixth of twelve. That was quite encouraging when all was said and done, the horse showing no sign of giving up and actually accelerating as it passed the line. So we all knew it had the stamina to run on, if not the early speed to stay with the pacesetters. Something Dominic was keen to remind me of after a course doctor had passed me fit to ride.

'Get him settled early and push on, don't let him boss you, Sam, or he'll just become lazy as he did at Newton,' he instructed, even before I had gone off to put on my racing colours.

I had a reasonable wins-to-rides ratio at Uttoxeter and had even fared better there than both Nathan and Paul, who I was happy to see were not competing with me in the first race. Bradley Somerville was on a short-odds favourite and the improving Simon Mendes had also secured a ride on a very well backed locally trained horse.

Nine went to post and after some prevarications by the starter we all got away in a comparative straight line. My horse, Linear Motion, was soon third of a leading bunch of five and pulling hard on my arms, which didn't feel as though they were part of my body. In a two-mile race over relatively small obstacles you have no real time to dwell and so it proved as three horses rounded the last bend with no more than a length between them. I was last of the three but could tell that the favourite, accompanied by Bradley, was just fractionally ahead of me and not enjoying it at all and for sure he was not going to give the bookmakers a sleepless night.

The other horse of the three was now pulling ahead, leaving me in its slipstream but at least I had the favourite beaten. I settled for a very well-deserved second, six lengths behind a worthy winner. Work in progress indeed, and leaps and bounds too, I thought noting the mirrored looks of satisfaction on the faces of owner and trainer as I took my place in the winner's enclosure.

'Great ride, Sam,' Dominic praised me.

'Bloody well done,' said a suddenly animated Grant, shaking my hand like I was a dear friend. 'What did it feel like? Never thought he could run so fast. That was bloody amazing.'

'He's come on such a lot and it felt very good,' I said, getting my breath back.

'You left the favourite for dead and look at the starting price. Bloody twenty to one,' Grant shouted, frothing at the mouth.

I imagined the criminal lawyer had put a fair bit of last week's wages on it each way and was now mentally counting his winnings, and I found myself actually beginning to like the man. Would his heart cope next time if the horse actually won, which I thought it might based on today's evidence? It was always gratifying to see a contented owner and not receive criticism from a trainer for not winning. But there were two more rides for Dominic to come so it was still early days. With that thought I weighed in and relived the race with a few other jockeys back in the changing room, most with unhappy tales to tell.

Several jockeys referred to my fall at Stratford the previous day and there were jokes at my expense about my 'bounceability' which I took in good heart bearing in mind questions about my fitness had been unanimously answered by my admirable second place in the day's opener. But now I had it all to do again in the second race on a newcomer to chasing, following a switch by Dominic from hurdling, a decision taken after three frustrating and barren seasons. The persevering trainer had bought the horse from its disillusioned owner six months ago and during the summer I had helped Dominic and his staff school it over fences resulting in some optimistic signs and a 'last chance' attempt by the trainer/owner to get a return on his money.

Sadly when it came to the race absolutely nothing went to plan and at the fifth fence, whilst trailing behind the others, I was clinically dispatched with no fear of being kicked by another horse as I landed on soft turf, adding bruises to my pride and not my body on this occasion.

Fearing that a work in progress label wouldn't cover it, I gave Dominic an honest assessment and left him to decide what to do next, which I imagined would mean more perseverance on the practice jumps together with long soul-searching sessions should the mistakes not be eradicated.

A plethora of wise cracks greeted me back in the weighing room and Nathan Scully spared me nothing despite himself finishing well out of the frame on a horse backed down to joint favourite.

'So Sam, is it true you've taken to collecting grass stains on your breeches from every racecourse you visit?' he quipped loudly, drawing howls of friendly laughter.

'It's a hobby of mine,' I said, going with the flow.

'Look everyone,' piped up a so far redundant Paul. 'Sam's got himself another entry into the "fall of the year" competition and tomorrow he's aiming for a double somersault and a handstand dismount.'

'Highly amusing,' I shrugged, my dignity in shreds.

It was just another day at the fun factory and nothing had changed. Jockeys' banter sometimes got more serious than that, especially when the stakes were high, but generally it was good humoured and well meant. Paul in particular, given his previous problems, was suddenly demonstrative and brash. His eyes were bright and his mood positive. He had three back-to-back rides to come for the Jollys' stable, and nobody would bet against him winning all three and rubbing everybody's nose in it. The race for supremacy in the jockeys' championship was well and truly on and that meant, joking apart, the likes of Bradley, Nathan and Paul would be singularly focused on the job in hand, trying to get that all important edge which was very often the difference between first and second or success and failure.

For me there was no more action until the fifth race unless called upon should injury or illness befall somebody, so I deliberately wallowed under a hot shower while most others prepared for the next race. Afterwards I struck up a conversation with one of the valets who didn't stop tidying up as he spoke. Something he said intrigued me.

Knowing I had more time for Paul Eddison than most, he told me he had accidentally witnessed a row between Paul and Tristan Jolly a few days before, something to do with the jockey threatening a man with a gun. He said it sounded like something from a movie and he felt bad about eavesdropping and wondered if he should be telling somebody in authority. Although not a gossip by nature I sensed it would have driven him mad not to tell someone about what he heard, though why he had chosen me I was not too sure.

Unless there had been another instance I knew nothing about, I assumed the man being threatened at gunpoint was Bruce Fielding at a time when Paul's state of mind was as fragile as his marriage. Quite how Tristan had found out about it was a mystery but I could see it might harm his reputation as a well-respected racehorse owner and why he might therefore take Paul to task over it.

I briefed the valet on a little of what had gone on, and suggested it was best kept under wraps. He saw some light and thanked me for my honesty. But at no point did I think him totally incapable of spilling the beans after having a drink too many in a pub somewhere, so I viewed his powers of discretion as flimsy at the least, and decided to mention it to Paul later should the chance arise.

When I next saw him Paul was wearing one of those now more familiar smiles of success, having quite literally slaughtered the opposition and guided Gala Prince to its fifth consecutive win, by a mighty twenty lengths to boot. If there had been a fall-out between Paul and owner it certainly hadn't affected the form book or changed a thing for the punters who followed the stable like disciples.

The races came thick and fast, with Paul in the mood again, winning the fourth by a head from a disconsolate Nathan in second. Bradley had taken a tumble at the very first fence and that meant him being the butt of a few well-intentioned jibes which at least made me feel somewhat better. In the fifth I should have felt confident riding Capital Gain after its unlucky second at Cheltenham due to overzealous stewarding by the man I had grown to dislike less in the last twenty-four hours. For once I was the one on the favourite and no doubt the bookies in the ring were secretly praying Paul or one of the seven other jockeys would triumph over me, especially with my odds suddenly shortening to seven to four.

Neither Dominic nor the owners seemed unduly worried by the move in the market and when I resumed my telepathic partnership with the horse my confidence rose so much I barely noticed the others around me. The race was run and won in a style I could not have been more content with had I already rehearsed it in my head. Only Hologram of all the other horses in Dominic's stable could have matched or exceeded Capital Gain on that day's performance and though the odds were poor it felt like I had won a much more prestigious race. There would no more teasing jockeys to contend with, only envious ones.

From thought-provoking uncertainty Dominic was now ebullient and glowing with praise for both rider and horse, immediately being asked by a reporter for a quote regarding rumours Capital Gain would be going back to Cheltenham in March for the Gold Cup or maybe Aintree in April for the National, or both.

Soaking up the attention he said he would keep his options open and that anything was possible now the horse had realised its true potential. Feet on the ground, not getting carried away and every other cliché you could think of put in an appearance and the reporter scribbled everything down as if it was food from the Gods. Hallelujah to the victorious.

After the time-honoured sponsors' presentations and more changing-room banter I managed to corner Paul and ask him about current relations with Tristan and Trudy Jolly, in view of the valet's earlier comments to me. He looked taken aback but came at me from an angle I hadn't bargained for, shrugging away doubts about him continuing to ride for the said owners and playing down thoughts of a rift.

'It would be sheer bloody madness on their behalf to dump me and they know it,' he said, rather smugly. 'So don't get any ideas about replacing me, Sam, the position's not vacant. We are a team and right now the best fucking one around.'

He said it all with a smile on his face and with no real bitterness towards me, recognising my genuine concerns but also driving home a message that was akin to warning me off.

I threw him a cautious smile. 'The thought of muscling in on you never crossed my mind. Just thought you should know that somebody else knew about the gun threats,' I started whispering.

He took a quick glance around and nodded his head saying, 'Trust me, Sam, I'll sort it. I'll explain the circumstances and I'm sure he'll accept it was a moment of weakness. I'm sure it will be all right.'

Job done, I thought, feeling relieved and receiving a reassuring hand on my shoulder before he prepared his speech to the valet who had noticed us talking and had kept well away.

An amateur jockeys only race was next on the agenda so I grabbed what I needed and went in search of Dominic. I knew he would be keen to get away as he was making a detour on the return journey to allow me to collect my car from Stratford racecourse, where I had arranged to meet a member of the staff to whom I had entrusted its overnight safe keeping. But I had not allowed for a still jubilant Grant Ibbotson who was insisting on stopping somewhere en route to buy trainer and jockey a slap-up meal with his winnings and throw in champagne for good measure.

Gratuities from successful owners were perks you rarely turned down and I noted the expert deliberation of Dominic in finding the most expensive hotel with restaurant he could. He and Grant plumped for salmon en croute and I ordered a medium rare ribeye steak with a green salad. A bottle of Moet et Chandon complemented the food and for once I, like Dominic joined in and had a full glass, leaving the already well-oiled criminal lawyer to polish off the rest.

As owner and trainer discussed plans for Linear Motion and others in the string, I made a call to Father who told me he had earlier spent an hour at Cheltenham police station waiting whilst Lavender was interviewed about her son. He said they had called her pretty soon after she had taken him over to Sloane Farm and asked her to assist them in finding Anthony, whose name was now in the local evening newspaper under the headline 'Vet sought after terrorising couple at house'.

Though still hiding from the reality of what her son had done, she reluctantly agreed to see them at two o'clock, fielding a deluge of questions mostly about Anthony's mental state and where he was most likely to be holed up. Were there any special places he liked to go? Did she know if he had a passport and if so did he have it with him? Was the gun in his possession a standard air rifle or had it been modified? Did she know about the illegal use of equipment at the surgery and had he made any direct threats to anyone else recently?

So many unanswered questions and Lavender had been of little help, she said. Then there was more concerning the fire and his relationship with my father, with the police emphasising the fact Father had been staying with her at Castle Moat Lodge whereas Anthony had preferred to stay overnight at the surgery. 'Does your son have a problem with Sam Woodall or his son of the same name?' they asked her. Had Anthony seen something he might have disapproved of? Did she know about his addiction to gambling as reported to them by one of his victims Curtis Fielding? Why would he tamper with records at the surgery and had he ever mentioned this to her?

Father said Lavender came out of there looking like a broken woman and totally exhausted. The police, he said, had been bastards to her and he had told them as much for putting her through it without much consideration or care. And he had been intimidated by the most senior detective there for daring to question their interrogating methods and had come mightily close to getting himself arrested again.

It seemed he had gone the full circle, from being arrested for alleged criminal damage two weeks ago to now being threatened by the police with the same fate for airing his forthright views and probably swearing too many times for their liking.

I asked him where he was now and he said he was at the house. Lavender, normally a woman with boundless energy, had gone for a lie-down complaining of an unrelenting headache. She had even left him with the chore of feeding all the cats and I could tell from his voice he had hated it, though I'm sure not even he would have wanted them to starve. Telling him I would be back as soon as I could, I gradually shoehorned my way into the conversation going on between Dominic and Grant and it was a great relief to be able to talk racing again, even if I didn't get to say very much at all.

Though later than planned, I did what I had to do at Stratford and drove with some purpose, stopping to pick up a paper and reading the front page story which didn't seem to bear much likeness to what had actually occurred but did cover the basics. Oddly, my name wasn't mentioned, only a reference to a family friend of the Fieldings who just happened to turn up after the initial attack and prior to the gun-wielding vet firing off a shot and then escaping into the night. Whoever the reporter was he was loose with the facts and seemed just to want to sensationalise and speculate. Certain facts about Anthony were true and a comment from a local horse owner who claimed to know him highlighted the shock and level of surprise the incident had caused.

It had caused a stir with the Blackwood family too and Tamara, now on a Swindon-bound train from central London, contacted me after hearing of it from her mother.

'Sam, where are you? Hopefully nowhere near that madman I've just this minute heard about,' she worriedly enquired.

'Heading back to see Father who's still at Lavender's,' I told her.

'Is that wise?'

Perhaps it wasn't but I felt I had no other option. 'Can't just leave him there. Anthony's mother is in a real state. She's been trying to help the police but I fear the worst. Seeing Anthony last night has me doubting he'll just throw in the towel and face up to what he has done.'

'You saw him? You were there?'

'I was sort of invited. It was a set-up for my benefit. Needless to say I've gained a few more grey hairs.'

'Sam, why? Did you know he had a gun?' She sounded horrified.

'I guessed but wasn't sure. I had little choice because he had Curtis and Caroline held captive and got Curtis to phone me. Had I not gone I might have had their deaths on my conscience forever. You know me, like most jockeys I'm stark raving bonkers and have this incredibly strong threshold to pain.'

313

I heard her gulp. Pain thresholds were irrelevant. 'And what if he'd shot you?'

'We wouldn't be having this conversation. Just be grateful he didn't.'

'Grateful, Sam for God's sake.'

'Tamara, I'm OK. I had to do what I did, I knew it would be too risky to involve anyone else,' I explained. 'That maniac pumped anaesthetic meant for horses into Caroline Fielding and though I didn't know that when I went in there she could have died without urgent medical attention. He used her and her husband to get to me because he was sure I had set the police onto him. I took a calculated risk and I'm alive. The only disappointing thing is that he is still out there somewhere. But hopefully the police will find him before he can wreak more damage.'

There was a sigh of resignation and I pictured her expression. 'When I get back I'm coming to see you,' she said without fear of contradiction.

'Why don't I meet you at the station?'

'Because Daddy's already on his way and I don't want you coming to the Willows. Mother just wouldn't leave you alone, she'd pester every little detail out of you and I'd never get a look in. I'll look in on Emilia and drive straight over. About two hours. Don't get into any more trouble, promise.'

I said I wouldn't and held my breath.

The last time I had seen a house in complete darkness before normal lights out was less than twenty-four hours ago when a somewhat deranged man was waiting for me, shotgun in hand. I could understand the upstairs lights being off if Lavender had taken to her bed, but not the downstairs ones. There was not even the flicker of a light coming from the front lounge window where I would have expected to find Father watching one of the Sky channels – a novelty given he had never invested in it himself, insisting he didn't have the time to spare.

Lavender's Peugeot was where it was always parked, in front of a junk-strewn double width garage that hadn't been home to a vehicle in years and had some crumbling brickwork on the side furthest from the house and missing tiles resulting in a leaky roof. And it was unusual not to be able to make out the outline of a cat anywhere on the approach to the part gravel, part tarmac drive or on any of the silhouetted roofs of the dilapidated outbuildings. Nor was there one sitting on the bonnet of the car as usual which Father and I had so vehemently disapproved of.

I parked thirty feet from the front door and sat and waited for ten minutes. Still no lights and no cats. Father's phone wasn't in receiving mode and neither was Lavender's. I telephoned the police and made myself anonymous, gave them the address and hung up. My phone rang out straight away. It was Anthony. He said he knew I was there and invited me inside. This time he said nothing about a party. He just said he was waiting for me. That we had some serious unfinished business.

28

How could I be so stupid as to let it happen again, I asked myself, and why this time had I phoned the police and put lives at risk? My own father's, for God in heaven's sake. I swiftly prayed for an unprecedented traffic jam or that the emergency services were too stretched to attend quickly. I might have even prayed for an earthquake. Being so close to the motorway I expected the sound of sirens to be echoing through the valley in a matter of minutes or less. So I found myself walking at a pace I would never usually consider in darkness, with the light from a nearly full moon obstructed by tall, unkempt trees which formed an arc at the point where the tarmac finished and the paving slabs of a pathway to the front door began.

There would be no need for the door to be opened for me this time. I had a key; the spare one Lavender had so readily given to me a few days ago when I first stayed over. She had quite liked having me around I thought, though she knew the demands of racing wouldn't allow me to be there for long. Even when I upset her with talk of Anthony not being what he seemed she hadn't shown me the door or taken it out on Father. We had a friendship of sorts and now I didn't want her to be in real danger, though the signs or lack of them for her were not good. And presumably much worse for Sam Woodall Senior. Please God let me be wrong.

As I got level with the bottom step of three rising to the dark-stained wooden front door I picked up something and put it in my right-hand trouser pocket. There were no CCTV screens to worry about as I did it, so for sure it had gone unnoticed. That small insignificant action probably saved my life – but at the time I imagined it was a pretty futile act. Even perhaps my last.

I fumbled with the key, swore under my breath, and pushed the door wide open at precisely the time Lavender's large, transparent mantelpiece clock sounded. It was ten thirty and there was no time to reflect. All the doors leading off the rectangular hallway were open bar one, which just so happened to be Lavender Thompson's least favourite place, the cellar.

I called out and heard faint scuffling noises. They sounded as if they were coming from under my feet. Did Lavender have rats in her cellar or was there somebody down there wishing they weren't? The noises didn't stop; if anything they grew louder. I shouted out again, fairly bellowing this time. Just the same noises persisted, nothing else.

With police sirens imminent I addressed Anthony.

'Anthony, if you are here show yourself,' I said, pausing for a few seconds. 'Let's get this over once and for all. There's no need to involve anybody else, especially your mother. Let her and my father go and we'll talk. You can salvage something from this if you're sensible and give it up now. I even know a criminal lawyer who may be able to help you. The Fieldings are shaken up but fine and my father's cars can be restored. Suddenly it's not looking so bad. Please, Anthony, put a stop to this now.'

There wasn't the sound of a creak in the old house but the noise from the cellar didn't relent. Then I swore I could hear breathing and moved towards it. And from behind the sitting room door the sinister shape of Anthony appeared, dressed as he was yesterday but minus the hat, the air rifle held high and pointing straight at my head, making it difficult for me to see his face.

The weapon he was holding looked no less menacing

than the shotgun he had aimed at me the previous day, and just because I knew it could only dispatch pellets didn't make it any less harrowing to be the prime target.

'Did you know,' he spoke suddenly, his voice very precise, 'a correctly aimed air rifle pellet at very close range could kill somebody?'

I avoided any movement and just stood perfectly still.

'Failing that it will surely leave you blind in one eye,' he added. 'How many one-eyed jockeys do you know, Sam? Perhaps you can start a club.'

He was laughing inwardly, egging me on to make a move he was more than ready for, his index finger poised on the trigger.

'Why risk a life sentence when you could be free in five years?' I said, guessing, not even daring to flicker an eyelid.

'It'll be worth it to know you suffered for what you did.'

'And what did I do, Anthony?' I challenged him. 'Did I break the law like you did? Commit fraud? Arson? Embezzle my own mother? Not to mention attempted murder?'

The angle of the gun wavered and for the first time in the gloom of the doorway where he stood I saw the outline of his face. It looked cowardly and evil at the same time. He was beginning to sweat. Buckets of the stuff.

'Fuck you, Woodall, fuck everybody. I'm the one on top here not you. You're no fucking angel, Sam. As for that money-grabbing bastard you call your dad he's nothing but a parasite and you know what happens to parasites eventually, they get splattered.'

Now it was my turn to sweat. 'If you've harmed him I'll make sure you rot in jail. Your beef is with me. Getting his hands on anything belonging to your mother was never further from his mind. It was all in your imagination.'

The noises from the cellar had ceased, almost as if our voices had quietened them. Apart from the faint drumming of traffic on the M4 we stood in absolute silence and

CAUGHT

Anthony's aim was still as focused as before with my head
as conspicuous a target as there could be despite the darkness
all around us.

'You're full of bullshit just like your old man,' Anthony
grizzled, baring the white of his teeth. The barrel of the
gun dropped a few inches as he said it but it was soon
levelled at my head again with a distance of about six feet
between us. Twenty-four hours ago in an almost identical
scenario I at least had somebody else next to me to distract
him, but now there was just me looking straight down the
smaller barrel of a weapon that could maim me for life if
I made one false move.

'This is madness,' I told him, wanting to sustain some sort
of dialogue. 'Do something right, Anthony, and give yourself
up now before matters get worse. Your mother's told me
about what happened after your father died. You need help
and there are people out there who can do just that if you
let them.'

He shuffled his feet and it brought him even closer to me.
'Just words, Sam, I know your game. You are so transparent.'

'I want the best outcome, that's all.'

His head shook slowly from side to side. 'For you, Sam,
for you. Why should you fucking well care what happens to
me? All you think about is saving your own skin. Why can't
people just be honest and leave all the bullshit out? Stop
playing games with me now and start believing this is for
real.'

The barrel of the gun was shaking, as was Anthony, and
though I couldn't see it properly I imagined his index finger
was twitching in harmony with the rest of his tensed up
body. I turned to pleading with him.

'Anthony, think about what you are doing. Think about
your poor mother.'

He was no longer receptive to persuasion though, and
he took another agonising step towards me.

319

It was then that I was sure I could hear a siren in the distance and I knew there was nothing left for me to do but imagine I was astride a falling horse. My hands and arms came up in one instinctive movement and I ducked my head low to employ it as a battering ram. But he had already pulled the trigger and I felt something sharp explode against my left cheekbone. It did nothing to halt the forward momentum of my body which achieved what I had hoped it would, knocking him clean off his feet. He landed on his back, retaining his hold on the air rifle with his right hand. I should have worried more about the left one.

Just beyond the doorway into the sitting room lay the open holdall. He had reached inside it in an instant to pull out a fully loaded syringe which he now clasped like a dagger and lashed out with, narrowly missing my right leg as I desperately fought to maintain my balance.

The siren was now much louder and I knew that he had heard it because he shouted at the top of his voice, 'You bastard, Woodall, why did you do that?'

I didn't have the time or inclination to answer. Whoever was employing the siren I just wanted them here now because I felt I needed them.

Any hope I had of Anthony running out into the night as he had before had gone, there was too much hatred in his eyes and destructive energy in his wiry body. A few more attempts to stab me were fended off but he was focused on his goal and I felt there was no escape. If only there was some light to help me or I had a weapon to use against him. Then I remembered. Reaching into my pocket I took aim with the handful of soil I had plundered from an outdoor flower pot. He flinched as it hit him square in the face and I capitalised on that to rub some of what was left in my hand into his eyes. It bought me priceless seconds and I now had a firm grip of the wrist holding the syringe.

In what was then akin to an arm-wrestling contest I

mustered every grain of my strength to try to disarm him. The butt of the rifle he was not prepared to let go of was hindering me as he had dug it solidly into the ribcage that still bore remnants of pain from yesterday's fall.

As long as I could keep him from stabbing me I was safe and encouragingly the vehicle sounding the siren was crunching the gravel at the far end of the drive. Sensing it too, Anthony then brought his teeth into play and like a rabid dog he shaped to bite my arm. I pulled it away from him which only meant he could tighten his grip on the syringe and resume his frenzied stabbing motions. With brakes screeching outside he summoned all, producing an inhumanly deadly cry and launching one concerted attack.

Energising my reflexes I shouted something back and, judo-style, threw him up against the wall of the hallway, twisting his wrist, which I had managed to regain a grip on, inward and applying pressure to it. His face looked aghast at the realisation of what was happening to him.

'What have you done, you bloody fool?' he asked, as if I had stabbed him intentionally. 'Oh God, no!'

The syringe was embedded in a fleshy part of his upper thigh. He was now no longer a contestant and certainly not a threat to man nor beast. I watched his eyes flicker and they looked at me appealing. Then his crooked torso slumped and he slid as if in slow motion into a sitting position, the contents of the syringe now inside him. With his eyes closing his legs flailed and his head fell to one side. He looked pitiful and suddenly there was no movement at all. If I had not known better I'd have said he was dead.

As one of the uniformed officers checked Anthony's vital signs the other radioed for assistance and I caught my breath. The left side of my face was throbbing and there was blood on my clothes. A reluctant look in the full-length hallway mirror opposite where I now knelt revealed to me the full extent of the damage done, but this was no time for vanity. Choking back any pain and ignoring police advice to remain where I had landed after Anthony went down in a heap, I staggered to the cellar door and, relieved it was unlocked, prised it open.

As soon as I turned on the light and lowered myself down the first few steps I saw Father lying on his side, an extension cord wound around his body and legs and tied in an untidy knot at the back. There was something with a striped pattern that resembled a tea towel pulled taut and wrapped around his face which acted as a makeshift gag and was seriously restricting his nose and mouth and his breathing. Behind him lay the unbound Lavender, stretched out on her back and in an identical position to the one I found Caroline Fielding in almost exactly twenty-four hours ago. Alarmingly she wasn't moving whereas Father was frantically talking to me with his eyes and demanding to be set free.

I freed his mouth first, asking him if Anthony had injected his mother with anything. He looked back at me, puzzled, and shook his head,

'She just collapsed soon after he shut the bloody door. I can only think it was a heart attack. Oh God, Sam, I think she's dead.'

'She's breathing,' I exclaimed immediately, putting my face to hers and trying not to get my blood on her. 'Help's on its way. Let's get you out of this.'

With difficulty mainly because of his inane impatience I slowly unravelled the cord and released him by which time the second officer had arrived on the scene and gone straight to Lavender's side. Father speculated again that it was a heart attack, but the policeman stuck to his basic training and amazingly he had her conscious again in a matter of minutes and she was asking him to allow her to sit up.

'Just get me out of this place before I pass out again,' I heard her tell him and then the penny dropped for me – her phobia for spiders was the obvious cause of her collapse. In effect she had hyperventilated and fainted. Father let out an animated sigh of relief and shaped to give her a hug, but I thought about what she might see upon exiting the cellar and went up ahead to find the first policeman hovering over Anthony's prostrate body looking pretty desperate and talking on his radio.

Anthony's skin was naturally pale with a liberal sprinkling of light-brown freckles on his forehead and on the bridge of his nose. But they were barely noticeable now because he looked bereft of any colour whatsoever. I got the impression the policeman, who didn't look a day over twenty, was in contact with a doctor or perhaps a paramedic. More sirens were rushing to us but it was looking awfully grave for the vet and any second now his mother would arrive back in the hallway and see him. Then the policeman finished on the phone and asked me a question.

'What was in the syringe, and how much was there?'

'Anaesthetic, I think,' I said. 'It looked about full.'

'He's not breathing, I can't get a pulse,' the policeman shivered.

I reacted the same way, and then suddenly there was Lavender dusting herself down and looking less concerned than she should have been.

'What's happened to him, and what's that I can see? Anthony, can you hear me? That was a very bad thing you did, I nearly died down there.'

The second policeman appeared too with Father close behind and they stood staring at the scene.

'Lavender, have you any idea what Anthony might have had in the syringe?' I asked her. 'The one now sticking out of the top of his leg?'

She stared at me and then at the syringe. Her head shook

slowly and she thought out loud. 'All I know is he uses things like that all of the time up at the surgery,' she replied. 'What's happened? Who did this to him?'

I gave her the only reply I could. 'He tried to stab me with it after he shot me with the air rifle.'

'But why would he want to do that?'

I thought it best not to answer and was glad for the noise of screeching tyres and brakes and people running.

Father held on to Lavender and coaxed her away into the kitchen with a cup of tea offered but declined. Two paramedics, both young males, exchanged words with the policemen and set about trying to revive Anthony. I thought it best to join the others in the kitchen and wait. The second policeman followed, suggesting tea which was rapidly declined again. He had his notepad and a ballpoint pen at the ready but didn't seem to have the heart to ask any questions. I filled up the kettle and switched it on in case, and used several pieces of kitchen roll to clean up my face, at which point the policeman said it looked quite nasty and that I really ought to get it seen to.

All the noise came from the hallway until the kettle began to hiss as it got hotter. And when it clicked itself off nobody moved from where they were standing and nobody dared to sit down. The door from the kitchen into the hallway was half open and we all tried to listen in to what the paramedics were saying to each other. They had brought equipment in from their ambulance and I imagined they were using it on Anthony, but it had been some time since he had gone down and the omens were bad.

His totally bewildered mother was standing with her hands clasped together as though in prayer but I didn't think for a minute that she doubted she would soon hear that Anthony was all right. Five minutes became ten and then the second policeman, still with an empty notepad, ventured into the hall to see for himself what was happening and presumably report back to us. We heard him and his colleague talking and Father then said something.

'Go and ask them what's going on, Sam, and we'll have that cup of tea to help calm our nerves.'

Lavender immediately protested. 'No tea for me until I'm sure Anthony's OK, but I think I will sit down. Why are they taking so long?'

'Routine, I suppose,' I said feebly, watching her pull a kitchen chair away from the table and lower herself on to it with a resounding sigh. Father dragged another chair across the floor and sat next to her, his hand hovering over her hands which had been joined together again in a prayer.

'They know what they're doing,' he told her in a reassuring voice, glancing at me and nodding towards the door. Routine or not it did seem to be taking the paramedics an insurmountable amount of time, so I did what Father asked but was stopped from entering the hall by the returning policeman.

'Not a good idea sir, I think it best you stay in the kitchen. I'll need to interview you and the others, but just at the moment I have things to arrange.'

His young face looked gaunt, his eyes unmistakably solemn. What arrangements did he have to make, I asked myself? What did he mean?

For Lavender Thompson I feared the worst. And in spite of everything he had done, for her son I feared the worst too. What would I tell her? How would I explain what had happened whilst she lay in the cellar waiting to be rescued? How would she react to what I told her and would she blame me forever more, and also blame Father?

It had been him or me. It could so easily have been me lying in the hallway awaiting arrangements, whatever they were. Things could have turned out completely differently. But things were as they were for a reason. Nothing I could do could change that. Looking up at me for news of Anthony, two faces shared the same expression although Lavender's was the one I could not focus on for long.

'Well?' Father asked me.

'We've been asked to stay in here and wait. The police will have to take statements from us in due course.'

That wasn't answering the question and his impatience got the better of him. He got up and I couldn't stop him getting to the door and making it into the hall. I just didn't have the strength left in my body to stop him. He had to see for himself what was going on. And despite the efforts of the policemen, he did. And from where I was after trying to block his path so did I. Both of us just stared at what was, for sure, a corpse; its head and upper part covered with an appropriately coloured black raincoat that had been taken from a peg and which probably belonged to Lavender.

One of the paramedics was returning equipment to a carryall and the other was presumably outside, their work done. They had worked tirelessly to try to save Anthony. Nine times out of ten they would have succeeded in reviving the victim and now be taking him or her to a hospital bed. This was one time they wouldn't be making that journey. That ordeal would be carried out by a different vehicle and when it had been loaded up it wouldn't be heading for A&E.

We returned to the kitchen and our combined expressions must have said it all, though Lavender still looked at us with a glimmer of hope in her heart, believing that her prayers might yet be answered. Then with cold resignation her hands parted company and she used them to cradle her head as her eyes shut tight. They stayed closed and I felt numb. Returning to his chair Father sat beside her and muttered something to her which I presumed included the word 'sorry'.

I decided to make tea whether it was wanted or not, and also went to the cupboard where I knew Lavender kept medicinal brandy, finding glasses and pouring it out in even measures. The tears she had held back in hope were now in full flow, and without the support of the chair and Father close beside her she would surely have collapsed onto the floor again. This time it had nothing to do with darkness and spiders. But it had everything to do with the death of her son. A death I had been very much part of. A death that might haunt me for the rest of my days.

Lavender was in no fit state to be answering questions and we were all now in the lounge, having shielded her from the harrowing scene in the hallway and persuaded her to sit in her favourite armchair. There was a mortuary van outside with its lights still glowing and the two men from it were doing what came naturally to them. Some job, I thought. I'll stick to being a jockey.

Red and white tape had been strung around the crime scene and a man with forensics written all over his protective clothing was busy within the cordon, no doubt cursing his loss of sleep.

One of the paramedics had put an antiseptic dressing on my face before they had left and I had taken painkillers which had still to take effect. They had advised me to go to hospital as a precaution but said the wound was clean and that I had been lucky. I wondered just how being shot was construed as being lucky. Then I imagined it could have been much worse and was thankful for having all my faculties intact.

A discreet call to Tamara had told her not to travel over from the Willows and the reason why. She was naturally shocked and said she wouldn't be able to sleep, insisting on seeing me sooner or later. But later seemed a long way off as Father and I still had to give the police statements, having now been told a detective constable would be along presently to mop up after the uniformed officers had finished securing the site. I couldn't fault their thoroughness. But it seemed to be taking an age and the inconsolable Lavender was totally exhausted, unable to even put more than two words together when we tried to engage her. She sat with her head bowed and eyes mostly shut, the woman I had laughed at over her antics with Father at Sloane Farm not so very long ago now a broken shell.

About an hour later, with our statements meticulously compiled, I was allowed to leave. I headed straight into Tamara's arms and trusted her not to bombard me with questions about Anthony's dreadful demise. My left cheek felt swollen but the throbbing, burning sensation had almost completely gone, though I suspected it would be back in a few hours. I would avoid having to go to hospital if I could but wouldn't argue with Tamara if she insisted. Already in the short time she had known me I had acquired quite a few injuries but this latest one was like nothing I had experienced before. An inch higher and a fraction to one side and the pellet would have surely left me blind in that eye or at the least with blurred vision. Not good for someone needing to judge distances and make calculated moves out on the racetrack. So luck was a contributing factor after all. On another day the outcome might have been different. And Anthony Thompson might still be alive and awaiting to be charged with his many misdemeanours. Thin lines and small margins. Tears and sad faces. Life and death encapsulated.

I felt sorry for his mother of course, but I felt just as sorry for my father and for what he had been put through. In the absence of anyone else he was the one Lavender would now have to lean on, which was bizarre in the extreme if you accepted that he might have perished in the aftermath of a fire started by her insanely jealous and highly vindictive offspring. Not a basis for friendship and certainly not one to help evolve a lasting relationship. If only I had read the signs sooner and reacted to them accordingly. If only Anthony had had somebody he could have turned to for help and understanding, given the very different world he appeared to inhabit when he wasn't examining horse flesh or studying blood samples at his surgery.

Time, it seemed was on nobody's side. But for me I felt sure it wouldn't stand still for long.

Epilogue

I had no stomach for racing, and Dominic had no use for someone who was both traumatised by events and suffering from sleep deprivation. It was Saturday, I should have been plying my trade at Ascot but instead I was trying to make some sense where there was none at all.

There had been some small pockets of sleep as I lay next to the woman I loved but it was questionable if they would sustain me. Tamara had been my shining beacon in a black hole of uncertainty, and she had neither pressured me nor persuaded me into reliving a very real nightmare.

From my father's point of view he was mightily relieved by the sudden appearance of acquaintances and relatives that Lavender had never mentioned, who rallied around her in her hour of need. A niece had been contacted by a police liaison officer and she had made further calls so there was a steady stream of offers of help. By midday Lavender had left the hospital where she had been checked over and had moved into the niece's house near Bath for a few days, away from inquisitive eyes and any perverse incriminations. This meant Father was freed up to accompany me and collect his car from the Cirencester side street where I had parked it the morning before, and to mull over things in a very disorganised manner which didn't seem to matter to either of us.

'I still don't know why he did what he did,' he puzzled.

'What made him think I was going to rob him of his inheritance? I never thought he gave two hoots about his mother or whoever she spent time with. I hardly ever saw him at the house. He seemed to live at that surgery of his and eat, drink and sleep there. I found it strange that a vet should hate cats like he did and they should dislike him too, making themselves scarce when he was around. But perhaps they knew something about him that we didn't and we misread the signs.'

It was unusual for Father to analyse or sound so profound but when I thought back to the previous night and to when I first arrived at the house, the noticeable absence of cats now disturbed me. Were they trying to warn me? Did they indeed have a second sense?

'Doctors don't have to like their patients to treat them,' I added, quantifying what he had said. 'The same, I suppose, applies to vets. And animals can be incredibly perceptive. You don't have to look any further than a horse for a perfect example. Some of them are remarkably astute.'

Father took no more than a few seconds to think about that. 'And some of them couldn't win a race for toffee,' he said, lightening the mood. 'You've ridden a few of them in your time, Sam, remember?'

I shared a smile with him and started to miss Ascot, though I knew it was the right thing to do to withdraw my services. It was only two races and we were still only in October. There would be plenty of racing to come. And plenty of time to reflect.

With Father returning to the fishery to brief Big Dave of events, I drove to Stroud to re-acquaint myself with my bed. Later I confirmed with Dominic that I would be available for Huntingdon the next day and likewise with Heath Coultard, who had asked me to ride his wife Felicity's Leap of Faith again in the day's opener. It felt good to be getting on with normality.

Unsurprisingly, over the next few days my life was full of extremes. I won three races, got pipped in a photo finish that I was convinced later was a dead heat, had two uncomplicated falls without further injury, and picked up a seven-day riding ban for excessive use of the whip. All part of life's rich tapestry.

Off the racecourse much had become clearer, and questions had been answered. A painstaking autopsy on Anthony came to one overriding conclusion – that he had died from an overdose of the strongest type of anaesthetic, the kind a vet would administer to a large animal the size of a horse to put it down humanely. A drug called Thiopental which was also widely used to perform euthanasia on dogs and cats. Bizarrely, the needle of the syringe had inadvertently found a vein in Anthony's leg and because the drug was fast acting he would have been dead before the paramedics reached him. They would have stood no chance of saving him.

'What have you done, you bloody fool?' he had asked me. And unknowingly I had watched him die.

But the police exonerated me of all blame and they didn't have to spell out to me what would have happened had he stuck the syringe in me, which made my blood go cold. At the same time I found out the truth about who blew the whistle on Anthony, which subsequently sent him into fugitive mode, led him to Curtis Fielding's home and twenty-four hours later to the final showdown at his mother's house.

A very informative detective constable confirmed to me that, although my suspicions and Anthony's pen might well have proved useful, they had acted upon another person's observations; Anthony's newest receptionist at his surgery. This was the same girl who was manning the desk the day I saw Anthony in his office. She had remembered seeing him some time ago shredding files behind closed doors, which was unlike him because that task was usually delegated to someone more junior. Initially he was rude to her, saying

she shouldn't be spying on him but although acting erratically
he had managed to shrug off her concerns, and she thought
no more about it. But just over a week ago, when she went
back to the surgery late to pick up something she had
forgotten, she said she had spotted him loading what looked
like a petrol can into the back of his car together with
several heavy-looking tools that for sure he did not use on
his regular rounds. Then followed my row with Anthony,
much of which she overheard. She mentioned these three
combined things to a friend whose husband was a traffic
cop based in Bristol, and it was flagged up to Gloucester
CID and followed up with the visit that triggered Anthony
to go into hiding.

No DNA, no fingerprints. Just the power of observation
and nothing more than routine enquiries. But I didn't feel
like I'd been let off the hook. Anthony was dead, nothing
could change that.

More diligent police work had established that Anthony
had gambling debts amounting to five figures and regularly
drove into London at night, coming back in the early hours,
hence the sleeping in lay-bys his mother had brought up
in conversation. Additionally there were investigations under-
way into methods used at his surgery and into the bogus
heat wrap he had tried to dupe Fielding with.

No comfort at all for poor old Lavender, who was having
a prolonged stay in Bath and paying some local animal
lover to go round and leave food daily for her cats. I
wondered if it would be best to give the funeral that she
still had to arrange a wide berth. And whether Father should
too.

Tamara, who had been a rock and had a soft spot for
Lavender after Emilia and Grace had gone there, was of
the opinion she would insist that we go. That nothing we
had done had caused the loss of her son's life and that we
had only ever tried to help both of them, her especially.

I thought about the syringe and fought away a sick feeling inside.

A week later I heard through the bush telegraph that doubled as the racing grapevine that Bruce Fielding, sporting a very black eye, had been seen out at a public function pawing his hands all over a provocatively dressed Gabrielle Southgate and dancing with her cheek to cheek. In the same bulletin someone who sounded suspiciously like Paul Eddison said that her father had been suspended on full pay pending enquiries into a charge of assault. Or Actual Bodily Harm to be precise, as it would appear on the charge sheet.

I thought immediately what a dangerous place the world could be and wished that it had all been a bad dream. From nowhere particular in my memory I also remembered that Bruce Fielding owed me a new leather jacket, though I quickly decided to write that off to experience.

Some things were just not worth pursuing. And some people were just best left alone.